Autumn in the Rearview

LINNEA MARCH

To Rusty, you're my Sedona.

ALSO BY LINNEA MARCH

<u>*Prevalent Notion Series*</u>
Faultless Notion
Treacherous Notion
Ruinous Notion

<u>*Seasons of Us*</u>
Wren's Winter
Villainous Summer
Second Chance Spring
Autumn in the Rearview

<u>*Other Titles*</u>
Reckless Liar
The One You Chose

CONTENTS

A NOTE TO READERS

This book contains pregnancy, discussions of death, infidelity, emergency contraception, abortion, and pregnancy loss

And the overuse of one stuck The Very Best of the Eagles album circa 1994.

One

POINT A-ILLAHEE, WASHINGTON

Autumn

EARLY AUGUST

How could someone grow so much hair on their neck but not on their chin?

Marcus tipped the last of beer into his mouth, and the sparse neck hairs glimmered in the glare of the LED strip lights lining the ceiling.

Of all my harebrained schemes, going to a party three towns over with a customer from the brewery might have been the worst.

Not that I could even call this date a scheme. More like an impulsive choice, fueled by that day's affirmation delivered to my phone. *"I will say yes to the universe."*

This party was filled with the same damp, flannel-wearing men of the Pacific Northwest. Despite never seeing these people, I knew them. Men in the area were all alike, falling into different camps of Pacific Northwesterners. From the coffee-black, rugged outdoorsmen who prided themselves on being men to the kombucha-loving hikers to the performance fleece-wearing tech guys. All so frustratingly predictable.

Including Marcus, whom I begrudgingly agreed to go out with after weeks of him asking after I delivered each pint of Liberty Double Hazy IPA. He was nice enough, I guess. And with all my friends pairing up, in love and settling down, I was once again left behind.

So, here I was at this tightly packed party with a guy my friends would absolutely skewer me for giving a second glance to. Because I had to do something, right?

I had long believed in the power of positive thinking and staying at home would not get me to the next aspect of my life.

Marcus put his arm around my shoulder, his empty IPA bottle resting on my collarbone. One would think after working for six months at a brewery, I would grow to appreciate the smell of beer, but IPA was a particularly rank scent.

As Marcus told an off-color joke to one of his friends, I glanced around the room. Sheets hung over the windows, and butter knives were stuck between the stove's burner prongs.

"Get me another, August?" Marcus handed me the empty bottle.

I didn't correct him for getting my name wrong. This terrible night and the even more terrible date had to end, and I stupidly had agreed to ride in his car. At least he didn't know where my house was—or, rather, my parents.

A month before, I had to move back in with them when my job at the Marine Science Center was eliminated because of budget cuts. I made okay money at the brewery, but I was new to the position and thus only worked part-time to prove myself. The tips weren't enough for the rent on my downtown Ridgewood apartment and college tuition.

But I was definitely going to need to call for a ride soon. Of all my friends, Devin would be the least judgmental. My cousin, Summer, the most. Plus, Summer might pick a fight with Marcus for getting drunk on our date. Or put sugar in his gas tank. She was fiercely protective and a hothead on her best day.

Devin, it was.

Plan set, I would get Marcus this beer and then call my friend to pick me up at the gas station a mile down the road. After heading to the kitchen, I pulled out a new IPA from the fridge with its trademarked skeleton with an army helmet on it.

"That's my beer."

I straightened and was met with piercing green eyes and sharp cheekbones. His lips were full and pink, the kind people in Manzanita spent hundreds on to perfect. Shaggy hair, not quite brown or blond or red but somehow all the shades put together, hung over his forehead.

His thick brows furrowed as he took me in. "Autumn?"

"Nico."

Nicolai Evjen. My oldest brother's best friend stood before me. Nico, the boy who once locked me and Summer in a bedroom while he and my brother Oliver had a house party. Nico, twelve years older than me and called me kid since the age of five.

Nico, my silliest, most unattainable crush since age twelve, from when I watched him help my three older brothers fix their car in the driveway. Shirt off and grease smeared on his cheek like something out of an action movie.

He had gone off to college and then he had lived in California, working for some tech company. Oli told me he sold software that helped with tracking pets or something. Apparently, he made a chunk of change.

Wrapping one arm awkwardly around my shoulder, I realized it was giving me a side hug like you gave your grandpa. Still, I couldn't help but suck in the scent of his skin as my nose grazed his neck. Sandalwood, grass, soap. Clean and male. Greedily, I sucked in a lungful of him before he stepped back, rocking on his heels.

"What are you doing here?" I asked.

Nico was far older than most other people here. If this wasn't my scene, it certainly wasn't his.

"Todd, my coworker, asked me to stop by to look at something in his garage. I think most of these kids are his younger brother's friends."

Kids.

They were all in their twenties, but to Nico, well into his mid-thirties, they would be kids. Just like I was a kid to him.

"What about you?"

"Oh, I came here with—"

A loud crash reverberated through the house, followed by shouting and shattering glass. We rushed through the doorway to see a scuffle in the living room.

A large man in a dirt biking T-shirt had Marcus in a headlock, stumbling, as shouts of encouragement mixed with the homeowner's plea to take it outside.

The bigger man tackled Marcus, his wraparound sunglasses cracking under his falling body.

"Idiots," Nico muttered.

I had to agree, though a small, misplaced loyalty to Marcus tugged at me. "I'm sure it's a misunderstanding. Marcus is—"

"Is one of those guys your boyfriend?"

"No, I barely know him. This was our first date but . . ."

Two lines appeared between Nico's brows as he frowned down at me. Had he always been so tall? Or had I stopped growing and would always remain so short?

"This is your first date? Not a nice dinner or a movie or a litany of five hundred other things? You go out with some guy, and he takes you to a skeezy house party? Why would you agree to that?"

"He asked me," I mumbled. My arms wrapped around my waist. With my chin raised, I shot him my most penetrating glare, which, in my experience, wasn't very effective. "I'm saying yes to the universe. I figured, what's the harm?"

"And now your date is getting his ass kicked beside a Buick LaSabre."

Apparently.

"Let me give you a ride home. You don't belong here, kid."

Holding back a flinch at the word, *kid*, I swallowed hard. "I'm not a child. I can take care of myself."

Most of the time. Sometimes, really, these things almost always ended up okay in the end, but I managed to find myself in sticky situations often. Sure, there was the time I went to a concert at the Gorge with girls I met the night before, and they left me at the diner in Vantage. Or when I flew down to visit a guy I had been chatting with online at his dorm in North Carolina.

How was I supposed to know he had a girlfriend and that *I wish you were here* was code for send naked pictures, not hop on a plane? And didn't I always figure things out in the end?

"I really shouldn't leave Marcus. He drove and—"

The fight had cleared, and a woman helped Marcus to his feet, placing him in the passenger side of his car before getting in the driver's seat.

He ditched me. This jerk drags me to a lousy party, forgets my name, starts a fight, and leaves with another woman?

Beside me, Nico clicked his tongue against his teeth. "You were saying?"

What was the affirmation for today? *I will say yes to the universe.*

Repeating it in my head, I steadied my breathing, in through the nose and out the mouth.

Silly, silly girl. What did you get yourself into this time?

Visualize a blank space, draw the sides of a box—up, across, down, across—with each breath in and out, until the panic clawing at my chest stalled. With a hard swallow, I gazed up into deep green eyes, his hair curling around his ears.

"You've had a few beers. I can drive."

"More than several, I was going to call for a ride, but having you drive would be better."

Keys in hand, I climbed into the front seat of his brand-new car.

His house was enormous. I wasn't sure what I expected, but it wasn't this. A mile south of the reservation on high-bank property, it sat on a cliff overlooking Jasper Pass between Ridgewood and Manzanita Island. A sprawling one-story with floor-to-ceiling windows boasted a peekaboo view of Seattle to the southeast.

"Oli wasn't kidding. This place is wild. And the view?" With my nose against the glass, I squinted in the dark. "Is that a staircase down to the beach?"

"Yeah, you want to see the boathouse?"

He shoved his hands in his pockets and rocked back on his heels.

"You have a *boathouse*? Like a legit one?"

"It's not that nice, but it's a house for my boat."

"You have a boat?"

"We live on a skinny peninsula in a state that has over a hundred islands. It's not that big of a deal."

Easy for him to say. The only other person I knew who had a boat was Summer's boyfriend, Van, and it was just a little one he used to putt around. We could squeeze five people on it earlier in the year, but it was a tight fit. Something told me Nico's boat would be much nicer.

"Waterfront home, a boat . . . Next thing you're going to show me is your helicopter."

"Sorry to disappoint, but I left that at my winter home."

The quirk of his grin had me questioning his honesty.

"Take me to your boathouse."

As the house's darkness fell away, Nico's hand brushed my lower back, guiding me to the path. In his other hand, he carried his beer while leading me down the steep stairs. The boathouse itself wasn't big or flashy, with a dock on each side with a boat up on its lift between them. Above the space was a second-story studio overlooking the water.

Across the water in Manzanita, the lights of a mansion were twinkling. Sandals shucked, and to the side, I plopped down at the end of the dock, my feet dangling.

"You know, I heard that one of the guys from Prevalent Notion lives over there." I jutted my chin across the water.

Nico sat beside me, his feet ghostly white in the water alongside me. "I heard it's two, actually."

"Really?" I grinned.

In the low moonlight, his hair shone almost black.

"Those kinds of guys are never really around, though. Pretty sure the band is touring in Europe right now."

"I wish I had met them before they all got married. I had such a crush on Nathan Ayers in junior high."

"He's a little old for you, isn't he?"

Cocking my head to the side, I pursed my lips. "He's, what, in his forties? For a man like that, who cares about an almost twenty-year age gap?"

Nico choked on his beer. "Are you serious?"

Shrugging, I took a sip of my sparkling water. "For the right guy, what's a few years?" Glancing over, I caught him staring at me, but he quickly turned his head. "Doesn't matter, though. Have you seen his wife?" I whistled low. "Like supermodel gorgeous. And a designer and owns a bunch of companies. Meanwhile, I can barely keep my job as a bartender and live with my parents. I'm the only one of my friends who they won't consult about fashion. And then there are the looks—which, I mean, yeah, I'm okay, but I'm no Ilsa Kruger."

"I think you're beautiful."

My breath hitched, the confession slicing through my rambling like the crack of a whip.

"What?"

The word eluded me as a breathless huff, barely audible over the rapid thrum of my heartbeat. Nico set his drink down with a faint clink on the wooden deck. His hand rose, deliberate and careful and brushed a loose lock of hair from my braid, his fingertips grazing my temple. The heat of his touch lingered, fire against the cool night breeze skimming off the water.

"When did you get beautiful?" His thumb traced my jaw, long fingers searching through the hair on my nape.

"Is that a compliment about me now or an insult about how I used to look?" I asked, trying to sound sharp, but my words gave way to the hope unraveling in my chest, betraying me.

He cocked his head, surveying me. "Last time we saw each other, you were, what, fifteen? I wasn't thinking about how you looked back then, kid."

The edge in my voice softened as I leaned closer, emboldened by the heat pooling low in my stomach. "I'm not fifteen, and I am certainly not a kid anymore."

The sweep of his gaze down my body, slow and deliberate, sent flickers of fire over my skin. The air crackled with an unposed question.

Was I flirting with Nico? Was this really happening?

I had years of childish daydreams and more adult fantasies to consider how Nico might kiss. Imagined it in dozens of ways—playful, soft, demanding.

But I never expected his eyes to trace down my body and back to my lips, as if he needed to savor the moment.

"I can see that."

The warmth of his hand against my nape as he pulled me against him, air escaping my lungs as I studied him. Millimeters from my face, the wash of his breath against my lips was sweet. Ferocity flared in his gaze, hunger I had never experienced searing over me. The tension of his fingers in my hair, his thumb pressing deliciously at my jaw, before he claimed my lips with his own.

The sandalwood of his skin flooded my senses as my fingers tangled in his hair softer than I expected it to be. My tongue traced the seam of his lips, tasting the tart beer and mint gum. Behind us, the bottle tipped over, rolling away with a hollow clatter. He pulled back, gasping, the air between us thick and charged.

As the back of his hand wiped away our kiss, his brows knitted as he shook his head. "Fuck, I'm so sorry, Autumn, I shouldn't have—"

My voice trembled, my heart pounding so loudly it drowned out everything else. My cheeks burned, warmth radiating all the way to my ears. "It's fine."

"No, it's not. I'm drunker than I thought and took advantage."

"And I'm completely sober and kissed you back."

Something held him back, even in his more drunken state. If anyone was going to make a move, it would have to be me. This whole week I repeated to myself over and over: *I am in charge of my happiness.*

I pressed a hand to his chest, warmth seeping through his shirt, then swung a leg over his lap and straddled him. Uncertainty clouded his eyes as he leaned back on his hands against the deck, careful not to touch me. Still, through the thin fabric of my linen shorts, I could feel him hardening against my core, his body betraying his reluctance. Wind whipped over the water, sweeping a cool breeze over my blazing skin.

"We shouldn't."

The words muffled against my throat as his lips traced a fiery path on my flesh.

"It's just sex, Nico." I gasped, tugging on his nape as his teeth grazed the sensitive curve of my collarbone, sending jolts through me.

With my feet under my thighs, I could feel the water of Puget Sound soaking through my shorts.

"But Oliver and your parents and—"

"I won't tell if you won't. Don't overthink it."

His hands, hesitant at first, came to rest on my hips. I guided them lower, pressing them against my butt. A low hiss eluded him as I ground myself onto his growing hardness. "Do you want to?"

Reluctance flashed in his eyes as his gaze traveled up my throat to my lips before his mouth crashed against mine. The tension broke, raw and consuming, and then he was hoisting me up, my legs wrapped around his waist. Ragged breaths and the faint creak of wood punctuated each step as he climbed the narrow boathouse stairs.

He lowered me, the leather of his couch cool against my exposed skin as his body covered mine.

His kisses blazed a trail down my body, the rasp of his stubble and the warmth of his lips imprinting on my skin. It burned so good.

"Sweet girl, tell me you want this, or I'll stop."

His voice cracked rough against my stomach as if he couldn't decide which he wanted to hear.

"You have no idea how much I want this." I gasped as his teeth nipped at the soft skin of my pelvis. The whisper of his fingers dragging my shorts down as I nodded, the words chanting in my head.

I was saying yes to the universe, after all.

Yes, yes, oh God, right there, yes.

POINT B-PEORIA, AZ

Nico

THE MIDDAY DESERT SUN simmered over the street, and bent over the car's hood was the nicest ass I'd seen in a long time, plump and full. The kind you held onto while driving between that cleft, with hips to grip and legs wrapping around your waist.

Then she straightened, her long auburn hair loose down her back, and I recognized that body.

Autumn.

Fuck.

It had been over two months since I last seen her. After the best sex I had in years, I fell asleep on the couch in the boathouse. When I awoke to the sun scorching my retinas and a pounding headache, Autumn was gone. By my head sat a bottle of water, and on the carpet by the couch lay a turquoise earring, the only signs she'd been there.

It was better that way. Sleeping with Autumn was a huge mistake. If I'd been a little less drunk and a lot less sex-starved, I would've remembered the facts.

Autumn was twelve years younger than me. Her brother was one of my best friends. I had sworn off serious, complicated relationships. Even though Autumn said she only wanted sex, no way would that would last. Women say those things all the time. I didn't have what it took to commit myself to anyone, let alone Autumn, and she deserved better.

Bringing to mind the most important issue, if Oliver found out, he would murder me. Or make me marry her. I wasn't sure which one I'd choose. Not that marrying into the Townsend family would be a bad thing. As a kid, I spent more time at their house than at my own. Lorelle was like another mom, not that I had much of a comparison since my own had left me with her brother when I was twelve.

Uncle Isaac was alright. I never went hungry, and if I needed something, I could ask. Whether I got it was another question. But he wasn't a father and certainly wasn't a mother.

But the Townsend house was always welcoming, the fridge bursting with snacks, Victor Townsend saying *You hungry? You boys want a hot dog?* as we walked in the door. The rabble of three teenage brothers bickering fused with Autumn's screeching and their cousin Summer playing whatever little girls play. It was such a chaotic, loud, loving *family*.

Every time I thought of Autumn beneath me, her whimpering as I sucked her clit, the flush over her freckled chest as I sank inside her . . . Well, okay, in the last two months, I jerked off to the memory. But other times, an immense weight of guilt would settle on me.

She was Oliver's little sister. Victor and Lorelle's daughter. Seventeen years ago, I dropped her off at dance practice, and when she got out, she shot me a grin with missing teeth. Until two months ago, I still pictured her as that gap-toothed girl with pop star posters on her walls.

Of course she was an adult. I had run into her cousin Summer a few times, and she had certainly grown up. So, why was I shocked to find Autumn before me at that house party, all lush curves and full lips, a woman?

It had been sixty-seven days since I woke up alone in my boathouse, not that I was counting. Until today, four thousand miles away. A week before, Oliver asked me to come down to drive his old car back up to his parents. How could I say no?

Over the years, he'd been my most loyal friend by visiting me in San Jose, lending money for rent while I waited for the app to launch. Beta testing things and offering his opinion.

When the dark time came, Oliver was there, distracting me with video games, cooking his terrible spaghetti just to make sure I ate. And he never asked for anything in return. When I sold Fetch Spot, I repaid everything with interest, but Oliver refused the extra gifts—a watch, a motorcycle—saying he didn't need them. And how do I repay him? By fucking his baby sister.

The same sister walking inside the ranch-style stucco home.

Twisting my hands on my bag, I ignored my driver, who was staring at me in the rearview mirror, her brow furrowed. "This is the address you put in, right?"

"Yeah, it is." I struggled to find an excuse to stay in the little sedan a minute longer, my mind racing with what might happen if I got out. If Autumn was the first one who saw me, would she hug me? Pretend what happened was no big deal, avoid me? Hand in my bag, I searched around my duffel bag, my fingers skimming over the tightly rolled shirts. "Let me just . . ."

What, stall for another five minutes, turn tail, and run away from my last one-night stand?

"Look, man, I've got another fare, so pay me to take you somewhere else or get out."

"Right." I cleared my throat. "Sorry, yeah."

After handing her an extra twenty, the smallest bill in my wallet, I climbed out of the car and into the blazing desert heat. Autumn was nowhere to be seen, the hood still popped on the front of the old blue wagon.

The door opened, and a small, round-faced girl came running out onto the porch, her strawberry-blonde hair up in two spiky pigtails.

"You not Uncle I-ben," she lisped.

"No, I'm . . ."

"I said Uncle Ivan and Auntie Bea will be here next week, baby." Oliver followed her, his freckled hand landing on her head. "Carys, you remember my friend Nic, right?"

The toddler shook her head, her big blue eyes narrowing at me. Townsend eyes, the same shade of blue as her aunt, though these were far more judgmental.

Oliver chuckled, stepping around her to pull me into a bro hug, slapping my back with his fist. "Man, I'm glad you made it. You're just in time. I was about to order some food."

"Oli, Janie needs—" Emerging from a hallway, Autumn appeared in the doorway with a stack of towels. Her hair was in small ponytails that stuck up everywhere with little jeweled barrettes.

"Look who's here, Guppy."

Autumn's freckled cheeks turned pink, probably from seeing me or the childish nickname her brother used. Autumn faltered for a split second but recovered quickly, a bright smile stretching across her face. Her nose was pink from the desert sun. A smear of red dirt marked her cheek, and blue smudges shadowed her lids up to her brows.

"Nico, always nice to see you."

"You too, Autumn." Her name was thick on my tongue, and I swallowed hard to clear my throat. "It's been a while . . ."

Nice, vague and unassuming, I totally played it cool.

At her feet, Carys raised her hands. Without breaking eye contact with me, Autumn scooped the toddler onto one hip and passed the towels to Oliver. She cocked her hip to the side to look me up and down. "You coming in or not?"

As I passed her in the doorway, I caught that deep scent of her skin, sweet earth, and sage. She didn't move out of my way.

"Nice hair." I motioned to the clips.

With her free hand, she patted her temple. "Oh, this? Courtesy of Chez Carys, only the finest styling here."

On anyone else, it might have looked ridiculous, but the ease with which Autumn embraced her niece's childlike styling tightened my chest. How odd.

"I did makeup too," Carys chimed, her pudgy hand winding in Autumn's hair.

"I see that." I smirked at Autumn, then brought my attention back to the child. "Your aunt looks lovely."

"She's beautiful now."

I wouldn't fall into that trap. The last time I called her beautiful, I ended up between her thighs. There could be no repeats. Bag in tow, I brushed past them and into the kitchen where Oliver's wife Janie was standing at the counter, hands on her belly.

"Nico! Finally, I'm starving. Put your stuff down, and I'll order dinner. I've had a wicked craving for curry. How spicy do you like it?"

"Oh, Nico likes it real hot, doesn't he?" Autumn said behind me, Carys still on her hip.

Her innocent expression never gave away the double entendre.

My bag fell, and I gave Janie a tight-lipped smile, a strangled laugh escaping me.

I was so fucked.

"I can't stop eating it. I know it will give me the worst heartburn, but it's so good," Janie moaned as she piled another scoop of chicken vindaloo on her plate.

Pushing around my helping of the same butter chicken Carys was eating, I gave her a weak grin. They added two seats for Autumn and me, and I ended up beside her, my thigh brushing hers each time I shifted. The sweet smell of her skin somehow overpowered the spiced food. It was the slowest torture being so near her after what we shared. Her lips wrapped around her fork, and the little moan reminded me of the one she gave me as I sucked her clit.

Fist up to my mouth, I cough, hoping to clear away the lusty thoughts ruining me. I could not be thinking about our night together when her brother was only a few feet away, blissfully unaware of my growing hard-on.

"Pass me the naan, Nico?" she asked.

As the plate moved between us, her finger grazed mine. A slight touch but enough to make me nearly drop it as a spark flickered under my skin. Big blue eyes widened at the contact, long dark lashes fluttering, and the blue smudge of makeup Carys did, still faint on her auburn brow. Her hand was on the plate, but I couldn't let go, my finger still beside hers. The skim of her tongue against her lower lip before pulling it between her teeth.

"Why did I think you were a vegetarian, Aut?" Janie said from across the table, her eyes on her daughter's face, wiping away a smudge of orange sauce from her nose.

The words broke through us, and our heads snapped to the middle of the table.

"You would think, wouldn't you? But I tried going off meat for a week, and I felt myself slipping away. I can't do it. Plus, working with animals, you develop an appreciation for the food chain."

Only I seemed to hear the waver in her voice as she answered.

"Doesn't your work mostly involve the touch tank at the Marine Science

Center? What appreciation is there for a sea cucumber?" Oli joked.

Blush flared her cheeks at the comment.

"Says someone who's never seen a sea star eat a clam."

"How does it eat a clam?" Carys asked, glee in her voice at the image.

"They flip their stomachs through their mouths, pry open the shell, and digest it outside their bodies."

Carys and Janie answered at the same time.

"Cool."

"Gross."

Janie shot Autumn a warning look. "That is not dinnertime conversation."

"No, it's not. So, instead, let's raise a toast to my buddy here." Oliver raised his beer in the air, pointing the neck at me. "For helping me out with my car and, more importantly, with my sister."

A feeling descended on me. He didn't mean . . .

"Thanks for driving with Autumn back to Ridgewood."

The thigh that had brushed softly against mine a moment ago tensed.

"Wait, what? I thought—"

"He's driving my car with me?"

After a glance at her, I processed what I was learning. "Your car?"

"Yeah, my car. He's giving it to me. My truck stopped working a few weeks ago, and he said I could have it if I drove it back up."

"But he told me I'm driving it back up."

The rest of the table fell away as Autumn and I stared at one another. Panic gripped me as I assessed just how I got myself into this mess. Surely, Oliver hadn't mentioned it, or I wouldn't have come. Maybe. Damn, I probably still would have. But at least I'd have been prepared to travel with Autumn—or better yet, talked Oliver out of bringing her.

A chair scratched against the hardwood floor and then Oliver was there between us, his arm wrapped around each of our shoulders, nudging us.

"You both are. Originally, I was going to drive up with her, but the doctor said Janie needs to take it easy—preeclampsia—so I can't leave her to take care of Carys by herself for an entire week."

"I'd be fine, Oli. I'm a grown—"

Oliver laughed. "Yeah, right, guppy. Trust you to handle a multi-state road trip on your own? We'd never see you again. You'll forget to put gas in the car."

"That was one time."

"Or take a wrong turn and end up in Kansas City."

"It was Canada, and I figured it out at the border, didn't I?"

"You need someone with you. Someone trustworthy." The rock in my throat was growing larger at his words. "And who would I trust with my baby sis more than my best bro?"

If I thought I was fucked before, it was only getting started.

POINT C-PEORIA, AZ

Autumn

WHILE I'VE NEVER MINDED a change of plans, I had to admit Nico show-ing up at my brother's house was an obstacle I hadn't foreseen. Sure, I thought about our night together every day and had filed portions away for use when I was alone with my vibrator. But really, we lived close enough to each other that he could have seen me at any time. Instead, he had to surprise me at my brother's house while I was caked in cheap makeup, my hair a mess like Angelica's doll Cynthia in *Rugrats*.

It's unfair.

Utterly, ridiculously unfair for someone to look as good as he did. His hair had grown out longer, falling over his brow as he stooped to talk with Carys. His beard grew a shade darker than his hair, a true auburn, the deep red of the setting sun before the sky turns violet. A nightfall red.

While I had to watch as my older brother talked with him, joking and teasing. In the long breadth of a second, his green eyes refused to shift from mine once, and I was sure he didn't blink as I stood before him. Then Oli clapped him on the back, and as he glanced away from me, I could breathe again. The white-knuckled grip on his bag the only betrayal on his smooth face.

All night I had to sit near him, scrutinizing every inch we shared. Was I sitting too close? Would my leg pressing against his mean something? Would he notice how my eyes were fixed on his mouth as he ate? Or the way I grinned like a fool as he listened intently to Carys as she shared the plot of her favorite super-pup movie? As we washed dishes together at the sink, did his finger linger on mine too long?

The blankets in Oliver's guest room were far too heavy for this heat. Since he moved down to the desert, he talked of how the climate had thinned his blood. When he visited the family, he would complain about the cold, even in the depths of summer. But I wasn't a desert girl. I liked the cold biting my ankles as I slept, the chill on my skin as I replayed the day and whispered affirmations before drifting off.

I am in charge of my life. I am strong. I make my happiness.

None worked. The tepid air was heavy on my skin as I flung the blanket off my legs. The hallway was silent as I tiptoed past Carys's room, past the soon-to-be nursery and into the living room. In a fit of gallantry, Nico insisted I take the guest room, and he would take the couch. For a while, I thought about reminding him that my back was only twenty-six, while his was thirty-eight, but it felt low.

Shirtless, Nico was on his side, facing the back of the couch. An enormous pink stuffed cupcake plush wedged between his arm and his head. The night lights scattered around the room lit up his muscled back. Quietly, I stood over him, watching his breaths coming in and out of his mouth. His face was slack and seemed years younger.

He let out a jagged puff of air, and I stepped back, not aspiring to be caught ogling him in his sleep like some creeper. It was enough that he never sought me out after our tryst, but to find me hovering over him in the middle of the night? No, thank you.

When his breathing evened out, I stepped back. Hard plastic crashed and echoed as my heel caught the magnet tower Carys had built, snapping tile after tile as they fell. Still, I put my hands up as if that would diminish the sound. Nico shifted on the couch, and I sucked in, counting to twenty before letting it out. With his eyes still shut, his hand went from tense to falling almost to the floor.

Close call now. Get out and stop staring at him.

In the kitchen, I gripped the counter, tracing the blue-and-white swirls of the marble as I tried another affirmation.

I am flawed, and in those flaws, there is beauty.

Well, the first part was right, at least. Pathetic. I didn't get like this over boys. Sure, it had been a while since I had gone home with a man before the night Nico and I spent together, but I was normally more rational than that. I didn't need much. A nice guy who would make me smile, maybe give me an orgasm once a week? Was that really so hard to find?

All my life I had been told I was so cool, so nice, so laid back, and so easy to talk to.

And I was so over hearing it.

Those words never led to my finding someone who liked me enough to stick around. The number of times I had been told the dreaded "it's not you, it's me."

A girl can only hear it so often before she thinks that it's the opposite.

And now the worst evidence of never being enough was sleeping feet from me. With a shaky hand, I filled a glass, gulped the terrible, acrid tap water, and set it down with a clunk.

Despite what people thought of me, I was pragmatic about relationships. I wasn't hesitant about love—that was for my friend Devin, before she fell for her boyfriend Cedar. Or that I had impossibly high standards and a penchant for making men cry—that honor went to my cousin, Summer. Even *she* found someone.

I would never begrudge my friends their happiness. Seeing the way love changed them was a sight to behold. But when was that kind of love coming for me?

With the bag of bread in my hand, I pulled out the heel slice and set it down beside the toaster. A glass of water stopped halfway between the counter and my mouth as Nico shuffled into the kitchen, his hand wiping at his face. His chest was bare, and he wore only a pair of low-slung boxers. Scratching his stomach lazily, he walked to the fridge. I followed the trail of dark hair from his navel into his underwear, shamelessly taking him in before he realized I was there.

After pulling out the pitcher of water, he turned, his hand outstretched to the cabinet before he caught sight of me.

"Hey."

His voice was gravelly with sleep, and something clenched between my legs at the sound. Knowing I was too sleepy to fight the emotions on my face, I turned away, popping a second slice of bread in the toaster. The red-hot coils sizzled as I trained my expression into something passably casual.

I turned to face him, my arms crossed. His green eyes pierced mine, my breath hitching as I remembered how those same eyes had watched me fall apart beneath him. The sudden pop of the toaster broke my gaze. As I turned back to slather peanut butter over each slice, I heard him shuffle on the linoleum floor, his feet squeaking.

I could do this, be cool, and not jump into his arms the second we were alone. Holding one out to him. His finger brushed against mine. It was so much worse than dinner when he passed me the naan. This time, it was dark, he was half dressed, and we were alone.

As he took a tentative bite. I followed his movement, biting into my slice. His eyes darted from mine down to the toast.

"Do you like the heel?" he asked.

I shrugged. "Not particularly."

"Why did you toast it?"

With a short nail, I scratched my forehead. "Well, no one likes the heel, and I feel bad. So, whenever their heel is left in a bag, I always eat it."

"You feel bad?" He paused, his eyes narrowing. "For a piece of bread?"

I huffed. "No, not for the toast. I just figure no one else wants to eat it. So, I will."

His brow furrowed, and he shook his head slightly. A dense silence lingered in the kitchen, punctuated by our soft chews and the dripping faucet. Silence has never been something I could handle, needing to fill it up with something, anything.

"Look as nice as it is for you to do Oli a *'solid'* and drive with me, you really don't need to. I've gone on plenty of road trips with my friends before." As I wiped my crumby fingers over the empty sink, I chewed the last of my toast.

"With your friends," he corrected, his head tilted to the side, a lock of hair falling over his left brow. My fingers itched to tuck it back. "But not by yourself."

Well, no, not exactly. But how hard could it be?

I wasn't lying. I had gone on plenty of road trips with my friends. Last year, Summer and I took a trip to California, where I dragged her on a hike while she grumbled about her aching muscles.

"You don't need to be chivalrous or whatever you think you're doing here. I don't need another brother figure bossing me around."

"Brother?" he choked out a laugh, sauntering over to me until I had to back up into the counter. The edge of the marble top doused the heat rising under my skin at his nearness. I reached back, pushing my palms into the cold surface, centering myself. A *tick-tick-tick* in my core strengthened as he leaned closer. "I'm not your brother, Autumn."

Placing one hand beside mine, his body caged me in. Even in the darkness of the night, I could see the depths of his eyes, all winter moss and wet earth.

"And I'm not a little kid anymore," I strangled out.

Months before, I had been so sure of myself when I swung my legs over his lap and kissed him. Yet I could barely breathe from his nearness. Where was my courage?

"You think I don't know that?" he whispered.

His eyes skidded down my body, taking in the tiny sleep shorts and loose tank top hanging off one shoulder. He didn't need to step closer for me to feel the heat of his gaze.

The last time I said that, I ended up on my back on his couch, legs over his shoulder as he drove into me.

Flames licked my cheeks, and I was glad for the dim kitchen light hiding my blush at the memory.

Did he think about it, too?

Down the hall, the faint sound of Carys's white noise machine droned on. The fridge clicked and groaned, and far away, a car was driving down a nearby street. All I could take in was his body's heat pressing into me, the hint of peanut butter on his breath, and the clean musk of his skin.

Fractionally, I leaned forward, my mouth inches from his. Not moving back, I felt the deep intake of breath as my upper lip almost brushed against his lower. Beside me, his hand fisted and his forearms tensed as I held still, letting his sweet breath wash over my face as he groaned.

"Fuck." His hand shot out, his fingers in my hair as he pulled my face back. His green eyes darkened as his vision roamed over my face. An internal battle raged in his jaw, his brows, in the grip he had on my neck. Then he was blinking, his hand falling away as he shuffled back. "You can't fucking do that."

"Do what?" I asked, the air coming out of me in short bursts.

The glare he sent me was vicious.

"We're in your brother's house."

"I know that."

"He's sleeping just down the hall, and you're here with your—" His Adam's apple bobbed on his straining throat. The roaming look he gave me sent flames over my skin as if he could see right through my clothes. Screwing his eyes shut, he shook his head. "He's trusting me to keep you safe on this trip. You can't kiss me."

"That wasn't a kiss, and you know it. You, of all people, should know what kissing me feels like, or have you forgotten?"

"Forgotten?" he hissed through clenched teeth. "You think I could forget about that night?"

Training my face to look impassive, I tilted my head to the side. "I couldn't be sure because I didn't see you afterward."

"You're the one who left in the middle of the night."

"And, what, you were going to make me waffles in the morning, sit together on your expensive leather couch drinking coffee, and chat?"

"Maybe? We'll never know. Will we?"

In the weeks following our night, I had pictured it. I allowed myself the daydream of my feet tucked under his butt as we sat on that same couch together. Of reading his horoscope to him. Of his kiss as he held my face in his palm. But that was all they were. Dreams.

I couldn't go beyond imagining the what-ifs with him, so I summoned my courage to deliver the casual speech I'd rehearsed for two months in case we met again.

"That night was great—wonderful, even. I've felt things with you I didn't know were possible. But I know what kind of woman I am. And I might be delusional about a lot of things, but to think you're going to ask me to stick around? Even I can't imagine that."

"You couldn't let me prove you wrong?"

I couldn't respond to this because he would flip out. No, I couldn't stick around.

I had spent years half in love with the idea of this man and then spending a night with him confirmed all my worst desires. Because of that night, I was falling. In that boathouse, I woke up with my head on his bare chest. I had to get out. If I didn't get distance, I'd scatter apart when he didn't want me in the morning. I had to be the one to let go. To allow that night to be what it was. A wonderful time, meaningful but short.

"Would you have?" I raised a brow.

When he didn't offer an answer, I nodded. "Right. I'm going back to bed. I'll see you tomorrow. We have a big day ahead of us."

Point D–Highway 17

Nico

A MAN WITH A plan. In college, when I would enter the room, my roommate, Daveed, would call out, "There's the man with a plan."

I enjoyed having control over my life. Surprises rarely lead to anything good. If Oliver had told me Autumn was coming on this trip, I would have made a plan. If I hadn't been surprised by seeing Autumn at that party, maybe I could have kept my dick in my pants. In a world where Noemi had—no, I wasn't going there.

There would need to be a plan if I was going to survive this trip with my friendship with Oliver intact. Have set destinations each night and only stop when we absolutely had to. We'd only have to stay two nights maximum with the right timing. I wouldn't subject Autumn to driving all night the way I used to travel with my buddies. But I could handle two nights on the road.

Most importantly, I couldn't think about Autumn naked.

All points of this plan were blown apart only an hour and a half into the trip. We didn't leave the house until well into the late morning. Janie had insisted on making us a big breakfast until Oliver shouted her back into bed. When he returned, he informed us we weren't allowed to leave until after we ate. And then Oliver wanted to go over the details of the car with me. Where everything was as if I hadn't been driving for more than half my life. I rocked on my heels as he pointed out the section that held the spare tire, warned the power steering was finicky, and hoped I liked The Eagles since their greatest hits was stuck in the tape deck.

The 1980 blue AMC Eagle, pristine after twenty years under a tarp in his parents' garage, was brought to Peoria when Oliver married Janie. For how much this trip could've cost Autumn, I was surprised she was willing to drive it up. Wouldn't a mid-twenties girl want a cute little coupe or something? Something with a sunroof and stereo system. Not an old wagon with wood paneling and bright orange interior.

I was embarrassed to admit that it had been over a decade since I had driven something older than five years old.

Autumn piled bags and suitcases into the oversized trunk. Carys cried and clung to her aunt. Oliver hugged her, picking her up off the ground and squeezing her around the middle. When it came time to say goodbye to me, Carys gave me her hand to shake, her brows knitted together. As warm of an exit as I'd get, I suppose.

"Take care of my guppy, right, bro?" he asked, slapping me on the back. "She talks a big game, but she needs someone looking after her."

Guilt swam in my gut as I nodded at him. My impulsive action the night before floated through my mind. An almost kiss. That warm smile in the indigo and yellow of the kitchen. The clearness of her gaze as she looked right through me. We hadn't even left, and already, my composure was stretching thin. What would three days in the car be like?

"Of course."

Barely off the 101 loop, she reached between her legs. Flipping open the cooler, she pulled out a soda, popping the tab. She held out the bright orange can, and I glanced from her to it and back again.

"For me?"

"Is it still your favorite?" she asked.

It had been years since I had one. A drink like that felt childish. I hadn't allowed it for myself in San Jose, and now it seems silly to buy for myself.

"It is, or it was—" A tug in my navel had me swallowing down my explanation as I took the can. The fizzy sweet drink hit my tongue, and I was transported back to my college days. Of studying with Daveed, of parties and late-night drives. In the Townsend driveway, Oliver and I tinkered under the hood, the sun on our skin, while Victor watched from a lawn chair, shouting tips.

In her own hand, she popped open a ginger ale, taking a long swig.

"Oliver just had these around for us to take?"

Another sip, and I was almost done with the can. Damn, I had forgotten how much I liked these.

"No, I ran to the store this morning for snacks and drinks."

"You bought this?"

She nodded, head tilting back and her lashes fluttering shut. White blond at the root darkening to auburn at the tips. The air still in the mid-nineties as we drove away from the metro area and into the long stretch of desert.

She wrestled the manual crank with both hands until the window creaked down inch by inch. By halfway, sweat dotted her forehead.

One hand out the window, she let the wind pick up and drop her arm as the car drove on, a waving motion I used to do as a child, carefree and delighting in the sun on my skin. Her head tilted back, a small smile played over her full pink lips.

"Look, I think we need to set some ground rules for this trip."

From the other side of the car, her head lolled toward me, but her eyes remained shut, her long lashes casting shadows on her freckled cheeks.

"Rule away, Nicolai."

My full name on her lips. Her tongue against her teeth at the last consonant sent a spark under my ribs. The scratch in my throat worsened as I coughed to clear it away. "Right. No kissing, no touching. Nothing."

With one eye opened, she squinted at me. "Are you still going on about that thing last night? I told you that wasn't a kiss."

How could she say that? It took hours for my cock to calm down after she left me in the kitchen. I finally had to go into the bathroom and rub one out, something I hadn't done since my early college days before I could fall asleep. Her gaze lingered as my eyes closed, breath warm on my lips as she leaned in, her body's heat caged against mine. Was I the only one affected by this?

"Don't be a child, Autumn."

At this remark, she sat up straighter, her blue eyes narrowing. "I think you want to act like you felt nothing. To act like you didn't want it, like you want to forget both last night and what happened a few months ago."

Forget? That was impossible. There was no forgetting her. I was utterly distracted for weeks afterward. But I wasn't a dewy-eyed schoolboy. I knew better than to allow my dick to destroy me.

"What I want is not the issue here. Your brother is my best friend, and I'm not going to ruin my relationship with him over what I want. My own needs."

"So, you want me." She cracked a grin, sunlight breaking over the windshield and bathing her in a bleaching beam. She brought one hand up to shade her eyes. "Aw, Nicolai, you big softie."

"I'm serious. We can't do—" I swallowed the lump in my throat. "What happened last night can't happen again."

She raised her hands in mock defeat. "Fine. I won't almost kiss you again. Message received."

Beside me, she gripped the bottom of her sweatshirt and pulled it over her head. Underneath, she was wearing a tiny white top, if you could even call it that. A flimsy scrap of fabric was a better term.

"What are you doing?"

"I'm hot. It's like one hundred degrees out in October."

Hands gripped tight on the steering wheel, I trained myself not to look over at her, the smooth swatch of skin between her shirt and her shorts, the white against her freckled shoulder, the deep cut over her breasts as they strained against the cotton of her top. Was she even wearing a bra?

Fuck, I couldn't think about that. In a millisecond of a glance, I took her in. Nope, no bra, and somehow her breasts looked bigger. Not that I had much of a comparison—I had only seen them the one time—but still. Maybe it was the shirt.

And no bra.

Fuck.

Adjusting myself discreetly, I wiggled in the driver's seat, hoping she wouldn't look down at my lap and see my growing erection. That wouldn't help things stay platonic.

Then her hand was on my arm, her body leaning over the bench seat as the scent of cloves and soap invaded me. Her long hair whipped into my face. "Wait, take this exit. One mile, take it."

Her voice was so frantic, I put on the turn signal and drove down the ramp. Was she sick? What was going on?

"Turn there." She pointed at a street, and I followed her instructions, still unsure.

"Okay, park."

As I shifted into park, she opened her door, stepping out and stretching her arms. A swath of freckled lower back exposed as her shirt rode up. As she stooped into the car, she glanced at me, a grin filling her face and her shoes in her hands. When had she taken those off?

"Come on. Let's go see it."

"What? Where are we?"

"The castle. We have to see the castle."

Frowning, I pulled the key out of the ignition. Side treks were a bad idea and not part of the plan, but we were here, and I couldn't refuse when her blue eyes lit up.

A few yards into the parking lot, she stopped at a VW van with Washington plates. An older couple was getting out. "Hey, I like your bumper sticker."

In cartoon green letters was the phrase: *Geoducks for the state bird.*

The woman laughed. "Thanks, it's always nice when someone recognizes it."

"I love geoducks. All the bi-valves, really. I went to school for marine biology."

The woman's face brightened. "Oh, and what are you doing now?"

"Working at a brewery."

The woman's smile faded, but Autumn didn't seem to notice. "Anyway, nice chatting with you."

We were a few feet away before Autumn stopped in front of a large sign featuring a map of the area and sites of interest.

"I didn't know you went to school for marine biology."

"Going, actually. Yeah, I didn't finish when I was younger. I struggled with a few of my classes, and with the student loan payments piling up, it just got too hard."

"Aren't there tutors or someone who could help you?"

"Tutors are expensive. I didn't want to ask my parents for help."

"I'm sure they would've."

"But that's what everybody does. Everybody always helps me. I'm not saying I'm not grateful, but why do I always have to be the one who's saved? You know, in my friend group, in my family, everywhere I go. I'm the little sister. *Autumn means well, doesn't she? Oh, don't bother Autumn with that.*

As if I can't handle these hard things. As if I'm not strong enough or smart enough or hard-working enough to accomplish things. They just let me be, and I know that's a silly thing to be frustrated about, but it does. When I went back to school, I told myself I was going to do this on my own. I'm going to figure it out, and while it's taking me years and years, one class at a time, I'm almost there."

"Your family must be ecstatic."

"They don't know. I didn't tell them. When I dropped out at twenty, they were so nice about it. They said, 'It's okay, you'll figure something else out.' It's fine, but I knew it wasn't fine. I knew they were just letting me off easy, like they always do. I don't want to tell them until I know it's for sure. Until I know that I've really accomplished what I said I would. I have only three more classes to take. If I'm able to finish these classes, I should be done by March."

"You should tell them. College is hard, especially when you're alone."

"We'll see. It's not that impressive when it's taken me so long to finish."

I reached over, grabbing her hand to squeeze it. As I slid her palm against mine, I realized I already broken one of my rules. No touching. Too late now. Besides, the gesture wouldn't hurt anything. Right?

"I think you're the one who will continue to impress, no matter what you do."

The wide grin that broke over her face almost had me smiling back. Like the first crack of dawn after a long, starry night. "Come on, let's see this castle."

Point E-Montezuma Castle, Camp Verde, AZ

Autumn

Of course Nico stopped to read every plaque on the path, so I walked ahead of him, wanting to see this castle. As I rounded the bend, the cliff dwellings came into view, towering eighty feet above me. Carved into limestone, the square windows, and walls of an ancient civilization sat frozen. Marveling at the structure, the knowledge that people had been here since time immemorial. They had loved and fought, cried over skinned knees, and laughed at silly jokes. Lived, loved, and died on this very earth, and here was the evidence carved into rock.

A way behind me, I saw a woman in white linen shorts and a short-sleeved light pink button-down approach him. She motioned with what was likely a perfectly manicured finger at the sign they were both reading. Nico had his hands in his pockets as he nodded to her, giving her a polite smile, no teeth, just a slight curve of his lips. Still, this woman was gorgeous. Rocking my left foot to the side, I felt the strap of my hiking sandals dig into my ankle. The rough edge of my self-cut jean short overalls ruffled in the breeze. I'd meant to fix the unraveling threads before we came but never did, and the hem knotted and frayed worse with each wash. That woman seemed like the type to throw away a fraying hemline.

From the other side of the viewing area, bits of the tour guide's speech filtered over.

"Sinagua people—pre-Columbian—1100 AD—some Hopi clans and Yavapai people trace their heritage—return for religious ceremonies—"

There was more I wanted to see, but I couldn't bring myself to walk out of Nico's line of sight. What if he gave that woman a genuine smile? I had to be there in case of something. On principle, I didn't indulge in negative self-talk, but I couldn't help but stand there, frozen, as this woman chatted him up and—were her fingers on his elbow?

No, she didn't touch him. She was pointing at something, and her finger grazed his arm.

Still, that was enough of that.

Before I could tell myself it was a terrible decision, impulsive and child-ish, I was at his side, setting my hand on his arm. "Nicolai, come see this."

Upon closer inspection, she was younger than I thought. Mid-thirties maybe and, unfortunately, much prettier, with straight dark hair and per-fectly lined pink lips. My hair was frizzing out of my braided pigtails. I didn't even own lip liner. What was the point of it anyway? Summer would know, and why was I obsessing over this woman's perfect lip liner in the desert?

His green eyes widened at my hand on his arm, but he didn't try to remove it.

The woman's eyes flashed to my hand and up to my face. I fought back the self-satisfied grin I wanted to give her.

He gave the woman a curt nod. "Have a good day."

Leading him away, I didn't take my hand off his arm, reveling in the light dusting of golden hairs under my palm, the way his muscles tensed as we walked to the viewing area. Once there, I dropped my grip and motioned to the roughhewn buildings.

"How do you think they got up there?" I asked.

"Very large ladders, I would guess." Nico pushed his hands in his pockets, his neck craned up to the cliff side. "It's an engineering marvel." With a brochure in his hand, he ran a finger over the tiny printed words. "This says the construction is almost entirely from the limestone found at the base of the cliff and the clay from Beaver Creek. It's an example of early stone and mortar masonry, and they used sycamore for the roof hatching."

"And you didn't want to come." After I bumped my shoulder against his, the corners of my mouth turned up.

A muscle ticked in his jaw as his Adam's apple bobbed. Green irises darted from the paper to my face, a slight quirk of his lips before smoothing them into a straight line. "It's not a good idea to drag this trip out. We should get back on the road as soon as we can."

"But if we hadn't stopped, we wouldn't have seen this." With my right hand, I motioned to the cliff. "There's nothing like this in Ridgewood."

"Because we live on the ancestral home of the Coast Salish. It's an entirely different ecosystem, culture, and people."

Resting my hands on the wooden guardrail, I gazed up at the cliff, leaning forward and arching my back to stretch. "Yeah, and aren't you glad you get to experience this?"

A large huff of air escaped his lips. "Sure. If you say so."

Over my shoulder, I glanced back at him. His gaze was on my back, but when I turned my head, it darted up to my face, the slightest pinking of his cheeks. Was he looking at my ass?

"Careful, Nicolai. If I didn't know any better, I'd think you were enjoying yourself."

"Just because I'm not an endless ball of energy and optimism doesn't mean I don't know how to have fun."

"I'm not endlessly energetic. I sleep." Phone in my hand, I waved for him to come closer. "Now come here. We need to document this trip."

"This isn't a vacation. We need to—"

Frowning, I shook my head. "It is for me. I'm not like you. I don't get to go on vacations to the Greek Isles and Iceland and Sweden and—"

"Norway. I went to Norway."

"And the farthest I've been out of the States is Kamloops, BC. Any adventure outside the confines of our little town can be an adventure. And I want to remember this trip with you for later."

Because, later, I won't have you with me.

"So, get your booty over here and take a selfie with me."

The woman I saw chatting with Nico earlier strode up, her hand out to us. "Do you want me to take a picture of the two of you?"

Grinning, I handed my phone over. "Yes, please."

Before Nico could argue, I slid my arm around his lower back, wedging myself into his armpit. His arm tensed beside me as I grinned at the camera.

The lady lowered the phone and quirked a brow at Nico. "Put your arm around your wife."

"Oh, she's—"

"Closer, lover. Let's make it a cute one, huh?" I wrapped my arms tighter around his middle, my chin pressing against his chest as I beamed up at him.

Slowly, his arm slid around my waist, his thumb drifting to the bare skin of my hip. In the desert sun, his eyes looked lighter, sage green with little flecks of gold. His fingers brushed softly on my stomach. A small smile played on his full pink lips. As big of an expression as I was going to get.

"So cute. You two make a lovely couple. " The woman was in front of us, my phone extended. "I took a few. I hope that's okay."

"That's the best. Thank you."

As the woman walked away, I saw the brief flash of want in her eyes as she looked Nico up and down.

That's right, walk away. He's not for you.

For one last time, I took in the castle in the rock before clapping my palms together. "Alright, that's probably good. You said we need to get going, right?"

The well-worn path curved around sparse brush as I started walking back to the car, his footsteps falling behind me as he caught up.

"Why did you let that lady think I was your husband?"

With a brow raised, I chuckled. "We'll never see her again, so what does it matter what she thinks we are? Correcting a stranger is far more awkward than letting her think we're something we're not, don't you think?"

He considered me, a muscle in his jaw ticking. "I guess."

"Besides, what would you have me say? 'He's actually known me since I was seven, and he was nineteen? Three months ago, we had sex on his leather couch, and he gave me three orgasms before I left him while he was sleeping, and now we have to drive this old car back up to Washington?'"

"When you put it like that." His face screwed up, and he grimaced. He was silent for a few minutes as we walked back to the car. With his hand on the roof, he paused, looking over my shoulder at the path leading to the cliff dwelling. "Three, really?"

"You couldn't tell?" I smirked before dipping back into the passenger seat and taking off my sandals.

At the gas station beside the highway on-ramp, the lowered Yukon beside us had a "battle-tested" bumper sticker and neon LED lights. The guy who got out was wearing a black baseball cap with rifles crossed over one another.

With soda, licorice, and spicy chips on the counter, I scanned the impulse buys and snatched the black-wrapped package before the cashier finished ringing me up. As I walked back to the pumps, I slowed, admiring Nico as he leaned against the side of the blue car. Strands of gray were growing at his temples, catching in the sunlight. Somehow, it added to his attractiveness. I meant it when I joked about older men. His long legs stretched out before him, his toned, muscled arms crossed.

That chest I fell asleep on months before. Arms that caged me against the counter less than twenty-four hours before.

The gas pump clicked, and his eyes darted from the rolling numbers to me. Light-green irises finding mine, sage. My favorite scent in the world, sage and earth and warmth.

"I got us matching keychains!" I handed him the plastic neon green cactus, mine saying *Looking sharp* while his said *Don't be a prick.*

The corner of his mouth twitched up before smoothing out.

Brandishing the small package, I grinned. "And a few other things."

His fingers brushed against mine as he took it from me, sparks sizzling up my arm.

Brow creasing, he tore the plastic off, and his expression grew more confused.

"It's a sunglass holder. I noticed you put yours in your bag. But I always think you need car sunglasses, especially for a trip like this." My hand delved back into the bag, and I pulled out the rest. "So, to go with the holders, I also got you—"

I drummed a beat on my leg with one hand. "These!" With a flourish, I presented him with thick gold-rimmed aviators. "Like Elvis Presley."

"I'm not wearing those." He scowled at the glasses.

"Of course you will. They're just for the car if you want to wear your boring ones—"

"Those boring ones are Tom Ford."

"Well, Tom can stay in your bag. These"—I pushed them in his hand—"are for you to wear on this trip. No complaints. They go wonderfully with mine."

He scowled at me but took the glasses, sliding them on his face. There were slightly too big for his face and crooked.

"Just like The King. Don't act like you don't dig it, man."

"They'll probably turn my skin green."

"Good thing I like green." I smirked as I put on my plastic, flower-shaped bright yellow glasses.

Behind the dark lenses, I could see his eyes roll. "Get in the car. We're wasting daylight."

Rounding the front of the car, I climbed into the driver's seat. "I'll take this leg."

Nico seemed to think that this trip needed to be over quick, but I had my own plans. The desert was a new adventure for me, and I wanted to see as much of it as I could.

Only eight miles on the highway was the sign for the next turnoff. I knew Nico would fuss a bit, so I waited until the last minute to put on my blinker, taking the exit at the last minute. Luckily, there were few cars on the road and none in my way.

As I got on the ramp for I-179, Nico glanced over at me, the corner of his mouth turning down. "Is this the way to—"

"Just taking the scenic route."

He sat up straighter, looking out the window as if he could determine how off track we were from his plans. "How scenic?"

"You'll see." I grinned, fixing my flower glasses.

In the Pacific Northwest, we have blue-and-gray mountains that dominates the skyline and towering green trees that surrounds you everywhere you go. But we have nothing like these formations. Red, brown, and orange rock towers stood stark against the pale blue sky.

He hadn't wanted the detour, but slack-jawed awe spread over Nico's face as we neared the town center. On the other side of the road are neon lights of two cowboy boots, the shapes flashing. "Oh, a cowboy bar. We have to go there tonight."

"We're not going to a cowboy bar."

"Why? I bet they have line dancing."

His voice edged with panic. "I don't line dance."

"Who says you have to dance? I'll do the dancing, and you can watch."

I can't help but notice the slight creep of color in his cheeks at my words. Really, he was so easy to rile up, how could I resist?

Going by the sign for the hiking trail to my left, I flip on the turn signal a few moments before taking the tight turn toward the east. In the passenger seat, Nico grabbed the ceiling handle, what my dad called the "oh shit" handle when I drove.

"Autumn. What the fuck are you doing?"

The grin I flashed him as I took the next left had him gripping the handle tighter. "A little detour. Are you scared, Nico?"

"You're driving like a maniac!"

Under our tires, the car bumped up and down on the uneven road. I stuck out my lower lip, cocking my head to the side. "You look tense."

We hit an especially big pothole, and I had to twist the steering wheel to right the car.

He scowled at me. "I'm driving the rest of the way. You can't be trusted not to brutally maim us."

I smirked as I pulled into the parking lot. "No one has ever been *brutally* maimed with me. *Slightly* is a better description. What's a few bumps along the way, right?" Two other cars were parked alongside a single vault toilet and a chipped-paint brown bulletin board. "Here we are. A quick hike to watch the sunset."

"I'm not hiking. We need to—"

"If you think I'm going to come all the way to Sedona and not walk among those rocks, you have another thing coming."

Arms crossed against his chest, he shook his head. "We shouldn't have come here in the first place. If we had stayed on Highway 17, we—"

"And miss this? I don't think so. Live a little, Nicolai." Stuffing the keys in my back pocket, I climbed out of the car, stretching my arms over my head.

Inside the car, I heard the low muttering, "I think I've lived enough, thanks."

When I duck my head back into the car, I realize he was staring at my middle. My crop top rode up as I drove. His eyes dart away as I fish my sweatshirt out of my bag to wind around my waist in case the weather gets chilly once the sun goes down. "So, wait here, then. I'll be back in an hour."

At my words, he scrambled out, shaking his head at me. "There could be strangers up there or scorpions or snakes." The Elvis glasses were sliding down his face. I think he forgot he was still wearing them. "I'm not letting you go up on a mountain by yourself."

"Wonderful, then we'll do this together."

The gravel crunched under our feet as I made my way to the trailhead. After ten seconds of nothing, I heard his footfalls behind me as he caught up. "If I die falling off a cliff, Autumn, I will haunt you."

Glancing over my shoulder at him, I grinned. "Don't make promises you can't keep."

Point F-Sedona, AZ

Nico

Ten minutes into this hike, I brushed my hair off my forehead, and my fingers bumped into the sunglasses I forgot I was still wearing. Those ridiculous, garish, gold-rimmed monstrosities. Normally, I'd have refused something so silly, but with Autumn's big blue eyes shining behind her equally absurd glasses, I couldn't say no. Not only the glasses but the sunglass holder. A cheap plastic contraption clipped to the sun visor, but when she handed it to me, something sparked in my chest.

She noticed where I kept my sunglasses and knew I liked orange soda. Saw I needed something and sought to take care of it for me. A foreign sensation sprouted beneath my skin. I couldn't remember the last time someone had done anything like that for me. It had been years since I had received a gift. My uncle was never much for holidays. I hadn't realized how nice it felt to get something.

The last actual gift I received was probably from Noemi, and that was—well, that was in the before. Besides, her gifts were designer, bought with my money—bespoke dress shirts and a Piaget watch, examples of a life

I should aspire to. That same pair of designer sunglasses that were sitting at the bottom of my bag.

In comparison, this gift from Autumn was cheap. Off-brand soda, ill-fitting glasses, and a few pieces of plastic. But they were for me, not who I should be, not what she wanted me to be. But mine.

She was several feet ahead, kicking rocks down the path, pebbles skittering as they ricocheted off the red stone. The hike was simple, and the trail was well-worn for thousands of others who had traversed it. The red and orange dust puffed up as we made our way to the summit.

Before us, the city opened, sprawling to the west. Hundreds of miles away lay the ocean, but here, everything was umber and orange, sparse trees with dying leaves darkening to black with the setting sun. Lowering myself to the bright, rocky floor, I rested my hands on my knees.

She pulled out her phone, angling it until we were centered, with red and orange crags around us, the sky a brilliant blue beyond. This time, I leaned in closer, sucking in her flower and herb scent as the side of my head rested against hers for the picture. She took several, sending them off to someone, likely her family, if I had to guess.

"You know, I've heard there are seashell fossils here?" Autumn sat beside me, her thigh inches from mine.

It was all so reminiscent of sitting on my dock months before, her feet kicking out in front of her.

"Really."

"Yeah, I know how you love those little factoids." She grinned at me, her blue eyes lighting up behind those ridiculous flower-shaped glasses.

I couldn't stop my lips from curling up in response. The fading sunlight playing on her burnished hair, the shades so similar to the rocks around us, red, gold, orange, brown, blonde. Blindly, I reached forward, tucking a wayward strand behind her ear, my fingers burning from the heat of her skin.

She sucked in air through her teeth, her expression somehow softening even more. Then her fingers were on my face, tapping at the corner of my mouth. "I love your smile. It's rare. It feels precious and hard earned. I wish I could see it more."

I wish I had more reasons to smile.

Her words are frank; no ridicule, no ulterior motives. She loved my smile and wanted me to know. It had been so long since someone looked at me the way she did. I couldn't help my smile, the urge to give her everything, to let her know she's the one I couldn't deny. For so long, I felt like a ghost, moving like a whisper through the world, never feeling, never wanting. Then she glanced back, big blue eyes on me, and as I grinned, I felt I could be happy if she saw it.

"You bring it out in me." This was true. "You always have. You were such a sweet kid—"

"Please don't call me that."

Pain laced her voice as she drew her knees to her chest, and something inside her shifted.

"What, sweet?"

"Kid." She shook her head. "I can't handle you seeing me like that."

The name slipped out so easily, I hadn't realized I'd said it, but now that I could recognize the word, it felt wrong. She wasn't a kid to me, hadn't been for months. I spent far too long over the past three months trying to fight back the images of her under me. The sounds she made, the feel of her skin.

"I know you're not a kid anymore, Autumn. I see you."

"And what do you see?"

Her voice was meant to be light, but I could hear the strain in the question as if she wasn't sure she should ask.

Danger, danger! This is bad. Lie and say something blasé.

The lies wouldn't form. "I see a woman who eats the heels of bread because she feels bad. A woman who won't stop taking her shoes off in the car and who has the worst taste in spicy chips I've ever seen. But I can also see someone who loves her family more than anything. Someone who doesn't mind looking foolish in blue eyeshadow and wearing those little snappy hair things for her niece."

"Barrettes, they're called barrettes." She gave a whisper of a correction.

"—A woman who, even when I'm grumpy, still puts a smile on my face as she pulls me up the side of a mountain. I see someone who makes me *want* to smile. You're incredible."

"I wish I could see that in myself." Her words were low as she gazed out at the desert. A sudden fall breeze kicked up, cooling our skin. "I don't feel incredible right now. I'm not sure what I have back home. I don't want you calling me a kid because I still feel like I must still be one to be where I am now. It's like everyone is moving on to this next stage, and I'm still stuck behind them. They have their careers and their boyfriends and dogs and houses, and what do I have? Half a degree, the ability to pull two beers at once, and my old full-sized mattress from my parents' house waiting on me. When you call me kid, it reminds me that not only am I undesirable but also immature to everyone else."

Undesirable? Is she serious?

All day long, I've battled with all things I desired to do with her. This entire trip was fraying my restraint faster than those little jean shorts she was wearing. That wouldn't do. I wasn't going to try anything with her, but I couldn't have her feeling like she wasn't an amazing woman. Despite knowing it would make things harder for me, I wrapped an arm around her shoulder to pull her to my side.

"There's no timetable for success. So what if you didn't graduate when your friends did? If you have a job, that isn't quite a career. Even being back with your parents for a bit. We all take our own paths."

"When you were my age, you already made your first million," she reminded me.

Yeah, and I was a miserable prick who lost everything I thought I wanted.

"That life, when I was living in San Jose; my job, the company, my relationship with—" The name died in my throat. I had to bear this weight. "Even when you think you have what you need, it doesn't always work out."

Looking back, I could pinpoint why I said the words, but before the sunset—auburn streams fading into night—I felt safer than I had in years.

"When I say that I admire you, it's not empty words. You are joy and kindness, and sometimes . . . I don't know if I deserve to be around someone so pure."

Her big blue eyes, the same shade of the sky once we reached the summit, widened as she took in my words. My gaze darted down to her mouth, the way her teeth dragged over that lush bottom lip. For the first time since we arrived on this red rock, I realized how alone we really were. No one else was around for miles. I could kiss her, and no one would know. Give in to what my body had been begging for all day, for three months, really. This honest confession had me struggling to steady myself. Why had I said that? Why was I saying far too much to this woman I swore I would only have distance with?

"You think I'm pure?" She gave me a half-smirk, the somber tone fading. "I think we both know I'm not pure."

The joke broke the tension between us. A tease, nothing to wallow over as I drifted off that night. As if it didn't mean everything to me to say. I was both relieved and disappointed she didn't close the gap, claim my mouth, run her hands over my chest, take me like before.

You said you'd look out for her. Remember what you told Oliver.

It was for the best. The rough scrape of my hand against my unshaven cheeks was the only sound in the still evening air. "You know that's not what I'm saying, and if I didn't know any better, I'd think you were provoking me."

The bump of her shoulder jostled us, and I leaned into her, the warmth of the sun still clinging to her freckled arms. "Just figuring it out now? What was your big clue?"

She grinned at me as the sun set in the west and the sky darkened. I could watch as the fading light played over her face, the freckles across her nose and the little scar under her right eye.

Silence had never bothered me, but I knew it was something that she was apt to fill. Except, this time, she didn't. My arm still held her as her head fell to my shoulder as we took in the valley beyond us. In the dying light, her eyes fluttered shut, the corners of her mouth slightly turned up. With her gaze elsewhere, I took her in. Her lashes were blonde at the root and dark at the tips, a heart-shaped mole sat by her ear, freckles dotted her collarbone, and a thin tattoo traced a sideways V of dots ending in small circles.

"What's this?" I asked, my finger hovering over her skin but not quite touching it.

"The constellation Pisces."

"Is that your sign?"

Astrology always seemed like a bit of a joke to me. When I was in college, I saw a student get kicked out of my astronomy class for arguing with the teacher. If that was the belief, I wanted nothing to do with it. I wasn't even sure what my sign was.

"But I'm a February Pisces, not a March Pisces."

"Is there a difference?"

"If you look closely enough, there can be, but you have to earn it." With her eyes still closed, her tongue came out, licking across her bottom lip.

You have to earn it.

That lip that I held between my teeth as her legs wrapped around my waist. The weight of her breasts in my hands, the heft of her ass as I carried her up the stairs. I knew those lips, that ass, those breasts. And yet, there was so much more I wanted. Things I hadn't allowed myself to want in years.

What would it feel like to earn her? She seemed like an open book, warm to everyone, but I knew something simmered beneath her self-deprecating words, at odds with the personality she showed others. Could I earn that knowledge?

"We should head back down before the scorpions come out," she murmured.

"One more minute."

Long ago, someone told me that Sedona had vortexes, spiritual centers for healing and self-exploration. I was too practical to believe in such things, but with her head on my chest and auburn ponytail spilling over me, I almost did. Even knowing I was breaking my own rules, I reveled in the wonder of her weight and the falling dark.

Country pop played on the speakers as I nursed my beer. I was far too old for this bar scene.

Two hours before, she directed me to a campsite where we could park the car for the night. I offered to get us some hotel rooms, but she insisted we needed to camp. When I returned from the camp store, the car was already set up with a blow-up mattress in the back. The mattress looked far too small for both of us, but Autumn insisted we'd be fine, calling it another adventure. Deep down, I knew she was wrong. The more time I spent beside her, the thinner my restraint. The herbal-floral scent clinging to her hair threatened to undo me. But what could I say to change her mind?

Sorry, I can't sleep beside you because the idea of you gives me a massive hard-on, and I don't know if I can control myself?

I was thirty-eight, not some fourteen-year-old spilling in his pants after a school dance.

So, I got her to agree to hotels for the rest of the trip after tonight.

Since we didn't have food for dinner, we ended up at a little cafe, which then led us to the country bar. She was damn hard to say no to.

Fresh from the dance floor—where, true to her word, I'd seen her terrible moves—she set a hand on my shoulder and chugged half her ginger ale. When we arrived, she made me take the shorter stool, standing between my legs, saying that way we were almost the same height. That if she took the stool, she'd be face-to-face with my crotch. That only brought to mind how her lips would feel around my cock. Something we didn't get around to the first time. And wouldn't if I could keep it together.

Something made even more difficult as the bar filled up. Her thighs wedged between mine as the people around us got more and more drunk.

"That was so fun, Nicolai—"

Fuck, if I didn't love the way she said my full name.

"No one calls me that."

She furrowed her brow. "It's your name."

"Yeah, but no one uses it." I tilted my head to the side.

"So, are you telling me not to?" She placed her other hand on my shoulders as someone jostled her from behind.

My fingers found her waist, pulling her closer to me.

"No." I spoke too quickly, panic inexplicably lacing my voice. "No, I like it. You can call me it. I just—"

What was it about this woman that had me on edge? The curl of her tongue around my full name, the sweetest sound I ever heard.

A smirk curled on her lips as she stooped, her mouth brushing against my ear, her breath washing hot on my neck. "I'll get us another round, then, *Nicolai.*"

As she walked away, her hips swayed in those fraying jean shorts. The threads fluttered over her toned thighs as she moved. Had they gotten shorter than when we left the campsite? Out of my line of sight, I could shift the growing hard-on I was sporting from her last word.

Her brother is your best friend. Her brother is your best friend. Her bro—

"So, what's up with your girlfriend?"

I glanced over at the guy beside me, mid-twenties, dark hair flipping out under a pristine Rams cap. "Pardon?"

I hated how the word sounded so proper, making me feel older—especially beside the twenty-something douchebag ogling Autumn's legs and licking his lips. Sure, he was closer to her age than I was, but he was a twat. "Yeah, you two—"

"Todd, you made it!" With two drinks in her hand, her blue-sky eyes sparkled as she approached us.

Autumn gave him one of her sunny smiles, the smile she offered everyone, whether they deserved it, and this guy definitely didn't. Where did she meet a random frat guy? What the hell was going on?

"He's staying at the campground, too. We got to chatting a few hours ago, when you ran to the store. I told him we were coming out here."

She met some random dude at a campsite and invited him along on our—whatever this was—date? No. Friend hang? That sounded worse. Night out? Sure.

"The more the merrier, right?" She set my beer down, then gripped my shoulder to steady herself, her short nails dragging through my thin T-shirt.

The guy's stare darted to her hand and then back up to her face, his smile slipping.

With my hand on her hip, I pulled her closer between my legs. Yeah, I was breaking my rule again about touching her, but I sure as hell wouldn't sit by and watch this fucker take what was mine.

Wait, what? She isn't mine.

This swirling coldness settled over my skin, and I hated this dude even more. I wasn't even sure what this sensation was. I hadn't felt it before.

"No." Not even trying to keep the annoyance out of my voice, I glared at him. "Not to me."

This guy seemed to get the hint, the smile falling from his lips as he backed away. "Imma head back to my friends. Good to see you." He addressed this to Autumn alone, as if I cared.

Once he was far enough, I snatched my beer and downed half, hoping the cold would soothe the itch under my skin.

"You don't have to scare away my new friend."

Glowering at her, I clicked my tongue. "He's not your friend, Autumn. He wants to fuck you."

She threw her head back and laughed. "Unlikely." Did she have any idea? She couldn't. "God, you're as bad as Summer. She thinks every dude has ulterior motives."

"Your cousin's a smart woman. They do."

"What? I can't make new friends?"

Lacing my finger into the belt loop on the front of her shorts, I pulled her closer between my legs. Her breasts brushed against my chest. She still wasn't wearing a bra. "Not with a guy like that, you can't."

"Are you jealous?" She smirked down at me.

"What, no, that's—" I swallowed the rest of my beer down.

Her auburn brow arched, white teeth flashing as she looked up at me, tongue tracing her top lip as she hummed a soft *mm-hmm*.

"Okay, if you say so."

"I don't think you should leave the bar with some guy."

"Why? I left that party with you."

Light danced in her eyes.

"Yeah, but I'm me, and you're you, and—"

"And, what, Nicolai, you think I'm going to have sex with him, too?"

She said that word so casually as if that was all we did. As if that was all we could be. She didn't really think that, did she?

It's just sex, right? That was what she said to me that night.

It's just sex, it's just sex, it's just—

"Was it just sex with me too, then?" I asked.

Why did I do that? I was hoping she would say yes, that we could still play this game where that night together was a blip. That we were two consenting adults who made a single mistake. But a larger part of me wanted her to admit it was different. That she wanted more from me, expected more, needed more. Needed me.

Her blue eyes darkened as she glanced down at my lips. "You made those rules, Nicolai. Don't make me want things I can't have."

Leaning forward, I pulled her hip into me, my words soft against the shell of her ear. Her hair smelled of flowers and something herbal, the scent of it my whack-off fuel for months. "Sweet girl." The endearment came out before I could take it back, and I relished the light in her eyes. "Who says you can't have them?"

This was the beer talking once again. My common sense wasn't listening.

Her fingers tensed on my sleeve, a sharp breath escaping into a low moan that would be my undoing, before she pulled away, eyes bright. "You are such a frickin' tease."

The grin playing over her face was warm and wide, the corners of her eyes crinkling as she shook her head from side to side. As if I didn't mean the words, as if she couldn't feel this too. By then, she should know me well enough to know I wasn't funny.

Stepping back, she held out a hand, pulling me from the barstool. "Come on, let's get back. We've got a big day of driving ahead of us."

With her hand in mine, I pulled her along and gave a self-satisfied wave to Tom—Trent?—who'd spent the night alone, not with her. Even though I knew nothing would happen between her and I. Most likely, maybe.

I opened the driver's side door and let her climb in before shutting it and circling to the passenger seat. As we pulled from the neon-lit lot, my eyes caught a jeep with a UFO on the tire cover and the words: *Get in, loser. We're doing butt stuff.*

This trip would take all my composure to get through.

She climbed into the back, the full-size mattress barely big enough for two. Already, that flowery herbal scent of her hair was filling the small space.

I turned away, fist clenched to keep from reaching for her.

If you can earn it. Earn it. Earn—

"Just so you know, it wasn't just sex for me," she said to my back.

Then her fingers were on my shoulder.

I could have stayed turned away from her and the tension between us, but I didn't. In a shimmying movement, I allowed her hand to guide onto my back, my head falling to the side to face her. Palm still on my shoulder, she tucked the other one beneath her cheek as she stared at me. It was too dark to see her features, but they were there, the perfect triangle cluster of freckles at her hairline, the white scar under left eye, those full pink lips.

Little space separated us, her face at my neck, my breath stirring the auburn strands on her head. A tendril of hair curved over her clavicle, and my fingers itched to wind around a wayward strand, to pull her face to mine. To claim that spot on her throat, mark it. I clenched my fist tighter.

Me too. Why can't I say it?

"And what you said earlier about me? I think you are more than you believe yourself to be. I know I'm not nearly as good as you think I am."

Her sweet air was soft on my throat.

It was a dangerous game. We had several more nights together. After the sun went down, these lines blurred, but in the dark of this car on a blow-up mattress, I couldn't pull away. Instead, my forearm slid between her shoulder blades as I pulled her against my chest.

"Yes, you are," I murmured into her hair. She didn't pull away—just wrapped her arms around my waist, one hand on my hipbone, the other tucked beneath her cheek.

Despite my frequent attempts to resist, she was etching herself into me. In this tight space, I let her face burrow into my chest. Her breath fell over my skin, evening out until she was asleep. I could blame it on my three beers at the bar or the confined quarters of the car. The next day, I'd regret this slip-up, but that night, in the darkest of this night, I clung to her as assuredly as she held me.

POINT G–GRAND CANYON, AZ

Autumn

THIS TIME, HE WAS awake before me. Everything was warm and sticky from the condensation of our breath all night. The windows fogged up against the cool desert air. A deep crease formed on my cheek from how hard my face was pressed to his chest all night. All night. He held me all night.

When he reached out and pulled me to him, I was surprised. For all his big speeches about rules and boundaries, he sure seemed to barrel through them. Never one not to act on my impulses, I wouldn't be this voice of reason over what we craved in one another. I didn't always realize when I was being hit on—a fact my friends found funny. But if you press against a man in a bar and his dick hardens, he wants something.

That same dick tented in his thin sweatpants. Not moving my head, I opened my eyes more to see the evidence clear as day. From his breathing, I could tell he'd woken only moments before me, more alert but not enough to notice I, too, was awake. No bother, I could take this time to catalog the lines of his body flush with mine, the way my thigh bracketed over his. The tense pectoral muscle under my cheek. That erection got larger as I shifted, my center rubbing against his hip as I adjusted myself.

Above me, I heard a low groan and the scrape of a calloused hand over his unshaven cheeks. In mere moments, he would push me away, regretting being so close to me all night. Savoring the last second, I rubbed my core against his hipbone and hummed low, my eyes on his pants. Sure enough, his dick twitched at the sound.

Gotcha.

His arm slid out from under my shoulder blades, depositing me onto the mattress as he shimmied down the small area to open the back hatch. Cool morning air flowed into the car as he climbed out. Dramatically, I played up the sleep in my voice as he adjusted himself away from me.

"Morning, lover."

Over his shoulder, he scowled at me. "Aut—"

I propped myself up on my elbows and cocked my head to the side. The blanket fell down my lap as I studied him, the corner of my mouth crooking up. "How did you sleep?"

His eyes darted down to my chest, my nipples hard in the cool morning air, my thin top leaving little to the imagination. Good, he's seen them before. I was rubbing them against his side only five minutes ago.

"Fine."

A muscle ticked in his jaw.

Offering a sleepy smile, I rolled my neck around, my eyes drifting closed. "I was so comfortable. Car camping can be hit or miss for me, but this car is perfect for it, don't you think?"

A snort of air came out of his nostrils as his gaze dipped to my chest again before he grabbed a small bag from the car. "I'll be back soon."

His long legs ate up the gravel path as he stalked to the bathroom, and I couldn't contain the giggle I let out. He was so easy to rile.

But was it embarrassment?

As attracted to him as I was, I wasn't foolish enough to think I was casting some spell over him. He was firm on those rules the day before. Was it for my benefit? Was I making a fool of myself flirting with a man who didn't want me?

He might react that way to any woman. I could have been anyone, and his response would have been the same. Flopping back onto the mattress, I stared at the ceiling, the smile fading from my face.

Nothing special, nothing worthwhile, nothing—

No, I wouldn't go down that path. Pulling out my phone, I opened my favorite daily positivity app. A few years ago, I started doing these affirmations.

I am confident in myself and my abilities.

I could do that. Empowerment. The hour was early, but I texted the group chat my daily affirmation, something they grumbled about yet admitted they appreciated. Devin gave it a heart reaction first. I'd have to wait for the rest to wake up beside their perfect boyfriends in their perfect little houses with their perfect little dogs. Okay, it was only Wren who had a perfect little dog but still.

Scooting my butt across the mattress, I grabbed my bag, pulling out my toiletries. Confident. Confident.

When Nico returned over twenty minutes later, his hair was damp, the ends curling around his ears. I had changed and scarfed down a handful of spicy chips from the snack bag, followed by a lukewarm ginger ale. *I would kill for a pumpkin spice latte, maybe we could stop by on our way out of town.*

Toothbrush hanging from my mouth, I watched as he rifled through his duffel bag in the front seat, pulling out fresh clothes. With a fluid movement, he pulled off the shirt and changed, facing away from me. The lean taper of his back, the band of his underwear a thin line as he dragged the fabric over his head. Those arms that held me the night before. It was a tragedy he was hiding them.

"Should we get breakfast somewhere or just hit the road?" I asked as his arms were still pushing through the sleeves.

"I guess we have time to get breakfast at a little diner or something." His head popped out of the neckline, and he looked at me for the first time since returning to the campsite. "Do you—" His jaw tensed, his eyes darting away. "Never mind."

Toothbrush stowed safely in its plastic sandwich baggie—I really should get a nicer toiletry kit—I pulled out my favorite sunscreen.

"What?"

His cheeks were flooding with color.

"Do you own a bra?"

With the lotion absorbed into my hands, I rubbed it on my décolletage and up my neck. "Of course I do. Several, in fact." I grinned.

"Then, why aren't you wearing them?"

Men like to talk about women with big boobs, but they have no idea of the hassle they could be. I got my first bra when I was ten and was a D cup in my freshman year of high school. I got dress-coded for tops that would be appropriate on almost any other girl, including one Summer wore with no issues. After a while, I leaned into the whole big-boobs thing. They weren't going away, and I wouldn't hide or wear torture devices like minimizer bras just to look smaller. Plus, anything over a DD stopped being cute and started looking like Auntie Murial in a housedress.

"I don't like the straps showing. Plus, they can be uncomfortable, especially when it's so hot out. Really, with this top, I'd have to wear a strapless bra with it, and with boobs as big as mine, those things are such a hassle, made for smaller busted girls. So, it's way more comfortable to go without. Besides, this top is tight enough it's confining enough to be like a pseudo-bra."

Nico tilted his head back, eyes shut, Adam's apple bobbing as he clenched and slackened his jaw.

I couldn't help myself once I started going. Even if he didn't want me flirting with him like this, it was so fun to see these little cracks in his armor.

Confident.

Tossing the sunscreen back in my bag, I shimmy my shoulders. "I'm so glad you noticed, though. Was wondering how long it would take you."

Truly a highlight to watch him losing it over me. It was a fun little thrill.

Behind his hand, he mumbled, "So fucked."

"What?" I pulled my hair up with both hands and asked, angling my chest forward.

Electrifying, really.

"Get in the fucking car, Autumn," he grumbled as he slid on the gold-rimmed aviators.

Hands on the observation deck's railing, I peered down into the colossal rip in the earth, millions of years in the making.

The air in Northern Arizona was wildly different from that in the desert valley. At least twenty degrees cooler than when we left Oliver and Janie's house. I relished the chill as it whipped over my bare arms. Finally, it felt like fall. Finally, we could see the change of the leaves, the briskness of morning settling over the ground, the scent of the end of a plant's natural life cycle, and the decay that would lead to rebirth after the winter. As a scientist, I rejoiced in the season.

Pictures truly could not have done the area justice, the sheer scale of the rock split apart from the Colorado River. The water itself was a thin line so far beneath me as I peered down the canyon. The varying colors on display, millions of years of earth and elements standing witness to time. Red, brown, yellow, white, gray, orange again.

My display of bralessness must've distracted Nico enough not to question when I typed in the next destination on my phone. The tension in his jaw didn't abate until we made our way through the hairpin turns of Oak Creek Canyon. He didn't question the route until we were passing Flagstaff, heading farther north and off the main highway. The bright orange and red foliage grew thicker as we left the desert. When he realized I'd hijacked navigation for another side quest, he only shook his head and let me ramble while staying on course.

For a long stretch, Nico and I stood side by side on the observation deck, taking in the view. He'd been here once in college on a spring break trip after Lake Havasu—a place he insisted he never wanted to visit before I could ask. Silently, he listened as I gushed about all the features I loved seeing, his eyes flickering over the brochure he grabbed from the visitor's center. Once again, that smile crept up on his lips as he extolled the history of the park. He loved facts and teaching others, and I loved that light in his eyes when he was excited about something.

When he saw I wanted to take a few extra minutes, he offered to get us snacks and coffees.

Hands in my back pockets, I stopped at an interpretive sign about local wildlife and conservation efforts.

"Questions?"

I startled at the sight of a man wearing an olive-green-and-gray park ranger uniform. The little tag on his chest read *D. Collins.*

"What about marine life?" I motioned to the sign.

Ranger Collins scratched his chin with a thumbnail. "There's two clam species that are thought to be introduced to the area, not native, but we have some aquatic snails."

"Really?" I brightened. "What kind?"

"Pond snails. Fresh water ones. Itty bitty things."

"Lymnaea?" I asked and thrilled at his surprise. "I'm in school for marine biology. Though most of my focus had been on saltwater clams, specifically geoducks."

"Not sure I'm familiar with those. But I'd be willing to hear more about them."

He was cute. In another day, if I wasn't so caught up in thinking about Nico, I might be interested. But this man's eyes were blue, his hair black, his face too narrow.

He wasn't Nico.

Realizing I was assessing him, I turned away, my eyes searching the other side of the canyon beyond the fence. "They're so fascinating, the largest of the saltwater clams. And they can grow to over three feet long and have the longest lifespan, around one hundred and forty years old. Plus, they're pretty famous because of their phallic shape."

The ranger rocked back on his heels, his lips thinning, and brow raising. "Well, now you're teaching me something. That doesn't happen often." He smiled at me, his wide face brightening as he dug in his small bag. "We keep these for the kids, but I think you deserve it."

He handed me a small plastic gold pin, with the words *Junior Park Ranger* written on the top.

"Aww, I'm honored." I clipped it to the strap of my tank top before grinning back at him.

"Now, you were saying something about the shape of clams?" he asked, leaning in closer.

Nico approached, two coffees in hand, his narrowed gaze on the ranger, his knuckles white.

"Nico!" Taking the coffee from his proffered hand, I motioned to my new acquaintance. "I was telling Ranger Collins here about geoducks and how they look like—"

"I know what geoducks look like," Nico snapped, his jaw tight.

Really, he was going to need dentures by forty if he kept grinding his teeth like that.

The ranger's smile faded, and he stepped back. "Well, I hope you two enjoy your visit to the park. Let me know if you have questions. The visitor center is open until four today."

Nico scowled at his retreating olive-and-gray form before his eyes snapped to me. "What was that?"

"Nothing." I took a sip of my coffee, the pumpkin flavoring mixing just right with the sweet cream and coffee. Humming, I closed my eyes and nodded my head to the taste. "Dang, that's good. Who knew they'd have such great coffee here, right?"

The day before, he'd teased me about my sugary coffee—plain black for him—asking if I wanted Fruit Loops in it. This time, Nico didn't take the bait.

"I didn't know it was part of a park ranger's job to flirt with visitors."

Smirking over the top of my coffee, I shook my head. "He was being nice. It's his job to be friendly."

"No, his job is to make sure assholes don't wander too close to the cliff edge, not talk about dicks with pretty girls."

The corner of my mouth hitched up as I studied him with bright eyes. "You think I'm pretty?"

Scowling, he sipped his boring coffee and shook his head at me. "Don't change the subject."

"And I wasn't talking about dicks. I was talking to him about geoducks."

"Something in abundance here at the Grand Canyon," he mumbled before stalking away.

This time, I trailed him. In minutes, we approached the car, and he unlocked my door manually before moving to his side.

Climbing into the passenger seat—I was still banned from driving after the Sedona incident—I tilted my head and frowned at him. "He was interested. And he gave me this pin, see?" I kneeled on the bench seat, feet tucked under me, and plucked my tank top strap with my thumb, tugging the pin closer to him.

His eyes darted to the plastic, and somehow his jaw tensed harder.

He slid on the gold-rimmed sunglasses, his grip on the tan-and-white leather turning each knuckle white. "Why is it you flirt with every guy who comes within fifty feet of you?"

The keys hung in the ignition, but he hadn't turned the engine yet.

With one finger, I slid my sandals off my feet. "I wasn't flirting. I was being nice. Something you clearly don't know how to do."

The huff of air through his nose combined with his closed eyes gave the appearance of a man on his last thread. "Sorry if seeing you throw yourself at every guy you see isn't making me want to get up and cheer."

"I—how dare—I'm not."

Rarely did I get mad, but when I did, I could never come up with retorts. Summer always had a dozen at her disposal, quick and acerbic but me? I got speechless.

"You don't need to be nice to everyone."

The words erupting from me weren't polished or well-thought-out, and I wanted to take them back. They were too personal, too raw, but I couldn't bring myself to stop.

"Maybe I do. Maybe nice is all I have going for me? Maybe it's my only redeeming quality, and I have to hold on to what I can."

"What the fuck are you talking about?" He threw his glasses onto the dashboard as he turned to face me, his gaze cutting sideways.

A furrow in his brow and a sneer on his lips as if my words were ridiculous. Which, apparently, he thought I was. Big surprise.

"I have to be nice because if I'm not, then—" I swallowed hard, a burn arching through my chest. My gaze grew hazy with tears as I faced the open canyon beyond, the words spilling out of me, unbidden. "Once, when I was about eight, I woke up early in the morning and decided I was going to make a breakfast feast for everyone, make it a party for the whole family. I spent hours making toast and juicing every mandarin we had in the house into a pitcher. I even spent over an hour cutting out little animals from construction paper to make a mural I hung in the entrance of the dining room. When my mom came down, she looked around at the table, then went into the kitchen. She returned a minute later with the empty fruit bowl and asked me, 'Did you really have to use them all, Autumn?' And it stung so bad.

"She wasn't mad, wasn't anything, but I could see how all my work was for nothing, just another silly thing I did thinking I was making the right choice and failing to understand why no one could see all the hard work I put in. I had envisioned this big celebration where they would say, 'Oh, thank you for making this morning so special for us, for getting up early and putting all this effort into our day.' But it was her grumbling that I left scraps of paper all over the living room floor. It was Ewan complaining that the juice was too tart, Ivan knocking into the mural and ripping it on accident, my dad grabbing a single slice of toast on his way out the door and not sparing me a second glance.

"It's such a silly memory to hold on to. They weren't being cruel. They said thank you and ate the food, but the reaction I built up in my mind, the acknowledgment I craved, I wasn't going to get it. That's what it's been like growing up with them. I've always been an outlier. My brothers were athletic and intelligent and went to school. Dad, a whiz at all things mechanical. Mom is a formidable mathematician. I can't help but compare myself to them all, even my cousin, Summer. She's so bright and vivacious and doesn't take any flack, and everyone is always won over by her.

"They would never think they're better than me. I know that. They love me endlessly. But I'm always *sweet Autumn who tries hard. Give her a break.* I always mean well, but try as I might, I can't seem to figure out how to do the right thing. Didn't finish college, can't find a career. In an impressive family, I've only ever been ordinary. My only saving grace is being nice. It was a simple thing, nothing special, nothing worth its salt . . ."

Reaching across the seat, he pulled my hand to him, and I couldn't help but delight in the way his palm fit against mine. "This world is cruel. We could do with a little more nice, don't you think?"

"And where does that get me?" I snorted, turning my head away, feeling more broken. The past thirty hours of wanting him and receiving nothing but sneers and rudeness took their toll. "Every time I try to be as assertive as Summer, I get this pain in my chest, and my whole body feels cold. It's like I can see their disappointment in me, see the way they think. *Oh, she's not nice now. She's nothing special.* And I know I shouldn't care what others think of me. But I do. There has never been a day when I haven't. I'll read self-help books and recite affirmations about bravery and practice speeches in my mirror to end up capitulating the moment someone argues. It's not a virtue. It's a sickness."

"Nothing about you could be sick, Autumn."

His grip on my hand tightened as he snorted the words.

"Really, you sure about that? I see the way you look at me." His face paled, but I barreled on. "And I know it's the same. She's so nice. Such a nice kid. I'm not blind. I can tell you think what happened between us is a mistake, that I'm being a silly girl throwing myself at you this way. I know I should stop. You don't want me like that. You never did. That it's foolish and childish and that there's nothing between us, and once again, I'm putting my idea of how things should be on someone else and—"

"Stop. Please, don't say another word." Unexpectedly, he raised our clasped hands to his mouth. His soft lips brushed against my knuckles.

It was a reverent kiss, not something born of passion or want but chaste and innocent. Platonic even.

I swallowed, the shame of my word vomit cascading over me. *Oh gosh, oh no. No, no, no, no.* What was I doing? Harmless flirting was one thing, but that was wholly something else I could never get back from.

"Sweet girl, don't think for a moment that I don't want you"—he swallowed hard, his gaze focused on my hand as he formed the words—"like that. Because I've spent the last three months trying to get you out of my head. Trying and failing miserably."

"You have?" I breathed out, my chest expanding at the admission, my breathing growing staccato.

At this, his eyes snapped to mine, and his jaw once again tensed as if he was determining how much truth to give me. "But you are my best friend's sister. Not to mention more than a decade younger than me. I can't take advantage of you like that."

"Even if I want it, too?" I rushed out, scooting closer, my knees knocking with his right hip.

He turned my hand palm-down, his finger tracing from pinky to wrist, fire burning a line across my skin. He followed the bones, up and down each finger, then reached my thumb. The air thickened as his gaze stayed fixed on me.

"You have beautiful fingers, you know that?"

If I was honest, I had no clue what we're talking about anymore. All I could think of was his lips near my skin, my knee against his hip, and how little it would take to swing my leg over him—just like that night on the dock. The heat of his breath tickled the back of my hand until he held up our entwined fingers in the space between us. "I do?"

"Long and graceful and the skin here"—he pressed down below my knuckles— "is still so soft and young. You know, I've been around a lot of people who get plastic surgery, and one way you can always tell someone is older is by their hands. The hands always give it away."

Again, he brought my hand up to his mouth, pressing another kiss where this thumb had pressed down. "But yours, these freckles, the give of your skin. You're young, Autumn, too young for me."

"I'm not." I shudder out the words, wanting to sound confident, but need coated them, weakening them.

"But I can be your friend. I can look after you the way Oliver asked me to."

These words were bars coming up between us. *Clang.* Slammed shut from all I could want. *Clang.* A promise made by a brother. *Clang.* The guilt and doubt of what we did weighed on him.

"I'd like to be your friend." He hesitated, his fingers still laced with mine, his thumb tracing over the apex under mine. "Though I doubt I'd be a friend to you. Not the kind you deserve because you are a good person. There is a lot you don't know about me, things Oliver doesn't know. No one really does, but suffice to say, I've had my share of complicated friendships. Maybe it would be good to have someone who is kind, who says what they mean. Maybe I'm ready for some nice. Don't downplay kindness. It's pure, like you."

With this, he dropped my hand, the sensation of his skin against mine searing up my arm straight through me. His eyes caught mine, those sage green so light it's unreal, eyes burrowing into me. What the heck was I supposed to do with this sharp ache in my chest whenever he looked at me?

Somehow, despite not understanding how, I knew this frankness, the vulnerability as he studied me, the earnest green of his gaze was for me alone. No one else would get the privilege of seeing this version of him. Only me. Only them.

"Don't let me ruin you."

His arm slid over the backrest of the bench seat, his fingers inches from my shoulder as he shifted into reverse. His biceps flexed as he gripped the headrest and glanced over his shoulder to pull the car from its spot. As the car idled in reverse, he dipped one finger over my shoulder to pull at the strap of my tank top. A whisper of a touch against my skin scorched a path that led straight down into my center. With a clenched jaw, he studied the side of my face, his expression unreadable. Between his finger and thumb, he gripped the pin, twirling it.

"It's a nice pin." Then he pulled it loose, closed the clasp, and stuffed it in his pocket.

"What are you—" Huffing out a breath, I narrowed my eyes.

"I don't want you wearing this."

"Why? Because it's silly?" I waggled my head mockingly, my voice coming out like a song.

His gaze crashed into mine, his expression hard. "No, because another man gave it to you." He shifted the car into drive, the parking lot giving way to open road until the Grand Canyon shrank in the rearview.

POINT H-LAS VEGAS STRIP, NV

Nico

THE BREEZE PICKED UP a business card with a picture of a naked woman and hit Autumn in the stomach. Card in hand, she studied the picture before shooting me a wicked grin. "Do you think if you called the number they'd really look like this?"

I glanced at the escort car. The woman in the picture had big hair and poorly done clip-art stars over her nipples. If I had to wager, that photo was at least twenty years old. "Doubtful."

The sun was hanging low over the Strip as we made our way between casinos. Even in the late October afternoon, it was warm in our shorts and T-shirts. To the left, a sign advertised two-for-one canned micheladas. To the right was a video billboard cut from a comedian to a sizzling steak.

"Should we call the number?" Autumn asked. "I've always wondered."

"About hookers?" I scoffed.

"Sex workers, and yeah. You've never been curious?"

I snorted. "No. Definitely not."

"Don't be snide. It's the oldest profession in the world."

Tapping a finger on the lip of my aluminum beer bottle, I studied her. "I'm not denigrating their work. I'm just not interested in hiring one."

"I bet they have the most fascinating stories to tell. I'd love to talk with one."

I stopped on the sidewalk beside a kiosk for tourist T-shirts. *Save water, drink beer, Las Vegas.* Turning to face her, my brows together. "You can't be serious. You want to call up some hotline and what?"

Tilting her head to the side, she surveyed the escort card, flipping from the front to the back. "I'm not trying to have sex with them. I'd want to ask questions."

"Questions? You can't do that."

Keeping Autumn safe on this trip was becoming much more than I bargained for. From now on, when Oliver asked me for a favor, I would let him know all debts were cleared.

"Says who? You? Is that one of your rules, Nicolai?"

Fire danced in her eyes as she said my name, and she had to know how it affected me when her lips shaped the letters.

I glowered at her as she reminded me of the rules I couldn't keep. The softness of her skin as I pulled that stupid pin off her shirt still tingled over my fingers. Not to mention the way her hand felt clasped in mine. Like it belonged as if I should never hold another.

"You can't say you've never been curious?"

This woman was going to give me a headache. Between my thumb and forefinger, I pinched the bridge of my nose. "The thought has never crossed my mind, no."

"Who knew you were so puritanical? Where's your sense of adventure?" she teased, tucking the card into her back pocket.

"In the same place as my common sense."

She looped her arm through mine. "Fine, don't let me call the number. Be the boring voice of reason or whatever."

The smile she gave me told me she had only kept the conversation going in that direction so long because she liked my reaction. Shaking my head, I led her toward our next stop. "You know what I said earlier? I take it back. You're not nice. You are a vixen, mean and calculating."

With this, she threw her head back and laughed, the cords of her throat straining with the sound, her shoulders shaking with mirth. "I can't calculate a tip at the Olive Garden without my phone, let alone with another person."

This wholesome laugh, the way her arm felt so right tucked through my elbow, I couldn't help but lean in closer, bumping into her. Why was she so hard to stay mad at? "I know, and maybe that's what I like so much about you."

In Autumn's free hand, she brought the gigantic straw up to her lips, the strap on the yard-tall plastic cup over a shoulder.

Thick orange liquid of her virgin slushie was stuck halfway up the straw as she offered me a sip. My expression must've said more than my words because Autumn laughed—that throaty, sweet sound I'd grown too attached to in our short time together. Sensation expanded in my chest and down to my cock.

"Come on. One sip won't kill you."

Her lip gloss, a thin sheen of raspberry color, was left on the edge of the straw. Even though I knew I would hate the drink—too sweet, too thick—I couldn't help but put my lips where hers were.

Just as I thought, the drink was disgusting, cloying and viscous. With great difficulty, I swallowed it down, trying not to gag.

"See? Delicious."

I hummed my assent before opening my beer, the aluminum bottle icy in my hand. Here, I was glad of the open-container laws in the city. The taste of fake mango and sugar washed from my mouth as we continued down the street.

"I can get you your own if you want, the girls, and I always get these when we're here."

"No, I'm good. I'll stick to beer."

"Suit yourself. I'll enjoy mine, then." She bit the straw's tip while looking up at me. My cock twitched before she wrapped her lips around it, sucking until her cheeks hollowed.

Fuck me.

Her eyes stayed on mine as she swallowed hard. She had to know what that would do to me—to any man, really. Now all I could think of was those lips around my cock, her gaze heavy on mine as her hand pressed into my upper thigh. I had to drop my arm from her, angling myself away so she couldn't see the bulge in my pants.

"—No one was drinking the blue one after that."

"What?" I missed the front half of her story completely.

"The neon blue slushies. Devin had one last time we were here, and it led to some surprises in the bathroom later that day. She'd be so embarrassed. I told you that. Don't let her know." She grimaced. "Sometimes, I start talking and things just come out. I'm the worst secret keeper in the world. You wouldn't believe the pickles I've gotten myself into because I couldn't keep my trap shut."

"Do you ever swear?"

She pulled the straw from her lips, her head tilted in consideration. "Not too often. I mean, if I hit my head on a cabinet or something, I might now and then. But I've never seen the point of cursing. There are so many other fun words to use."

"Curse words have actually been shown to relieve pain better than their counterparts."

Her eyes narrowed as she assessed me. "Is that true, or did you make that up?"

"I read it somewhere."

Hoisting the strap of her ridiculous drink higher, she pulled out her phone from her pocket and began typing on it.

"What are you doing?"

"Checking with Summer."

"How would she know?"

"She knows everything. She and her boyfriend Van are the trivia extraordinaires. You wouldn't believe the random tidbits they have about every topic."

Though the phone was upside down, I could read the group name, *Seasonal Obsessions*.

I'd have to unpack that one later.

"So, you don't trust me."

"Did I say that?" She raised one auburn brow, the fading sunlight catching the loose strands of her hair that had come out of her long braid.

My finger itched to wrap around it and tuck it behind her ear. To trace that freckle just below her jaw, to wind my palm around her nape and pull her lips to mine. To taste the fake mango and sugar on her tongue.

A text came through, and Autumn scrunched her nose. "Wren says you're right."

"Told you."

"Do you have to be so cocky about it?"

"I like to think of myself as confident."

She sucked on the straw, a light twinkling behind her eyes. "What else does that confidence get you?"

Since we left Sedona that morning, she had been goading me—with low-cut tops, double entendres, fingers brushing mine, her hand lingering on my forearm.

But, damn, if I wasn't falling for each and every one. It had been years since I let myself flirt with a beautiful woman, since I loosened the inhibitions warning me not to get attached. But Autumn made me want to, even if only for a short while.

"I don't know if you could handle it."

Her teeth closed around the straw as her smile widened at me, happy to have me flirt back. "Oh, I don't know. I felt like I handled you fine before. You're not the only one who can be confident with their prowess."

That night flashed before me. Her cry as I pressed her to the couch, breasts too big for my hands, her warmth as I sank into her, the way she shattered against my tongue. And now here she was before me, with the same pink cheeks, the soft hair escaping its braid, the same brightness in her eyes. Could I have that again?

"I'm completely sober, and I kissed you back."

She kept talking about this trip as an adventure, a break from the reality of the world. Standing on this neon street with a drink in my hand, I could almost allow myself to let go of all that was holding me back. Maybe for the next thousand miles, at least. Still, I couldn't stop the little voice of her brother in my head. More than once, I tried to push Autumn away, but she barreled past my fears, and each excuse grew tenuous. I wasn't sure how much longer I could hold on to them.

Autumn refused to get two separate rooms, even after I offered to pay for them, saying in front of the desk clerk, "We've already had sex and slept together last night. Don't get your undies in a wad over this."

I had the sense to slide my credit card across the counter to the clerk with downcast eyes and a knowing smirk. We walked in expecting two queens but found a single king in the center. No fold-out couch and not enough blankets for the floor.

Once again, I offered to get to another room.

Autumn leaned back on her elbows, her tits pushed out and her head cocked. "Now, who's being a kid about things?"

Once again, I was committing myself to a night of temptation, fraught with what my body wanted and what my mind knew I couldn't have.

"Au—"

She squealed, her gaze leaving mine as she pulled my arm with one hand and pointed across the wide street with the other. "Oh, look! A wedding party!"

A woman wearing a white poofy dress and a big veil stood beside a man with khakis and a Hawaiian print shirt with a bow tie.

"Did you know Keller Grant married his wife here in Vegas?"

"Who?"

Did I know a Keller?

She rolled her eyes. "Keller Grant? From Prevalent Notion, remember we were talking about them after that party. The musicians."

Right, the famous band that owned summer houses across the water from me. The night she was talking about how sexy she found another member, Nathan Ayers. The hot rock stars she talked about loving. That part, I remembered, then another comment from that night came back to me.

For the right guy, what's a few years?

"I always liked the idea of a Vegas wedding," Autumn mused.

Her gaze stayed on the couple posing, a patriotic song blasting from speakers in the cement pillars beside the fountain.

I choked on my beer. "What?"

"I'm not proposing to you, silly. Don't blow a gasket." Her blue eyes darted to mine, and she graced me with a wicked smile. "I'm just saying, there's a certain romance in falling in love and getting married so quickly that you can't wait another day."

But now that she said the words wedding, love, marriage. Words that I had stashed far away for years, buried under guilt and deceit. But now here they were, simple, sweet and full of hope, I couldn't help the vision flashing before me. Autumn in white, the brightness of her smile at an altar, the cool press of her hand while reciting those age-old vows. Nearly a decade had passed since I welcomed such a thought. Yet here it was—unbidden but welcome, if only in my head.

"I would have thought you'd want a big wedding with your family and friends and several hundred townspeople." I allowed myself a single glance at her before resting my gaze back on the couple across the street.

"Oh sure, that could come later, of course. But there is something terribly romantic about a moment being between two people alone, isn't it? After all, that's what marriage is, right?"

"How should I know?" I asked before draining the rest of my beer.

"Are you acting like you've never thought about your wedding?" She quirked a brow, that sunny smile never leaving her face.

"Guys don't think about that stuff." I swallowed hard.

She snorted, her face never losing its humor. "I don't believe that. I think you know exactly what kind of wedding you'd have. Let me have it." She waved in a beckoning motion. "Give me all the details."

The coffee table, with its bridal magazines, vineyard, or beachfront—east or west direction, fabric swatches, and cake samples.

I glanced away from Autumn, swallowing hard. "Since I'm not getting married, I don't know why it matters."

"Because it's your life."

A too-short life.

"A party to celebrate love, it's a beautiful thing." Her smile never wavered as memories flooded through me.

Filet mignon or prime rib, summer or fall? The cold sting of a platinum ring with its three-carat diamond solitaire. Such a disappointment. Such a disappointment. Such a—

"I'm getting another beer," I grumbled, stalking into the greasy windowed storefront.

"Who do you think Tactil is?" Autumn motioned to the framed photo on the wall of the small Italian restaurant we found ourselves in.

The Vegas strip is one of the worst types of optical illusions. Every building so vast it seems like it's closer than it is, and by the time you reach your destination, you've walked miles. After walking around all day with me and my mercurial moods, Autumn deserved the world. The least I could do after snapping at her for no reason was to buy her pasta. It wasn't her fault. None of this was.

And that made it all the worse. Her sunny smile faded, and I did that to her. I would do worse if she kept allowing it. Why couldn't she listen to me when I told her to stay away?

Earn it. Earn it.

I never would. Never *could*.

For the rest of the day, she stayed by my side, pointing out street performers and sharing stories of past trips with friends. By the time we reached the restaurant, I'd heard too much about her friend's life, about her cousin breaking into a boyfriend's house, her ex likely fired. Good riddance to that rubbish.

In the years I had been friends with Oliver, I formed a protective feeling over Summer. When I found out her ex was showing naked photos of her to his coworkers, I made the uncomfortable decision to tell her. When the asshole was fired a few months later, I suspected Summer was behind it.

They were only months apart in age, but my protectiveness toward Summer was nothing like the way my body reacted to seeing Autumn again that night. The moment Autumn stood up, one of my pilfered beers in hand. It was as if I had taken a punch to my chest. With Summer, she was an adult, but she was still gawky Summer. But Autumn, I recognized her immediately, but she wasn't the girl I knew.

Her big blue eyes stared up at me. The sweet scent of her hair enveloped me as she hugged me, and I knew then what I was trying to fight so hard against.

I'm in trouble.

No, how I was feeling about Autumn was very, very dangerous for us both. Maybe it was pragmatism, maybe cowardice. I couldn't be sure, but I would break, and if I wasn't more careful, I would pull her down with me.

Ruin her just as much as I ruined all before her.

Standing beside her as the hostess helped the family before us, I studied the old picture on the wall. A middle-aged couple stood in front of a small house, their arms around each other. Beside the photo was a hand-written letter. One version in Italian if I had to guess and below the translation.

TACTIL,

The distance from you has rendered me in despair, but I treasure the memory of your kiss. Know I will fight ceaselessly to return to you. Until we are wed, hold to my word that my heart has always and will always be yours.

TACTIL

"The letter, it's to and from Tactil, so which one do you think is Tactil? What kind of name is that?"

"That's not Tactil, it's T-A-C-T-I-L," an older man in a suit declared behind us. We whirled around to face him. "Ti amo con tutto il cuore. *I love you with all my heart.* It's how my grandparents signed each letter." He touched his finger to the picture. "Giovanna and Enrico Vitale. She was Catholic, and he was Jewish. They weren't allowed to date. She used to come into his father's bakery every day. She was sixteen, and he was nineteen. They would write letters in secret to each other, slip them in the paper they wrapped the rolls in. They could only be together in secret until they escaped Italy and eloped."

Autumn's eyes softened at the story. "That's beautiful." She turned to the photo. "I adore stories like that."

The man grinned at us, beckoning us to follow him. "And I adore young lovers coming into my restaurant. Sonny Vitale, welcome."

"Autumn Townsend." She stuck her hand out, shaking the older gentleman's hand. "It's a pleasure. I love the ambiance in here, and is that—" She motioned over his head at a black-and-white photo on the wall.

"Betty Grable. She had a show here with her second husband. My father worked at the show. That's where we got many of these photos. My parents met quite a few stars in their day. Back then, Vegas was new, flashy, with the mob still running a few things."

"The mob?"

Autumn's eyes lit up the same way as when we were discussing the escorts earlier, full of curiosity and wonder.

"There's no mob in Vegas anymore," I chided.

"Unless you call the corporations that own all these hotels mobsters, which some might, I'd have to agree." Sonny laughed at me, shaking his head. "Come, my nicest table for you two."

As we walked to the back of the darkly lit place, dodging tightly spaced white linen tables and carts, my hand hovered over Autumn's lower back. She had changed from her shorts and tank top of earlier into a little pink sundress, the fluttery hem dancing over her thighs as she moved. The crisscross back showed off the smooth freckled expanse of her lower back. Again, she wasn't wearing a bra. A server emerged from the kitchen, and I stepped closer to Autumn to not get separated, my fingers brushing her soft, exposed skin. Over her shoulder, she glanced at me, her blue eyes alight with surprise and warmth. Slowing, she pressed her back to my hand, the heat of her flowing up my arm and straight to my chest. I kept my fingers on her until we reached a small back table, where a white taper candle burned over a wine bottle beside a fake red rose.

"Thank you, Sonny." Autumn beamed up at him, the corners of her eyes crinkling.

Disregarding the implications, I pulled out her chair, and the smile I received in return was darker, the sight of it going straight to my groin. Good thing I was sitting.

Two carafes of house wine, one white, one red, were placed on the table beside Autumn's sparkling water with lime. As I helped myself to the red, I became emboldened by the wine and her proximity and leaned closer. "So, what's up with your group chat?"

Her mouth fell open.

"Nicolai Louise Evjen, I can't believe you snooped on my phone!" Swatting my arm with fake outrage, she shook her head. "Shocked and appalled by your behavior!"

"Louise? My middle name is Thomas."

"I know, but it's mine and Summer's, so we use it as a placeholder. You're changing the subject."

"It wasn't reading your texts. I just saw the name of your group, is all."

"Seasonal Obsession. That's me, Autumn." With one finger, she pointed at her chest, and I rolled my eyes. "Summer, obviously, and then Devin because her last name is associated with spring." Her hand clapped on my forearm, heat drawing into me. "And then—get this—when Wren marries Adrian, guess what her last name will be?"

"You can't be serious." I asked over the rim of my short-stemmed wine glass.

"Yep, Winter. Isn't it the cutest ever?" She grinned at me.

I did not think it was cute, but I wouldn't dash her happiness.

"Are they engaged?"

Her gaze took on a dreamlike quality, the corners of her mouth turning up. "Not yet, but it's a matter of time. He's so good for her. You should see the way he takes care of her. After that asshole we had to put up with for *years and* then Adrian was right there, and it was like fate or something. It's sweet. They have the cutest dog, Maizie. He's such a nice guy, we all love him. Plus—"

Is that what Autumn would want, someone sweet? Someone good? It would be so easy to imagine her with a man like that. Kind, outgoing like her, someone who didn't scowl at everyone. Someone who would encourage her to drive roughshod over logging roads and not lecture her. Someone more like her.

"—And then saved her from an icy river in the middle of February."

Well, shit, how could I compare to some guy who rescues her best friend from freezing waters?

"I think you'd like him. You'd like all the boyfriends."

With this, I raised one brow. "Why would I meet your friend's boyfriends?"

I didn't mean for the question to come out as harsh as it did, but the blow landed. Sure enough, the smile faded from Autumn's face, replaced by a red flush up her neck and over her cheeks. "Oh, I don't know. I was just talking, you know how it is when I get going, I start and then I can't shut up and then I say the wrong thing, I know it's annoying."

With a shaky hand, she picked up her drink, sucking all the water through the straw down to the ice. Shame washed over me. Autumn didn't mean anything by it and wasn't making assumptions about me or pressuring me into more the way other women might be.

Even though it would be an idea, I set my hand over the top of hers. Had it only been half a day since I held her hand in the car at the Grand Canyon? The warmth of her knuckles against my mouth as I admitted I was all wrong for her still scored my lips.

"I'm sure I'd like your friends just fine."

Her gaze was on my hand over hers, her throat bobbing with hard swallows.

"It's okay. You don't have to say what you think will make me feel better. It may seem like I'm oblivious to the effect I have on others, but I'm not. I try hard not to let it get to me, but as you can tell from my outburst earlier today, I know it all too well. I know I rile you up. That I can be difficult."

"Difficult? Is that what you think? Nothing about you is difficult."

Thick auburn hair fell over her face, and she pushed it back with a huff of air. "That's not true. If it was, I wouldn't be where I am right now. Do you know I haven't gotten past the third date with a guy in over a year? And then there's this disaster between us, which I know you don't want to talk about because you're trying not to hurt my feelings. And I know I should be coy or whatever, but it's really hard for me, pretending that what we had together didn't happen and then have you touching me the way you do. I'm an open book—some would say too open, maybe, but I don't know how to play those games. I'm not mysterious or flirtatious. I'm just me. And, sometimes, it's like you want me back but then you pull away. I don't know what you want from me. I can't keep going back and forth with you, Nicolai."

There she went again, with my full first name.

This complimentary carafe of wine was a mistake, but I couldn't stop the words from coming. "You'd be the easiest person to fall for. Everything about you is effortless. What's hard is staying away. You have no idea of the thoughts that have been running around my head. You're impossible to stay away from, impossible not to want. But I have to. I told Oliver I'd take care of you."

You promised her brother. Don't forget that he trusts you.

"If anyone here is difficult, it's me."

She laid her palm on my face, her fingers curling over my cheekbone, her nails brushing against the hollow of my jaw. "You really think that, don't you? I can see it in the way you won't allow me close. And it's not just me, is it?"

Her words were too earnest, too truthful, not to sting. Her big blue eyes bore into me, and I should've pulled her hand away, stepped back, and forgotten I'd leaned into her touch.

"It's everyone. You have to let someone in eventually. To let people care about you. You're worth it." Her stare dropped to my mouth, her thumb tracing my lip before my tongue touched it—the salt and sweet of her skin exploding on contact.

What she tasted of when she came on my tongue. The press of her breasts against my chest as I drove into her. Her eyes grew glossy, and she had to have been thinking the same as me.

The loud clink of dishes against the table broke us apart as our food arrived, steaming dishes of pasta, breadsticks, and meat. I was relieved for the break. If I could get some food in me, maybe I'd sober up enough to get a handle on myself. Maybe then I wouldn't maul her in the back corner of a restaurant.

So, you can wait until you're alone to do it, then?

I shook off the thought. I could do this, could keep my word to her brother.

POINT I-LAS VEGAS, NV

Nico

WINE ALWAYS MADE MY cheeks blaze red, the heat scorching under my skin as we made our way to our room. She chuckled as I fumbled with the door three times before taking the key card, flipping it around, and sliding it through the slot. "Seeing you let loose, it's times like this I'm almost tempted to drink."

Plopping down on the bed, I toed my shoe off. "Why don't you?"

The bed shifted as she sat beside me, her shoes already off, her knees tucked up around her and her dress fanning over her upper thighs. "Never liked the smell of it, for one, which is ironic, considering what's been paying my bills for the past year. But also, I'm impulsive enough, completely sober. I don't need something making me worse."

"Who says your impulsivity is a bad thing?" I asked, leaning back on my elbows.

With one imperious brow raised, she blinked at me. "You, when I was driving in Sedona."

"That wasn't impulsivity. That was a vagrant disregard for the treads of your tires and possibly my life."

She grinned at me. "Plus, my dad is a drinker and—"

"Your dad is a fun guy. He's not so bad."

A line formed between her brows. "I'm sure that's how it may seem to you, but he's not always—it's no fun when he's forgetting to pick me up from dance or calling my friends by the wrong name or when you have to drive him home every time there's a family event because he never can. Most of the time, I don't mind it, but sometimes—" She swallowed, her eyes darkening. "I know how I appear to people. Silly and flighty. I couldn't handle out of control being another descriptor. I know I don't always make the right decisions, but at least they are my own, born from my own choices and not because I had a few too many. The idea of losing control, of regretting something because I was drinking, I can't do it."

"So, you don't make choices you regret?"

Her blue gaze fixed on mine. "Not very often, I don't. Sometimes I say the wrong thing, but most of my choices I've made, I don't regret."

I opened my mouth, then closed it, then glanced away from her. Beside her on the king-size bed, the heat of her leg radiated inches from my arm. The scent of her shampoo and the warmth of her skin soaked into me.

"Ask me, Nicolai." She ordered. "Ask me what you want to hear."

Not what I was wondering but what I wanted . . . in a terrible way. She was giving me permission to hear those words.

"Do you regret sleeping with me?"

With her hands folded in her lap, her fingers twisted together as she took a steadying breath and then another. She ordered me to ask her and then backed into herself.

This was it. She was going to say everything I deserved to hear. That, while the sex was good, I was right to push her away. We needed to keep this dance at arm's length I was failing to hold. That line from the letter in the restaurant's entryway shot through me. *Rendered me in despair.*

Is this what her rejection would be? In my mind, for the practicality of it, I needed her to tell me no, to say she didn't want me. Whether it was the wine, the burn of silk from her back on my fingers, or her hair brushing my arm in the elevator, I couldn't shake it. I was sure if I rolled over, my hand would find her knee, slip under her dress, and discover her wet. I craved that in equal measure.

"No. I'm not good at secrets or keeping things close to the vest—or whatever you call it. And while I try to focus on the positive as much as I can, even I know that wanting something fiercely doesn't mean you get it. And I had to be okay if that included you. So, when that night happened—"

"You wanted me?" I asked.

She wanted me. She wanted me before that night and still did. This wasn't flirtation or a way to pass the time. This was craving and want, and, fuck, if I didn't savor those words.

Her big blue eyes shot up to catch mine, her brows furrowing as she stared at me. "Of course I want you, bright, sturdy, brilliant you. I've wanted you for half my life, but that doesn't mean you're mine. I know that. Knew that. But I don't regret the night we had together, even if you only want it to be the one."

Reaching over, I cupped her chin, bringing her closer to me. "Why do you keep saying these things? I'm poison, Autumn. You deserve someone better than me. You deserve so much more."

Her words were the sweetest torture. "There is no one better than you, not to me."

That was a lie. I would never be enough. I shook my head, allowing my hand to drop between us, and flopped back on the bed. Stupid house wine and loose tongues.

"I don't know what vision you have of me or what kind of man you think I am, but you're wrong. If you knew me, really knew me, you'd run as far away as you could."

Her head tilted, those big sky eyes boring into me, seeing something that I couldn't imagine because they softened when they should do the opposite. Her blind faith in others. I couldn't understand the kindness she so easily gave, the optimism in this future only she can see. "You really think I don't know you? I know you better than you think. So, why don't you let me decide what I deserve? Because to me there has always been you and then everyone else. No one has measured up."

Slowly, she lowered herself to lie beside me, her chest rising and falling as her head fell to the side and her eyes bore into mine.

Too old for her, too broken, her brother's best friend. My personal mantra to keep my hands to myself. Those ridiculous rules I created broke so quickly. All reason was fading.

"We can't keep going like this. I don't want to destroy . . . whatever we could be. Things always—"

My voice faltered as a line formed between my brows, and my eyes fluttered shut as I tried to form the words. A deep breath shuddered out of me as she slid her palm to my cheek and then through my hair. Bringing one hand up, I cupped hers, holding it in place on my skin. I was allowing myself too much, but I couldn't pull her hand away, couldn't grieve the loss of contact.

"No matter how desperately I want something, eventually, it'll shatter."

"Then, we can put the pieces back together." She inhaled shakily. "You'll be amazed how good I am with a little glue and a little more gumption."

My chuckle was a staccato against her hand as I leaned into her touch.

I could feel my control slipping, bit by bit, wine drunk, and sloppy decisions. This was all coming to a head. It would be days or hours before I snapped and succumbed to that overwhelming need to take her in my arms. To kiss her the way I wanted. To feel the softness of her body and pull each devastating cry from her mouth as I sank into her. Would it be her touch?

Or just her voice? What would the last thread be?

I slid my hand over her throat, thumb leaving a pink wake before stopping above the swell of her still-braless breasts. With one flick of my finger, I could slip past the fabric, baring her to me. *Mine, mine, mine.*

"I can be," she whispered, and I was mouthing the words, watching the way her skin reacted to my touch. "Say the word, and I will be."

With that, I pulled my hand away as if burned. It will take more than a few well-placed remarks for her to convince me. In the dark, I could almost believe them, but to touch Autumn, to see the sunrise in her. She wasn't darkness. She was light and was shining on all that I could never offer. My fingers twitched, wanting to pull her closer, wanting to back up and never allow her to be ruined by me. This tongue that drove happiness away, these hands that bruised and bled and would inevitably destroy.

Earn it, earn it.

I hadn't. Who knows if I ever could? Yet she was there before me, giving it away, trusting me to take care of her. If she had the faintest clue, she wouldn't allow me to touch her this way.

Swallowing, I let my hand drop between us. "We should get to bed."

Point J–Birch Creek Springs, California

Autumn

THE SHEETS TWISTED UP around me as Nico pried open my thighs. Twisting my nipple between his fingers, he traced my entrance with his length. "I'm too old to play games, Autumn. I know what I want, and it's you, under me. My cock deep inside you as you're screaming my name."

"Maybe I need it, too." I coo, bringing my hips up to meet him.

He hisses, his hand moving from my breast to press against my throat. "You're playing with fire."

My legs tighten around his waist, pulling him closer, his cock rubbing against my clit torturously. "I like the burn."

Then he lines himself up at my entrance and tugs my head back with a fistful of my hair again. "Eyes on me when I sink into you, sweet girl. Nowhere else."

I keep my eyes wide for him as his finger circles my clit, the buzzing in my veins winding up tighter.

"Now let me hear you scream around my cock."

As he slammed into me, I cried out.

My eyes flashed open, and all I see is darkness. Heat flared through me, and my hand was between my own thighs, one finger on my clit. Slowly, I pulled my hand away, aware of the wetness. I've soaked my underwear.

Just a dream, just a dream.

It wouldn't be the first time I had a sex dream about Nico, but it was the first since we started this trip. The sensation lingered—his grip bruising my hips, the burn of him stretching me, the slick press of his sweat on mine. A shaky breath escaped as I closed my eyes, desperate to return to the dream, to feel us join again. It didn't work.

Beside me, Nico was on his back. With the window light behind me, I could see his profile, his jaw clenched and his hand down his pants. Taking a low, steady breath, I watched him. His eyes are on me, and after a long minute, when neither of us moved, his jaw relaxed. The way the light came into the room cast my face in shadows, and he must've thought I was still asleep. I must have said something in my sleep. Maybe his name? Something else? I do that sometimes.

As carefully as I could, I steadied my breathing. The musk in the air, my arousal, and something else.

Then he shifted, rolling over on his side to face me, so carefully I was shocked when he made contact. His fingers landed on my throat, his thumb brushing over my clavicle. Heat raced under his touch, and if the light were on, my skin would be pink from the single trace of him.

Somehow, I knew he was testing me, seeing how asleep I really was. If I let him know I was awake, this spell would be broken. He'd go back behind those rules and the guilt and won't let me in. And I need in.

So, I didn't move, allowing myself the low, deep breaths that mimicked sleep. As his fingers brushed over my skin, I gave him the darkness where he could have a piece of me without shame.

Arduous minutes dragged before his other hand slipped between us, and for a moment, I thought he'd place it on my hip—but he didn't. It was so shadowy I couldn't see it, but the sound of him pulling down his pants was unmistakable. The soft brush of his hand as it gripped his cock. A slow tempo as if he were trying to be silent. The rasp of his hand around himself the only sound in the room, steady and low. A singe of want still pulsed between my legs, demanding to be sated, but I couldn't stir, couldn't break whatever this is. When I didn't move, his pace quickened, the slap of his hand against his base getting louder as he worked himself to the edge.

His fingers on my throat tightened, and it took all I have not to lean into his touch, to let him know I'm there, to push his hand between my legs to find me soaked for him.

It is filthy, perverse really. Any other man jerking himself off while lying beside me would send me running away, but the heat between my thighs built up as he stoked himself harder, the inaudible gasps as he fisted himself growing louder. I clenched my legs together, the burn of my dream orgasm lingering. The deep sounds he was making shaped my release that I knew I couldn't have yet. Then he rolled away from me, his back tense, and the same guttural groan I replayed for weeks sang around the room.

His breathing was shaky as he pulled his hand away from my throat. Low curses and words escaped as he pulled himself into a seated position.

"So fucked. You're so fucked," he murmured as he grabbed the pillow off the bed and threw it down on the floor.

The bed was empty, save for me. In the bathroom, I heard the water running, low curses, and then he was on the makeshift pallet. Shifting and scratching noises sounded as he tossed himself back and forth before his breathing evened out, and he fell asleep.

I may good at feigning sleep, but I knew he wasn't.

At his first snore, I plunged my fingers inside me, finishing what he started.

"Why did you let me drink that whole carafe of red wine last night?" he groaned as he pulled on the gold-rimmed shades and sank lower into the passenger seat.

We had been on the road for over two hours by this time, the Vegas strip in the rearview long before. Somewhere in the rolling crags of the Mojave Desert, he had fallen back asleep, his normally tanned face pale in the stark fall sun. "Lyin' Eyes" playing low, I sang along with the tape that had been stuck in the deck since 1999.

Hands on the wheel, I shot him a grin. "You're fun when you're wine-drunk."

"It's not so fun the next day. Red wine hangovers are the worst."

Glenn Frey sang about strong drinks and regrets, of lost love and cold hearts. As a child, my father played this album while working on the car, swapping the radio with its clothes-hanger antenna for this tape. Now, even through the sadness of the song, I was back on his creeper seat, legs splayed as I rolled across our one-car garage.

"I wouldn't know."

"Trust me."

"Summer always said tequila was the worst, but Wren says it's those fruity mixed drinks, and I know my brothers complain about the time they went to Emerald Downs and had too many Kentucky Mules and—"

"Please, for the love of God, can you stop talking about booze? I'll throw up."

"Sorry." I shot him a sly grin. "I don't know much about hangovers. I feel fantastic, by the way, very refreshed from the night's sleep."

Eyes tensing shut, he leaned his head against the window and groaned. It was a pained sound, but its richness echoed the noise of him coming on his hand the night before, and a flutter stirred between my legs. The real noise, coupled with my dream, made my grip on the steering wheel tighten.

The night before, something shifted between us. We had been walking this fine line for days, and for all my pushing him to his limits, he wasn't breaking. But then there were his words.

How desperately I want something. Desperately.

He admitted wanting me. That was something, more than something. It could be enough to create everything, if only he'd allow it.

And then the sounds he made beside me.

Desperately.

The bed shifting beneath us, his hand slick on his cock, a low moan in his throat, a whisper of my name. I may have been sleeping with my hands between my legs, but he was the one who came all over the blankets. As if I didn't know every note of his orgasms by now. As if I hadn't played it repeatedly in my head the past few months.

As if his hand on my throat didn't change all the rules he made. This want was a living thing, curling and dark inside me, demanding to be sated. Need, need, need. Not want. And I've never been good at denying myself.

And I can't allow Nico to keep denying me what we both want.

A sign ahead on the highway catches my attention. Nico had dozed off again, and with him half incapacitated with his hangover, I made the split-second decision. This time, I took the forest road slower, navigating the bumps and potholes with more care so as not to jostle him awake. We were winding through the forest before Nico even noticed we've left the freeway. The parking lot at the hot springs was a gravel space with four spots. I pulled in beside a ranger truck and killed the engine.

I grabbed my phone and texted the girls my daily affirmation. *The answer is always in front of me, even if I haven't seen it yet. As long as I continued to search, I would find the answer.*

The response was instantaneous.

I got three chorus texts of *what* and exclamations before Nico stirred beside me. Shoving my phone back in my bag, I glanced over to the passenger seat to find him stirring.

"Where are we?" Nico asked as he straightened in the passenger seat, his voice deliciously rough as he pulled down his Elvis shades.

While I got them as a bit of a gag, his expensive glasses had been in his bag the whole trip.

"A little pit stop for us. Trust me, you'll like this one."

Years before, Summer and I took a road trip together. We had to split the activities we both enjoyed up evenly, with poolside drinks and tanning on her agenda and hikes on mine. This spot was one we discovered that fit both our needs.

When I returned to the car, I opened the passenger-side door, where Nico was glaring up at me behind those shades. "Why do I feel like I'm going to regret this excursion you're forcing me into?"

"No one is forcing you into anything, ya big baby. Now, come on. We have an hour to get there and then two hours to ourselves."

Set against the side of a mossy cliff, the pool was rough stone piled around an even rougher hole in the ground. A wooden railing plunged the three steps into the steamy water and had seen better days. Standing on the edge of the pool, I could see down into the valley beyond us. The tops of trees brushed a cloudy sky to the south. West of us was a taller mountain, the dusting of permafrost keeping it snowcapped and waiting for the winter to cover it with white.

To the left of the open pool was a cave face, carved out with billowing vapors mixing with the cool air. The switchbacks on the way up to the site had both of us sticky and overheated. A few times on the hike, I worried that bringing Nico after his hangover complaints was a mistake. But the color in his cheeks as he took in the view said otherwise. Fresh air, a car nap, and granola bars seemed to snap him out of his wine headache.

"There's this pool, which is pretty pleasant, but there's another one in that cave over there that is even hotter. Last time I was there, I could only handle a few minutes in it, but Summer likes to be boiled like a Dungeness crab, so she had to be bribed out."

"You know, most people would say lobster." Nico wiped a hand over his face as he surveyed the small pool.

"Yes, but I like crabs more than lobsters, so." Shrugging, I turned my back to him as I hung my bag on a small hook screwed into a pole.

"I didn't bring my swimsuit." Nico glanced around as if there would be a store three miles up the side of a mountain beside the primitive outhouse.

I flashed him a devilish grin. "Me neither, but our underwear is the same, right?"

Brows furrowed together, he tilted his head back, his jaw flexing as his Adam's apple bobbed, his words low on the mountain breeze. "Of course. Fucking hell."

"Where is your sense of adventure? Huh? Where was the guy who hiked up here, who went four-wheeling in Sedona and talked about escorts in Vegas?"

With one foot raised, I tried to pull my sandal off and teetered before Nico snatched my elbow, steadying me. Under his hand, my skin felt flushed, heat searing up my arm and into my chest at his quick save. When I switched feet, his grip moved as well, balancing me on the other foot.

"None of those were my idea. I'm a boring guy who likes to play it safe and didn't want to do any of those things."

With both shoes off, I wiggled my toes on the dead leaves and gravel path leading to the pool. He let go of my arms and stepped back, his fingers twitching.

"But didn't you have fun?"

His green eyes flashed to mine and then slowly his gaze drifted over my mouth, down to my throat, then lower. Everywhere his eyes fell upon heated as if his focus were burning me. My breasts, my stomach, my hips, the space between my legs was left woefully empty after watching him the night before, a place my fingers could never fill. Then down my thighs, my calves, my bare feet and back up again. Was he thinking of the night before? Picturing me in my sleep. Or was he thinking of that night months ago the same way I was?

"Yeah, I did." Something stirred between my legs at the growl in those three words. "Doesn't mean it was smart. Or right."

"Why does everything have to be right for you?" With one hand on the edge of the shirt, I teased it up over my stomach, his scrutiny catching on the slow exposure of my bare skin. "Why can't you allow yourself something a little now and then?"

"Because there's nothing little about this. It's wrong, so wrong, and I—"

My shirt came over my head, and I stood before him in my bra. For this entire trip, I didn't wear one. Not for his sake—my shirts made it cumbersome—but I still reveled in how he reacted whenever he noticed. This bra was a thin white thing, lace-edged against my breasts with a little white bow between them. It wasn't strappy or sexy. Didn't push my breasts up or pad them.

Still, his jaw was tense, his fists clenching.

He rarely gave things away. He liked control. So, those little signals were practically the equivalent of him moaning my name and kneeling at my feet. I knew his tells, and he was about to crack.

Slowly, I stepped into the pool, the water up to my waist as I settled on my knees on the stone seat. Motioning to his still-clothed body, I raised a brow. "Your turn, Nicolai."

Studying me, he huffed, the decision to join heavy in his expression. "You're going to bruise up your knees sitting like that."

I quirk a grin before pulling my bottom lip between my teeth. His eyes followed that movement, his gaze steady on my mouth.

"Perhaps I like having bruised knees, especially for when the activity"—my eyes dart down to his crotch and then back up to his mouth—"makes it worth the pain."

Once again, his hand covered his face, scraping over his eyes and then covering his mouth as he looked down at me in the water. The underwear I had on is yellow cotton with a scalloped hem, even less sexy than the bra somehow.

"You are slowly killing me." He huffed again as he gazed down at me.

"A soak. I'm talking about soaking in a hot spring. Get your mind out of the gutter." Smacking the water, I send a splash up onto his feet.

"I'm going to regret this," he mumbled before reaching behind him to grab the back of his shirt and pull it over his head.

I had seen flashes of him shirtless. He changed into bathrooms, slept in his shirt. Even the night we spent together had been so dark I couldn't have described him by sight. Now describe by touch? That, I could have done.

His body was lithe, sinew and muscle. A smattering of different shades of hair caught in the noonday sun peeking through the surrounding trees. Gold, brown, blond, auburn. He wasn't muscular in the way that meant he spent time at the gym but lean in a way that can only be explained by genetics. His stomach was flat and firm, with a small scar above his belly button. I knew I lowered my hand, it would be firm under my palm. That the hairs that led from that scar to under his briefs would be soft.

As much as I'd like to say I love my body, I am a woman in the real world and have struggled with my image. No matter what diet I have, no matter the exercise, I was soft. My large breasts, courtesy of my mother's side of the family, always make me appear larger on top, my shoulders broader than was fashionable. My torso, a soft straight line, with barely a curve to my waist compared to my hips. As a kid, I admired Devin's curves, the way her body had that hourglass shape. For years, I focused on body neutrality. This body can carry me up a mountain, and this body can be nourished. This body can dig for clams on the beach and haul supplies. Mine was strong and carried me through life. Most days, I was fine with myself, but on rare days, I sank back into comparisons.

Under Nico's eyes, I felt beautiful.

On his left side was a small inked mark. A white flower, a tulip? No, not a tulip, something smaller, more delicate.

"I didn't know you had a tattoo."

His fingers traced over the mark, not quite touching it but acknowledging it the same. "Yeah, I got it eight years ago."

"Of all the tattoos I thought you'd have, a flower isn't one."

His jaw ticked, and his gaze was unfocused over my head and into the trees beyond. "Lily of the Valley, I got it for—" He swallowed hard, blinking a few times. "Someone I knew."

Someone he loved. The unspoken weighed heavily between us. While I knew Nico as a teen, and in early twenties, there was a decade where he lived somewhere else. Where he was with someone else. And whoever that person was, they fell in love. Did he still love this person?

Oliver never mentioned his relationships with women, but then again, my brothers were the worst source of gossip out there.

While I could run my mouth, I had the sense not to press on this. If he wanted to tell me, he would. So, instead, I cupped the water and threw it at his ankles, breaking his reverie. "The water's getting cold."

"I thought this was a hot spring. Isn't that impossible?"

"Get down to your skivvies and find out." I quirked a grin as I shimmied my shoulders.

"Skivvies," he chuckled. "Is that what you're in? Your skivvies."

I huffed out a shocked noise. "Obviously not. I'm in my chonies."

"Right. Of course you are."

The black boxer briefs gripped his muscular thighs as he made his way to the steps of the pool. His bulge was barely contained behind the fabric, and I had to glance away lest I ogled him. If the night had been lighter, I might have seen it—but then he would have known I was awake and never touched himself beside me.

Still on my knees, I squeezed my thighs together, the pressure building.

As he stepped into the pool, the water came up to the waistband of his briefs, and he let out a low groan at the heat. "Fuck, okay, yeah, this water feels amazing."

"Told you." I smirk at him.

"You want me to say you're right? I will."

His chiseled jaw tilted toward the sky as he leaned against the pool's edge, arms stretched wide, fingers inches from mine.

"What's that scar?" I motioned to his stomach under the water.

"Laparoscopic appendectomy, I have another one lower that matches. Two incision sites."

I brought my arm up, touching the keloid on my elbow. "Longboarding down 288th when I was fifteen."

Chin down, he touched his hair at the crown, a small raised pink mark parting his strands. "My uncle Issac dropped a hammer on my head when I was eleven."

With my hand raised, I wiggled my pinky. "Summer stabbed me with a fork when we were seven."

"She is ruthless, isn't she?"

I laughed, thinking back on all the insane things my cousin had done over the years. "You have no idea."

Nodding, he flashed me a knowing smirk. "I think I have an inkling. I was the one who told her about those pictures her ex was showing around."

Summer told us about the day she found out about her cheating ex. A night of too much drinking, puking on the man who'd become her boyfriend, and calling one of Devin's neighbors by a cartoon character's name. I wasn't sure how much Nico knew about Summer's revenge plot after that day. Heck, there were many details Summer never shared with me, but I knew my cousin could be downright vicious if she was crossed. Despite our differences in problem solving, it was nice to have on your side. And a pain when it isn't, thus the fork in the pinky scar.

"That was a kind thing you did, telling her about it."

"It's not a big deal." He shook his head. "Anyone would have done it."

"No, they wouldn't." I reached forward, placing my hand on top of his. Warmth that had nothing to do with the water flowed up my arm at the contact. "You're a good man, Nicolai."

Flipping his hand over, he slid his palm against my own, lacing his fingers between mine. "I'm not. I wish you could see that. Being here with you . . . what would your brother say?"

"Oliver isn't my keeper—"

"I know that."

"Do you?" Sitting up higher on my knees, I glared at him as I tried to pull my hand out of his grip, but he held it steady. "I'm an adult, perfectly capable of making my own decisions. Where this archaic sense of duty you have is coming from, lord only knows, but you need to let it go. I want to be here with you, so I am. I wanted to walk around the Vegas strip and hike Sedona and see castles in the cliffs, and I wanted to do those with you. That night on your dock, I wanted to kiss you, and I've wanted you inside me every day since then. And you know what else I want? To take off this stupid bra because I actually hate them, and a wet bra is insanely uncomfortable."

The change in conversation had him sitting up, his hand slipping from mine as he opened and closed his mouth like a fish. "You want to take off your bra?"

"Yes." I reached behind me to unclasp it, the first of four hook-eye closures snapping. "It's already damp, and I don't want to get it wet."

"But you'd be naked in front of me."

"No more naked than you are."

"It's not the same, and you know it."

"Oh, Mr. Evjen, how will I face you again if you've seen me naked?" I cooed. "Maybe I only wore it, so you could take it off."

Across the pool, his eyes darkened at the comment, but he didn't make a move.

Shaking my head, I clucked my tongue. "They're just boobs. I went topless with Summer the last time we were here. It's no big deal."

"I'm not your cousin."

"No, you're certainly not. She isn't a prude."

"I'm not a—" He groaned, and a spark fired at my clit from the sound.

That same groan. That same rasp of his hand over his face. Him squeezing his cock as he wrung each little drop only inches from me.

There was a limit to my coyness, and I couldn't dance around this any longer. Once again, I was crummy at keeping secrets, and this was no different. "Turnabout is fair play. I watched you last night. Now you can see me. Now you can feel me. I know you want to. I saw it, Nico."

This information stopped him, his hand freezing on my hip, all the muscles in his arms tightening as my words sunk in.

"You—" He gasped out. "Knew? You were awake when I . . ." The hand he brought to his face was shaky. "Autumn, I'm so sorry. I had too much to drink, and honestly, I thought maybe it was a dream and—"

I sat up on my knees and unclasped the last closures, catching the bra before it slipped into the water.

"I don't want your apology."

"But what I did last night. Why didn't you stop me? Why didn't you say anything?"

I tossed the bra over his head, where it landed squarely on his folded clothes. An excellent shot, if I say so myself—before finally meeting his eyes. "Because I knew if I did, you would stop. And I couldn't have that."

"But I—you—oh." He buried his face in his hands.

"I liked it, Nicolai."

"You did."

I nodded again. "What did you think I was dreaming about?"

His Adam's apple bobbed as his gaze traced from my clavicle, down to my nipples beneath the water, and lower still to the apex of my thighs.

"Why did I cry out your name in my sleep? With my fingers between my thighs, what do you think I've been needing?"

"Tell me."

His voice was husky, his chest rising.

"You really want me to? It was dark last night, and I know how you like to pretend that we—"

"It's daylight in my dreams, sweet girl. And I can see it all now. So, tell me."

Sweet girl.

His words washed over me, hotter than the steam from the pool. My dream from the night before, the press of his cock at my entrance. His whispers as he thrust into me.

My dreams, my dreams.

"You know, I think the view is so much better on your side of the pool." Before he could stop me, I stepped through the water and slid onto his lap, wedging against his groin with my thighs pressed between his.

Settled, I feel his cock pressed against the thin fabric of my underwear, twitching under me. "Why are you making this so hard for me?" he gasped as I leaned further back into him, tilting so he could see the rise and fall of my breasts.

He still didn't relent, only the taut lines of his forearms beside me and our ragged breaths betraying the struggle.

I worry he won't give in—that I've gone too far and he'll shove me away, back to the kitchen's awkward silence after I nearly kissed him. I know he is at a breaking point, and I am the one hammering away at it. But still, I can't stop, the smile curving on my lips as I whisper, "When have I ever been good at following rules, Nicolai?"

This was what I wanted—he was all I wanted, and if this were all I could have, then I would take it.

Longing gnawed at me like hunger until I was nothing but need, starving for his touch, for proof I wasn't alone in it.

He was holding steady, not allowing himself this in the daylight, but I couldn't have that. I saw it in him the night before, and I would feel it again. I abandoned subtlety, grinding hard against his cock, the thin fabric the only barrier keeping him from sliding inside me.

"If you keep moving like that, I'm going to fuck you in this hot spring."

His growl was low in my ear as he leaned back, his jaw tense.

I rolled my hips harder, my voice husky with want as my head lolled to his shoulder. "What are you waiting for, then?"

His resolve snapped. He groaned, and his hands moved from the seat beside him to my hips, pulling me down harder against his stiff cock.

"You'd like that, wouldn't you? Been begging for it for days. No, when I fuck you again, it's not going to be in some hole in the ground. I'm going to lay you out on a bed. I'm going to mark these tits with my teeth, suck them until they're bruised and red, and then I'll feast on your cunt until you're screaming for me—"

Just like my dream, oh Lord . . .

"—And only then will I slide into you, wringing out one last orgasm from that cunt. But not now, not like this."

"So, you're the only one who gets to come on this trip?" I said as his hand stilled on my hip.

"You want to come?"

Still leaning against him, I nodded. One hand still on my hip, his other one tangled at my nape, snapping my head back. The delicious burn of his fingers gripping me coupled with his breath against my cheek.

"Fuck it. You want to play this game? Prove it. I want you to sit on the edge of this pool and show me how you come."

Oh. Oh.

I expected him to touch me, to kiss me, turn me, slide my underwear aside, and fill me. But with his hands on my hips, he moved me off his lap and pushed me to the other side of the water.

"I—but—"

"Go on. You started this. You sat on my hard cock, grinding yourself all over me. So, hop up there and show me how much you want this."

Somehow, this is more than I was expecting. More raw. He still hadn't kissed me again, and he was expecting me to finger myself in front of him? To get myself off on the edge of the pool?

"Or are you all teasing, but no action?"

That taunt wouldn't do. I was many things, but a coward, I would not be. The water dripped in rivulets over my breasts as I pulled myself up to sit on the edge. The rocks were wet and cold under my butt, but the heat from his stare was more than enough.

"I don't know—I've never—"

"Oh, sweet, sweet girl, you know what to do. Don't you?"

This switch in him sent flames to my clit. As if he had been tightly wound, every second we spent together increased, and he wanted me to pay equally.

An excruciating moment passed as he studied me on the other side. His eyes roamed over my bare breasts, my damp stomach, the way the cotton of my underwear clung to me.

"I—" Swallowing hard, I slid a hand under my underwear, pulling the waistband from my damp skin and tracing a finger over my mound.

"No, not like that." He was sitting back, watching me with heated eyes. "Start at the top. I want to see you touch your body."

With my hand out of my underwear, I trace a slow line over my stomach before brushing my thumb over one nipple, hard in the mountain air. The sizzle of my touch sparked as I circled the areola. The water made a low splashing noise as my calves clenched at the sensation.

"Harder, pinch them."

I complied, rolling them between my finger and thumb.

"Harder, make it hurt."

The sting only added to the heat building inside me. I recalled the way his fingers felt on me, the tug and scrape of his own hand against my skin.

"Does that feel good?"

His voice was rough, and I opened my eyes to find his on my face.

I nodded, shaky exhales moving my chest up and down.

"But it's not enough, is it?" he asks with a sinful smirk. "No, you need more, don't you?"

"Yes."

"I knew you would. You need so much more. Now lick them. I want to watch you lick yourself."

Heavy in my hand, I pulled my breast up, darting my tongue out to lave at the pert nub. My nails scratched at the sensitive skin.

"Imagine that's my mouth, my teeth on you. My fingers."

The image made me groan. If my breasts were smaller, this wouldn't be possible. But their size let me lave one while pinching the other nipple, the sting pulling a hum from me. It's not the same as his hand—a poor substitution. My fingers were all wrong, too weak, too small—but it was something. Back arching, I keep my gaze locked on him. His arms stayed at his sides as he commanded me, but he shifted in his seat, and even through the water, his erection swelled. I scratched at my skin, my nails harsh against its tenderness.

"Enough."

Releasing my breast, I let out a shaky breath. The sear of his gaze moved down to my center.

"Now I need you to touch yourself over that pretty little cotton thing. Don't go under it yet. You understand?"

I nod, my fingers stuttering over my stomach and over my center. A pulse ticking between my thighs as I circle my clit behind the thin fabric.

"Does it want to be touched?"

I nod at him.

"Tell me."

"Yes." My fingers drawing up and down with varying pressure, my center already so tender from his gaze alone.

"What does it want?" His voice was ragged but firm. As if he was barely holding himself together.

The awareness of how I'm affecting him shot arousal through me, and I gasped.

"More. You. It wants you. I want you."

"You're so fucking sexy when you're thinking of me. Go ahead, slide a finger in. You've earned it."

Despite being in the water, I know it's my wetness that is guiding my middle finger inside, and I let out a small sigh. In and out, I curl my finger to the front the way he did, but it's not enough, not even close.

"Oh, sweet girl. You can fit another one in, can't you?"

Obliging him, I slid a second finger in, curling it deep as I rocked my clit against my palm, not being able to stifle my cry at the zing of pleasure with each pass.

"What are you imagining?"

"You, it's you." I gasp out.

"My hands or my cock?"

"Your—" I'd never been much for dirty talk—it always seemed absurd in the moment—but I was too far gone. "Your cock, oh God."

"That's right. Look at me."

My eyes caught his, and this time, his hand was under the water, his cock distorted as his hand wrapped around it. The sight of his long length gripped tight had me pressing harder on my clit, a moan escaping my lips. "Look what you do to me."

His arm was moving under the water, slow and leisurely as if he had all the time for this orgasm, as if I'm a meal he was savoring.

I imagined that cock inside me, the agonizing press at my entrance, the slight burn of the tip. The rigid thrust of him as he filled me up. The hot spurt of his cum deep within. My breathing turned ragged, little gasps escaping as I moved faster, thumb grinding my clit while my fingers thrust and curled inside me.

His gaze was dark, hooded, and deep as he watched me.

"You're so fucking dirty, my sweet girl."

His sweet girl. That's what I aspired to be. So much better than the Nico of my dreams.

His.

"Yours."

The flash of possession in his eyes and the increase of his hand on his cock told me he liked my words. My body made him this way, my hands on my skin, and my fingers inside. A surge of power coursed through me as I writhed against my palm.

"Please, Nico, I need you." I gasped.

His grip on himself tightened, his motion harsh as he moved up and down, his eyes never leaving mine. "No, you do this to yourself, you filthy girl. Show me how you come for me and me alone."

I gasped again, riding my fingers, going deeper, harder. My other hand pinching my nipple to the point of pain.

"Let me see it. Show me what I do to you. I want to watch my sweet girl come undone. Fucking come."

His sweet girl. Come.

The words hurled me over the edge, my wall constricting around my fingers. My thighs clamped over my hand as the water quaked with my jerky motion. Drawing out the orgasm as much as I could, I cried out.

My legs were jelly, and I collapsed back on my elbows, my hair falling onto the moss and pine needle floor. Slowly, I opened my eyes again, the trees above us waving in the soft breeze, and a bird dipped low and disappeared. The orange, red, yellow, brown of leaves about to fall to the forest floor. A sunset of colors as I fell apart. In and out, I sucked in air.

I had just fingered myself in front of Nico. While our night together before had been hot, this was another level I had never experienced.

And he hasn't kissed you again.

The cool cut of his body through the water sounded, and I lifted my head to find him between my open thighs. My underwear still pushed to the side. Slowly, as if it would spook me, his hand came to rest on my knee.

"You okay?" he asked, a low tremor in his voice.

Nodding, I brought myself up to balance on my elbows. His dark brows furrowed as he looked me over as if to see if I was hurt, protectiveness but also an undercurrent of need in his expression.

"More than okay." I murmur, opening my legs wider as he moved full between them.

Tentatively, his finger traced up my inner thigh to my still-pulsing core. His hand hesitated at my entrance as if he was waiting for something, and I nodded slowly. With one finger, he swiped through my folds, taking with him my arousal. As I watched in wonder, he sucked that finger into his mouth, humming around the digit. His gaze never left mine as his tongue swirled around the tip. "How can you taste better than my memory?"

Despite the mere minutes since I last climaxed, I felt a new surge ticking, needing.

His finger swiped at me again, and this time, it came to rest on my lips, smearing my cum on them. Before he could pull away, I snatched his wrist, swirling my tongue around his finger, my taste exploding in my mouth. His green eyes darkened, his thumb rubbed a circle on my jaw until I let it go with a pop.

His other hand reached down, and I thought he'd slide a finger in, but he fixed my underwear, covering me before stepping back.

Disappointment flooded through me as he distanced himself.

"You didn't." I motioned to his lap, where he was tucking his sizable erection back into his boxers.

"No, as you reminded me, I already came today."

"I can take care of that." Dropping, I stalked toward him, my fingers dancing over the water.

He caught my hand as it was dallying towards his lap. "No, I already told you, when I come again, it's going to be inside your cunt."

The way he talked to me was so raw and filthy. He called me his sweet girl and then asked me to be so depraved.

My arms wrapped around Nico's neck and his around my waist, the sliver of space between us gone as I was consumed by the burning desire I'd carried for months. A distant voice warned he might change his mind, that it couldn't last, but all that mattered was the thought. *Fuck, I'm ruined.*

And before I could think about the expletive in my head, he pulled me tighter against him, his hand tensing on my hip.

"You haven't kissed me again," I said, tracing a circle at his nape.

"Is that what you want? A kiss?"

With a shake of my head, I said, "I want a whole lot more from you." Needing to touch him more, I relished his embrace.

I wanted everything from him.

"It's still wrong."

"Nothing you could do would be wrong," I whisper, my lips a breath away from his.

"That's not true."

His words washed over me as I pressed my lips to his. Once, twice. Silently begging him to kiss me back.

His mouth was still beneath mine, and I urged into him. Three times, and then his arm wrapped around my waist. Before he captured my lips, I could feel his words.

"But what's another sin to a sinner?"

Point K-Sol del Mar, California

Nico

THERE IS A LINE between being rational and being a masochist, and I was straddling it full force after our time at the hot spring.

To not give in, to not break while we were in the mountains, would have been impossible.

It was bound to happen. I had only so much composure, and Autumn knew exactly how to press into me, stripping away every hesitation I thought I could hold.

It was wrong.

As she pulled off her shirt, the cracks burst. That white cotton bra would turn transparent with the slightest splash of liquid. The second she glided under the water, I was done resisting.

It was a foregone conclusion. It had been for days, and to delay it anymore.

And now that I had broken, all I wanted to do was touch her. See that light in her eyes as she came, feel the heat of her skin and watch as she came undone all over her own hand.

Autumn had always been free spirited, this was true, but there was a hesitancy in baring herself the way she did. Somehow, I knew the show she gave me wasn't something she did often. She may be friendly and flirt and joke with others. But to bare herself in that way.

Autumn was still the sweet girl I'd always thought. But, damn, she was also a wild, unnamed thing that I couldn't quite put words to. She was a decade younger than me, and still, in a matter of days, she held all the cards. She wasn't afraid of teasing me, of driving me to the edge. If anything, I was slightly afraid of the power she already had over me, though I'd never admit that to another soul.

Fuck, if it wasn't the sexiest thing I had ever seen in my life. More than any porn I've watched or strip club I was dragged to. It was raw and emotional. And she trusted me with that.

True to my word, I didn't fuck her in the hot spring—only kissed her long and deep while my cock strained in my briefs as she rubbed against me. But I wasn't a pubescent boy. I knew how to delay pleasure. Knew to wait until we had time. The space would only intensify everything. So, I kissed her, our tongues warring and her nails scraping at my nape but didn't allow for more.

She seemed to like it when I took charge.

After the second—or was it third?—side trip Autumn had led us on, I took over driving. If I hadn't been hungover and flustered from the night before, I would've in the first place. But then we wouldn't have gone to the hot spring—and who knows what might have happened. I couldn't bring myself to regret the way things ended up. Denying myself a taste of Autumn had been an exercise on the best of my restraint.

I was broken.

After a long nap in room 3 of the Salt of the Sea Motel off the 101, I woke to find the room empty and the car gone. I was sure we'd pick up where we left off on the mountain, but once we lay down, the past days' exhaustion caught up with us. The side of her bed—she had a side of the bed—was mussed, the pillow bunched in half.

On a small water-stained notepad, I found Autumn's looping script.

Grabbing some snackies. ~XX~A

In the time she was away, I showered, scrubbing the muck of the sulphuric hot spring off my skin. Autumn's toiletry bag was already on the counter, open and messy. Two towels were already damp and hanging on the back of the door. Even though the bottle was small, I opened her shampoo and found the same floral, herbal scent I knew as hers.

My sweet girl.

Just as I held so tightly at resisting her, now that I had given in, all I could think of was how to get her again.

I aspired to be strong enough to resist, to not find myself under her spell again, but less than a day later, here I was. One hand finding my cock, the other braced on the shower wall as I replayed our time at the hot spring. I let my head fall back, the water sluicing over my chest as I worked my fist up and down my straining cock. Muted gasps as her fingers circled her breasts, a pinch to her nipple, a moan as she slid a second finger into her gleaming cunt. Her words washed over me as she cried out for me, told me how much she wanted me. Those ocean eyes on me as she fell apart from her fingers and my words. The taste of her arousal, tangy sweet, and nothing compared to the way it would taste fresh with her clit against my tongue.

My release paints the wall, mixing with the water and running down the drain before my mind has time to clear.

From the other side of the door, I heard footsteps and the shuffle of bags. Quickly, I turned the water off and got out. The door swung open as I finished wrapping the towel around my waist.

"Darn, I was hoping to catch you naked." She smirked at me, her eyes darting over my wet chest. "A minute too late, it appears."

This coquetry of hers wasn't new. It was the same one she used for days, but I was going to give in to it. Whether it was my loss of control or her sense of spontaneity rubbing off on me, I wouldn't deny myself this today. I should have felt sluggish, hungover, hiked miles up and down a mountain. But I wasn't.

Autumn giving herself over to me so readily lit something inside me.

But still, she stayed where she was, and I didn't bring myself closer. The room felt too small, the weight of our actions at the hot springs right there but still somehow removed. As if it was another set of people on that mountain.

"Say the word, and I'll drop the towel."

Even I was surprised by the flirtation in my tone, something I hadn't allowed in myself in years.

"Don't threaten me with a good time." Autumn raised a brow before her face softened. "But we actually have a party to get ready for."

This news shouldn't have surprised me. I wasn't sure how we'd been in this beachside town only three hours and she'd already been invited to a party, but if anyone could manage it, it was Autumn.

"A party?"

"Martina's quinceañera, actually."

"You want us to go to a fifteen-year-old's birthday party?"

"It's more than that, and her mom invited us or me, but I asked, and she said you were welcome to join us."

Us? As if she were long-time friends with these people. "How did you get invited to a quinceañera?"

"Isabel has a food truck next to the store where I got the snacks. She makes the best empanadas. I ate three already. I brought you back some, but she assured me there would be plenty tonight for the party, too."

Hiking in Sedona, hot springs in the mountains, a random girl's quinceañera. Nothing about this trip was according to plan, but with the gleam in Autumn's eyes, I couldn't bring myself to tell her no. I'd go to a dozen quinceañeras, hike miles, and suffer through long stretches of the Las Vegas strip and mango slushies to see her this happy.

"What time does the party start?"

A band set up in the corner, beside a long table piled high with various steamy dishes in aluminum containers. A young woman with an intricate updo and a bubble-gum pink dress that was wide as it was long was laughing with a group of similarly aged teens. The disco light above caught on her silver-and-pink-stone tiara.

Not that I had never gone to a party where I wasn't friends with the host, but crashing a teenage girl's party felt odd. Outside the house, Autumn must have noticed my hesitation because her palm slid into mine, fingers entwining as she pulled me through the crowd. The steady warmth of her skin on mine calmed me.

"Isabel," she cried out, raising her free hand to pull a woman with chin-length highlighted hair and big beaded earrings to her for a hug.

My hand still clasped in hers, she straightened, beaming at her new friend.

"Thank you so much for inviting us. Where's the present table? Nico and I got Martina a little something."

More like I followed Autumn through the store as she picked out a bunch of items, and I put my card down at the register.

"Over by the cake," Isabel said, glancing at the lines around my eyes, the slight gray hairs at my temple.

While I looked good for my age, I still looked my age, and Autumn looked even younger than her twenty-five years.

"Isabel Cordero." She stuck out a hand, and I accepted it. Her handshake was firm and warm.

"Nico Evjen. Thank you for the invite."

The music switched from a teen pop song to one in Spanish.

"Well, after she here told me all about your adventures, I had to extend one to this lovely lady and her—" Isabel raised a brow.

What had she said I was? Not boyfriend, certainly. But with a simple glance around, I knew this family was likely more traditional.

Autumn's attention was over my shoulder as she waved at someone else. How many friends did she make while I napped?

Isabel's brow stayed up on her forehead as she took in our non-answer. "Right, well, enjoy yourself. If you'll excuse me, I have a brother I need to rope into doing some work." Leaving us alone, I heard her yelling out behind us. "Aye yi, what are you doing, pendejo? I said not until after six."

I tightened my grip on Autumn's hand. "What did you tell her I was?"

She beamed at me, oblivious to my concern. "Oh, I didn't. Does it matter?"

Despite not having the words myself, I wanted Autumn to say them, to give us a name. Every exchange we shared, she had been the braver one, the one who took charge, and I was the one fighting ceaselessly against what was inevitable. I couldn't fault her for not giving us a name, when had I ever shown I would want a label, and what would it even be?

Autumn grinned at me, squeezing my hand. "Come on. Let's get some food and then I'll introduce you to Isabel's husband, Joseph."

The disco lights flashed above us, red, blue, green, yellow, the light flashing a dark rainbow over us. After a dinner of empanadas, tamales, rice, and beans alongside tater tots, egg rolls, and mini sandwiches on Hawaiian rolls, I nursed my second beer while Autumn clutched her tamarind soda. Isabel's suspicion hadn't wavered, but her husband was kind enough, and I got strong-armed into a shot with a circle of cousins and uncles. On the side of the dance floor, Autumn was being swung around by one of the younger uncles—or was it a cousin? It was hard to tell at this party. The boy couldn't have been older than twenty, but the way he looked at Autumn set me on edge, the same as that douchebag in Sedona. The short red dress spun off her thigh as she moved, halter straps tied at her nape flying loose and brushing her bare back.

This would not do.

The song changed, and Autumn laughed as she stepped back from the young man. Before she could leave the floor, I took her hand in mine, pulling her body close. Her bare lower back warmed beneath my palm as she leaned back, eyes glinting while I began to sway.

Though I hadn't danced in years, the steps felt familiar when I held a woman on the dance floor. As her body melted into mine, I could lead her. Walking her back and moving our hips in time to the music.

A tendril of hair curled around her collarbone as she gazed up at me, the corners of her mouth turning up. "I didn't know you knew how to dance."

As I stepped away, I lifted her hand in the air to spin her out and away from me before pulling her back against my body. The cords in her neck stood out as she threw her head back in laughter at the twirl. It was a low, heady sound, the ringing peal of joy, and I gave that to her. For a brief, shining moment, I made her laugh. I pulled her close, one hand splayed on her bare back, the other gripping her hip, fingers digging into her ass. Her breasts brushed against my chest, no bra again, and her nipples were hard despite the heat of our bodies and the crowded room.

It was all so much like that night we spent together, the way her body reacted to mine, the way she fit perfectly in my embrace. I had spent months failing to get the images out of my head, but I welcomed the honeyed memory.

"In Sedona, I said I wouldn't dance, not that I didn't know how."

Her fingers found my nape, her hips grinding against mine as I stepped us around the floor. The dance wasn't complicated, and Autumn wasn't skilled, but she was loose in my arms, feet moving with mine as she yielded to me.

The sensation was a dichotomy to the last time I had danced like this. The rigid set of arms, the counting each step, the admonishment when a toe was out of sync. Eye rolls and the snap of *again* until it was perfect.

Dancing with Autumn was far from it. Messy and clumsy. Full of vigor and laughter when she stepped on my toe and sparks of light in her eyes after every dip and twirl. Other couples on the dance floor were moving far more skillfully than us, but as the outliers, I wasn't sure that could be helped.

After our trek to the hot spring, her honesty and bravery were rubbing off on me.

"I took dancing lessons with my fiancée."

Autumn leaned back, a line forming between her brows. Her foot collided with mine, not moving to the beat anymore but still holding my hand, her breast pressed against my chest. If she said anything, I might have stopped talking, but she only held my gaze, waiting me out. Autumn knew how to fill the silence, but she also somehow knew how to draw out my own words.

"Noemi."

With a start, I realized I hadn't said it aloud in years. Not since moving back to Ridgewood, not since the sale of the app. Her name was a bitter phantom on my tongue. "We were supposed to be married, but she—" Autumn's grip on my hand was warm and steady and sure as I said the rest.

"I lost her eight years ago."

Our hands were clasped together, and as she pulled back, finally, my admission made her see sense. She tightened her fingers on mine, big blue eyes wide as she studied me, finding in my admission what she'd been searching for.

"I'm sorry, Nico."

"Thank you."

In the wreckage of losing Noemi, I found that accepting the apology always felt hollow. It wasn't mine to accept and never was, with no way to explain that to Autumn. Not without sharing the rest. And for an unfurling, selfish moment, I wanted to hold her for a few minutes longer. It had been years, and until I held Autumn, I hadn't realized how lonely I was, how much I savored her gaze, how she might even care for me. Want me. Had anyone ever looked at me that way before?

"Oliver never told me, I didn't know."

Her voice was raspy, as if she were the one to cry over the truth. As if she was the one with the loss.

"I don't really talk about it. When it all happened, he came and stayed with me, made me eat, forced me to shower, stuff like that. I was—"

Over her shoulder, I saw a teenage boy approach the birthday girl, Martina, and ask her to dance. They stood stiff on the floor, her hands rigid on his shoulders while his froze at her waist as they rocked back and forth. The innocence of a whole life stretching out before them, when all you had to worry about was where to put your hands during a slow dance. It had been so long since I worried about stakes that low, but I still remembered them, the unknown, the fear of rejection. It was so trivial, yet I knew the bone-crushing weight of it on a teen's mind. Of thinking that it would never feel this good or this bad ever again.

"It was a dark time for me."

With her free hand, she placed her fingers on my side, the heat of her touch searing through my thin shirt. "Your tattoo?"

I nodded. "Her favorite flower."

She nodded, not asking anymore. The song ended, and I loosened my grip on her waist. Autumn stepped away but still held my hand. "You want to walk to the beach? It's only a few blocks away. I heard it's lovely."

I nodded, allowing her to lead me out of the party and into the falling night.

Sandals shucked, we sat side by side on the low steps, feet buried in the sand. Her red dress rode up, exposing freckled thighs as she leaned back on her elbows. All the way from the party, she talked about nothing important—a tip from an aunt on frying chicken and how Martina's crush danced with another girl instead.

"If we were seahorses, would you let me get you pregnant?" she asked.

I raised a brow. "What kind of question is that?"

"A completely legitimate one."

I shook my head, the scrape of my hand over my unshaven jaw making a rough noise. "Sure, Autumn, if we were seahorses, you could fill me with millions of little seahorse babies."

"They can only carry about two thousand at a time, so you're off the hook for a million. But glad to hear you'd be an equal opportunity fish."

The waves crested white against the darkened sand, falling and rising like breaths. Autumn straightened, her gaze on the inky night, the line where the ocean met the sky a blur beyond us. "Tell me about her?"

"Noemi? She was—"

The name was thick on my tongue. It had been years since I said her name and even longer since I had talked of her to anyone who didn't know her. In the years that passed, I stopped meeting with our friends from San Jose. Stopped accepting invitations from her parents for dinners. They weren't my family. It wasn't my life, not anymore. If it ever had been.

"What do you want to know?"

Autumn leaned her head on my shoulder. "Anything, everything, whatever you want to share."

Describing someone like Noemi was a lesson in contradictions. Maybe if I'd gone to therapy like her mother urged, I could have compartmentalized the joy and pain of thinking about my former fiancée. But I hadn't. I shoved her down into her own partition, beside my mom leaving, beside the vacant stands when I won awards and an empty house on holidays. She was another tally of the happiness thought I deserved, only to be proven wrong.

"She was dynamic. You know, the sort of person who everyone looks at when they enter a room. She had this confidence that was unreal. I thought she was the most beautiful woman I had ever seen. We got set up by my roommate in college, Daveed, who was dating her cousin. We had one disastrous first date. I had a cold that week and had some medicine and then had two beers at the restaurant and fell asleep at the table. She refused to go back out with me after that. I had to send her flowers and ask her five more times. I was a borderline stalker if I'm being honest before she agreed to a second date."

"That's a lot of effort to go on a second date," Autumn mused, her words tinged with a longing I sensed had nothing to do with me.

"From the second I saw her, I knew. She had blonde hair, brown eyes, always wore the same shade of pink lipstick, *Roundez-vous*, and I would watch as she reapplied it every morning. Swipe, blot, swipe, blot. Our coffee mugs always had little half-moon stains on the rim from her lipstick. She called it her power color. She always smelled faintly of the expensive face cream she wore to bed, like powdery flowers. Funny, but in a dry, witty way.

She thought I was too silly."

"You? Silly?" Autumn pulled her head off my shoulder, her expression incredulous. "There are a lot of words I'd use, but silly isn't one of them."

"You didn't know me back then. I could be immature. I didn't take myself seriously, wasn't living up to my potential. She was smart. Smarter than me, for sure."

In the low shine of the waning crescent moon, Autumn studied a line creasing between my brows.

"When we met, I didn't know the difference between Matisse and Monet, but she taught me. She saw something in me, this scruffy kid who thought a pair of jeans with no rips meant they were fancy enough. She made me aspire to be better, pushed me into making the app. Pushed me in a lot of ways. She expected perfection in herself and everyone around her. Including me and when—" I swallowed.

I didn't want to go there. Autumn didn't want to hear about all the ways I let Noemi and myself down.

"You must miss her."

I miss who I wanted to be for her.

"It's been a long eight years."

"Do you still love her?"

"Who I am today is because of her. There's no getting around that. I wouldn't lead the life I do if she hadn't been in my life. But I'm not that man any longer. Sometimes, I don't even recognize him. That man loved her, and while he's a part of me, he's not all of me. But the person I am now—" Autumn turned her body on the step, pulling one bare foot up under her and rose to her knees. She reached between us, fingers on my jaw to turn my face to hers, thumb tracing my cheekbone as I searched for words. "She wouldn't love the man I am today."

Pain lanced my chest at the admission. For years, I had tamped down these thoughts. Guilt, yes, I let that flow through me, anger sometimes, sure. But the certainty that I was failing Noemi's vision of me lingered beneath the surface, never spoken.

"If things were different, if she hadn't gotten in that car that night, if we hadn't thrown that party, if—"

In the distance, a ship's bow light blinked—a red dot on the endless horizon. Even though miles away, I could blot it with my thumb, yet it remained steady and massive. "Who knows where I would be today?"

"You don't like talking about her, do you?" She wrinkled her nose at the question, shaking her head from side to side. "Sorry, I don't know why I asked that. Forget it."

"No, it's okay. You're right, I don't, but you make me want to share. This trip, spending time with you—it's like I'm living someone else's life. I don't allow myself to do these things, to—"

"Be happy?"

Her expression was one of innocence and cunning.

I snorted, pulling my lower lip between my teeth, biting back the truth of her statement. "I was going to say be casual."

Casual. The word was wrong. Nothing about the way Autumn felt under my hand was casual. Not the gleam in her eye as she glanced at me in the passenger seat. Not the way her body curled into mine as we slept in the car or a dingy motel. Not the way her smile struck like flint against my walls, ready to burn them to ash. With any other girl, it could have been, I could have been. But not Autumn.

And the worst was, despite using Oliver as an excuse or our ages or any myriad of reasons we could never work, I knew it was me. Deeply scarred, ruinous me. All other rationales of why this would implode were merely fodder.

"You deserve happiness, despite you trying so hard against it." She picked up my hand, entwining her fingers with mine.

Her lips grazed my knuckles, echoing the moment at the Grand Canyon when I held her hand and spoke of her youthful skin and why we'd never work. A speech we both barreled over and obliterated together. The kiss was reverent, a balm to the ache of memory. With my hand still clasped in hers, she pulled it over my head to rest my palm against her nape.

"You have no idea what I deserve," I told her.

Our lips inches from each other, her breath sweet from the fruit sodas at the party. So badly, I wanted to give in to her. To accept this tenderness and think I could earn it.

"Sure, I do."

So close, inches, and warmth and the sugar clinging to her lips. It would take nothing to close this gap, to concede. "I don't deserve this, not from you, maybe if I were a better man. You shouldn't want me."

"Don't tell me what I should want, Nicolai. You think I don't know myself?"

"I'm serious. Maybe if I could change myself to be better."

At this, she pulled away, her thumb pressing against my wrist, her head cocked to the side to study me. "Why would I want you to change, Nico? When who you are is what I want? You think I can't see it? The way you hold yourself apart, how you think you owe my brother some cosmic debt, for what? Making you microwave dinners a few times and not allowing you to fall apart?"

"It's more than that—"

"It's really not. You're not some burden. You're allowed to be human, to make mistakes and to be forgiven. To feel emotions the same way as the rest of us. Even if it's happiness. It's as if you enjoy hurting yourself, denying what would make you happy. Acting like you need to be another kind of man to atone. Someone who cares about you wouldn't want you to change, wouldn't want you to be anything but exactly who you are today."

As if it could be that simple. As if her words weren't blowing everything up, making me want, and want, and want. To not lose hope when I never had it in the first place.

"So, you don't think we should aspire to be a better person for those we care about?"

She studied me in the dark. I couldn't see the shades of her irises, but I didn't need light to recall them—the flare of cornflower, the lines of a desert sky. The blue of a bright day, of hope. "Better versions, yes. But a different version, no. You can improve yourself and still be the same at the heart of yourself. That's what someone who lo"—she pressed her lips together, her eyes darting out to the ocean—"cares about what you would want. They would want all of you."

Throughout the trip, Autumn made comments about how others saw her—silly, chaotic—yet her words cut to the bone. She made it all sound so simple, and for the first time in years, I wondered if I could let myself believe it. Could someone truly care for all of me? And if they did, what did that mean for all I've clung to?

It couldn't be. I wouldn't let it.

"If you were engaged, then she must have loved you, and I know that no one who loves you would want to see you unhappy. It's silly to think that because you're still here and she's gone you aren't allowed to enjoy life? I didn't know her, but I'm sure she'd be disappointed if you were wasting it."

Disappointed.

You're such a fucking disappointment, Nico.

Behind my head, I pulled her hands apart and stepped away from Autumn in one motion. "You have no idea what she wanted, and you don't know me."

Stalking away from her, I made my way toward the white break on the sand until the chilly seafoam hit my toes. Under my feet, the sand gave way, in and out, sinking lower with each wave crashing over my ankles, the ever-changing shoreline under the pulse of the ocean. Tilting my head back to gaze up at the stars, the Little Dipper alongside the dragon in the stars. Stories of navigators using the celestial references for millennia to guide their way. Of knowing exactly where to go by trust and the sky.

Then Autumn stood beside me, her hair whipping in the breeze, tickling my arm as her hand slid from my elbow to my wrist, twining with mine. I didn't pull away, despite knowing it would be for the better. Despite knowing the way I craved her was needy. Parasitic, even. Her trust in me. The way she offered herself up for heartbreak made me feel like I could be worth something. I was so fucking lonely. How did she make me realize how lonely I was, and why was her hand in mine filling something I hadn't realized was a lacuna?

"My dad told me about Andromeda and Perseus. Do you know the story? Her parents chained her to a rock as a sacrifice for her mother's vanity, but she was saved by Perseus. A bit archaic, but all those myths can be. And yet they are sent up to the heavens, together for eternity."

"Ceaselessly," I murmur, the love letter from the Italian restaurant coming to mind.

Her hand faithful in mine.

"Ceaselessly." With the echoed memory of Noemi's voice fading as Autumn holds me tight, the cool waves licked at our skin. "Swim with me?"

Salt brine filled my lungs, the heavy sea air thousands of miles from Ridgewood still feeling like home.

Home. Her hand in mine as we stared up at the boundless sky.

"Okay."

It was needy and selfish and so incredibly wrong, but I couldn't push her away. I couldn't say no to the warm grasp of her hand against mine. Couldn't say no as she untied her dress at her nape, pulling it over her head and tossing it as far up the beach as she could. And certainly wouldn't say no when she pulled those little lace scraps down her legs. The moonlight reflected off her creamy skin, the freckles across her chest a constellation all their own. My shirt landed beside her dress as I followed her into the water. Cold waves lapped against our thighs and hips. Then she went under, her hair blackened and flat as she emerged from the surf.

The water was cold, and it was far too late in the season—even for Southern California—to be swimming, but heat was building under my skin. I followed her deeper.

POINT L-PACIFIC OCEAN

Nico

As she floated flat on her back, her dusky nipples pebble in the cool sea.

Hands flat on the surface, I studied the way she floated, the moonlight bleaching her skin against the black of the water. "Aren't you freezing?"

"Of course I'm cold, but how many times do you have the chance to skinny-dip in the ocean?"

I raised a brow at her. "I did it all the time in high school, climb under the patio at Bella Luna? Jump off the dock? You didn't?"

She opens one eye and flashes me a wide smile. "But that's in the summer. And I always wore a swimsuit. I'm talking about this—here, you and me. Us together. This adventure."

I hummed, not wanting to give a full answer. She stood, the water sluicing over her body as she stepped closer to me, taking my hand in hers. "What I said earlier about Noemi, I'm sorry if it sounded like I don't think she loved you. You two obviously loved each other a lot."

If you only knew.

Turning her hand over in mine, I entwine my fingers with hers. Although it was selfish and wrong, I wanted the constancy of her touch—keeping me rooted in the surf, salt air mussing our hair as we stood before the ocean. Home.

"What are you doing with me? I'm not good for you. I'm a shitty person, and the more time we spend together, the more of a chance you're going to end up hurt."

She lifted our clasped hands to her face, rubbed her nose over my skin, breathed me in, then rested the back of my fingers on her cheek. "I'm not some delicate flower. Stop trying to protect me from something I so clearly want. I'm impulsive—I know I am—but that doesn't mean I'm wrong about you. Even if you can't see it yourself."

"Once you got to know me, if you really knew, you'll—" I drew in the brackish air as a foghorn sounded and waves hushed against the sea shelf. "I take things that should never be mine, and I ruin them until there's no going back. That is what I learned, and that is where I come from. That is who I am."

"No, it's not. I don't need to know every detail to know what kind of man you are. But you should know me well enough to say that I don't do things in half measures, and I trust you."

"Don't." The exhale shuddered. Trust. Earn. "I don't trust myself." My words cut the air, knife-sharp, and to the point. "Not anymore. How could you?"

"Easily. All this stomping off, your shouting and little tantrums." I scowl at the description. "You say you don't trust yourself? Fine. Trust me."

"I don't know how."

Every time I expect Autumn to finally pull away, to see my truth. Instead, she stood before me, her fingers finding my hair, dragging her nails over my scalp as she brought my face to hers. "Let me show you, please."

Maybe it was the wide-eyed way she was watching me, the press of her forehead pressed against mine. Or the hope in every word, affirmations washing over me as if they could heal, her hand cupping my cheek to lift my eyes to hers.

Or worst of all, the endless seconds of stillness, her lips a breath away, heat the only barrier between us. Each inhale was her exhale, in and out together in perfect synchronicity.

Whatever it was, I broke, her gasp sliding over my ocean-cooled skin as I took her mouth with the sweetest touch.

I kissed her as if I was good, as if the brush of my lips could forgive every wrong, the tensing of my fingers in her hair, the slow exhale of our shared breath. As if I had earned this right.

In the water, it was so easy to grab her waist and pull her up into my arms, her legs coming around my hips. She was weightless. It was strange and mesmerizing, the way the waves moved us, moonlight reflecting off the swaying surface. Breaking from her mouth, I found her jaw, the column of her throat, the little spot between her neck and her collarbone, where she tasted of sugar and salt.

"You're so fucking sweet," I ground out through a strained moan, my mouth tracing past her jaw to nip delicately at the area around her bottom lip. "Like something I need to ruin."

My cock wedged in the space between her legs. It would be so simple to pull her up a little higher and then bring her down around me. She would be so warm, so tight.

"Go on and ruin me, then," she urged, her legs tightening.

She doesn't know how true her words are. The little voice in the back of my head warning me, rationality saying this can't go on forever. There was so much she didn't know about me and the—man I was . . .

Her kisses grew deeper, her gyration against my cock growing tighter.

With nothing solid to push against, she only shifted her hips, but it was enough to make me swell as my hands held her steady.

"This isn't how I wanted to do this," I murmured against her mouth. "I wanted to take my time with you."

"We have time. We have days and miles and nothing but the open road together. Take it, Nico. Take what you want, and I'll give it."

Her trust again. The promise, the want and need and fire. How was the ocean not boiling with us in it? How was she simultaneously steadfast, yet the idea of her was still slipping through me like something I could never possess as much as the water around us?

I pulled her head to the side, my teeth scraping her tender throat as a canvas for my mouth. I wanted to see my mark there, to claim her as my own. To sink into her and never let go, to allow the waves to roll over us and dissolve as we came together.

"You have no idea what that means. The things I want to do to you, the depraved and wicked, the—"

"Then, prove it. Haven't I shown you? Don't you know?" Her moan reverberated between our bodies, my cock sliding in the space between her thighs.

"I'm not going to fuck you here." I grated against the side of her neck.

"Why not?" She gasped out as I slid my finger over her ass, between her cheeks from the back.

"I'm a patient man, not some boy you can tease into fucking you."

In the moonlight, freckles scattered across her chest formed constellations, ancient stories of love and loss, a world for me to trace with fingers and tongue.

"We both want it. Why are you denying yourself?"

Her legs tightened around my waist, hands on my shoulders as she pulled herself up. If it were up to her, she'd sink onto my cock. She was breaking me into pieces, trying to shape me to her whims, but I wouldn't allow that. If she wanted this, it would be on my terms, not hers.

With my free hand, I grasp the hair at the nape, pulling her head back to look at me. "You're filthy, wanting me the way you do."

She wiggled against me, her nipples hard against my chest as she inhaled with a stutter. "I am, I do." The groan she let out against my neck was low, her teeth scraping my collarbone. "Nicolai, Nicolai."

My name repeated in that breathless, sobbing whimper. My fingers danced over her slit, the velvet of her hot and wanting. Every repressed shred of desire from the last week was singing through my blood, her pleading and the pulse of my hand on her skin. I'd never allowed this need to become this strong for any woman, letting it build. Not by a long-fucking-shot.

Sliding one finger inside her warmth, she gasped. "Please, please."

"You want to come, sweet girl? You want to come all over my fingers? My tongue?"

"Please," she pled again, grinding her cunt into my hand. "More. Please."

"You're so gorgeous when you beg." Sliding a second finger inside her, I curled them to the front. The base of my cock rocked against her clit as I drove deeper. "Has any man ever made you feel this way? I saw how that boy from earlier was dancing with you. Just like that asshole in Sedona. Whispering in your ear, touching your skin, watching you and thinking they could taste you. If I didn't know any better, I'd think you wanted me to be jealous. But we know who you belong to, don't we?"

"Yes." Her breath hitched as my hand slid from between her legs to her front, rolling one pink nipple between my fingers.

"Do you think he could touch you like this? That he has the right?"

"No," she panted as I slid my cock against her folds, rough. "Only you."

Hitching her up higher to nestle myself firm against her core, I pulled one dusky nipple into my mouth. She leaned back, granting me access, her hips pressing hard on my cock as it moved against her clit. Her body shivering around me spurred me to suck it, my teeth scraping. "You need more, don't you? Beg me, sweet girl. All you have to do is ask."

With the waves around us, she was edging closer. Her only response was a groan as she rocked her hips against me harder, searching for relief. The little noises, pants, and gasps, lilting on her tongue as her ankles dug into the backs of my legs.

"Fuck, you're so good, sweet girl. So fucking good."

Needing no further encouragement, she ground against me, her movements becoming tight and short, her legs tensing and trembling. "Go on. Come all over my cock. I know you want to."

Our eyes locked as she crested her peak. Her legs pulsed around me, squeezing me harder, begging me to follow. She cried out, jerking against me, her pupils wide enough to swallow me whole.

I came in the space between her legs, into the water, the first time in over twenty years I had been brought to orgasm this way. No penetration, just raw friction like a teen. My mouth sucked the delicate skin between her throat and shoulder, groaning my climax into the salt of her skin.

Languid, she sagged against me, her head resting on my shoulder as her legs loosened around my waist. One by one, she put a foot down on the sea floor, her balance shaky.

"That was—"

"Yeah."

It would've been easy to step away, to create distance and blame this on hormones and the temptation of the moon. But I couldn't. Once again, she had broken me, and I savored the way these fractures fit exactly around her. With a firm hand on her chin, I pulled her mouth to mine. Salt lingered on our tongues as I delved into her mouth. The brush of lips and soft breath—this time it was a promise of something I couldn't yet offer.

As I pulled away, I rested my forehead against hers, breath to breath, heat to heat. Goose bumps popped up on her arms as the ocean breeze picked up. I would need to get her back to the hotel soon.

With my hands over her arms, her head dipped to rest on my clavicle, her warm breath drifting across my bare chest. "I haven't done that since Bobby Luca's basement party in tenth grade."

My hand stilled on her upper arm, where I was rubbing it to bring back heat. "I don't know who Bobby Luca is, but I hate him already."

She swatted at my bare chest, a grin stretching across her face. "Stop, you know you're way better."

"I would hope so, or else I'll have to track him down."

A blissed-out hum eluded her. "I kind of like you when you're jealous. It's hot."

"Only with you," I admitted.

"And also with you," she joked. Pulling her lower lip between her teeth, she gazed up at me. "You know, before you, I hadn't gotten off in a while."

"How long is a while?"

"A few years. I mean, if you don't count battery-operated toys."

That image burned into my mind. I couldn't wait to see that.

"But being with someone, no. Not even my hand can do it for me anymore."

"It worked earlier today," I reminded her.

"Yes, it did. I wonder why?" She shot me a wicked grin as she sauntered to the sand, her pale skin dripping with ocean water as she emerged like a nymph.

Despite her best efforts, the moment we got back to the hotel room, the awkwardness of what we had done sunk in. Had I dry-humped her in the ocean? Wet humped? What word was even right for what we had done?

It took me back to junior high dances, recession era rap blasting as I ground against a willing girl, careful not to spill my soda. Sweaty and clumsy, raw and real.

What was it about Autumn that made me feel so young, so full of life? She made me want things I hadn't allowed myself in years.

The harsh hotel lamps cast shadows over our faces as we settled into the room. All I want is to gather Autumn back into my arms, to carry her to bed and have my wicked way with her. But this hotel is small, dingy, and not the white bedding and streaming sunlight she deserves. None of what I've given her on this trip is. Myself included.

"Listen, I know we keep getting caught up. Skinny-dipping is one thing, but we don't have to do anything you're not ready for. I'm not a good man. I need you to know that—"

"Stop."

"No, let me get this out. That I'm giving in to this only proves I am not a good man. I know I should let you go, should have better control over myself, but I can't do that, not anymore. I'm moody and proud and have a temper. I don't know how to talk about my feelings, and I'm going to hurt you. We both know I will. Deep, dark marks that are rooted inside me. I am scarred."

A line formed between her brows, her deep blue gaze holds me.

"Nicolai."

She said my name like no one ever has before, and I can't deny her anymore. I've been shattered and reconstructed into a messy, flawed thing.

I'm good with glue.

Somehow, she knew all this and was still here and cared anyway.

"If I were a better man, I'd let you go. But I'm not. I'm selfish, and being with you makes me want things for myself I shouldn't want. I can't want. But, fuck, if I can say no to it. To you. You make me selfish, wanting you. You make me hope I could be better, even when I know I never will be."

"Let me decide that, then? I asked you earlier to trust me. So, do it."

The first kiss was warm, a low sweeping on her lips, on mine, a pleading on my skin. Then my hands were on her ass, her legs wrapping around my waist as I hoisted her up and walked three steps to the bed. My knees hit the mattress, and we fell together, my head landing in the crook of her neck, the damp ties of her dress cold against my cheek.

"Tell me again, say I'm the only one," I demanded. "I need you to say it."

"Only you, always you."

Her hands were scrambling at my shirt, pulling it up over my head. The hem of her dress rode up between us to above her hips as she pulled my cock between her thighs.

"Please, Nico, I need you inside me. I need to feel you."

"Not yet, sweet girl. I promised you, didn't I? First these breasts." With one hand, I untied the thin straps of her dress, pulling it down to pool at her waist, freeing her breasts in the low light. One finger traced her nipple, a slow circle that made her gasp. "I'm going to leave my mark on them, red and bruised, until you're begging me."

"Yes."

Her back arched, pressing her breasts harder into my hand. When I pulled my fingers away, she groaned, but I slid lower to cup her through the thin fabric between her legs.

"And then I'll lick this cunt until you're screaming my name, and only after I've tasted you on my tongue will I fuck you."

With one hand, I pressed down on her sternum, sitting up between her shaking legs.

"My sweet girl needs it. Doesn't she?"

Her blue eyes darkened, hands on my thighs. With my shirt tossed to the side, I shimmied her dress over her head, leaving her almost bare. So similar to the hot spring, with only her tiny underwear separating us.

The bob of her throat was all the answer I needed as I sank over her, my lips tracing devotion down her neck, across the curve of her breasts, and into the hollow between them where I held her still.

The arduous lick of her bud with the flat of my tongue had her panting, pushing her body up into me. As I took her in my mouth, kissing, and sucking, she let out a low cry that could only be my name.

My teeth scraped over one nipple, pert in the cool fall air. Under me, her nails dug into my scalp, pushing her deeper, harder. It was past pleasure, edging on pain, but she urged me on, writhing against me, mewing and gasping, "Please, please, please," with each pass.

When I pulled away, the purple marks around her nipples were angry, my selfish claim on her and, fuck, if it isn't sexy.

"Did that hurt?" I asked.

She nodded, a wicked smile grazing her lips. "But I liked it."

She was ruining me.

Slowly, I traced my thumb along the silk of her inner thigh, rising higher and higher until I reached the thin scrap of lace covering her mound. With one finger hooked over the side, I pulled it down her hips.

I was so fucked.

Returning to my home between her thighs, I stared at those pink folds, wet and warm for me. Parting her, I placed one arm flat against her hips to keep her from moving. With one finger inside her warmth, I watched as her lashes fluttered shut, her back arching. The tiny muffled groans she let out with each thrust spurred me to go faster, to add another finger.

My first lick was languid, curling around her clit before sucking it into my mouth. Sharp nails dug through my hair, holding me firm against her center and the taste of her, the tang of her arousal and the salt water exploding on my tongue. With two fingers, I parted her folds. "You're so wet for me, sweet girl, so ready."

With my thumb against her clit, I plunged my fingers in and out, the sound of her cunt taking me filling the room. Each pass of my tongue was meticulous, exacting pressure, where she needed it the most as she bucked against my mouth. Her legs quivered as I feasted on her, tongue and fingers, suction, and thrust. She was so close I could feel it in the fluttering of her body under me. I leave no area unmarked, slow, then fast and harder. She was wound around my fingers as I pressed up inside, her walls clenched around me as she fucked my face.

Just as I told her to, she gasped out my name, first softly, then louder and louder, a cry for me as she shattered beneath me.

Her chest rose and fell with each cry, her taste bursting on my tongue, and nothing would ever match this—her surrender, her giving herself to me.

Never before, never again. No one else.

Ceaselessly.

I had thought she would lie still after her orgasm, but she surprised me by pulling herself up, flipping me onto my back to straddle me.

"My turn. I let you do it your way. Now give me what I want."

Her breasts were heavy, my teeth marks marring her freckled skin beautifully.

"I thought I just did."

"We both know you have a lot more to offer."

Together, we fumble as I remove my shorts and boxers before I pull out the last condom from my wallet. Until three months before, I had two, and now it would be none. I would need to replenish them at our next stop.

"Here, let me," she said, her hand covering mine as she took the wrapper from me.

Clenching it between her teeth, she pulled the condom out. Fisting my cock, she dragged her palm along its length, harsh and frenzied. Her thumb traced the slit at the top, spreading my precum down the backside.

With one hand firm on the base of my cock, she placed the condom on my tip, rolling it down my length slowly.

"Just like with a banana." She mussed. "I've never done that with a man before."

"Never?" Something about being first in this, being the only one, made my cock even harder.

She was brash energy and innocence, clumsy and well-meaning.

"Only you."

It was barbaric. With every woman before her, I never cared about their pasts, never cared if I was the first. But each time Autumn admitted her lack of experience, it only drove me wilder. So many things I could be her first for. I could be her only.

Sitting up, I pulled her body against mine, with my cock jutting up between us, flat on her stomach as I kissed her. With one knee on each side of me, she straddled me. My mouth was hard on hers, and we melted into each other, my hands in her hair, holding her to me. Her fingers were wrapped around my cock, pumping it between us. The thin sheath of the condom slid on my bare length. Pulling away, we both looked down between us where the rubber had split.

"Fuck." I pulled away, grasping the useless protectant.

Autumn leaned back, her lips swollen and pink, her gaze bright and filled with humor as she stared at me. "Oh, no."

With her still above me, she handed me my wallet, hoping I had one more stashed away. Nothing but cash and a punch card for my favorite coffee stand inside.

"We could run to the store."

Lacing my hand in her hair, I pulled her in for another kiss. "I will. You stay here. I'll be a few minutes."

Flopping down on the bed, she ran a hand over her naked body. "Don't take too long, or I might finish by myself."

Once again, I took her mouth, this kiss bruising in its need. "Don't say that, or I'll never leave." Not bothering with underwear, I pulled my shorts off the floor. "Trust me, I'll go as fast as I can."

As I grabbed my shirt from the floor, I picked up the wrapper and narrowed my eyes to see the date. Expired one year before.

That explained it.

Buying condoms at an indecent market with half a hard-on was bad enough. But having to wait for ten minutes behind an elderly woman paying for her Virginia Slims with change was torture.

The lights were on in the room when I returned, but when the door closed behind me, Autumn didn't stir from her side of the bed. She had slid under the covers, the sheet not fully covering one pale breast as she lay on her side. With one hand tucked under her cheek, her slow, even breathing ruffled the pillow beside her. Her freckles on her nose spread over her closed eyelids. Ignoring my erection, I turned the harsh bedside lamp off. I wasn't going to wake her. We had enough time. Slipping beside her, I took her hand in mine, lacing our fingers together.

POINT M- SAN JOSE, CA

Autumn

IT WAS THE SUN that woke me first. The night before, I got cold waiting on top of the covers for Nico to return, so I slipped under the blankets. My eyelids grew heavy, and before I knew it, sunlight was harsh on my face, water running faintly in the other room as I blinked into morning.

I fell asleep. We were finally about to have sex again, and I fell asleep. What an amateur.

Still half in bed, I grappled for my phone in the bag beside me, bringing it up to my face to see my daily affirmation.

I belong here, and I deserve to take up space.

I quickly copied the message to my group chat and sent it to the girls, who would barely acknowledge it but still relied on it, even as they teased me.

Devin liked it. Summer sent the sarcastic Jennifer Lawrence thumbs-up gif—her favorite, and Wren was likely still sleeping.

The door to the bathroom opened, with a billow of steam coming out as Nico stepped back into the room, his boxers on but nothing else. His hair was darkened, a bead of water clinging to a strand that hung over his temple. We were naked together the night before in the water, but this was different. The morning light was bright, stark and real. Was that a love bite or just a small mark on his chest? Did I do that? I knew my skin bore a few marks.

"You're up."

I set my phone down beside me, schooling my face to appear as if I hadn't been ogling him like a teenager. "You could have woken me up last night. I didn't mean to pass out on you."

His muscular back rippled as he searched through his bag. "Nah, you were tired. I'm not going to have our first time together be when you're half asleep."

Sitting up, I pulled the sheet above my chest. "It wouldn't be our first time, though."

He turned to face me, his jaw ticking. "No, but this time it's different, isn't it? It's a first of something."

That acknowledgment was more than he had given in the past few days. I wouldn't let it go.

"Yeah, you're right."

With clothes in one hand, he held out a paper cup with a lid. "I got you a coffee."

The coffee was exactly right—the milk, the flavor.

Every morning, my mom would get up and make my dad the same breakfast: two eggs, scrambled, and an almost burned English muffin. Every spring, my dad would be in the front yard, pruning the blue hydrangeas, her favorite, helping them bloom gloriously in the later weeks. He would take her car to the car wash once a month, scrub it down, and vacuum it out. Van would bring Summer her favorite food for lunch, the right flavor of sparkling water—lemon, not lime—a sandwich with extra sun-dried tomato compote. The bottles of wine with their tarot card labels that lined the cabinet in Devin and Cedar's house. The way Adrian would place his hand on the back of Wren's neck, over her scar, his thumb tracing it.

Is that what it feels like to have someone know you? The right coffee, their hand in the right place, a thousand little acts that build up to simply being right. As a teen, my friends mocked me for thinking each new guy was the one, my rose-colored glasses making every red flag look the same. And maybe that was true. I often looked the other way, content just to be cared for. The guy who worked at a seafood restaurant, whose truck smelled like clam chowder, but I still cried for days when we broke up. The boy who took me up snowboarding every Saturday, kissed me behind closed doors, and then loudly boasted to all his friends, *"She wishes I was her boyfriend."*

No, I wasn't always the best at finding a guy, but I tried. Still, I waited for those flutters, that yearning. Over the years, I had gotten used to the disappointment of those men not living up to the idealized version in my head. Until Nico. Because this was more.

Everything about Nico was different.

It was the tides, in and out, lapping around our bodies as we came together. It was inexorable. Nothing before and nothing again. Those celestial beings far above us the night before, spinning, spinning, spinning, and always out of reach. Steady and true. Even the stars will burn out someday, but to burn with this man would be an honor.

It was such a simple thing—the coffee, the way he placed his hand on my lower back. The ridiculous sunglasses he wore for me and the stops he made because I suggested them.

My tongue coated with the pumpkin spice and coffee, and nothing had been so sweet as this act of remembrance. I was gone, had been for days, months. Since the house party, since the dock. The waves lapped at our bare skin as we dove into the ocean. Bound by the moon and slick of the sea.

Sitting back, I watched as Nico dressed, the long planes of his back flexing as he pulled his shirt over his head. It was a shame he couldn't be shirtless all the time. Rising from the bed, I gathered the blanket around me. While he had seen me naked the night before, slept beside me that way as well, in the morning sun, it would be too much.

"I never washed the ocean off me before being distracted last night." Gripping the blanket around my body, I let it drop slightly. His eyes darted from my face down to my cleavage and back up to my eyes. "You want to join me?"

With one hand, he gripped my chin, moving me closer. A breath away, sweet and coffee tinged, his gaze took in my face, tracing over my lips, my brows, my nose. His thumb pulled my lip down, and I had to hold myself back from sucking that digit into my mouth, to swirl my tongue around it.

My voice was breathy, lower than normal. "Don't say you haven't thought about it."

"All I've thought about was you." His teeth found my earlobe, nipping at it, and I had to stifle the moan burning my chest. "And sweet girl. If I join you in there, we're going to end up fucking ten ways to Sunday, and we'll never leave this town."

Holy heck, what his words did to me. My core tingled, and wetness grew between my thighs.

"And that's bad, why?" I allowed the blanket to drop lower, one nipple showing.

The blackness of his pupils grew as he hazarded a glance down my body, and a muscle ticked in his jaw. "Check out is in an hour, and while you can do your coursework on your laptop, I cannot and have to be back at work in five days. We still have at least two more nights on the road."

"Boo, that's no fun." I pouted.

"I know, but so is the way of the world. Now, hop in the shower. We're wasting daylight." He sent me off with a little smack to my bum, a more playful gesture than he had ever given me. Squealing in delight, I made my

way out of the room as he adjusted himself in his pants when he thought I
couldn't see.

This was his town, and he drove it as if he were coming home. Never once
did he use the GPS, navigating through the streets with ease. With our bags
already dropped off at the hotel, he insisted we go out to one of his favorite
restaurants in the area.

The air was crisp, shedding the last traces of the afternoon sun. A light
breeze drifted through the valley, rustling the amber and gold leaves carpeting the sidewalk. A late afternoon shower had the lights reflecting softly
against the darkening street.

"You look beautiful." During the five-block walk to the restaurant, our
fingers brushed, my pinky grazing the whisper of his calluses—but it wasn't
until we reached the crosswalk opposite Trattoria San Nicola that his fingers finally entwined with mine. He hadn't let them go since. Throughout
dinner, the drinks, the food, he touched me. A hand on my knee, his finger
tracing a circle on the back of my hand, leaning in, whispering in my ear.
Under his touch, heat sizzled, this need to have more.

Heat flooded my cheeks as I looked down at my white dress. It wasn't
anything special, not as dressy as what others wore, but under his gaze, I
felt like a queen.

"You look pretty good yourself." I chuckled, tucking a hair behind my
ear.

His hand cupped my cheek. "If only I could earn you."

I tilted my head to the side, studying him. The candlelight flickered
shadows over his cut jaw, catching the reddish hue of his beard a shade
darker than his hair. Those full pink lips. His hand turned over, lacing his

fingers with mine and pulling the back of my hand up to press a kiss to the soft skin there. It was an innocent gesture.

I'd had his tongue inside me and cum on his face just the day before. But this, a moonlit walk on a city street, his favorite place, the warmth of his palm and the lines of his wrist in mine at this little restaurant, felt entirely different. It was another level of intimacy. With his hand covering mine, I was done. Nothing had ever felt so right.

"You keep saying that. To earn me."

Head cocked to one side, he brushed his thumb over my wrist, addressing the space between us. "Because you said it first. You told me to earn it, so I'm trying every day. I'll try to earn you."

For so long, he was careful with his words around me, but it was still perfect. He was perfect. The right person, the only person.

"I don't remember saying that. If it did, I'm sure I didn't mean it the way you're taking it. As if you don't—"

"I can take it however I want, sweet girl. You don't get to decide that. Because, no matter what you say, I don't understand why you would do all this for me. Why you're still sticking around?"

"Yes, you do. You understand. You just don't want me to say it, but you understand."

Green eyes studied me, wary. Everything unsaid simmered. It was too soon for him, but I was already gone. Perhaps we were both damned, but I didn't want to let anyone burn me but him.

"You know, I thought for a long time I wouldn't feel this way again. Noemi, what happened—" He let go of my hand to scrub a palm over his face. "It's been a long time since I was happy. And I'm not going to lie, this . . . us. Whatever you may call it. It's scary, but I can't deny that you're the happiness I'd choose for myself. All those nights I lay awake and wished for a future I knew would never be mine."

For a man who liked to pretend he was all practicality, he sure knew exactly the right words to string together.

Love was too solemn a word. It was the rush of a strenuous hike. All adrenaline of the climb, the irrevocable wash of calm at the pinnacle, the land stretched out to the edges and you at the top to enjoy it. No matter how my heart was racing, I was exactly where I needed to be.

I'd rather be ravaged by his love than be without. No guarantee waited for us in Ridgewood, but I'd take the shattering loss of loving him over never knowing it at all.

I was never a cautious person. Never learned to control my emotions. Much like my cousin, Summer, only my impulses were more genial, while hers erred on the side of vengeance.

I brought his hand up to my mouth, pressing a kiss to the back, the same way he did for me. "You want to get out of here?"

He leaned down, his words a whisper against my ear. "More than you know."

As Nico stood behind me, holding out my coat, a man stopped before us. "Nic?" His dark brows furrowed as he took us in. "Is that you?"

Beside me, Nico tensed, his hand dropping to the small of my back. He blinked at the man before him, his throat bobbing with thick swallows. "Drew, yeah, how's it—" He coughed into his fist. "How have you been?"

The man's face broke into a wide grin, and before either of us knew what was happening, Nico was being wrapped in this man's arms. "I knew that was you. I told Sanvi it was you, but she didn't believe it."

"It's me. In the flesh." Nico's shoulders were tight, coming up to his ears as the man smiled up at him. We three stood in silence for an arduous moment, the man's gaze darted from Nico to me and back, his grin never faltering.

"I'm Autumn," I interjected, putting my hand out between them.

"Autumn, so good to meet you." This man's wide-open face was brimming with mirth. "Come on, have a drink with us. We have a table at

Whelan's. I know the gang would love to see you."

Nico hesitated, his eyes flickering over me. "Who will be there?"

"The usual, Daveed, Sanvi, Reese."

Something on that list made Nico relax. He glanced down at me. As much as I wanted to get back to the room and have my way with him, I knew he hadn't been back in the area for a long time.

Deep down, I wanted to know more about him. He kept much of his past walled off, revealed only in fragments of conversation and drunken slips—the fiancée, her death, his fears. Understanding Nico was a battle, and watching him with his friends promised another piece of the puzzle.

"We would love to, right?" I smiled, nodding.

I saw the fight in his eyes, the want to keep me separate from this part of him but also the way he couldn't say no now.

His thumb rubbed a circle on my lower back. "Sure, we'll join you."

The bar was one of those pseudo-dives, with well gin and tonics for seventeen dollars, but they don't clean the graffiti off the bathroom wall to maintain authenticity. Nico pulled out the high-backed wooden chair, motioning for me to sit first before he took his spot beside me.

The three-block walk from the restaurant to the bar had been filled with his friend chatting nonstop. At one crosswalk, someone had hacked the signal so instead of the robotic "Walk," a fake AI voice of a famous tech billionaire blared that he sucked dick for the oligarchy. We passed a ginger beer restaurant beside a new-age crystal store.

At first, I sat back and watched the group. They weren't my friends.

This whole trip, Nico was many things, a bit of a jerk, stringent, grumpy. But what he wasn't was uncertain. As we sat, I could feel the unease coming off him in waves, his fingers fidgeting clumsily around mine, his lower lip pulled between his teeth, his gaze darting around the room.

My friends and I would tease each other. I grew up with three older brothers and was around my share of rude or offensive language. My cousin could be brash and spoke before she meant to, her words sharp. But never had I seen friends spend their night one-upping one another with sharper and sharper remarks.

Did these people even like each other?

For the most part, Nico was quiet, and I followed suit. The group talked of their jobs, all tech or tech adjacent, their families. Daveed had a three-year-old daughter. Reese, twin boys. They spoke of people I had never heard of, but with a reverence that meant they were someone important. They spoke of mortgages and annuities and taxes. The very grown-up conversation flowed around me as I tried to avoid audibly slurping my virgin mojito. My twenty-dollar bargain bin dress, which had seemed nice earlier, now felt slick and plasticky on my ribs. A few times, Nico would answer direct questions, but there was a hesitancy in his speech as if he didn't want to give away something. Until that moment, I hadn't realized how easy conversation was between us.

"How long has this been going on?" Daveed asked, his warm brown eyes shining as he motioned between Nico and me.

What was there to say? A week? A day? When did this tension turn from flirting in the front seat of the Eagle to more? The hot springs? That first night in Sedona? The night before as we swam in the ocean, the boundless salt and sea crashed over our bodies?

"Almost three months. We reconnected in August."

Nico traced a line down my nape, a frisson of heat coursing from every glancing touch and those two words. Three months.

"Reconnected? Sounds like there's a story there." Reese waggled her brows.

I laughed, the sound hollow. "It's not as tawdry as it sounds. Nicolai and I have known each other for years. Old family friends."

Behind my back, Nico snagged a tendril of my hair, wrapping it around his finger casually. "More than that. Her brother was my best friend growing up. Her family's practicality raised me."

A glance passed between his friends. I got the sense that Nico didn't talk much about his life before he moved to San Jose. Admittedly, he didn't talk about it much, even when he was in Ridgewood. I knew his uncle passively. I could probably even recognize his mom if asked, though it was well known that she had taken off years before. Nico had a side these people would never know, but I did.

"We saw each other at a party and got to talking and—" I waved in what I hoped was a coy, mysterious gesture, but probably just looked tongue-tied.

Nico caught my gaze, his green eyes so warm, the corners crinkling. In the dim bar light, shadows veiled his smile, but I recognized it anywhere: the grin of a man who liked what he heard, who knew what he wanted, and in that moment, it was me. At least Nico saw I could hold a conversation when I wanted. Wasn't that all that mattered?

"So, Autumn." The woman with the red bob—Kim? Kara?—narrowed her eyes at me, a smirk playing on her lips. "What is it you do?"

Blinking away from Nico, I found the woman. The corners of her mouth were turned up, but sharpness flared in her stare. To steady my hand, I swirled my straw around in its ice-filled highball glass, my drink long past gone. "I worked at the local marine science center for a few years, but with budget cuts, I had to find something else. I'm working as a beer-tender until the next thing comes up."

"A beer-tender?" She echoed, her dark brow raising. It was obvious that the shade of red she had on her head was not natural. "And what does a beer-tender do?"

"It's a local craft brewery, so I pour beer," I say, reaching in front of

Nico and grabbing his full glass of water, taking a sip out of it. At my back, Nico's fingers traced along my spine, and I glanced over at him. His green eyes were warm and full of humor. Bolstered by his reaction, I kept talking. "Sometimes wine or cider. On Sundays, we even do mimosas."

"And you like this"—her lip curled—"vocation?"

I shrugged. "It's only until I get done with school."

"Autumn is studying to be a marine biologist," Nico offered to the group.

"Oh, so you're in college, a college student." Her gaze rested on Nico, hard and unrelenting. "Cute."

Beside me, Nico's hand on my neck tightened, his Adam's apple bobbing as he swallowed his bourbon. Under the table, I slid my hand onto his thigh, squeezing it in reassurance.

"Really, Kim? Some of us had to work while in school." One of the other women at the table, Sanvi, laughed, offering me a smile. "I was a server for years."

"Yeah, Kim, we didn't all have a trust fund growing up," Drew said.

The redhead quirked a brow. "Apparently." She rolled her eyes at the group before setting her gaze back on Nico, the red wine was staining her once-white teeth a garish purple.

Leaning in close, my lips touched his ear. "Maybe we should head back to the room?"

"Yeah, Nic, get your girlfriend home. Surely, it's almost past her curfew." Kim snorted into her red wine glass.

Under my hand, Nico's forearm tightened, and he leaned forward, his glare on the woman across the table. "What is your deal, Kim?"

"My deal? I have no idea what you're talking about."

"Autumn has been nothing but kind. She is a sweet girl."

I cringed at the word, *girl*.

"—And has done nothing to warrant your being such a bitch to her all night."

Kim tapped a bloodred nail on her wineglass, eyes narrowing at Nico. "You show back up here after years, and we're supposed to forget how you left? How you abandoned all of us?"

"I didn't abandon you. You're being dramatic, as always." He scoffed, his hand clenching around his almost empty old-fashioned.

"Not abandon. No, just leave while we're all still mourning her. You gave up your dreams and this successful life you had to, what, work some blue-collar job in your hometown? Come on, Nic, is this really what you should be doing? What would Noemi think?"

"That's not fair," he bit out.

"It's more than, and you know it."

"You don't even know Nico anymore." Instinctively, I laced my fingers with his. "You can't—"

"Let the grownups talk, little *girl*." Kim hisses.

"Don't speak to her that way." Nico leaned forward, his elbows on his knees, his jaw tight. "She had nothing to do with this."

"Oh, please." Kim rolls her eyes. "You really think you can bring a girl like that around, and I wouldn't have an opinion?"

"What right do you have to say anything, Kimberly? I haven't seen you, haven't seen any of you, in years. No calls, no texts. Nothing." His hand tightened in mine, a quick squeeze. Then his fingers slid to the back of my neck, brushing my hair from my shoulders in a claiming gesture before his friends. "Believe it or not, I stopped caring what Noemi would think about eight years ago, and I think we all know why. But as someone recently reminded me, what my *loving* fiancée should want, is for me to be happy."

Around the table, the group exchanged glances of pity. There was more to Nico's story, I knew it, but now was not the time to ask.

"Is that what you are? Happy? Because ditching all of us so soon after—" Kim shook her head, swallowing the rest of her wine. A drop clung to the corner of her lip and slid down her chin as she lifted her empty wineglass, eyes on a passing server who wasn't ours.

"I think you've had enough," Daveed scolded.

"No, I don't think so." Kim shook her head, her long nail tapping on the rim of the empty wineglass. "Nic, we all deserved better than to be ditched by you."

"And what about what I deserved?" Nico lowered his voice.

This conversation was going in circles, double meanings, and so much unsaid that it was hard to follow. The glances were heavy.

Kim seemed to ignore Nico's question, her slurred speech blanketing the table. "You show up here after years, a completely different person with some prepubescent girlfriend, and I'm not supposed to be concerned? What about all the progress you made? It's like you're backtracking into the same grungy weirdo from college."

"Before Noemi fixed me?" Nico nodded, finishing her sentence. "Because that was better? You know, I'm still the same person I've always been. And someone who cared for me would want all of me. Not just the part they can recreate in their image."

I sucked in a breath between my teeth, my own words repeated back for all his friends to hear. Heat bloomed over my cheeks, down my throat, and across my chest. I was never a pretty blusher.

"Noemi would be disgusted with you."

A hush fell over the table and around us. Everyone was darting glances, their eyes wide at the words.

"Too far, Kim," hissed Sanvi. "That was uncalled for."

A quick glance at Nico told me her words hit their mark. His fist clenched at his side as he shook his head slowly. "I don't know what I was expecting from you. You're all the same backstabbing assholes you've always been."

He stood, taking me with him. A fifty was tossed on the table, and his hand was on my back. "Let's go."

Nico's touch steadied me as I drew in a breath. Confrontation wasn't me. Protecting my own feelings and ensuring my peace never came easy, but I couldn't help opening my mouth. "You know, it's a shame you never truly knew Nicolai because he is amazing. He's a great friend and an even better person. And if you had more respect for who he is, you could have had that in your life."

It wasn't a takedown like Summer would have used, with no name-calling, no rapid insults, or snide remarks. But its vagrant assertiveness made me queasy, not because I doubted a word I said but because I had contradicted strangers. Because for the first time in recent memory, I didn't care what they thought of me, only of what they thought of him. "But that's your loss, and it's a shame because it's obvious from your attitude that you're all already miserable."

With an ardent clasp of hands, he led me out of the bar. Trying to ignore my shaky legs and the adrenaline from my comment, I walked beside Nico in the brisk fall air of the northern California night.

Point N- Santa Clara Hotel, San Jose, CA

Autumn

WITH A SOFT WHOOSH, he sank onto the crisp white bed, his elbows on his knees and his hands over his face. I pulled at a lock of hair at my nape, twirling it around my finger to stop the urge to ask questions.

I couldn't understand much from that conversation with his friends, but it wasn't my place to ask. Nico had a life before me. A fiancée, a different career, a world so much bigger than the tiny carved-out existence I created in Ridgewood. I had never lived farther than ten miles from my parents, never had a boyfriend longer than a year. My own experiences were quaint and silly in comparison. How could I possibly understand, and why would he share?

He had defended me, but why did he need to? I should have kept my mouth shut. My outburst had obviously embarrassed him in front of his more cosmopolitan friends.

When minutes passed without a word, I couldn't hold my tongue. "I'm sorry if I overstepped with your friends. Sometimes, I start talking, and I have no idea what I'm going to say, and then I keep talking and I put my foot in my mouth and—"

"Stop." His voice was rough, a muscle in his jaw ticking, his green eyes assessing my face with a furrowed brow. "Don't apologize."

"But I don't know them, and I was so rude to Kim."

"If that's you being rude, I'd take it over anything else. Besides, she deserved it. They all did." In front of his mouth, he folded his hands in a prayer pose, his pointer finger knuckle bumping on his top lip. "No one has ever—" His throat bobbed as his eyes rested on mine. "You defended me."

My hand fell from the nervous twirl around my hair, landing along my hip with a muted smack. "Well, yeah, of course."

"Of course," he repeated low. "You say of course like it's normal. As if I should be used to it."

"You should. That's what friends do for one another."

A shrewd expression crossed his face. "Is that what I am, Autumn? Your friend?"

I opened my mouth, closed it, opened it again. He was my friend, but he was more; friend was such a weak word to describe him to me. He had been my childhood crush—the older boy who was my brother's best friend, already a man while I was still a girl. I didn't know him, not really, not the way I wanted to, and certainly not as a friend.

When I didn't respond, his hands came apart, opening to beckon me. "Come here."

His gaze didn't leave mine as I made my way across the room to stand before him. The hem of my dress rested on his knees as I slid closer, snagging on his jeans.

The blending of green in his eyes: deep forest moss, sage, grass. The green of the thick leaves from the salal bush outside my childhood window, waxy and bright. Every late spring they would blossom, the light pink heart-shaped blooms that in August turned to the darkest berries. My mom told me she would dig up a start of that bush when I had my place to plant it. It was the green of a future to cultivate and a home to belong in.

"*. . . You're the happiness I'd choose for myself. All those nights I lay awake and wished for a future I knew would never be mine.*"

His head tilted to the side as he studied my face. Standing between his open thighs, a frisson passed over me. I can feel the warmth of his legs, smell the musk of his skin and the hotel room shampoo from Sol Del Mar that morning.

The air around us grew fraught. Thick and heavy on my warming skin, his hand hovered over my elbow, hip, thigh, then the back of my knee. A kindling of flames sparked at the first pass of his finger. It was an innocent place, delicate and sensitive. Years before, Devin told me that the back of the knees was an erogenous zone, and I laughed at the description. Now I understood. With Nico, anything could be. It wasn't my breasts or between my thighs, or even my throat. It was my knee, yet the sparks from the lightest of touches had my center clenching for more.

He drew his lower lip between his teeth, white flashing against the full pink cushion of his mouth. Those teeth that scraped over my breast the night before. Those lips that kissed over my body and brought me to the brink.

"I shouldn't want this. You're so good," he murmured. His finger drew a circle over the back of my thigh, heat rushing at the slight touch. "So, so good, Autumn."

Breath was stolen from my lungs, a numbness in my limbs. Almost as if I were floating in a dream, fragments of pleasure and mild pain. Of knowing this might never be and still welcoming the sting.

I only wanted this with him. I always had.

His heavy gaze never left my face as my dress bunched on his arm and his hand slid up the back of my thigh, fingers skimming my butt to my lower back. Cool air hit my exposed skin as he bared me.

"Take this off," he demanded, my dress bunched in his fist. "I need to feel you."

There was a hopeful desperation in his stare as I grabbed the hem of my dress, pulling it over my head.

His gaze traveled over my curves, every inch of me scorching as if his eyes were a touch. My collarbone, the length of my arms, the freckles over my chest dwindling to nothing on my breasts. Standing before him, in nothing but thin lace over my hips, I should've felt self-conscious. But this exposure had a different weight to it. He wasn't looking at my body. He was seeing all of me laid bare for him alone.

"Lovely, you have no idea how many times these past few months I've thought of this skin." His finger tapped a freckle on my side. "This little mark here." Bringing my wrist up between us, he traced a line over the blue veins of my inner arm. "Of the delicate skin here and how it tastes."

After the buildup we'd had, I expected his kiss—for his hands to find me soaking between my legs, my nipples hard from want of him. Instead, his fingers spanned my waist, his thumb on my hipbone. Then, slowly, he lowered his forehead to my belly, his nose below my navel and his warm breath in the softness above my underwear. "Sweet girl."

Back and forth, he rubbed his face into my stomach, nuzzling it. Tentatively, I raised my hand to his hair, my nails on his scalp as he breathed me in. The drag of his nose on my belly, the rasp of his unshaven cheek on my skin. An inferno licked deep inside from the contact.

"Only you, Autumn. Why is it you?" Words washed over my stomach, soft and warm, his lips brushing tenderness along my skin. The sentiments weren't for me; it was his own conflict raging in every brush. His own want and guilt battling. "No one had ever done that for me before. I'm thirty-eight years old. How sad is it that I didn't know what I was missing?

But you? You're so fierce, my sweet, sweet girl." His mouth pressed against the soft skin above my belly button as his arms wrapped around my middle.

"So good, so good." It was a chant on my skin, burning into me until I could feel it, too. "My sweet, girl."

"Yours." My fingers hitched in his hair, through the soft strands as he inhaled me.

Slowly, I pulled one knee up to rest on the side of his leg, then the other until I was balancing over him. Space lingered between us as I kneeled over him, not yet sinking onto his lap. As I moved closer, his nose skimmed my sternum, my collarbone, until I was at the same level as his face. With one hand on my waist, he brought me flush against him.

Darkening green eyes traced over my face, my lips, my cheeks, to meet my gaze. Words curled like smoke, and I couldn't scrape them out. How could I say what I was thinking? Every time I spoke, I gave more away, and he was never ready to receive it. Leaning forward, I rested my forehead on his, skin to skin, sweet breath to sweet breath, in and out. His fingers dug deeper into the curve of my waist.

With his free hand, he gripped my chin, pulling my face back as my eyes snapped up to meet his. He brought his mouth to mine, stopping a whisper away, his breath brushing over them but not touching.

"Can you be mine?" I whispered. Sweet and warm, the air mingled with our pants. My hand in his hair, coaxing more, needing to remove this space between. "Even if it's only for this trip, for the next few days. Let me have you."

Desperate for more, I ground myself on him, needing his lips on mine. His grip tightened on my cheek, on my lower back as my hips swiveled. The growing length of him hard on my barely clothed clit. Still, he won't close the gap, won't take my mouth the way I crave.

"You already have me." His hand ghosts over my temple to push my hair off my face. His thumb traced my lower lip as he studied me. "You have for some time. I'm no one if not yours."

"Then, touch me."

This plea is all air, not volume, but it is the last crack before he breaks.

This kiss was tender and deliberate, his thoughts in every brush of his lips on mine, a gentle murmur of his tongue. He showed no rush in his embrace, hands holding my face steady as he mapped my mouth with his own. The delicate rasp of his thumb on my cheeks, his pinky on my jaw.

He took my mouth like no one else. Knew my signs, the moans, and the curling of my hand in his hair as I pulled him closer. Mapping my skin, charting new roads deeper inside me, to where no one else could ever touch. I wanted to do the same, to learn the secrets of his arms, count the scars on his chest. To discover the virtue only I could know.

"More, please." I gasped out as his mouth left mine, trailing hot over my jaw.

With this demand, his resolution snapped, his teeth finding my throat, his fingers gripping my hips as he pulled me hard onto his cock. Rocking back on himself, Nico hissed through his teeth.

"Are you going to be sweet for me?" he murmured against my ear, his teeth scraping my lobe in a sting. Goose bumps raised on my skin, and I bit back the groan in my chest.

"Yes," I gasped out as his tongue found that spot where my jaw and throat connected. "For you, Nicolai."

"Fuck, I love the way you say my name; you have no idea what it does to me."

Something primal stirred in the way I hovered over him, bare but for my underwear, while he remained fully clothed. The coldness of his shirt buttons on my stomach, the rasp of his pants on my upper thighs as I worked my soaking center over his cock. The layers between us did nothing to mask his reaction to me.

"I have some idea." I snake my hand between us, slipping under his pants to feel the hot length against my palm. "You've earned it. Now take it."

With this, I'm being twisted in the air and then falling back onto the bed, bouncing twice as he stands between my open thighs. His clothes discarded, he prowls over me, his hand on my ankle, opening my legs wider for him.

"What you fucking do to me. I can't stop myself. You're wrecking me."

"Good." My lips crashed onto his as my hand slid down his front, over the hardness of his chest, his dusting of hair, and the tight muscles of his clenched stomach. To what I need the most. Wrapping my fingers around the base of his length, I squeezed, and his groan in my mouth shot heat pulsing at my core.

Then, my underwear is being pulled down my legs, the motion harsh and burning on my skin. No patience given as his fingers were on me, parting me. One finger slid inside, rough and needy, and I gasped at the intrusion. Tightening my grip on his cock in my hand, I ground harder against him. My hips snapped in rhythm as he added a second digit, stretching me. The heel of his hand bumping my clit with every thrust. Building into a tempo, his long fingers carved me out as my hand slid along his length.

"You like that, don't you? Ruining me, taking everything I thought I needed and smashing it to pieces?"

"Maybe I do." I panted into his mouth, my hand finding his balls and tugging on them before sliding back up his length.

"I'm tired of denying myself. This wanting you, I don't care if it's selfish. For so long, I've wanted you. You feel too fucking good. I'm going to keep taking unless you tell me to stop, unless you make me."

We curved around each other, edging closer to what has been building. With my free hand, I laced my fingers in his hair, pulling his eyes to mine. "Don't stop."

Heavy-lidded and dark, we stared at each other as his thumb rubbed a circle around my clit. I nod at him and then his hand was off me, pulling on a condom.

Gasping, my hands found his arms as his tip slid over me, static on my clit and then down to my opening and back up again, teasing me.

"You want it?"

"Please, please," I moan, urging my hips up, my wet center rubbing against him.

"My sweet girl begs so good, doesn't she?" His hand brushed hair away from my face as his cock slid over my opening again but doesn't fill me the way I need yet. "Need me to destroy you."

"Yes," I gasp out.

And then he's sinking into me, stretching me in a single languid motion. "So fucking tight, I don't want to—"

The thrusts are shallow and slow. My hands find his ass, pulling him deeper, urging him on. "I won't break." As soon as the words left my lips, his body started to move again, causing the most delicious mixture of pleasure and a hint of pain to rush throughout my body. "Please, more . . ."

Seated to the hilt, he groaned into the crook of my neck, his desperate words hot on my throat. No man had ever made me feel like this, and if I thought before he was going to ruin me, now I knew for certain. With a slight move of my hips, Nico could thrust even deeper, causing us both to let out a moan.

"You take me so well," he hissed out as I bent my knees to allow him deeper. "Such a good fucking girl you are."

"Yours."

Whatever hesitation dissolved, sea foam on the shore as he bottomed out into me, each thrust harder and faster than before. His hands are rough on my skin, abrading my waist, my hips, his fingers plucking at my nipples as he drove deeper inside me.

My release came barreling over me, tingles in my limbs and fire in my belly as he chased after me, coming as I tightened around him. It's the stars over the ocean sky exploding into the dragons and the myths, the ceaseless waves crashing. The sweat slick of our bodies as his teeth bit down on the juncture of my throat, a sting followed by the soothe of his tongue.

Our bodies connected, breath by breath, mingling in the space between. So often this would be the moment for him to pull away. Yet his hand was tangled in my hair, tilting my head back to capture my mouth again. His lips moved over mine tenderly, as if it were a first kiss. My heart ached at the sweetness, the slow dip of his tongue. He rolled over onto his side, taking me with him. He slid out of me, but I cupped his face and traced his jaw, the bristle of his unshaven skin, the softness of his hair curling over his ear.

"Tell me it's more than tonight. Tell me I can keep you," I whispered, knowing he might back away, knowing this might be too much.

Darkness flared behind his eyes at my words, but I held my hand steady on his nape, not letting him go.

"You make me wish I could," he murmured. With the pad of his thumb, he traced my lower lip, swollen and sensitive from the kisses.

With one finger, I traced a line across his chest and his stomach. I could hardly believe all this was mine to touch: the delicious pectorals, ridged abdominals, a trail of golden hair on smooth skin. The urge to kiss it all, to taste him, to feel him under my tongue overwhelmed me. His eyes followed my movements as his beautiful lips quirked as if he could read my mind.

My hand rested on his chest, over his heart, my fingers playing in the dusting of hair. "Do you remember how that couple signed their letters in the restaurant in Vegas? Tactical? Or something like that?"

"Tactil, ti amo con tutto il cuore. *I love you with all my heart*," he repeated back, his eyes not leaving mine. Understanding coursed through me before he said the words.

"Yeah, that one?" I murmured, not keeping the edge of surprise out of my voice, that he not only remembered the acronym but the words in Italian. The way they rolled off his tongue, the curl and affection in each sound. "I like that."

Brushing a strand of hair off my cheek, I pressed my forehead against his. Love was too big a word, but this I could say. I could give, and he could hear. He could pretend for a little longer this was less than it was. Even in my romantic idealism, I knew it was too early. But this sensation was the edge. The skirting of rocks as they tumbled over the cliff side. Your feet on the precipice and the only direction to take is retreat or to fall completely.

Fingers splayed over my nape. His nose brushed against mine, glancing over my cheek until he reached the side of my face. "Me too."

It was overwhelming, the softness of his lips on my ear as he held me, the fingers buried in my hair, the hard lean of his body. The gentle wash of those two words, the promise of more.

POINT O-CAPE ROSE, OR

Nico

SHE FOUND ME IN the shower, sliding behind me under the spray of water, taking my cock. The scent of her shampoo in the steam as I bent her over and guided inside her for the fourth time. Her shattering around me on the bed, our wet hair and damp skin marking the comforter.

This was messy, raw, and the first splinters of her had long since broken through me. Before we walked into that bar, I knew having her meet my friends might be a mistake. In the wake of losing Noemi, I had changed, and my relationship with them had suffered. Kim, while rude, wasn't wrong about anything she said. What I never expected was Autumn's defense of me. Her purehearted fight against their snide jokes. Her words echoed as we strolled back to the hotel. As we walked in the door, I took her mouth, and she unraveled under me.

Was she right? Did they never know me? Did I even know myself? I clung to this idea of what kind of man I was, but with that fierce gleam in her eyes, I aspired to be the man she saw. To be more. She told me I had earned her, and while I wasn't sure this was true, damn if I didn't want to continue trying.

After lunch at a small diner in an even smaller town, Autumn fell asleep somewhere between Eureka and McKinleyville. It was just as well. It would be at least a few more hours before we got to the Oregon border to stop for the night. The radio worked, but the reception would fade far from the cities, and I'd have to choose between silence or The Eagles yet again. Really, for what the Townsend spent on fixing up this car, they couldn't figure out how to remove a seventies rock album from the stereo?

With her head resting on the window, the gray sky blanching her skin as she dozed off behind those silly flower sunglasses she insisted on wearing. Not that I even knew where my nicer pair had gone. For years, I held onto them, the status symbol of expensive shades beside bespoke shirts. The right year of a bottle of Napa Cabernet. Reservations at the Michelin-star restaurant. When I moved back to Ridgewood, leaving Noemi's ghost and the wreckage of that night behind, I thought I had left that man, too. But I hadn't. The night before had proved I still hadn't forgiven, and I certainly hadn't forgotten what that city did to me. What Noemi did. And how she would never answer for any of it.

Pain twinged in my neck, and I unclenched my jaw.

It was far too overcast to wear the fake gold aviators that were currently folded in this holder on the sun visor, but I grabbed them anyway. Hiding behind the plastic lenses, I could gaze out onto the road ahead, thinking of a future I never wanted to wish for.

I was hopeful once. Desperately hopeful, in fact. Autumn made me yearn for something I once thought was foolish. Maybe she made me foolish.

If so, I couldn't bring myself to regret anything between us so far. She told me to trust her, so that's what I would do.

On the other side of the car, she shifted in her seat, a crease from the sweater she was using as a pillow marring her cheek.

"How long have I been sleeping?"

Sleep coated her voice, thick and warm. I'd heard that voice all week, and the thought of hearing it each morning flooded me. Could I have that? What was really stopping me? Yes, I was older, but we were both adults. She had been a legal adult for over seven years. Her brother? Oliver and the rest of the Townsends might not love the idea, but were they going to like anyone with their little sister? I had more than enough money to provide for myself. I wasn't getting any younger. What was it I admitted to her the day before?

You're the happiness I'd choose for myself.

"An hour, we're about to Oregon."

Why couldn't I choose that happiness? As she rubbed her eyes behind those flower glasses, I studied her face. Each freckle told a story, the constellation across her face, kisses from the sun to paint the stars in the sky.

"I don't know why I'm still so tired. I slept so well last night." She yawned, stretching her arms overhead, and her dark green shirt rode up, exposing a strip of creamy skin beneath her brown overalls. When were overalls hot?

"We had some vigorous activities." I grinned.

"Yes, we did." Winking, she pulled her hair off her neck, wrapping it around her wrist and then securing it with a hair tie.

The oversized sign on the side of the highway was an outline of the state with its sunset over the ocean, blue to orange to pink to blue behind roughhewn rocks. *Oregon Welcomes You.* We passed over the Winchuck River Bridge and deeper into the state along the two-lane highway.

The soft click of her seatbelt sounded, and I glanced over to find her on her knees, leaning across the bench to place a hand on my lap. The flat of her palm pushed down between my legs, and my cock responded. "Aut, what are you—"

"Vigorous activities."

"I'm driving."

Her fingers had already popped open the top button and were in the process of unzipping my pants. "I'm not."

"You can't—oh, God." Her fingers wrapped around my cock, tugging it out and giving it a long stroke.

"Hands at ten and two, Nicolai."

On her knees, she bent over and took me into her mouth. First, a soft drag around my tip, teasing and coy, before she licked the underside.

Stars flash in my eyes as her teeth drag gently on the sensitive area. She would be my undoing. She obviously wanted me to shatter into a million pieces. Her tongue explored swirling patterns up and down my shaft as she applied more suction. One hand moved to cup my balls, and my cock jerked in her mouth. She hummed in appreciation, earning another twitch.

I wasn't going to last long. One hand buried in her hair, she gagged as I hit the back of her throat, her mouth tightening around me.

I was done.

Cum shot down her throat, and she swallowed it all. She sat back on her haunches, wiping the corner of her mouth with a single finger, a satisfied expression.

"That was not a good idea."

"No? Seemed like you enjoyed it." She pulled her lower lip between her teeth.

"You're a wicked woman." I smirked.

"Maybe, but—look out."

The rabbit darted out onto the road a second before I could react, and I yanked the steering wheel to the side, missing the animal by inches.

Autumn was thrown forward into the foot space, her forehead clipping my foot on the brake and her knee hitting the stereo. We stopped with a loud thud, my seatbelt catching me in the neck, my softening cock still out of my pants and the tire flattening with a low hiss.

"Autumn, oh God, are you okay? Oh, my fuck—are you—"

There was a long, silent moment.

Visions of a rain-slicked night, tires screeching, headlights and a crunch of metal. I didn't need to see it to know the impact. I had replayed the scene a million times.

My voice was growing higher, catching in my throat. "Autumn, Aut—"

Then she groaned, twisting her body until she could climb back up onto the bench seat. "Ow. You have hard shins."

A small pink spot was forming on her cheek where she caught something on her way down. With rougher hands than I should have used, I pulled her to me, checking her face over for bruises and blood. She batted my hands away, frowning. "Ow, you're hurting me. I'm fine. We were going five miles an hour. It's not the first car I tumbled around in."

My hands squeezed her cheeks again, holding her still. "You fucking scared me. Keep your seatbelt on at all times from now on. No more shenanigans."

She pulled back, a petulant furrow in her brow. "Fine, no more road head for you, then."

Ignoring her joke, I climbed out of the car and walked to the passenger side, where the front tire was completely deflated to the rim. Grumbling to myself, I went to the trunk and pulled up the old faded carpet to find the space looked wrong. A single finger poke into the smooth rubber told me what I already knew.

The donut tire was flat as well. What was Oliver going on about before we left? Fucker.

Cursing, I ran my hands through my hair, head tilted at the grey cloud sky, and let out an animalistic scream.

My throat properly sore now, I hazarded a cursory glance at my phone to tell me what I already knew. Reception was spotty around here, and I wasn't sure how far we were from the next town and, hopefully, tire shop to get this fixed. Autumn appeared beside me, her brow furrowed as she peered at the tire.

"It's not supposed to look like that, is it?"

"No, definitely not."

Just then, an expensive sedan rolled by us slowly, and Autumn flung her hand up to wave it down.

"What are you—"

"Getting help."

Red brake lights flared and then the car reversed down the deserted road to stop beside us.

"Do you have any sense of self-preservation? It could be a—"

In the driver's seat was a woman with a black chin-length bob and a retro North Face jacket.

Her question was directed at Autumn. "A flat?"

I nodded, and Autumn leaned down into the window. "Yeah, and no spare."

"Cape Rose is about two miles down this road." The woman pulled her lower lip between her teeth. Her green eyes shifted from me to Autumn and back to me as if weighing our predicament.

"Teddy's gonna kill me if I get murdered," she muttered before the telltale click of a door unlocking sounded. "Get in, I'll give you two a lift to the tire shop."

While the drive wasn't long, Autumn had our rescuer—Matilda, she told us to call her—chatting about her life in minutes. She and her husband were raised in Cape Rose but both left in their early years. She and her two kids, ages eighteen and twelve, were in town for her parents' fiftieth wedding anniversary. When the tire shop she mentioned was closed for the day, she directed us towards a hotel down the street.

"Might be expensive." She glanced at Autumn's old overalls and was likely thinking about the early eighties wagon sitting on three tires. "These oceanfront places always jack up the prices.”

“That’s fine. We can swing it,” I assured her. “We were going to find a place to stop soon anyway, might as well be here.”

She nodded at me, with a dark brow raised. “Alright. If you two are bored later, stop by the brewery.” She pointed her finger along the long road of small stores to a place at the end, a few blocks down. “One of the locals is playing tonight. He’s a character. You might like it.”

“Oh, that sounds fun, doesn’t it? We should go.” Autumn set her hand on my arm and grinned up at me.

“You don’t even drink.”

“Like that matters. Live music? Something to do. We have to go.”

An erstwhile expression curled my lips up as I shook my head. “Fine. We’ll go.”

“Good,” Matilda said. “My husband, Teddy, and I might stop by later. He likes to commandeer the mic.”

“Oh, does he play?” Autumn asked.

Matilda’s tongue clicked against her teeth, and a smirk played on her face. “Yeah, something like that. You two should come by. It will be worth your time.”

After Matilda left us, I turned to Autumn. “That was a little mysterious, wasn’t it?”

Despite the town appearing small and empty while we were walking over, the brewery was full when we walked through the door. At the front of the queue, Autumn chatted with the bartender, sharing stories from her job at Freedom Bay Brewery and even trading a sticker from it. The bartender placed the sticker on a large glass-front refrigerator beside countless other brewery stickers.

Autumn handed me our drinks, and I gave the bartender my card. Autumn tried to pay, but I couldn't allow that. Turning from the bar top, we glanced around the filling room, searching for an open seat.

The sight of our rescuer appeared on the far side of the room with a man following her. Stopped by almost every patron as they walked in, when she saw us, her face brightened, and she waved. "You made it. Nic and Autumn, this is Teddy."

An oddly familiar man with golden hair stood beside Matilda, his hand on her waist possessively. "Mattie told me about her little rescue mission earlier."

Autumn leaned in close, taking the man's hand that he hadn't offered. "We'd still be walking down the highway if she hadn't saved us."

Shaking my head, I placed a hand on Autumn's hip and pulled her closer as women slid past us, and to the bar. "Hardly. It was only a few miles to town. It would have taken half an hour, max."

"But riding in a nice person's Mercedes is always preferred." Autumn rocked back on her heels, studying Matilda's husband. "You look familiar. Why do you look familiar?"

He snorted and glanced at his wife. "I get that a lot."

Autumn narrowed her eyes, assessing, then shot open wide, and she snapped her fingers and pointed at his face. "Oh my gosh, you're Theo Blake. The Theo Blake. Like Prevalent Notion, Theo Blake."

"Here we go," Matilda muttered into her drink, her eyes rolling in humor. "Can't take him anywhere."

Autumn's eyes grew wide as she studied him. "You live in Manzanita."

This surprised them. Theo drawled suspiciously. "Uh, yeah, sometimes. We have a few different houses and—"

"We're from Ridgewood. That's where we were headed before we blew a tire." The sunshine grin grew wider. "Theo Blake. Who knew? This is so cool. Could you do me a big favor?"

"Autograph?" he asked. "Picture? FaceTime with your mom?"

Autumn shook her head. "I wouldn't say no to that, I guess. But no, I have a question. Is Nathan as hot as he looks?"

With this question, Theo and Mattie choked on their drinks. Cider and beer spilled on the floor. Mattie seemed pleased as could be, and Theo looked affronted, sucking his teeth.

"I told you you're not the hot one anymore," Mattie chided him.

"Yeah, well, Nathan doesn't have kids. They age you a decade in a week. He can look fresh when he isn't woken up at two in the morning by a barfing five-year-old." He turned to us with a scowl. "No, he's the same ugly fucker he's always been."

Behind him, Mattie was motioning, wiping off her brow and fanning herself. Theo turned to her with narrowed eyes. "That's enough out of you." He shook his head at his wife. "We're going to get another drink, you two, okay?"

The idea of a millionaire celebrity asking if I wanted another round was so bizarre, I just shook my head.

"We're good, but maybe we'll take you up on that later," Autumn chimed with a grin. "We can get the next round, even."

Theo chuckled as he looped his arm around Matilda, pulling her to the bar top. "Okay, sure. Next round is on you."

Left alone, I stared down at Autumn. "Does anyone intimidate you? What is this ability to talk to anyone?"

She sipped her ginger ale, the corner of her mouth quirking up. "He's just a guy, Nicolai. A nice one too. He and his wife. Though he didn't seem to appreciate my calling Nathan Ayers hot."

"Neither did I," I mumbled into my IPA.

"But still, a normal dude."

"Dude?" Wrapping my arm around her shoulder, I brought her closer to my side as an older man approached the microphone stand. "I can't take you anywhere. Park rangers, douchebag fake cowboys, rock stars, empanada restaurateurs. One minute with you, they're all smitten."

Bringing her thumb to her mouth, she bit the tip between her teeth, her eyes flashing. "Then what has a week in the car with me given you?"

Tucking a strand behind her ear, I let my thumb trace over her lower lip, to her jaw, to tangle in her hair at her nape.

For me, growing up with so little of my own, to not knowing the unconditional acceptance of another, it hardens a person. I knew enough of psychology to know I needed to sort things out for myself. It wasn't Noemi who started my fears. She was just the final and heaviest brick in my wall.

But Autumn, sweet Autumn, it was amazing to be near her. To be given her trust so freely, even with warning, even with everything I am.

A better man would think he was lucky, but I knew I was selfish.

The idea I could have her as mine, when, for so long, I lived on so little, was overwhelming.

I had lived for thirty-eight years, and without a doubt, there would never be another woman worth loving more than Autumn Townsend. And, fuck, if that wasn't the scariest thought of all.

"I can't stand any of it."

She reared back, her brows pulling together, but I kept my hand firm on her head, holding her close. "I can't stand the thought that I'm going to screw this all up, and you'll forgive me, even though I don't deserve it."

I pressed a kiss to the corner of her mouth, and she sucked in a ragged breath, her blue eyes falling to mine.

"Is that all?" Her voice a whisper as I press another kiss to the other side of her mouth.

"No," I huffed. "I can't stand how I had a plan of how the rest of my life was going to go, and in a single week, you've erased every line. The way your very existence is overtaking me, even when I was so determined not to let it. I'm glad you're good at mending because this will end in nothing but shambles."

With this, I took her mouth, a low sweep of lips together, soft and fleeting but warm and full of the promise of more later.

To love is to give away. The only love I'd ever known was fleeting. The trust had been in vain. When had the cost been worth it?

She didn't need to say the word. Just as she was natural in her own skin, she loved the same way. To fall would be effortless, to trust. To simply exist beside her and expect nothing in return.

Resisting was a hard battle, but what could I do?

The aching emptiness had been growing for so many years. The thought of feeling that again, of having the world I had so carefully built around myself be shattered, left me motionless. It was terrifying. And that terror sank its teeth into my marrow.

The love in her eyes, the yearning I wouldn't allow her to give voice to. In the depths of her tenderness, I saw it. In the arch of her brow. The ocean blue of her eyes when I approached. The upturn of her lips as my fingers brushed her cheek, and the press of her body each night fitting against mine. It all spoke not with sound but with the virtue of hope.

A hope I never asked for. A hope I never allowed myself.

Her gaze was steady on mine, a deepness of emotion shimmering on the surface. Trust, love, support. All the things she was offering. None of the things I should take.

The playback screeched on an amp, and we jumped apart, our gazes breaking.

Catching sight of a loft in the back, I grabbed her hand, pulling her through the crowd and up the stairs to the dark area. Up here, you could see over the whole brewery and the musician as he settled on a stool. A scratchy bass voice boomed into the room. "Hello everyone here, I'm Trawler McGee, and this here is Trisha."

The man held up his guitar. He looked like a pirate—if pirates lived to seventy and wore a brown leather vest over a Grundens long-sleeved T-shirt and black jeans. A gray leather pageboy cap was placed jauntily over his long white hair. Leaning forward. A gold charm in his gray scraggly beard caught the light as he placed his beer in a cupholder beside the music stand.

Small tables and chairs were scattered around. Autumn selected one next to the wire-partitioned balcony. We were the only ones up in the loft above.

With a warbling voice, the singer launched into sea shanties. Songs of mermaids and those left behind, of the waves' pull and the endless hunger for adventure and solace.

> *... The winds blew foul, and*
> *the seas ran high.*
> *Leave her, Johnny, leave*
> *her.*
> *We shipped up green and*
> *none went by,*
> *And it's time for us to leave*
> *her,*
> *Leave her, Johnny, leave*
> *her,*
> *Oh, leave her, Johnny, leave*
> *her ...*

In the loft's darkness, I could barely make out her expression, but whether it was the old shanty song or being in this space alone with her, I couldn't stop myself. Reaching forward, I grabbed her hand and pulled her to me, settling her on my lap. Her bare legs draped over me, her dress hiked up as she sat. Goose bumps started on her exposed skin.

"Are you cold?"

October on the Oregon Coast could get chilly in the evening, even without the wind picking up from the ocean.

"Nah, I always run a few degrees too hot, anyway."

With my free hand, I ran a finger over her bare knee, between her legs, to her mid-thigh. "I'm not complaining, but if you get cold, let me know, and I'll give you my jacket."

As my finger traced the delicate skin of her inner thigh, she gasped, her head falling to my shoulder, her mouth on my ear. "I won't be cold if you keep touching me like that." She moaned in my ear.

Fuck, what this woman did to me.

I hadn't intended to fool around. I only wanted her closer, but now that she was on my lap, so close to my aching cock, my thoughts were soon changing. She wiggled against me, and I had to place a hand on her hip to steady her.

"You're so pretty," I murmured into the shell of her ear. "Do you have any idea?"

"Thank you," she breathed out.

I was thankful she didn't refute it, didn't give the false modesty women were taught to have. I never wanted her to think she was anything but the most glorious, to bask in the warmth of her confidence. She was the sun, so was it any wonder I was the one being burned?

Downstairs, Trawler McGee was switching to a more upbeat song, and the crowd was clapping along poorly, missing the beats. Still, I kept going up her thighs until I reached her center to find her damp and needy.

"Nico," she gasped out as my finger traced over her core. "We can't."

"Shhh," I murmured against the side of her neck. "You were so good to me in the car before."

Hooking my finger around the wet cloth, I pulled it to the side. With the cool air touching us, she hissed as I sank a finger inside her. With her arm still wrapped around my neck, I added another, my thumb tracing over her clit.

At any moment, someone could come up here and catch us. Maybe that was part of the appeal. She let out a strangled cry as I curled my finger inside her, working her into a delirium.

"I'm only returning the favor," I murmured against her throat as I curled and thrust inside her. Her cunt fluttered around me, and I knew how to touch her the way she liked. "Will you be good for me again, sweet girl?"

She nodded as she ground herself harder on my hand, her words a staccato. "More, Nicolai. I need you."

"Quiet or someone will know how desperate you are for me." I sucked at her skin, the salt of her exploding on my tongue.

She slid her hand between us, palming my hard cock, rubbing the side of her thigh against it.

"You make a sound, and I'll have to stop, you understand? You have to be silent." I warned her as I adjusted her dress over my lap to shield us.

It took a moment of fumbling, but soon, my cock was out, and then it was sliding inside her in a single tight motion. I couldn't stop the grunt that eluded me as she sank down on me, taking me to the hilt.

"Who's the quiet one now?" she teased as she moved her hips, slow circles, her cunt wrapped around me.

"Fuck, you feel so good," I whispered in her ear. "You're so fucking hot taking me like this. Desperate for my cock, aren't you?"

She nodded as she moved. Thrusting into her again, bottoming out as her walls stretched around my cock. I couldn't find words to explain the feeling as I allowed her body to fully adjust to me. Feeling a gentle tug at my hair, my eyes met Autumn's, taking in the unfamiliar look in them. She was more gorgeous than anything I had ever seen in my entire life. Real and warm and mine.

Just below us, a rock star and his wife mingled with a pirate-turned-singer and craft beer drinkers. All while Autumn rode my cock, hips grinding faster, her cunt tightening with each slow thrust.

She fluttered around me, and she was almost there. Taking one hand off her hip, I covered her mouth, muffling her cry as she fell apart on top of me, clenching and hot. I was on the edge, about to fall behind her, when I realized with a jolt that I hadn't put a condom on. In this lust haze I was under, I had forgotten it.

Before I make a drastic mistake, I pull out of her, coming in the space between her thighs. The mixture of both our fluids coated our skin, sticky and hot between us. My breathing haggard as I slump against her, filling my lungs with her herbal flower scent of her shampoo.

I almost came inside her without protection. This woman was always making me lose my head. It was something I never did. But with Autumn, it was an afterthought. No, not even. It was something I almost wanted.

As her body slumped into me, I wrapped my arms around her waist. This didn't feel like sex. Maybe it never had. She felt more like home than anything I had ever felt in my entire life. And shouldn't that be terrifying?

Something about the idea of her cum dripping down her legs gave me a primal satisfaction I wasn't used to.

The idea of filling her up with nothing between us should have scared me. Instead, I craved it. Wanted the risk. For a brief flash, maybe even wanted the consequence. Because then I would get to keep her, wouldn't I? When she figured out what a mess I was, she would still need to stay with me.

I was a selfish, terrible bastard.

"Sorry about the mess. I didn't use a condom and—"

She blinked a few times, desire clearing from her eyes at my comment. "Oh."

"I—" How could I explain my lapse in judgment, the way a deep part of me was rising, to claim and mark her? Never to let her go. She was so pure, and I knew what happened to those I cared for in the end. How could I condemn Autumn to the same? And why couldn't I pull my arms away from her waist?

"Good thing you pulled out then, right?" She pulled her lower lip between her teeth, worrying the pink skin there. "I mean, that would bad, wouldn't it?"

"Yeah, bad," I repeated, a hollow sensation forming in my chest.

Why did I want to disagree? This was foolish. She was twenty-six. Almost done with college, and I wanted her pregnant?

No, not wanting her. But not *not* wanting it.

She shifted slowly, allowing me a moment to tuck myself back into my pants. She turned to face me, a furrow on her brow as she glanced at me.

My selfishness must have been written all over my face. It was too much risk for her; we were in two different stages of life, and I had almost condemned her by thinking with my dick. Why she wasn't running from me, I would never understand.

"Hey, it's okay. We'll be okay," I murmured against her cheek as I pulled her closer. "I'll take care of you, sweet girl. No matter what, you know that, right?"

Doubt trickled in, warm and familiar. Hadn't I said that to Noemi? Made the same promises, gave the same vows. And where did it lead me?

The thin white stick on the counter, two lines. Shouting in the doorway, a fist swinging at air, a car door slamming, and a lone pair of shoes by the front door. The tire tracks burned black into the pale concrete. Echoing voices.

You're such a fucking disappointment.

No, Autumn wasn't Noemi. I wasn't that man anymore.

I wasn't even sure what I was promising Autumn. But there was no use in denying myself any longer. I was drowning in her either way. At least I could choose to dive below. The idea of a future with Autumn sprawled out before me, a home, a family, happiness. Time and time again, I told myself I didn't deserve it, but didn't Autumn?

And if I was who she wanted, who was I to refuse?

Resting my forehead on hers, I laced my fingers through her hair, tangles, and waves and softness. Was there a word to describe this? Love seemed too terse a phrase. How else could I describe the dizzying high of the unknown, the fear of losing what I never wanted to risk again, and the placid wash of holding her against my chest, knowing it was exactly right?

Her lips brushed against mine, a breath of heat and want in the air between us. The kisses we've shared before were hard, punishing in their want, but this was sweet. It was everything a girl like Autumn deserved. Reverent in the press of our tongues, the slow tug of my bottom lip between her teeth, the curve of her cupid's bow, the softness of her jaw in my hand.

She nodded at me, understanding lacing her expression. "We'll take care of each other."

Sixteen

POINT P-YOUNGS RIVER FALLS

NICO ALMOST CAME INSIDE me the night before. As the youngest of four kids, I knew accidents happened all the time. Being so much younger than my brothers, I was fairly sure I was one.

Despite my impulsivity, I had never had sex without a condom with a man. To do so indicated a level of trust I never had with any of my previous—and admittedly few and far between—boyfriends.

But with Nico, everything was different. The press of his hand on my cheek as we recalled the letter from the restaurant in Vegas. The lingering of his kiss on my lips. How his gaze would settle on me as I spoke. He still held so much back, yet I knew he gave me more than he gave most others. The surprise in his eyes when I defended him, the weight of his touch on my hip the night before.

His fingers on my arm wake me, little lines and circles, letters I can't quite make out as I rouse from my slumber. I had never been a big sleeper, but lying beside him every night had me sleeping harder and longer than before. Even in the car, I found myself dozing off, safe with him.

Opening my eyes, I took him in, the long lines of his arm as it rested over me, the muscles of his shoulders, his stubble burnished in the morning light, and always those green eyes on me, soft and warm as I stretched beside him.

"This is the fifth morning I've woken beside you, and still, it feels like a dream." Nico's fingers skimmed across my cheek tenderly until he reached my chin, gently tipping my gaze up to meet his. "Maybe I never want to wake up."

"You are awake." With sleep still coating my vision, the corners of my mouth turned up as I wind my finger in his hair, my nails running over his scalp.

"Prove it." Nico bent lower, his breath over me warm and sweet.

The way he whispered it, his eyes dark as he stared down at me, softened the demand. It wasn't fair, the way his gaze alone could make me combust. I'd do anything to have him continue to want me this way.

Morning sex has always been my favorite. Languidly, I open my legs to allow him inside. With the cloudy gray sky filtering loosely through the filmy white curtains, it's him and me taking our time with each other.

His mouth kissed down my body, over my breasts, my stomach, the side of my knee. His eyes on mine the whole time as his lips continue their path over my skin.

"How did I get so lucky with you?"

"I'm lucky," I mused as his fingers dug into my calves with biting pressure, pulling them over his shoulders.

His hum was a vibration on my inner thigh. "That remains to be seen."

My fingers found his hair, pulling at the strands as he kissed the crease between my hip and my pelvis. "But you? You're gracious, smart, funny."

My eyes fell closed as his breath landed on my core, and a zing of pleasure arced inside me at the first run of his tongue over me.

"You're selfless and sweet. You make me feel seen." He pressed a kiss to my clit and then gave it a long, languid lick.

I moaned, my toes curling as I hooked my legs around Nico's broad back, pulling him closer as he settled between my thighs. His mouth is tender, sucking and laving at my delicate places as he held me. My hand fell to his head to grip his hair as his tongue sank inside of me.

"And fuck, are you ever the most beautiful thing, laid out like this."

As he devoured me, his tongue and lips, fingers and force had cut off all words, edging me close. Then he pulled up, his mouth still shiny from my arousal as he kissed me, the taste of us on his tongue. With his hand between our bodies, he thrust inside me in a single motion, deep and hard.

My eyes snapped open. The lingering of his finger on my jaw as he ghosted his lips along my throat. His control as he moved inside me, taking his time to bring me to the brink. The shuddering of our bodies as we came together, sweat mingling on our brows as he held himself against me. Those words sizzled over my skin.

My sweet girl, taking me so well. So good, so good.

I wanted to be. Countless times and miles between when we left, he warned me off. Told me I was making a mistake with him, but I couldn't care. Wouldn't. Not when it was like this between us.

With every stop on this trip, something had shifted. Not only between us but inside me as well. I can challenge others, and they will still care for me and him. I didn't need to be forgiving or complacent. I asked for what I wanted, and at every turn, he's given it. As if I were worthy, as if I had the right to it.

He looked at me as if I were precious and strong. A version of myself I dreamed of.

With sweat still clinging to our skin, he brushed my hair off my shoulder, his fingers lingering on my collarbone tattoo. "I should have been more careful with you last night. If I had better control, I never would have put you in that position. You should be angry with me."

Turning my head to him, I studied his face. Furrowed brow, his gaze downcast, already demonizing himself for something that never happened. "Why are you making me into the victim here? I knew what I was doing. I was sober, completely in control of my own actions. I could have told you to get a condom. I could have stopped you at any point. Instead, I asked you for more. Since that first night on your dock, I've had control over this. Don't act like I don't know what we're doing."

"And what are we doing?" he brushes my hair off my throat, fanning it on the pillow beside me.

"Earning each other." I lean forward, giving him my mouth once more and hoping it is enough.

At the continental breakfast in the lobby, he spread peanut butter on two pieces of toast, taking the heel for himself. "You shouldn't be the only one who feels bad for a piece of bread. I'm only doing my service to bakery kind."

Thousands of miles, popped tires, and hot springs skinny-dipping had passed since that offhand comment, and there he sat, with the heel in his hand, offering me the best piece from the loaf.

With all these little moments on this trip, when did I fall? Or had I always been in the air, waiting for him to join me?

After a short walk to the tire shop, a ride in the owner's old truck for the spare, and forty minutes of muted reality television in the waiting room, we headed to our next stop. Somewhere between Cape Rose and Astoria, I fell asleep again, my head resting on the cool window, The Eagles Greatest Hits playing softly on the old speakers. I woke bleary-eyed and sore to Desperado, switching to Tequila Sunrise.

"Where are we?"

He flicked the turn signal, the *tick, tick, tick*, echoing in the car. "Almost to Astoria. I know side trips are kind of your deal, but I thought you might like to see a waterfall?"

I pulled up in my seat, nodding. "Yeah. Absolutely."

The path down to the falls was a rough trail, and the sound of rushing water found us before we made our way around the bend to a clear pool. A large white log was floating in the middle, worn down from years of play. I could picture the spot in the summer, the swimming hole full of kids, families with coolers and sandwiches. The break of sun through the trees. Birdsong and simplicity.

A small rocky beach curved, and then the waterfall was there, moss and dark stone behind the white churning of the falling river. The pool it emptied into wasn't large, shallow enough until the very edge that if the air was warmer I could wade out until I stood under the spray and still have my head above water. To the side, a maple tree was hanging onto the last of its orange-red leaves, the bare branches of brown-gray blending with the rocks.

We settled on the rocky beach, the ground damp from that morning's rainfall. Tucking my knees up to my chin, I wrapped my arms around my legs and leaned my head on Nico's shoulder. The steady warmth of his body along mine, the smell of the forest and water, the dull rushing falls surrounding me.

This night could be the last we had together. Across the Columbia River was our state and, with it, home. What would we be once we returned? What would he want from me? I was ready to give him all of me. In a way, I had done that months before. If he hurt me, then so be it. It was my choice to make. My fall, my destruction. He had been nothing but clear from the beginning, and I wouldn't be the person I am if I could hold back these feelings.

"We'll be home tomorrow," I murmured.

My words were almost drowned out by the water. His arm around my shoulders tensed, and I entwined my fingers with his.

"Back to reality."

"When we get back, will you take me to dinner?" My legs stretched out before me, my heels digging into the tan clay and pebble beach.

"Isn't the guy supposed to ask the girl?" He nudged me with his shoulder, and I grinned. "Besides, one would say we're past the first date stage."

"When have we done things the right way? We haven't talked about what we'll do when we get back to town and—" I keep my voice calm, cool, not at all freaking out the way I want to. "I'm fine with whatever."

I wasn't, not at all. But like a skittish dog, Nico had to be eased into things, lest he bolt.

"This trip, this"—he tilted his head as he studied me—"you. Is that really what you want? Because we both know you can do a lot better than this mess I am."

"Let me decide that, okay?" Above our heads, the gray clouds parted for a sliver of sun to peek out, bright and clear over the green-blue water. "If I didn't know any better, I'd think you mistake softness for weakness. Not seeing the power of being unguarded with others. In using your strength to surrender willingly."

"Surrender." With one hand, he picked up a small stick on the ground, scratching a line in the packed sand with an audible scrape. His words came slow and contemplative. "I've never seen it that way, only that to give was to be hurt."

"We are all broken by something, but to keep vulnerability in the face of a harsh world? That's courage."

Reaching his hand back, he launched the stick at the falls where it disappeared into the foaming water, the corners of his mouth turning up despite his best efforts. "Is this supposed to prove to me I'm not bad for you because it's not working?"

"Maybe? I don't know. All I mean is you don't need to hold back because of some misplaced sense of chivalry or whatever. I'm tougher than I look." Despite my best efforts, my words came out strained. "As long as you tell me I'm not the only one who feels this. That I'm not alone."

"No, you're not alone but—"

Around his finger, he wrapped a lock of my hair, rubbing it with his thumb. A sensation expanded in my chest, creaking against my ribs at the pressure. Each breath was torture as I waited on Nico.

"Noemi's bouquet was going to be lily of the valley. It was her favorite flower." He pulled away, bringing my chin up with a single finger. "She loved it because it was beautiful. Because it was expensive in large quantities. But you know what else it is in large quantities? Poisonous. She loved having something so beautiful and so deadly at the same time. You met our friends the other day. She was exactly like Kim. For so long, I thought because she let me into her world, that meant I was special, that if someone that discerning cared about me, I must be worth more than I thought. I was this dumb kid from nowhere, but she liked me? Loved me, even? So, I adapted, changed myself to fit into her world. But in the end, it didn't matter what brands I wore or the nice restaurants I took her to or the job I worked myself half to a nervous breakdown over. It was never going to be enough for her. I was never enough."

"Nico, I—" Weight bore down on me, crushing the words I wanted to get out.

"She was eleven weeks pregnant."

I sucked in a breath, knowing he was giving me information he didn't want to share. So many times, I ruined the situation by talking, filling the silence with chatter. But I couldn't, not this time.

"When I found out, I was so happy, I thought, finally, here was my chance to prove myself. To show her I was worthy. I spent the last five weeks

I had with her elated with the idea of being a father and every day since that night, atoning with the knowledge it was never to be."

This wasn't my pain, wasn't my life, but the tears came anyway, hot and stinging as they escaped down my cheeks. A bird trilled from within the trees beyond the falls. The wind whispered through the leaves and the water rushed to the bottom, white foam, and force. His fingers laced together before him, a hard wall he was building with each admission. Moving from my spot beside him, I took his hands and pulling pulled them apart to settle on my hips. In the gray afternoon light, his gaze was heavy with hesitation as I dropped onto his lap, hands on his shoulders, straddling his waist.

My fingers laced in his hair, holding his face up to mine. Delicately, he brought his hands from my waist up to my chin. With his thumbs, he brushed the wetness off my cheeks, cupping my jaw.

"I'm trying not to think the same with you. I hear you when you say I don't need to change, but all I've ever known is this, Autumn. All I've known is"—he swallowed, the last word raw—"disappointment."

I cupped his cheek, resting my forehead against his as his fingers dug into my jaw.

"This . . ." He motioned between us. "I'm not supposed to feel this way. I spent so long telling myself that I deserved less because of who I am, because of what I had done. And then you come around, and you're so good and sweet and right. And I want it, Autumn, I do."

After a long-weighted silence, he scrubbed a hand over his face, his beard making a faint noise against his palm. "But I can't help but think of last night. What would have happened? Of Noemi and how I failed her. She created a life and then look at what my love did," he said hoarsely. "My love killed."

"You didn't kill her, Nicolai. You said it was an accident."

"It's not that simple," he whispered. "I've never been blameless. I may not have been beside her in that car that night, but I didn't stop her.

We fought, and she left, and now...I can never take back that night." He swallowed, a hollow expression sinking over him. "And the worst part is, I thought I loved her. I thought what we had was real, but it wasn't. You, sweet, wonderful, you. You're real and beautiful and kind, and I know you could be mine. To have that. You. How could I allow myself this? How can I be so selfish? And now I get this second chance at something, and I hate how much I want it. How much I want you."

I couldn't breathe. Couldn't respond. I wanted to soothe him, to say sorry, to take it all away, but before I could say anything, his lips crashed onto mine. His hands roamed over my body, needing me in a way he hadn't before.

Needing me the way I needed him.

"And I want you, you, you."

Each word was heat on my skin as he pulled my shirt over my head. Steam and promises as my hands skated along his bare chest.

"Someone might see us," I murmured, my voice catching as his teeth scraped down my throat.

"Then, let them see."

It didn't matter that we were at a public park. That anyone could come rambling down that dirt path and find us here. In a frenzy, I shucked off my pants, and he dropped his own, my bra pulled up to my collarbone, exposing my breasts to the chilly Pacific Northwest air. Small rocks dug into my knees, but I didn't care. I'll be bruised and abraded, but this is worth the marks. It's fumbling with a condom and shuffling on the rocks and then he's thrusting inside me. As the falls pounded into the water below, water droplets found us, cooling our skin as we came together. With his fingers between us, wringing out an orgasm from me as I take him deeper.

My orgasm came barreling through me as quickly as we shed our clothes, messy and wet and as sharp as the rock under my knees. Slick from the fall air and our sweat, we stayed together, heads bowed over each other, breath to breath, as I trailed a hand down his back to his spine.

His lips moved along my bare skin, the brushing of heat and air. Words I couldn't decipher, tracing over me, each whisper sounded almost like *I love you.*

POINT Q- ASTORIA, OR

Autumn

WE FOUND A NONDESCRIPT hotel on the water, an old cannery turned restaurant on the pier outside our window. We took the trolley into the heart of the city. With one hand, Nico holds tight to my hip as we move along the rail, the clacking of the track beneath us as the Columbia River flows into the Pacific Ocean. Signs pointed to the Goonie's house up the hill and a school featured in some Arnold Schwarzenegger movie Nico is appalled I haven't seen. He took me to a bar at the edge of town where the bartender was mean to everyone. Patrons played pull tabs at the counter, discarded losers dropped into yellow plastic baskets beside their Rainier tall cans. From there, we went to another bar, where heavy EDM played for an empty dance floor. A one-eyed, purple-haired server made me the best Shirley Temple I'd ever had, winking as they added two extra cherries.

We missed the trolley back to the hotel and had to make the mile-long trek in the chill of the drizzle. The spray of the Columbia River and the morning's rainfall mixed with the dead leaves on the walkway, a red and orange sludge that got caught on our shoes. We found a seafood place nestled between an antique mall and a children's clothing boutique. Nico watched aghast as I ate a dozen raw oysters, slathering them in hot cocktail sauce and slurping them down. When we tumbled into our hotel room, night had fallen hours before. Our clothes soaked from the rain and slightly grubby from the walk along the river.

He took his time peeling off each layer, our coats, our socks, our pants falling in a damp heap on the bathroom floor as we climbed into the shower together.

Under the spray of the hot water, our lips and teeth clashed together as he stiffened in my palm. His mouth traveled from mine down my throat to nip and suck bruises into my skin. Steam filled the small room, thick and clean-smelling. With one hand on his chest, I pushed him against the cool wall before dropping to my knees. The tub was cold as I sat on my haunches, his hard length at my eyeline.

The water clung to his hair, turning it almost black. Droplets hung on his long lashes as he studied me beneath him. With my tongue out, I took him into my mouth. As I sucked him down, I reached up my body, rolling one of my nipples between my fingers and thumb.

"Oh, fuck," he moaned, his thumb on my jaw as my cheeks hollowed around him, his eyes dark and glassy. "Let me fuck your tits."

Pulling him out of my mouth with a pop, I sat up higher and gripped his base. Slowly, I placed him between my breasts, surrounding him. "Like this?"

"Tighter. Harder." He ordered, and I squeezed myself around him, my thumb flicking over his tip. "Yes, just like that."

"Use them. I want to feel it." His grasp on my hair tightened as he cursed. With my hand clasping my breast around him, I moved up and down, the water and friction sliding our skin together.

His hips flexed with me, thrusting into the plane of cleavage I created. When he would come up, I dipped my chin lower, dragging my tongue over his tip. Between my mouth on him and the slip of my breasts, he was groaning, pumping harder against me.

"Y-Yeah, oh fuck, that feels so good," Nico keened, one palm flat on the shower wall, the other clenching my wet hair between his fingers.

"Where would you like to come? In my mouth, on my face, or—?" I gazed up at him, flicking my tongue over his tip.

"Tits—tits," Nico choked out before clenching his jaw, the tendons in his neck flexing with each slide of my breasts against him.

I stared up at him, the power I held on my knees beneath him, him completely in my thrall. "Come for me, Nicolai. I want it, please. Make me filthy."

The first jet of his come hit me on my chin, the second on my collarbone, coating me with him.

His breathing was ragged as he stared down at me, his come sliding over my skin in the shower's spray. Swiping a finger through his spend, I drew the digit into my mouth, cleaning it off and humming loudly. His gaze darkened, and his hand on my upper arm pulled me up to stand.

"That was the hottest fucking thing I've ever seen." With this, he crashed his mouth against mine, the taste of mint gum and his come on my tongue. His fingers parted me fast and viciously as he drove into me. My orgasm came on quick, his teeth scraping over the skin of my throat as he worked my clit.

Despite coming only minutes before, he hardened against my stomach, ready for round two.

"Please don't tease me," I beg.

"You don't want to come on my fingers?"

The question was a vibration on my wet skin.

"No, you. I need you."

"My cock? You want me to fill you up?" His voice came out almost depraved, dark and needy as if he could barely recognize it himself. My tongue soothed my swollen lips as I nodded.

A moment passed of fumbling inside his pants pockets outside the shower curtain. He spun me, hand on my back, pushing me forward to brace my palms against the cold tile wall. Sheathing inside me in a single move, I stretch around him, a low groan eluding me. I was halfway to climax before he even touched me, but now, with his fingers over my clit as he thrust faster, my thighs shook violently.

"That's it, taking my cock so good—going to come inside you," he hissed as his hips snapped against me. Over and over, taking him deep, stars behind my eyelids until I shattered apart in his arms, his admissions blurred into my skin.

"Sweet girl, take me so well. My perfect sweet girl. That's it, be my girl and come for me."

As I fell over the edge, I stifled declarations he wouldn't accept. His arm snaked around my middle, pulling my back flush with his front, his cock falling from inside me to rest between my legs. Our drenched bodies slid together as he placed his cheek on the top of my head.

With one hand braced on the wall, I straightened up, his hand sliding over my skin to hold me tight as I turned in his arms.

Behind my ribs, I felt the splintering of doubts digging deeper and more insidiously inside me. We were less than two hundred miles from home, a bridge, and highway and another full run of the Eagles, and he'd be dropping me off at my parents' house. Nothing promised, nothing agreed upon.

What do I have to offer him? The way he talked of me as if I were some good and precious thing, it wasn't real. Time and time again, he talked of letting me down, of not earning the right to me, but was that because he didn't understand me fully? Who was I to think that a man like that would want more with someone like me?

On a podcast, a relationship counselor talked about how often marriages would fail because the thing that attracted them to their spouse ended up being the personality trait they hated. My so-called sweetness turned to naivety, to foolishness. My spontaneity turned to recklessness. While I was shiny and new to him now, when had anyone ever stuck around long enough to see what more we could be?

"What are we doing?" I asked.

"Showering, sex, showering after sex?"

Tilting my head to the side, I glared at Nico. "You know what I mean. What are we doing when we get back to Ridgewood? Do you want to take me out? Is this some road trip fling or—"

"What do you want, Autumn?" His palm rested on my cheeks, his bright green eyes on me. Water clung to his lashes, falling over his cheekbones, down his throat.

If only all moments could be exactly like this. On the road, in this liminal space where I could be his sweet girl, and he could be mine.

"I—" Why was this so hard to ask for? To just ask? To receive? When did it ever work out that way? "Well, if you want to, if you want me—" I swallowed down the lump forming.

"I want to trust this. To think this could be real for me." His fingers were at my chin, pulling my face up to meet his. "There is no world I wouldn't want you, but I'm going to mess this up, I know I am. So, the only question is whether you want to be around to see it."

"I do. I want it." My answer was breathless, too obvious, and I should've been more reserved. Shouldn't act like it isn't everything I want. But I've never been that girl.

The corners of his lips turned up, his eyes crinkling as water ran down his temple. "Then, I'll give it to you. Whatever you want until you don't need me anymore."

There was no world in which I could picture not wanting him.

"I'm not going anywhere, Nicolai. I'm not leaving you. You know that, right?"

His head fell onto my shoulder, his breath hot on my skin. "Say it again."

"I'm not leaving."

We fell into bed, naked and still damp, his arm wrapped around my waist, pulling me into him. With the heavy weight of his foot on my calf and the burn of his hand cupping my bare breast, I breathed in the soap and musk of him and closed my eyes.

The soft brush of my wet hair off my shoulder, the press of his lips on the juncture of my throat had me sighing. As I was almost asleep, Nico's voice rang out through the dark room, low and sad. "It's funny in some ways. You remind me of her."

Some part of me knew this would happen. Surely it had occurred at the dinner in San Jose. They would compare. I would compare. He would. Despite never seeing a picture of Noemi, I could envision her: sleek hair, manicured nails, pressed shirts, and smooth skirts.

Cracking one eye open, I studied the shadows, dark edges, and long lines. "Confident? Put together? I'm a mess inside a chaos gremlin inside a crystal soaked in moonbeams. Or at least that's what everyone thinks."

"I don't. I see you. You're a little impetuous, but it's from passion, not a need for chaos."

In the corner, the heater clicked on, with a whoosh of warm air hissing.

"I wouldn't want to be some substitute for her." Somehow, my voice sounded assertive and not peeling apart at the seams.

"You never could be. I wouldn't want you to ever feel that way. I only meant the way you draw people in. Magnetic and charming. I think—" With the audible click of him swallowing, the bed shifted beside me as he rolled onto his back, bringing my head to his chest. "It's not that you two are similar. It's the way I know I'll never measure up."

"I would never want you to feel that way, Nicolai." Reaching between us, I rested my fingers on his cheek, the scrape of his stubble coarse on my palm.

"I know. That's why you're more. I spent years with her and even more getting over losing her, but in a few months, this week, being with you. It's like a sunrise after a long night."

His finger trailed up my arm, over my shoulder and along the column of my throat. I couldn't see his expression but felt the hesitancy under his skin.

"Sweet girl, you're my sunrise. The sunrise in Sedona. Since that morning when we woke up in the back of your car, you had your arm wrapped around me, your hand on my waist, and I didn't move you. Couldn't. Then the sun began to rise over the rocks, and it was you. The dark sky turning to light, the red rocks, the shades of your hair, the blue sky stretching on for miles full of hope and possibility, the same shade as your eyes. The pink of the dawn on your cheeks. You're my Sedona."

That moment on the red rocks, looking over at him and the inexorable sensation of a growing swell behind my ribs. The tick, tick, tick, of his heartbeat under my fingertips. The mix of our breaths. The way I knew, it was right, it was real. If only he trusted it, too.

"That's funny because I had the opposite thought of you. You remind me of the sunset, the last vestige of color before everything goes dark. The promise of more if only I'm patient." Leaning forward, I rested my head on his chest, my words heated over his bare skin. "Nico, I lo—"

He sat up, his muscles tensing beneath me. "Stop, don't say that."

Coming up to rest on my elbows, I studied his shadowed figure. "Why? Because if I do, you think you have to say it back? I'm not telling you because I need you to say it back. I'm telling you because I need to."

"I would say it back." An expanding in my chest at the words, bright and wide as a night sky, bursting with mythological tales. "But it will change everything—"

"Everything is already changed. We've changed."

The midnight hour approached, and light from a boat parked in the middle of the river. Outside our window, there was a loud laugh, a dog barking on the riverside boardwalk. Fourteen miles away was the mouth, flowing unbidden into the Pacific. He rested his face in his hands, his elbow on his knee. When he started speaking, it was deliberate and slow.

"I know I could love you. And that is terrifying. Because you give away love like it means nothing at all."

I pulled back, grabbing his chin and forcing his eyes to meet mine. His words did not offend me. It was the statement of a man who had never really been loved, of a broken man who was never taught how to put himself together. "It's everything to me. To love is everything, but there is no limit on it. My love for you won't be less if I share it with others. But the way I love you is different. Sacred. They may get my smile or a hint of kindness, but they don't have my heart. That's yours. There's nothing wrong with being loved, Nicolai."

In the dark, I could feel him watching me, as if I would take it back. As if I could ever refuse him. Then his mouth found mine, stifling anything more, the declarations falling away as his kiss devoured me.

An hour later, as I drifted off, I recalled a sign on the river walk. The Columbia Bar, the "Graveyard of the Pacific," where weather and coastal features caused thousands of shipwrecks. Lives lost because of shoals and shifting sandbars. From fog and storms, the ever-changing tide as it mixes with the fresh water. Of man against the power of the sea.

Was this my fate? Would I be a fool to believe in what we could have? On the other side of the Astoria-Megler Bridge was our home. A future I had never allowed myself to admit could be mine.

Eighteen

Point R-Ridgewood, WA

Nico

Victor grasped my hand, pulling me in for a half-hug, half-shake. His beefy fingers covered mine and crushed in his grip. "Nic, so good of you to watch out for our Little Autumn here."

Beside me, Autumn's lips turned down at the corners, and her eyes darted away.

"Not at all. It was nice to have the company. We took turns driving."

Victor chuckled. "Now, why the hell'd you do that? She could've driven you all the way to Kansas with her sense of direction."

"Dad," Autumn mumbled, her cheeks turning pink.

He ignored his daughter beside me. "So, no issues?"

"We got a flat tire in southern Oregon but—"

"Ah, let me guess, this one hit a curb. Always doing that, aren't you, guppy?"

I wasn't about to tell this man the circumstances of the flat tire and how my cock was in his only daughter's mouth thirty seconds before. But I couldn't let him assume Autumn was to blame for the biggest mishap on the trip. "I was actually the one driving. And the donut was flat in the back."

"No kidding. Well, better you than her, right? Knowing Autumn, you would've run into the ocean. Let me pay you for the tire."

"That's really fine, Victor. It was an easy patch. Consider it payback for the countless Costco hot dogs you made me over the years."

"I bet you're eager to get back to your little job at the bar," Victor said, jovially patting Autumn's back.

"Brewery—and it's been slow after the Oktoberfest. I'm not expected back for three more days."

"Well, now that you have a working car, maybe you can find a better job than some bar."

"Brewery—and it's not forever, just until—" She swallowed, her eyes darted to me.

They didn't know about school.

I don't want to tell them until I know it's for sure. Until I know that I've really accomplished what I said I would.

"It's not forever." Sucking in a steadying breath, Autumn hoisted her bag higher on her shoulder and offered me a tight-lipped smile that didn't reach her eyes. "I'll talk to you later, Nicolai."

Victor didn't acknowledge his daughter as she disappeared into the house, his hand cracking on my shoulder as he pulled me toward the garage. "Now that you're here, let me show you my new toy. It'll be a fun daily driver once I get a new timing belt put on."

Settled on my leather couch, with the sun setting over the Jasper Pass Bridge, I listened to the hum of an empty house.

When I bought the house three years before, I was pleased with the oversized windows, cedar shakes, and the expanse of hardwood panels. Marble counters and the shining silver appliances. It was all so new, so expensive. The kind of place Noemi would have approved of. Even the leather couch. Cold, rigid, sumptuous. Not particularly comfortable but beautiful. It was a house, but I hadn't realized until I returned that it never felt like my home. Had anything?

It all felt so lonely. One week in the car with Autumn, and now I was bereft. Her hums and snorts from the other side of the car. The squeak of her bare feet on the floor and the warmth of her body in my space. I almost missed the Eagles music. I missed her.

It had only been two hours. Before I could talk myself out of how foolish it would be to reach out, my phone was in my hand.

> **Nico: Can I take you to dinner tonight?**

> **Autumn: you still want to?**

> **Nico: see you? Absolutely.**

Three dots appear and then disappear. For over a minute, I see her typing.

> **Autumn: K**

> **Nico: Pick you up in an hour, is that enough time?**

> **Autumn: can you make it in 45?**

Idling in front of the Townsend home, I remembered picking up a girl from her parents' home, nearly twenty years prior. Autumn, and I had danced around what this was between us, but I had never come out and said what I wanted. Mostly because I couldn't parse it out. Did I miss her the moment she was away? Yeah. Was my house feeling lonely without her? Obviously. Did I want her to be my girlfriend? What a stupid word.

I wanted her to be *something*.

Had for a while now. But back home, what we shared on the road trip became all the more complicated. Dating would mean her family knowing; her brothers, her dad. Her protective cousin, who might be scarier than all of them put together.

And if you hurt her? Disappoint her the way you did Noemi?

I shook off the thought. Couldn't let it grow legs tonight, the way it had hitched a ride in my psyche for the first two-thirds of the trip.

Feet barely on the ground, I looked up the driveway to see the barrel-chested form of Oliver walking toward me. No, not Oliver, Ivan. All these Townsend brothers looked alike. After the standard back-slapping hug, he hoisted up a cardboard box.

"Mom found some old blankets or toys or something of mine and insisted I needed to take them home. Most of it's junk, but I'll throw it away once she can't see. I don't know why she insists on keeping every little thing from our childhood."

It was impossible for me to imagine anything of mine that my uncle would have kept once I moved out, let alone the smallest memento my mother had. I doubted she even had a picture of me. Would she even recognize me on the street? I couldn't reveal my thoughts to Ivan, so I smiled and nodded, pretending I knew about loving families.

"I heard about your trip with Autumn, and now you're here again. One week together, and you're still wanting to hang out with her?" Ivan laughed. "Braver man than I."

Autumn emerged from the house wearing a thick yellow sweater that looked so soft it could have been butter. I wanted to peel it over her body and drop it on the floor of my bedroom. I doubted she was wearing a bra. Dark-wash jeans and low-heeled boots finished her outfit. For anyone else, it would have been a normal outfit, but on Autumn, it was stunning.

Autumn's eyes narrowed on her brother, obviously hearing his joke, and shook her head. "So funny I forgot to laugh."

With his free hand, he wrapped his arm around Autumn's shoulder, pulling her to his side and messing up her hair. "Come on, Guppy, you know I'm only teasing."

Heat was building under my skin. How had I never noticed the way her family talked to her? Had it always been this way?

"And your jokes are only getting funnier, aren't they?" She smiled as her eyes narrowed.

"Back me up here, Nic. You spent a week with my little sis. You have to admit, she can be a lot to handle."

"Only for someone who wants less."

Who was I to comment on their dynamics? To defend her? Still, I couldn't help myself.

He snorted at my comment as if it were a joke as well. "I hope you still have eardrums after your date. This one likes to talk."

"I know what Autumn likes."

The tension in my voice was unmistakable to Autumn, but Ivan didn't seem to notice it. Instead, he was looking his sister up and down, frowning.

"Are you wearing makeup? And are those heels?" Ivan's gaze darted between us, blinking those Townsend blue eyes dramatically. "Wait, is this a date?"

"No."

"Yes," I said over her. Tensing my jaw, I glanced at her and shook my head slightly to dissuade her from making excuses for me. "Yeah, I'm taking

Autumn out to dinner. On a date."

Ivan's red brow shot up into his freckled forehead. "Wow, okay. So—" He scratched his nose with his thumbnail, his eyes darting. "Huh."

"Take a breath, Iv. It's no big deal," Autumn huffed out.

"Does Dad know? Does Oliver?"

"I'm twenty-six, not sixteen." Autumn crossed her arms and did her best imitation of being annoyed, which I figured, if your siblings couldn't do, no one could.

"And he's forty."

"Thirty-eight," I corrected. "Same age as Oliver."

Ivan stared me down. "Is that supposed to be better?"

"It's factual." I shrugged.

He clicked his tongue against his teeth, and I could see the temptation to punch me pass over his face.

"How did this—" He scrubbed a hand over his face. "Never mind, I don't want any details. I can put the pieces together. Long drives, alone time, ugh." He stuck out his tongue and fake gagged. After a minute of dramatic drying-heaving and eye rolls from Autumn, Ivan straightened. "I'm gonna need a bit to figure out how to feel about this, but you two better get your shit together because we both know I'm not the issue here."

"I'm an adult. My prefrontal cortex is fully developed. You are thirty-four and still stuff your socks between couch cushions the same way you did when you were twelve. Mind your business."

"When has anyone in this family done that?" Ivan glowered at her, and Autumn lifted a defiant chin. "Fine. Do what you want. I'll see you guys." He started down the driveway, the box in his hands. At his car, he stopped and turned to face us. "Danielle is missing her aunt. You should come by the house soon. Both of you."

That was likely the ringing endorsement I would need for whatever this was between us.

Her face softened at the mention of her niece. "Of course. Tell my baby Yellie I'll take her to ice cream."

Hand on her back, I led her to my car, opening the door for her to slide into the passenger seat. In the front window, there was a twitch of the blinds as someone was watching us.

Should have known that The Cabin was a mistake when Autumn waved at two servers and the bartender before we even made it to our seats. I didn't go out to local restaurants often. Too crowded, too overpriced, too many memories and opportunities for someone to make small talk that I inevitably failed at. But Autumn suggested it, so here we were.

The nautical themed restaurant was bustling with its professionally faded shiplap walls, the oversized dark wood boat wheel over the bar, and the anchors on all the menus.

With our plates bused, Autumn sat on the other side of the bench seat, her legs crossed under her. Outside the window was Freedom Bay Marina, the kayak, and paddleboard stand boarded up for the cold months. The tide was low, a long stretch of dark brown muck and barnacle-covered rocks dotting the beach.

Autumn had finished telling me about her last quarter of school, the internship she had been approved for at the Ridgewood Marine Science Center on the other side of the marina parking lot.

As a university student and a former volunteer, she would be finishing her capstone at the same place that drove her interest in marine biology as a teenager.

"—And while they can be shy, they have been known to attack divers on occasion, with their venom in their bite, and since they grow to—"

"Oh, no, are you boring Nico with talk about sea cucumbers?" Summer slid in beside her cousin, not bothering for an invitation.

"It's the giant Pacific octopus and—"

"Whatever." Summer took Autumn's glass out of her hand and sipped from the straw. "What's up, bitch?" When Autumn didn't say anything, Summer raised a brow. "Not you, Autumn. You're an angel. Obviously."

"I'm the only other one here, so I'm assuming that means me."

My annoyance had nothing to do with Summer calling me a bitch and everything to do with the way she interrupted.

"If the pretentious man bun fits." She handed Autumn her mostly empty glass.

"I don't have a man bun." I touched the ends of my hair, which were brushing dangerously close to my collar.

Summer stole my drink from the table and gulped down the rest. "Sure, Evjen. You're just in desperate need of a haircut."

"What are you doing here?" Autumn asked, twirling the straw in her glass, the tinkle of ice barely audible in the more crowded restaurant.

"Meeting Van for dinner. Like minds, and all that. So, you two are fucking?"

The change of subject sent me and Autumn choking on our drinks.

"Summer!" Autumn hissed. "Don't."

"What? Say fuck or ask the question?"

"Both." Autumn lowered her voice. "It's none of your business."

"Oh, you two definitely fucked." She smirked. "I thought Ivan was lying in the group chat. He always was a shit starter."

Autumn pulled out her phone, a wall of notifications showing up on the lock screen.

"It's one date." Autumn glowered at her cousin, who was far more trained in rude facial expressions.

"Yeah, okay," Summer replied in a mocking, sing-song voice. "As if you're not getting dicked down three ways from Sunday."

"Can you not—"

Summer slid out of the booth. "Call me later, cuz. I need to hear all about it."

She strolled off before we could reply, arm-in-arm with a muscular, dark-haired man who looked at our table, waved at Autumn, and led her out.

"Is she always like that?"

"Summer? Yeah, she's funny like that."

Funny wasn't the word I wanted to use. Autumn's interests were disregarded, and she assumed people wouldn't care about octopuses. But her passion for it, the way she lit up, was captivating. I couldn't think of a single thing that brought me joy the way Autumn did when she talked of the biodiversity of the Puget Sound, from hooded nudibranchs to dog whelks.

"Don't you find it interesting that you'll defend other people but never yourself?" Her hand tightened around her empty glass as it was poised halfway between the table and her mouth, her big blue eyes widening as she took in my question. "Your dad, your brother, Summer. Do you always let them talk to you that way?"

Pursing my lips, I studied her face for a sign that she was embarrassed, but she only responded with her own pulled brows.

"I'm not sure I get what you're asking me."

"Your dad today, assuming that you were the one to wreck the car, acted like you would drive us across the country on accident. Summer teased you about sea stars."

"Sea cucumbers," she corrected as if that was the point at all.

I tilted my head to the side, my jaw tight. "Why do you let them do that?"

"It's just a joke."

"Does it make you laugh?"

"What?" She blinked.

"You say it's a joke. So, what's so funny about it? Why are you the punchline?"

"You're overcomplicating things. It's just how it goes."

"You're not a joke, Autumn. You know that, right? You're smart and kind and beautiful, even if they can't see that."

She pulled her lower lip between her teeth, her brows pulling together. "Take me to your house? Show me your bedroom."

This was a change of subject, but I wouldn't be the one to call her out on it. She understood my question, even if she didn't want to answer.

The moment we walked into my house, I knew having Autumn here was right. Entering my kitchen, she went straight for the fridge, as if she'd been there many times, grabbing a ginger lime soda, preceded by her warmth, the sounds of her feet and her fingers.

"I like you in here." I lifted her until her butt was on the marble island counter and I could stand between her legs.

"In the kitchen? Is that some sexist joke?" She raised a brow at me.

Taking the soda out of her hand, I took a sip, my mouth over where hers was moments before. "Absolutely not. All I've seen you make is peanut butter toast, and I'll be honest, you burned it."

Her lips twisted up, fighting back a smile. "Maybe I like it burned."

Setting the can beside her, I leaned in closer, her pupils dilating as my mouth stopped inches from hers. "No, I think you felt bad for the heel once again and can't bring yourself to waste something."

"Who's doing the anthropomorphism now?"

Her fingers wound through my hair, her nails scratching at my nape.

"Such a big word." I clicked my tongue. "And what a big heart you've got. Heels of bread, ugly sunglasses, grumpy assholes. You want to save them all, don't you?" My teeth found her ear, nibbling her lobe before grazing down her throat.

"Well, I do like ugly sunglasses, yes." She gasped out, her legs tightening on each side of my hips.

"I think you don't want to admit you have a problem because you don't want others to think you're asking for help. You value the needs of the people you love, more than you do yourself." With one hand, I slid her shirt up over her head to fall soundlessly on the floor behind me. As I predicted, she wasn't wearing a bra, her breasts heavy and full.

"Are you going to psychoanalyze me or make me feel good?" Her hands found my bare back, pulling my shirt off to join hers on the floor.

With my thumb, I grazed over her nipples, the cool air, and pressure making them pucker beautifully. "Both, sweet girl. I think you need to learn to have someone take care of you without you having to ask for it."

"Do I? And what does that entail?"

The strain in her voice wove higher as I rolled her nipple between my fingers, the slight bruising from our night in Sol Del Mar still painting her pale skin.

My lips found hers, an urgency building with every pass of my tongue. Between us, she undid the top button with ease and slipped her hand inside my boxers to cup my cock.

A hiss escaped me as she wrapped her hand around my length. When she cupped my balls, I bowed forward, capturing her mouth with mine. She was going to make me cum, and we both still had our pants on.

Pulling away, I wrenched her palm from my cock, capturing her wrist and holding her hand up below her mouth.

"Spit," I commanded.

Her gaze dark, pupils blown wide, she leaned over her own hand, her cheeks hollowing before her tongue darted out and saliva dripped into her palm.

The sight of her, compliant, wanting, was more beautiful than anything I had ever seen. "Oh, sweet girl, you take such care of me, don't you? Want to be so fucking good for me?"

She nodded at me, her grip tightening on my cock. Up and down, her warm palm and her spit gave exquisite friction. I would allow this for only one more minute. I wouldn't come first. After fumbling, I could unbutton her jeans, sliding the zipper down, then cupped her fiery core. She lifted her hips, and then her jeans fell off her legs.

"And I'll be so good to you, won't I?"

"Please," she gritted out before my mouth captured hers again.

The last of the ginger lime soda and something uniquely Autumn lingered. My lips made their descent down the delicate skin of her neck.

Her back arched to meet my lips as they continued their trail down her chest, contemplating every beauty mark on her until she was squirming under me. I peered up at Autumn briefly as I ran my tongue along her skin, swirling it around her nipple before taking it into my mouth. Autumn gasped as I tweaked the other with my fingers. I had barely touched her, and her body heated, her core sopping and ready. The slow torture of her want against my hand.

With one hand, I pressed on her sternum until she was bowed on her elbows. "Lean back, sweet girl. One taste of you, and I am famished."

"Nico . . ." She breathed shakily as I kissed my way down her stomach, her chin dropped low to watch me, her body shaking from every caress of my lips on her bare skin. A small whimper escaped as my nose brushed against the front of her underwear. "More. Please."

"I know, I know what you need," I whispered, unable to hide the smug look on my face. I kissed the inside of her inner thigh, nipping it lightly as I hooked my fingers under the fabric. Inch by inch, I dragged them off, revealing her delicate skin.

Legs parted for me, I took in the sight of her, juicy pink and glistening with her arousal. "So fucking beautiful. You're going to be so sweet on my tongue."

My eyes trailed over her before running my finger through the center of her slick folds.

"You want me here, don't you?"

The soft moan she let out went straight to my cock, somehow growing harder with every gasp as I slid one finger inside her heat, then two.

"Need my fingers inside this cunt, want my tongue to lick you clean."

Her pussy clenched around my fingers, tight and perfect. I couldn't fight my smirk as she let out a small moan.

The first pass on her clit was languid, a gentle lapping of a wave on the shore. When her legs tightened around my head, I dove in, kissing and sucking, her arousal heavy on my tongue. Her nails sharp on my scalp as she pulled me in deeper. Each dip in and out of her, wrung out a new cry, a fresh shudder around me. I fucked her with my mouth, sucking her clit, our combined juices dripping off my chin as I devoured her. The quaking of her thighs on each side of me told me how close she was, her keening cries echoing as she came, hot and tight on my face.

The wrench of her hands in my hair, stinging, then releasing as she came down from her orgasm.

Hands splayed over her head, her chest heaved as I stood above her, my face gleaming with her. Fingers tracing over her body, from her wet cunt and up to her puckered nipples, I took her in, lying flat on my kitchen counter like a feast I could never finish. "Do you have any idea how beautiful you look when you come?"

"I—no?" Her breathing was still shaky as she propped herself up on her elbows to look at me.

"You love this, don't you? Dripping all over my counter. Defiling my kitchen."

"Yes," she shuddered out.

Swelling pride and possessiveness flooded me at her submission. With one hand, I gripped the back of her neck, pulling her body flush with mine, her legs wrapping around my waist where my pants still hung low. Desperately, I needed to be inside her.

"Good fucking girl. My girl." With my finger on her chin, I pulled her face up to meet mine, my thumb pressing on her lower lip. "I'll be the only one who sees this, you understand?"

"Only you. Yours," she repeated, her ankles hooked together behind me, pulling my hard cock against her dripping center.

"I could fuck you right here, and you'd let me, wouldn't you? Let me fuck you all over this house."

She nodded, her voice failing her.

In a few quick moments, I had my pants off and the condom rolled on. The slick heat of her coating my tip as I slid my hard cock through her folds. It was past the point of teasing. I needed to feel her around me.

She braced her hands behind her in time as I thrust inside, all the way to the hilt. Buried inside her, her heat gripped me tight as my knees weakened at the sensation.

"Fuck, you're so tight, so perfect for me." I pulled out almost to the tip then sink back in, my length dragging along her walls, and she keened at the motion, her legs tightening around me. "This is what you bring me to. Making me want you this way. Making me fucking insane for this cunt."

With one hand on her hip, the other finds purchase on the cold counter beside her. She clenched around me as I moved faster. She whimpered, her breathing speeding up again as I thrust in and out of her. "You love when I fuck you like this, don't you?"

Her response is a gasp as I drove deeper, faster. With one hand, I snagged her nape, angling her head down.

"See how you take me? You never look better than when you're taking my cock."

She stared down at where we were joined, the shiny evidence of us on my cock as I thrust in and out of her, and she moaned at the sight.

My grip tightened in her hair as she rolled her hips against me. "No one else, Autumn. No one. You're so fucking perfect, so tight. Mine."

"Yours." She cried as I kept the steady pace, marveling at my control so far not to blow it already with her. The way her tits bounced with each thrust inside, the sheen of sweat over her forehead, the constellations of freckles on her chest.

"You take me so good, sweet girl. I fucking love this. I lo—"

Two more driving thrusts, and her walls constrict in a vise grip. "Nico—" Around my waist, her thighs quaked, and she bent forward, her stomach clenching. Her hips jerk against me as she crests. "I-I—"

As I followed, I collapsed on her, my sweat-slick body flush with hers, our breathing in rapid sync. The edge of the counter was digging into my thighs as I lay on her, arms around her waist, my face buried in her neck. The salt of her skin was on my lips as I dragged my nose over her throat.

"You're going to kill me, you know that?" she murmured under me, and I raised my head to flash her a smirk.

"Did you think we're done? I'm taking you to my bed to finish what you've started."

After three more orgasms, two for her, one for me, we're on my bed, her hair spread, gazing upward.

Trailing a finger over her sternum to circle the pink bud of her nipple, I mused. "I don't want you to be with anyone else."

"Not likely." She snorted.

"Don't interrupt me." I dropped a kiss on her nose, and her response was a smirk. "You will let me take you out on dates, and you can chat my ear off about sea mussels and the life cycles of the booby-headed monkfish or whatever."

"There's no such thing. You're mixing up your anglerfish and your birds."

"And in return, I will give you at least three orgasms a day."

"Sounds like I'm the one who's getting the better end of this deal."

"Oh, no. It's definitely me. This power imbalance is unreal. I'm trying to catch up."

"Nicolai."

There she goes again, saying my name like it's a blessing as if I could be salvation.

Tucking my arm around her shoulders, I pulled her body flush with mine, my words lost in her thick hair. "You told me at the falls that it takes power to surrender. And you were right. You always had the power here. From the first moment, I was powerless to stop how I felt, to resist you. It would be so much simpler not to feel this way, but I do."

"I think . . ." I felt, not heard, the swallow as she tried to find her voice. "I think you might be it for me," she whispered, and I allowed the words to wash over me. It had been years since anyone had told me that. Almost a decade since I last felt it.

"Fuck," I murmured against her mouth. "I don't deserve that. I never will."

"Do you . . ." She pulled her lower lip between her teeth. "Sorry, I can't assume you would."

How I felt? There was no comparison. She wasn't Noemi, this heaviness in my limbs when she was away from me, the way my chest constricted into a tight ball, making every breath feel ragged. The way my fingers itched to find her face. Hugging her was like watching a sunrise paint the sky indigo, blue, yellow, and red behind jagged rocks, her hair and eyes reflecting the colors. Was this love? Whatever it was, I could never deserve it.

"I'm not worthy of it, you know. But I'm also selfish, impossibly so. I won't let you take it back."

"I wouldn't."

"You should. I take things that should never be mine, and I ruin them until there's no going back. That is what I learned, and that is where I come from. It's who I am."

I long prided myself on my composure, my restraint. Few things made me weak, but when it came to Autumn, I was powerless.

Long gone was the man who thought I could control myself around her.

"But we're past that point already, aren't we? Things will fall apart or together. But either way, I'm falling with you."

The deep blue of her eyes glimmered in the low light of the moon. She drew her lower lip between her teeth, grinning up at me. "I'm going to my friend Wren's tomorrow night for a party, do you want to come with me?"

Had it only been a few days since I hurt her feelings, asking her why I would meet her friends? It was like a lifetime before.

"If you want me there, I'll go."

"I want; I always want." She ducked her chin, the last part of her statement warm on my bare chest. "But I think we both know that, don't we?"

Wrapping my arm around her, I pulled her tighter. She fit under my arm, in my bed. In my house, that for the first time felt like it could be a home.

Fingers trailing down her arm, I listened as her breath became steady, the low wheeze of her sleep before I rolled over to my side to study her sleeping face.

Autumn was for the patient; it's not the end of things but the promise of all that will return if only you allow it the space. A season of rest. The assurance that all will be well if only you give it time.

If only time were enough.

POINT S-ICICLE CREEK, WA

Nico

THE PRESS OF LIPS, the weight of a hand on her hip, the arduous drag of a finger up the side of her throat to capture her chin between my fingers. It didn't matter the gray sky was threatening rain or that the siding on this A-frame cabin was in desperate need of a sanding and a re-stain. With Autumn in my arms, all that mattered was the two of us together.

If only things could be that simple. Her friend Wren had already dragged her away ten minutes into this party, leaving me with men I had never met before.

"A little birdie told me something," Summer sidled up to me, her eyes gleaming with knowledge that set my teeth on edge. Within thirty minutes of arriving in Icicle Creek, I was questioned by Wren, Summer and two other people I vaguely remembered.

"Oh?" I took a sip of beer and couldn't give myself away to this sly woman.

"I heard from Autumn that, while on your trip, you, buttoned up, uptight, stodger, were—" She leaned in closer, and I fought the urge to take a step back and cover my balls. "Drinking orange soda."

A whoosh of relief came out of me. Not about sex or our relationship or my age or a host of other issues that Summer could come up with. "I guess so."

She raised an imperious brow, her blue eyes the same shade as Autumn's. Really, how two people could look so similar and be so different was astounding. "You, who cornered me at the grocery store and berated me about my strawberry refresher."

"Cornered? Berated? I think you're being dramatic."

She fake-pouted her lips, placing a finger on her chin. "No, I'm not. So what, when others drink that kind of 'swill' it's gross, but you can do it?"

Shrugging, I glanced around the wooded area beside the cabin. Autumn was standing with her friend Wren and their other friend Penny in front of a fire pit. "Autumn kept buying them for me. What was I supposed to do?"

"Tell her no. You can tell her no, can't you?"

Not about things that actually matter, no.

"Of course I can."

She hummed noncommittally. "I thought so."

We stood side by side before she leaned in. "And she also says the sex was good."

With that parting shot, she left me alone, huffing. Good? Good? Not spectacular? Not earth-shattering? The best she'd ever had? Bullshit.

I liked Wren and so far. I liked her boyfriend, Adrian, even more. His neighbor across the street had opened her house to the group as well.

"Whatever you do, don't go in the hot tub," Adrian warned. "Trust me, things have happened in there you don't even want to imagine."

But I was never much for meeting new people. What I wanted was for Autumn to return to me, lace her fingers with mine, and drag me around the back of the cabin where we could make out again.

It was not to be.

"So, you're the newest import into the Seasons." Adrian handed me a fresh bottle, holding out his own for me to clink the neck against.

"I guess." I took a low swallow. He had good taste in beer, at least. "Though the way I hear it, you're the season name, not Wren."

"Winter, yeah. Matter of time for us, though. My Birdie isn't much for her last name, so I'm sure she'll want to hyphenate at least."

We watched the group, sipping our beers. Somewhere behind a copse of trees, the rush of the river could be heard. "Autumn said you had to fish Wren out of that river once."

He snorted into his drink, his eyes growing dark. "Makes it sound far more heroic than it was. More like slipping and sliding in mud and then yelling at her, but yeah, the bank is being eroded, and she fell in. In February, no less. Crazy girl."

A small caramel-shaded wiry-haired dog pranced around the clearing, jumping up on its hind legs to place its paws on Summer, who reached down and picked the dog up. I never took her for a tiny-dog person, more like a Belgian Malinois or an Akita, maybe. Not a dog of an indeterminate breed with bad manners. Wren bent lower and nuzzled the dog's fur, laughing when it licked her cheek.

"You know, when you date one of them, you're setting yourself up for life with the other three, right?"

Summer handed the dog off to Wren, who flipped it on its back and was cradling it like a baby. Autumn leaned over and gave the dog a belly scratch.

"I knew about Summer, at least. I'm friends with their family."

"It's lots of 'girl trips' and constant texting and inside jokes you'll never understand, and when she tries to explain, it makes even less sense than whatever you've made up in your mind. I like the affirmations Autumn sends every morning, though. It's been our routine that Wren will read it during coffee in the morning while I make her breakfast."

The dog had wiggled away, now prancing over to a group of sixty-year-olds that were on the other side of the clearing, Adrian's neighbor of the infamous danger hot tub, I guessed.

Adrian cracked his neck, his gaze sliding to me quickly before resting back on the women.

"She's a good girl. Been a wonderful friend to Wren. Didn't give her shit when we started dating, like some others did. Helped move her stuff up here." Adrian drained his beer, pointing the empty neck at the women. "And she seems like she's crazy about you."

Autumn threw her arm around Wren and tried to bring Summer in for a hug as well, but her cousin ducked out, grimacing and crossing her fingers, calling out, "No sappy shit, you two. You're the worst."

A smile ticked up at the corner of my mouth, watching Autumn with her friends, at ease, giving affection to all. "Autumn's crazy about a lot of things. She loves everyone and everything around her, like some damn fairy princess. The way Autumn sees the world, the joy and love she finds in everything, I've never been that way. When I care about something, it's singular. I've never cared about the world the way she does."

"But—" Adrian prompted.

"Like I said, singular. I only have the space to love one person."

"Love. That's a big word," he mused. "How long have you two been dating?"

I hadn't realized it, said it, but judging by the besotted way he was talking about Wren, he didn't seem like the type to give me a hard time about it.

"Does it matter?" I asked, raising a brow.

With a smirk, he knocked shoulders with me. "Come on, let's get our girls before Wren tries to kidnap another dog."

"Would she do that?"

"You have no idea." He chuckled, pointing at the golden-haired mutt now jumping on a couple beside a truck in the driveway. "That's my dog, abandoned at my house by some chick I picked up a few years ago, but would you know it by the way she prefers Wren? Of course not. She's a dog-napper. And if I had to wager, I'd say Autumn is one, too."

She was a thief, that was for sure.

A dark-haired man approached us, a bag of ice in one hand. Introductions were made. His name was Tam, and he and his wife, Penny, were Adrian's oldest friends, *only friends, you little fucker* and lived in town. Clapping Adrian on the back, Tam held up the ice. "Just as you ordered, right?"

"I said IPA."

Tam pulled out his phone. "No, you said get a twelve-pack of ice."

Adrian frowned. "Why would I want a twelve-pack of ice? And this is one bag."

"I can run back down to town if you need beer. This is my second, and I've only started."

Best to get in good with the friends, right?

"Let's all go. Penny said she wanted to talk to the girls, and if I can avoid listening to them talking about alien dick girth from their latest book, I'd like to."

Not ready to unpack that but agreeing all the same, I let Autumn know we were running into town, and I'd be back. She let me leave with a long, lingering kiss and the promise I'd grab her some spicy chips and more ginger ale at the store. Beside us, Summer gagged dramatically, and Wren teased her she was just as bad with her own boyfriend.

We climbed into my car to the sounds of Summer and Wren bickering over who was more disgusting with the PDA.

POINT T-ICICLE CREEK, WA

Autumn

SHOCKINGLY, IT TOOK OVER ten minutes at the party before Summer and Wren strong-armed me into standing by the fire and dishing all about how Nico ended up coming with me. Summer was slightly gleeful, letting me know she knew I had a crush on him and was ready to take full credit for getting us together.

Wren, who basically moved in with Adrian after a long weekend fling, refrained from giving me a hard time, on principle. *When you know, you know. I get it.*

Then her eyes got all glossy as if she was daydreaming about Adrian, even though he only stood a few feet away, offering Nico a beer and pointing out their dog, Maizie.

Summer grimaced and clapped her hands together. "Ew. Snap out of it. You two are disgusting. Makes me want to barf."

"As if you and Van aren't as bad."

At our feet, Maizie jumped up on my legs before moving to Summer.

"Van and I would never make moon eyes at each other in public."

Summer reached down and picked up the dog. "It's indecent."

"Didn't you and Van have sex at a park against a tree outside the Boathouse?" I asked.

She sniffed as if affronted. "I have no idea who told you that, and I'm sure whoever did would blame a generous portion of queso and too many margaritas."

Wren, who was nuzzling Maizie, snorted into her wiry-haired fur.

"You have to admit, this is all a little fast, Aut." Wren straightened, taking her dog from Summer's arms and flipping her to hold like a newborn baby. "And we both know I wouldn't judge you for that. Kettle meet pot but—"

She shot Summer a look that I read all too well. Wren had her head on straight. Wren was analytical. Wren never ignored the flapping noise in her car until the fabric pulled free of the convertible roof, and it almost blew off while driving up I-5.

"He's not a stranger I picked up at a bar. I've known him since I was a kid. He practically lived at my house growing up. He's Oliver's best friend. The best man at his wedding to Janie." I scratched the dog's belly, its little pink tongue lolling out.

"We don't want you to get your hopes up, is all. We know how much you want to see the good in a situation, and that can lead you to being—" Wren waved around, trying to find the word.

"A dumbass," Summer offered.

"Thanks a lot, Cuz." I sipped my cooling apple cider.

"Not the word I'd use." Wren warned with a head jerk. "I was going to say innocent and trusting. Which is never a bad thing, right?"

The dog wiggled in Wren's arms, and she stooped to place her on the ground.

"I appreciate what you're saying, even if I don't like the delivery." I shot my cousin a hard look. "But I'll be okay. Believe it or not, I have some experience under my belt. I know what I'm getting myself into. Maybe you two should take a page out of my book and *trust me* to handle myself."

A new car pulled into the driveway, with their friends Tam and Penny climbing out, a large fountain soda in Penny's hand and a bag of ice in Tam's. "Oh, good, the rest are here. Now we can party."

Half an hour later, the rain had broken up the bonfire party, leaving us to squeeze into their cabin.

"I know the guys said they're going to buy beer, but I know Adrian and Tam will want to give Nico the tour of Icicle Creek, and we'll probably have to pick them up at the bar later, so now we can have some girl time." Penny giggled. "And I know exactly what we should do. It's time to play a little game to jazz up the party—" With a flourish of her hands, she pulled out a plastic shopping bag and shook it around. "Pregnancy roulette."

Other women groaned, but I clapped my hands together, laughing at the game. "Scandalous! I love it."

Penny explained the game: we all take a pregnancy test, then place the test in the cup, shake it up and find out if anyone in the group is pregnant. One by one, each lady went into the bathroom alone with a box, returning a minute later empty-handed.

Following Summer's instructions, I peed on the stick, popped the lid over the gross part, and stuck it in the cup beside four others, already, I could see two lines on one of the other sticks. I had my suspicions about who it was. This would be an interesting night.

After calling for people to refill their drinks, Wren went around with the cup, instructing them to select one.

Summer pulled out the first stick, waving it in the air. "Negative." She fake-pouted and then held the cup out to the woman beside her.

"Negative." The cup was passed to the next woman, Marta, who owned the local cafe.

"Positive." Their neighbor, Agatha, brandished the two-lined stick.

A chorus of gasps and "ooos" sounded as we giggled and glanced at each other. One of these ladies had a surprise waiting for her.

My turn with the cup. I closed my eyes, waving my fingers over the three remaining sticks, before grabbing one and brandishing it. "One line—that's negative, right?"

The gals nodded, the cup moving to the next woman.

"Negative."

And then the last. "Positive."

And a cacophony of whoops and gasps as they all eyed one another.

"Alright, fess up, who is it? Wren, Penny, is it either of you?"

"It's me," Penny said, with a small smile on her lips. I had a feeling that was why she wanted us to play. "Tam, and I found out a few days ago. Tam wanted to wait to say anything, you know, until the first doctor's appointment, but it's me. I couldn't keep it in."

The gals rushed around the woman, hugging and kissing her cheeks. Even though I didn't know Penny and Tam well, I couldn't help but offer my congratulations, squeezing her hand and wishing her the best, extracting a promise she would drop me her address, so I could send a gift in a few months.

Once all the fervor died down, the woman with the dark hair, Agatha, spoke up. "There were two, though, so who else could it be?"

People talked over one another, *I'm on my period, so I know it's not me, it would have to be an immaculate conception, did you gals forget I'm sixty-seven?*

Once everyone had said their piece, their eyes turned to me. Summer's face paled as she asked. "Autumn, could it be you?"

I snorted, shaking my head. "No cause—" I thought back to the last few months.

My periods had never been regular, sometimes I would have two-week long ones and then three weeks later another and other times I could go sixty days without one. But how long had it been since my last one? August? Or was it July? No, it was early August, but that was before . . .

Color drained out of my face. "Well, I—"

"So, it might be."

"With a man like that, I'd be shocked if you weren't," Marta cackled. "He looks virile."

Wren slapped an extra box into my hand. "Only way to find out."

On jelly legs, I walked back into the bathroom, the pink wallpaper even brighter for the second time. What had been such a funny lark only twenty minutes before was pressing down on my skin, the bubblegum-colored walls getting closer and closer. I couldn't look at the test as it processed, my vision narrowing on the flamingo towel holder, a small chip in the black and yellow beak, a single glassy eye taunting me.

Stupid, stupid, stupid girl. How could you be so foolish? He wore a condom that night. I knew he did. But condoms fail. All forms of birth control can. The night we were in Marina Del Sol, the condom splitting as I rolled down his length, the expiry date from a year before—were they from the same pack?

If this were true, I had been—I couldn't even think the word—for over three months. The air that I sucked through my nose and out my mouth was shaky. What did I always tell the girls when they were struggling with something, focus on your body, where are your feet, your toes curling on the ground and the weight of the air around you, deep breaths, in and out.

I opened my eyes. The box said to wait five minutes, but it didn't need that. The results were instantaneous.

Breathe in through your nose like you're smelling a flower, now out like you're blowing out a candle, in and out. In and—

Wren knocked on the door. "Autumn, are you okay?"

"I'm fine. Still peeing," I called out. A second, more demanding knock made the door quake, and my voice rang out. "Give me some privacy."

Why I didn't open the door, I couldn't say. Maybe in the privacy of this little room, I could pretend this was all a game, that there was no way my entire world was being turned upside down in a single pee-tested moment.

"I pulled a lost tampon out of your vag before, open the door, Autumn." Summer shouted. Wonderful, now everyone knew about that encounter from when we were sixteen.

They would know, probably already knew, and still I grabbed my phone. With shaky fingers, I typed out a message to the group.

> **Autumn: Two lines mean positive, right?**

On my screen, text bubbles started and stopped, and with every ticking second, I knew my question was futile. Pregnant, pregnant. Oh God. What was I going to tell my parents? My brothers were going to be so pissed, especially Oliver. And the girls.

Fuckity, fuck. I hated cursing, but if there was ever a time, it was now.

That morning after Nico almost came inside me at the brewery. How he was so worried, how was he going to react? What would he say? What the heck was I going to do? My knees wobbled beneath me, and I gripped the counter to steady myself.

On the other side of the door, I heard Wren knocking, her phone buzzing in sync with mine on the counter. A second, louder knock rang out. Summer.

Then it rang, but it wasn't one of the girls.

It was Nico.

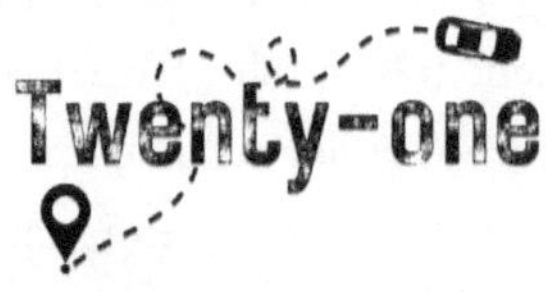

Twenty-one

POINT W-HORSE AND TRAILS, ICICLE CREEK, WA

Autumn

I'VE LONG LIVED INSIDE my head. Over my twenty-six years of life, I've created stories and worlds in my mind, played out situations with friends and insults I'd hurl at my enemies. As a teen, I would practice my reactions to things in the mirror, the shock of being asked out on a date, the hurt of being left out by a friend. The joy of receiving a compliment.

Nothing in all my daydreaming had prepared me for this. How do you tell a man you only started seeing that not only are you pregnant but almost three months in?

I had never been the best at math, but even I could do this simple addition, and if it had been from the sex three days before, there was no way the test would show it now.

The banging on the door got louder, then fell suspiciously silent. Test in hand, I squeezed my eyes shut, willing it to be different when I opened them back up again.

What is Nico going to do when he finds out? What am I going to do?

After a scraping, the doorknob jiggled, then clicked, and the door slammed open, the knob crashing against the wall. "Tell me you did not text me through the door," Summer warned, a skinny screwdriver in one hand, fire dancing in her blue eyes as she looked from the phone on the counter, the test in my hand and back up to my face. "Are you fucking kidding me right now?"

Beside Summer, Wren had her arms crossed against her chest, her lower lip between her teeth and brows furrowed. "Are you sure?"

Nodding, I extend the test out, the two lines bright blue.

"Fuck," Wren murmured, taking it from me. "Okay." She nodded as if she was coming up with a plan. "We'll just—" She swallowed, her eyes darting to Summer, who was panting and shaking her head. "We'll do— what? What do you want to do?"

"Heck, if I know. I—" Scratching my nails along my scalp, I balled my hands up, pulling at my hair from the roots. "What do I say? How do I tell him? And then what?"

"You have options. Nico doesn't have to know if you don't want to tell him. You can take Plan B, or I can make an appointment for the clinic I went to when this happened to me a few years ago, or—"

"No." I shook my head.

I didn't know how I would handle telling Nico yet, but whatever I did, he would be informed.

"And Plan B wouldn't work. I know when this happened, and I'm way past emergency contraception."

"How far past?" Summer asked, her eyes narrowing.

"Three months. August seventh. After I got ditched at that house par-ty."

It was going to come out no matter what. No point in hiding it now.

"You mean when you said Nico drove you home?"

"He drove me to *a* home. It just wasn't mine. It was his, and I didn't leave until the next morning."

"You little slut." Summer's grin sparkling on her lips. "Devious thing, you never told me. I can't believe you didn't give us all the details that night."

"Can you give me a hard time about not telling you later. I think I have bigger issues today."

"Right. Yes. Okay, so three months, that's what? A third of the way through?" She pulled out her phone, tapping on the screen. "What was the date? August 7th. So according to this—" She grimaced, huffing. "You are totally messing with the ads my phone is going to get now, by the way."

"Summer," Wren chided.

"Right, according to this, you are thirteen weeks. Second trimester. The baby is the size of a plum. That's weird. They compare it to fruit, but okay."

Penny approached, her phone in her hand, a frown playing on her mouth. "Hey, sorry to interrupt, but Tam called and was hoping we could all head down to the Horse and Trails. I guess they had a few while on their beer run and want us to join them and have Autumn and me drive them back up here? Agatha and the gals already left, it would just be us?"

Going to the bar was the last thing I wanted to do, but also what could I say? I couldn't take off without talking to him and certainly couldn't leave him at the bar.

Shoving my phone into my back pocket, I straightened. "Let's go."

"Aut, maybe we should figure out—"

"I said, I want to go." My voice had a hard edge. "I need to talk to Nico."

As I walked past Wren and Summer, I couldn't miss the glances of concern.

The Horse and Trails was exactly as I remembered it being from my last visit. Old terrible green carpeting, purple walls, an electric dartboard on the wall beside old neon signs for Budweiser. A young woman with short black hair and a colorful tattoo sleeve stood behind the bar, scrolling on her phone. She waved at Wren as we walked in, pouring a dark beer before we made it to the bar.

A bright smile stretched over Nico's face as he saw me, making him appear years younger. Would this baby have his smile? Those eyes that crinkled up at the corners? How was it I found out thirty minutes before and was already envisioning what our child would look like?

Child. *Child.* A real human baby. We made a baby.

Swallowing, I tried to paste on a convincing smile as he wrapped his arms around me, pulling me into his chest. "You're here. Settle a bet Adrian, and I have; he says that hot dogs aren't sandwiches, and I say they are."

Adrian laced an arm around Wren's waist, squeezing her hip and pressing a kiss to the top of her curls. "I'm just saying it's a slippery slope to call it a sandwich, what's next? A taco is a sandwich?"

"Tacos use a tortilla. This is meat between bread. What else could it be? Are you saying a meatball sub isn't a sandwich? A hoagie? Who's on a slippery slope now?" Nico pulled me closer to his side, his thumb tracing over my hip bone as if it was totally normal to have his hands on me in the middle of this bar in front of all my friends.

"It's its own thing, completely separated from sandwiches." Adrian waved, gesticulating wildly. "Birdie, back me up here."

"I don't know. It's a hard call—" Wren mused as she sipped from her beer.

Adrian shook his head. "Autumn, tell your boyfriend he's wrong. Hot dogs have never been sandwiches and will never be sandwiches."

I startled. *Boyfriend.* But what else would suffice? *Baby-daddy? Nope. Lover?* Ugh.

I clicked my tongue in pity. "I gotta go with Nico on this one. They fit all the requirements of a sandwich."

Nico gloated over my head at Adrian, his arm wrapping tighter around my waist. "See, I told you. Knew my girl wouldn't let me down."

His girl. It wasn't such a loaded word after all, hadn't I been that for a while? For over a week, really months. Since that moment in front of that yellowing fridge, with a stolen beer in my hand and a fistfight erupting in the next room.

Mine. That was the only word that felt right. But for how much longer?

"Traitors, all of you. Unbelievable. For penance for turning everyone against me, I think you should get the next round." Adrian told Nico, who gladly accepted.

The next hour was full of warm conversation, inside jokes, and stories of everyone's life. As I knew he would, Nico fit in perfectly. Sipping my warm apple cider, I let the remarks flow around me, nodding and smiling. Nothing was sinking in. On any other night, under different circumstances, it would be perfect. As it was, my mind kept flashing back to the test I stuffed in a plastic baggie, then shoved inside a pocket of my purse.

Nico's finger traced up my arm, his lips inches from my ear. "You okay? You've been awfully quiet since you got here."

I attempted a convincing smile. I would need to tell him soon, but the bar wasn't the place. Maybe once he finished his drink, I could ask him to come back to the house with me, just the two of us.

"Fine, tired." I grabbed my purse. "I'll be right back, okay?"

Getting up, I lifted my foot to walk to the bathroom when his hand wrapped around my wrist, pulling me down toward him. His fingers laced in my hair, and his mouth slotted over mine for a quick kiss. As I pulled away, I was sure my face was as red as Summer's mulled wine.

"Hurry back." He smirked at me, and I couldn't help the matching expression that graced my face.

Would he smile like that at me once he found out?

The water in the bathroom wouldn't get hotter than lukewarm as the sticky pink soap left a film on my hands. Kitschy signs around the neon green room hung over the toilet. A faint smell of pee and vomit clung to the porcelain. I dipped my wrists in the tepid stream; the water ran over my bare skin. What was I going to say to Nico? How do you start that conversation?

After a few tries of pulling and wrenching the knob, I opened the door to find a man standing on the other side, his receding hairline shining in the low yellow light of the hallway. "Well, hello there." The man grinned at me.

"Hi." I smiled back on instinct.

"What's your name?" He leaned in closer as I tried to step around him and into the hall.

"Autumn." I squeezed to the side, and he rotated with me.

His hand moved from his pocket to rest over my head.

"I'm Jarrod."

"Nice to meet you, Jarrod. Excuse me, I have to get back to—"

"Not so fast. We're talking, ain't we?"

"I really should get back and—" I glanced down the stretch. Our table was just out of view of the long hall.

I ducked under his arm, but he slid in lower, catching me. The man gripped my hip hard, his beer breath wafting over my face. "Now, come on, sugar, where's that smile for me?"

"Please let go of me." I wriggled away, clutching my arm to my chest.

The man stepped closer, his hand once again finding me, but this time lower on my butt. "We're just having fun, aren't we? Wouldn't like—" Suddenly, he was gone, pulled off me and sprawled on the floor. Nico stood between us, the tendons in his throat bulging as he glared down at the man.

"What the fuck do you think you're doing putting your hands on her?"

The man rolled onto his feet with surprising dexterity. "Who the hell are you?"

"The man who's going to kick your ass, that's who."

The man shoved at Nico's chest, knocking him against the wall. He stumbled slightly before rearing his arm, fist ready. At the bar, I heard Jordan yelling for them to stop and saw Adrian and Summer running over. Nico hit the man in the cheek, his head snapping back and the sound of flesh thumping against bone echoing in the hallway.

"Stop it," I shouted. "Nico, don't."

It was as if he couldn't hear me. Nico stepped forward with his fist raised, but before he could swing again, I caught his arm and pulled him back. The man took this opportunity to take his own swing, hitting Nico in the mouth with his fist. Nico being struck had his elbow connecting with my chest. Pain exploded in my lungs as I tried to pull in air. Falling back, I bounced against the wall, sliding down until I was sitting on the floor. With my hand over my heart, I watched as Adrian grabbed the man, yanking him down the hallway and toward to exit. Summer was still rushing over, screaming first at the man and then turning to face Nico.

"What the fuck did you do?"

"He was grabbing Autumn."

"And look at her now! She got hurt because of your dick-measuring contest."

"I'm fine, Summer," I gasped out. Leaning forward, I pulled myself up on my hands and knees, each breath wheezing out of me as I tried to pull air into my lungs.

"You're not fine, Autumn, you're pregnant."

The word echoed around the bar. It was as if the jukebox stopped playing, every patron had silenced their conversations, even the heater quit hissing.

Pregnant. Pregnant.

Nico's brow furrowed as he looked from her to me and back several times. The spot where his elbow hit me thrummed hot, pulsing over my skin. A bruise bloomed over his eye as he studied me.

"Wha—" He sucked in a breath. "Autumn, what is she…"

"I was going to tell you." Slowly rising on shaky legs, I set my hand on the wall to steady myself.

Color drained from his complexion, and he stumbled backward, hitting the opposite wall. His eyes large on me as he looked over my body, my face, my hand on my chest where I would surely be bruised tomorrow and then down to my stomach.

"No, no." He shook his head at us. Turning on his heel, he walked away through the dingy hallway with its neon purple walls. His shoulders hunched up to his ears, the other patrons stepping out of his warpath.

With one hand braced to keep me on my feet, I watched as he walked out the door and into the rainy night. Leaving me alone.

The bar was silent for several heartbeats, the thrum of my injury counting each moment as blood pounded under the surface. Slowly, people turned away, whispering low. A new song came on the jukebox. Despite the avoiding glances, I knew many were still listening and watching for what would happen next.

"What the heck did you say that for?" I yelled at Summer.

Her eyes grew large as she fumbled for the words. "He…you were…I thought—"

"I can handle myself." Rubbing the area, I hissed at the tender skin under my fingers.

"He pushed you down." Summer stepped to me, her hand grabbing my elbow to stabilize me.

Brushing her hand away, I retreated, my gaze burning into her. "He fell onto me after being sucker punched. That's not the same thing."

"I was only trying to—"

"What? Protect me? Coddle me? Act like I don't know what I'm doing and someone else needs to swoop in and fix me? I don't need you, my parents, or my brothers to save me. Despite what you think, I am an adult. So, start treating me like one."

As the words left me, I realized that in all my adult life, I had never yelled at Summer. I was born five and a half months after her. While I'm sure we had a few toddler tantrums between us in our younger years, I didn't have a single memory of ever raising my voice at my cousin.

Her hands out in front of her as if she were taming a wild beast, she must have come to the same conclusion. "I'm sorry, I didn't mean for—"

"You never do, Summer." Shaking my head, I stepped around her. Halfway to the door, I turned to face her. Drawing in a low breath, I let it out, in, out, in, out. Nico's words a balm in my mind.

You're smart and kind and beautiful, even if they can't see that.

How I told him, time and time again, to trust me. But no one else would.

"I'm so sick of everyone I love underestimating me."

"Autumn, I don't mean to..."

I put a hand up to stop her. "I have to go catch him."

"What are you going to say?" she asked.

Pausing, I scratched my forehead with my thumbnail. "The truth, what else is there?"

The night air was misty, the October chill seeping through my fleece jacket in minutes. His car was still in the parking lot, the keys in my purse from earlier. It was presumptuous to take his car, but I had bigger issues. I would find him, and whatever happened between us would be my choice, my responsibility. Mine and Nico's.

Twenty-two

POINT U-SIDE OF THE ROAD SOMEWHERE IN THE OLYMPIC MOUNTAINS OF WASHINGTON.

Nico

IT HAD BEEN OVER a decade since I tried to walk home after the bar. The old sensation of rage and intoxication heated my blood as I trekked down an unfamiliar road, rain-filled potholes and rocks skittering against my shoes.

The chill of the damp fall air had already taken the sensation from my fingers. My toes wouldn't be far behind, despite the speed at which I was walking—to, where? I didn't know this town, had no sense of it. But I couldn't be there.

Pregnant.

Autumn on the floor, her hand over her heart. The red mark on her chest already blooming into a bruise. I did that.

Another man's hands on her body.

Pregnant.

Hands in blond hair. Mouth to mouth, fingers on her hip. Whispers on skin.

Pregnant.

You're such a fucking disappointment.

A cold, cruel laugh.

The shove out the door.

Get your hands off her.

Items in a trash bag tossed onto the lawn.

Pregnant.

Autumn, shaky as she rose, pink stealing over her cheeks.

Was going to tell you—

It was all blending together. My chest was tight, too tight. The cold air got stuck in my throat and never made it to my lungs, my vision blackening.

Such a fucking disappointment.

Autumn hurt on the ground.

Pregnant. Pregnant.

Disappointment.

Leaving her.

Fuck. I left her on the ground. I hurt her and then I left her.

Didn't I warn her? Didn't I say? *I ruin things, break them.*

And her sweet voice, that hand on my cheek. *I'm good with glue.*

There was no going back. How could this ever be repaired? What was I doing? What was she doing with me? I told her. Over and over, I told her. This was a mistake. I was a mistake. And wasn't this the proof?

I left her, pregnant, alone, on the floor.

It was all so familiar. The same hurt in their eyes. The same guilt.

No, Autumn wasn't Noemi. This was different, wasn't it?

Was this chill seeping into my skin from the air or from all I had done? Each breath a battle to pull air into my lungs, icy, bitterly tinged with regret. Farther and farther from the bar, I walked. My toes now numb. A car passed me, gray and brown mud splashing up from the tires. How long is this road? How far to the bridge across Hood Canal? How far to my home? My house.

It was never a home. Not until her.

And it wouldn't be again.

I knew you would be this way. Why I thought you could be better is beyond me.

A voice screaming. Hers? No, mine.

Then, get out.

Her amber eyes flashing, the parting shot. *You're such a fucking disappointment, Nico.*

The headlights caught me in the eyes, blinding me as the car slowed, parking on the other side of the dirt road.

With the dome light on, catching an air freshener on the vent, the beanie I kept on the dash.

My car. It was my car.

Door opening, her legs came out. Shadows fell over her face, but I knew every freckle on that nose. Had kissed each mark on her cheeks. Loved them. Loved her.

Stock still, I stared at her as she slammed the door. So many questions, so many things I want to say.

I'm sorry.

I'm an ass.

How long did you know?

Did you keep this from me?

Are you exactly like Noemi and about to break me in two?

Or am I the one who broke this apart?

Looking both ways across the street, she crossed until she was before me, pink cheeked, healthy and beautiful. She had a bruise hidden under her coat. My bruise. My fault.

I should've been on my knees begging forgiveness. Groveling, telling her she's the best thing I never knew I could have. Instead, my words were sharp-edged. "What are you doing here?"

"Picking you up." She put her hand out, the way a mother would with a petulant child, patiently beckoning. "Come on."

I stepped back, shoving my tingling hands deeper into my jean pockets, the lint and dust rough on my knuckles. "That's a terrible idea. I'm not in the right headspace right now."

Head tilted, she pursed her lips. "And you think I am?"

Eyes closed, I willed her to back away, to see reason, to leave me before I made things worse. How I didn't know, but this night proved I could do it. "Leave me alone, Autumn. I'm not worth running around town for."

The glare she sent me was so reminiscent of the expression her cousin gave me. I almost reared back. "That's not your choice to make. It is forty-two degrees, raining, and you aren't even wearing a jacket."

Oh, maybe that was why I was so cold.

"I'm fine. Leave me be." I started walking away, the gravel crunching under my boots.

"Nicolai Thomas Evjen. You get in that damn car right now," she hissed through clenched teeth, and I stopped at the tone and the curse word.

The first I had ever heard her say. It was so out of character for her, so harsh and demanding, I could barely process it.

"What?"

She stalked to the car, opening the passenger-side door. "Get in. We are adults, and I will not have you running off like some sullen teenager before we discuss this. You want to be mad at me, fine. But you're not going to walk back to Ridgewood to prove a point."

The car was warm, warmer than I normally kept it. A low song was playing on the radio, a song she played for me once. At a gas station some-where on the PCH, she showed me a video on her phone and described the symbolism: blood on a woman's red dress, a decaying pomegranate, and golden light across water. The loss of innocence and the aching desire.

Now, as the singer broke into the bridge, she jabbed the button on my stereo, shutting off the sound.

"Make yourself at home in my car," I grumbled as I buckled.

With a cold fury simmering under every word, her muscles tensed as she shifted into drive with a white-knuckle grip. "Is that really the issue here?"

"I suppose not." Slumping lower in my seat, I waited for her to speak, to berate me for all my misdeeds. All that I deserved.

The road lit up as she turned the car around, heading east instead of toward Adrian and Wren's town.

The hiss of the tires on the rain-soaked streets was the only sound in the car until we pulled out onto the main road. The headlights caught the green rolling hills of newly cut forestry and Department of Natural Resources signs. *This area was sustainably harvested in 2022, replanted efforts started in 2025.*

Miles and miles we drove. It wasn't until we reached the electronic sign about ferry wait times that I realized the low sniffling sound was Autumn beside me. In the dark, I could barely make out the track marks of tears bleeding down her cheeks.

"Are you—"

No, I couldn't ask her if she was okay. Of course, she wasn't. Neither of us were.

With one finger, she swiped the tear from her eye. "All my life, I've known what people think of me, *oh, that Autumn, she can be so naïve, so silly.*"

With a steadying breath, the truth of how she was feeling poured out of her. "But this is the first time I've ever felt like that was true. To have my hope twisted. So what? For you to get what you want from me and then leave me behind? Our baby."

"Our baby," I echoed, a hard swallow moving in my throat. "I would never do that to my child."

She nodded. "So, it's just me you don't want. Me, who you will leave at some bar. Got it."

"Don't be ridicu—"

"Don't you dare, Nicolai Evjen. I am allowed to feel however I want about this."

"You don't need to yell at me about it."

"Don't I? You don't get it both ways, Nico. You can't string me along, make me fall for you, get me pregnant, and then act like I'm the cruel one. It doesn't work that way. You lost the right to tell me how to feel when you walked away from me."

She was right. Of course, she was. I sat here in the passenger seat of my car, sulking like a child. I was wrong. But I couldn't wrap my mind around the right choice. The vision of her on the floor, of Noemi, blending into an amalgamation of all I had destroyed. Autumn wasn't her. I wasn't that man any longer, yet I still lashed out, fear stinging my questions.

"And what about my right? How long have you known and kept it from me? How long have you been lying beside me in those hotel rooms, fucking me, letting me think everything was—that you were—"

I couldn't get my words out. To the right was the last turnoff for Dabob Bay before we crossed the floating bridge. Three motorcycles parked on the side of the street overlooking the dark waters of Hood Canal.

"Was this some trap?"

My voice cracked. Under the tires, the staccato bridge grate sounded until the road gave way to cement again as we passed the western trestle.

The car jolted as she tapped on the brakes reflexively.

"A trap? What kind of trap? Do you think I planned this? Nico, do you really think I can trap you?" Her gaze darted from the bridge road before snapping back, incredulity in every breath.

Clearing my throat, I sat up straighter. To the south were little lights of the cliff-side houses along the canal. A sailboat moored east, the waxing moon cast a wavering reflection on the smooth water. The tide was going out. "I didn't think you could lie either, but here we are."

"Lying? When did I lie?" We passed the drawspan tower in the center, the county line sign ahead. The last stretch before we were almost home, before this would have to be a conversation in the real world and not in this car.

"You've been lying since the moment you knew you were carrying my baby and didn't tell me. The moment your cousin knew, but I didn't. I should have been the first."

"It was thirty minutes. I took a test. It was supposed to be a silly party game but then—" Pulling her lower lip between her teeth, she bit down until the pink flesh was white.

"So, you didn't know? You weren't keeping it from me?"

She snorted out a huffed laugh. "I found out half an hour before we showed up at the bar. Do you really think me capable of keeping something like that for you?"

No, of course she wouldn't. Autumn was never the type. And wasn't that almost worse? Pure and sweet and good. Getting to have this part of her would be my greatest sin.

"My friends don't tell me secrets because I accidentally blurt them out. I wish I could be mysterious, and all, but I'm not Nicolai. And you should know that."

I did.

"That you think me capable of deceiving you, of being some—I don't even know what kind of woman—is so insulting. And then you left me. You heard the news, and the first thing you did was leave me."

"You fell. My elbow struck you, and you fell." I bellowed, shocking both of us with my volume. "Tell me there isn't a bruise on your chest right now.

You can't. I did that."

She shook her head, slowing as the bridge grate once again clacked under the tires, and then we were back on land. "No, the man who sucker-punched you did that."

Anger boiled up inside me.

"Don't make excuses for me. I know what I did."

In a sudden motion, she slammed on the brakes, jerking the wheel to the side where we passed over the rumble strips to rest on the highway. The car's gearshift clunked as she rammed it upward, and I would have winced at the transmission's impact if I were thinking clearly. She faced me, her eyes big with fury.

"And what do you think you're supposed to be punished for? I'm not making excuses for you. These are the facts. You got into a stupid fight with a drunk guy; you bumped into me. You didn't try to hurt me. You were, in your misguided way, thinking you were protecting me."

"Yes, but—"

"I'm not finished. Until that point, you did nothing wrong. Until you left me. Until you heard that word and ran off like a scared child instead of the adult you've been telling me you are. That was what hurt me. I don't care about a bruise. I was in the wrong place at the wrong time. But you took off like I mean nothing to you, as if what we shared was—was—" Tears streamed down her face, angry and blotchy. "I'm scared. Nico. And all I needed in that moment was for you to help me up and to tell me we'd be okay. Instead, you were a coward."

The words exactly how Noemi said them. I was a coward. A disappointment. My head hit the window as I stared up at the ceiling. "I told you not to get involved with me."

Hand over her mouth, she squeezed her eyes shut, the shimmer of wetness clinging to her lashes. Her voice was sorrowfully low. "So, it's my fault?"

The splinter of ice that wedged itself into my chest for the past hour split me open, a dread coursing through me. It was nothing I didn't already know. Nothing that I didn't tell myself. Yet seeing Autumn, tear-stained, the words I deserved coming from her sweet mouth, the sensation was worse than anything I said to myself.

"No, of course not. That's not what I meant." I was so exhausted—the weight of all that was discovered, the drinks, the fight, a baby. It was too much. "I did. You do but—"

"But what?"

"It wasn't supposed to be this way. You can't come into my life, turn everything upside down in a single fortnight and expect me to know what to do. Because I don't. I was fine before you. Almost happy and now—" I swallowed. "I freaked out, okay? I was a massive asshole; the same way I told you I would be. And I'm not blaming you, but trusting others, having faith? That's who you are, not me."

Autumn's jaw tensed, her shoulders rising and falling as she stared at me for five long heartbeats before blowing out through pursed lips as if a candle was before her. "I'm tired of everyone else telling me who and what I am."

Without a word, Autumn straightened in the driver's seat. A long-stretched silence settled between us. During the ten minutes on my way home, the only sound was the rain on the windshield and the whoosh of cars as they passed in the opposite direction. A large rain-blackened maple leaf clung to the side mirror, battered by speed.

The lights had been left on in my kitchen, a white beacon of a home Autumn might not want to be a part of.

"Are you coming in, can we talk more?" I asked.

The set of her mouth resolute as she followed me into the house. "I need my keys."

The dull slap of her tennis shoes on my hardwood floor as she made her way into my kitchen. The same place where I kissed her soundly only days before. Where I laid her on top of the counter and devoured her like she was my personal feast. The place where I loved her.

The keys to the Eagle in her hand, she wound her fingers through the little keychain, the neon cactus she got outside Sedona still hanging from it. *Looking sharp.* Sharp. Everything was cutting tonight, slicing my world apart.

Her bright and warm face weary as she stared at me over the island.

"So, what are you asking me to do? To forgive this? To act as if it never happened? Summer saw you. She's probably already told my entire family about it, and we're going to have enough of a mess without you taking off on me." She pursed her lips, tapping out a rhythm over her closed mouth as if to keep the words inside.

"If I could go back, I would—"

What? Not punch that guy? Catch Autumn before she fell? Not yell and accuse her of things that she would never do?

"—I'm just sorry."

"I know you are, Nicolai," she breathed out. "But sometimes sorry isn't enough, is it? We have so much more we need to talk about and—" With a steadying inhale, she dropped her hand, her eyes determined. "Actually, I take that back. I don't want to hear anything more from you. You were right to warn me. Neither of us is in a headspace. It's been a stressful night, and I think I need some time to think."

"So that's it? You're done with me?" I asked. "You said you wouldn't leave me."

Snorting, she squeezed her eyes shut, squinching up her face as if in pain. Once again, she exhaled as if she was blowing out a candle. Those perfect lips rounded in an "o." shape, a cupid's bow pink. When she opened her eyes, the blue was darker, wary and sad. "We both said a lot of things, but no, I'm done with *tonight.* You and I are a wholly different subject. I'll be back in the morning when you are sober, and I've had more than half an hour to process everything."

It was the soft pad of her footsteps down the hall, the click of the lock and the empty hum of my fridge as I was left alone.

Allowing myself time to wallow, I sat on a stool at the counter, the cold marble hard under my elbows as I reimagined the whole night. How everything had gone spectacularly wrong. The feel of her lips on mine as I kissed her against Wren and Adrian's house only hours before. The weight of her hand on my leg at the bar, steady and warm. The betrayal on her face as I turned away as she tried to get up from the floor.

You can't string me along, make me fall for you, get me pregnant and then act like I'm the cruel one.

The moment I kissed her on my dock, I was fucked. But it was too late to take it back. In no world would I be enough to deserve her, but I had her, didn't I? So what if it was selfish of me to take this golden opportunity? Hadn't I already wanted this? That moment at the brewery in Cape Rose. I wanted to see her full of me, to know that she was mine in a way no one else could claim. That if we made this mistake, she would have to stay with me.

I wanted this, and selfishly, I wouldn't let her go.

It was wrong and possessive and horrible of me. But it was mine. She was mine.

If only I could figure out a way to prove it all to her.

Flipping my laptop open, I had some research to do.

The indigo sky turned to pink streaks of dawn through the east-facing window. My eyelids grew heavy before I pulled my aching body from the stool to crash onto my covers. Two hours later, I awoke and continued my search. No matter what, I wouldn't ruin this opportunity for us. I may have been the one in ruins, but maybe this time I could be the one with glue.

POINT V-RIDGEWOOD, WA

Autumn

WHEN MY FATHER WAS seventeen years old, he told his mother he was going to the local fair in town. Instead of denying him, my bird-boned grandmother hurled a family sized can of soup at his head as he was leaving. Over fifty years later, he still has the scar. When his hairline began to recede, the pink and white jagged mark shone against his weather-worn skin.

In today's world, the life he lived would have been abusive. But in rural Idaho, years ago, it was just the way it was. He never called her mom, only referred to her as Gertie.

A few years ago, I saw a clip of one of those cop reality shows. An officer came to a woman's home and took a report for a domestic incident. A woman, insulted by her daughter-in-law being rude, picked up a full can of corn and threw it at her daughter-in-law. The cameras followed the woman into the woods, where the grainy footage focused in on the exploded can, yellow kernels dotting the brown pine needle ground beside broken eyeglasses.

"She pissed me off something bad, so yeah, I threw that corn a 'er. And

I'd do it again," the woman said, taunting as her washed-out gray bra strap fell off her shoulder.

When I showed my father, he laughed harder than I had seen in years. "Just like Gertie."

To this day, he texts me out of the blue. *Just watched the corn video. Still my favorite.*

When my dad would talk of his mother, it was never with malice. He would regale strangers with the soup can story as if it was a funny anecdote and not a cause for potential head trauma. He told a lot of stories this way. The time she threw his favorite stuffed animal in the fire because he was too old for toys. The way his father would hit him with the frying pan cord. To him, it was just another joke, another kooky thing parents did back then.

Never once did my father raise a hand to me, but he would squeeze my upper arm tight in his grip and hiss through his teeth to *knock it off*. He would fill his travel mug with box wine and sip it all day.

My mom told me once that all parents want is to do better than their parents. I guess, in a way, that was him doing better.

Was this baby going to be better off with only me? Was forgiving Nico for his mistake dooming us to a life where his first instinct would be to run? I knew he would have a reaction; it was a life-changing revelation, but I never imagined he would run from me.

I was never good at listening to common sense. It took all I had to be rational to leave when all I wanted to do was sink back into him. To tell him his reaction was only trauma. But what was I doing to myself if I allowed him this?

The second the line appeared on that stick, my entire world shifted beneath me. I was going to be a mother.

The other three tests I picked up at the store on my way back to my parents confirmed it all. One false positive might happen. But four—or five, depending on which one from the roulette game was mine—there was no way.

Not sure why I was doing it, I stuck the tests in a plastic bag and shoved them in my purse. It was gross, sure, but I needed the little lined reminders. I wasn't imagining it. Needed the proof when I spoke to Nico today about our future, whatever that may hold.

A dark part of me reveled in this. I could never aspire to be conniving or malicious, but this opportunity to have a piece of him? Since I was eight years old, I had held Nicolai Thomas Evjen in a corner of my heart. To know irrevocably that whatever came next meant I could keep him? I hated how much I wanted it.

It was foolish. I always had been. This wasn't an impromptu trip to Eastern Washington for a concert. Or the time Devin forgot the marina keys, so I had to jump off the dock, swim around the entrance, and let everyone in—dripping boat oil, salt water, and who knows what else across the decking. It wasn't half-baked business ideas or my countless crafts I abandoned after they got too boring. This was a child. A baby.

My parents would be pissed, my brothers more so. Summer would absolutely skewer me for this, call me an idiot, immature, irresponsible. And yet a deep, aching part of me knew I wanted this baby.

Nico's house was still as I approached. He really needed a pet here, with all those cold corners, with not a single furry creature? It was obscene. At the door, I raised my hand to knock, only to have it open before my fist hit the wood. Nico stood on the other side, purple circles coloring under bloodshot eyes, his skin washed out and gray.

"Hey," he breathed out, relief coating his voice at the sight of me.

"Hi."

With his hand on the door, he pushed it open wider, so I could come in but didn't move his arm, so I had to duck under. Stopping at the threshold, I glanced up at him. Barely ten seconds in his presence, and I could feel my resolve crumbling. Those serious green irises studied me, deep forest moss and shallow tides kelp. His gaze raked over my eyes, my mouth, before dropping over my throat, lower to linger on my chest, where his elbow struck me the night before. His jaw tensed at the discoloration there so faint I had to squint earlier to see.

"It doesn't hurt." Touching him was a mistake, not when I was all mixed up about the future, but still I took his hand, placing it over my heart. "See? Barely even a mark."

"Barely isn't enough," he mumbled, his thumb rubbing along the base of my throat.

Heat flared from his touch, and I dropped his hand, stepping away.

With his hands shoved in his jean pockets, he rocked back on his heels. "You want some coffee or, um—" He furrowed his brow. "I looked it up last night and peppermint or lemon tea is supposed to be good for morning sickness, I don't have any, but I can run to the store if you, I mean, do you have—do you feel—" He swallowed, his chin tilted up as he struggled for words, his eyes on the oversized light fixture embedded in his high exposed wood ceiling.

"You don't need to go to the store. Water would be fine."

Down the hall, I followed him into the kitchen. On the marble counter was his laptop, open to a baby website, with a picture of a poppy seed on the screen. As he filled the glass from the faucet, I read over the page.

"Were you looking up pregnancy stuff before I came over?"

With the glass set beside me, he turned the laptop to himself. "Yeah, a few things." He scratched his jaw with his thumbnail, his cheeks flaring pink. "I kind of went down a research hole last night, and this morning and—"

"Did you sleep?" I raised a brow.

"A little. An hour."

"That's not enough."

"I had some stuff on my mind."

Didn't I know it? Trailing my finger over the rim of the glass, I opened my mouth to say something, then closed it. The night before, when I had been so full of indignation and fear, I had plenty to say, but since then, all I had was uncertainty.

Yes, I knew what I wanted, but there was only his reaction at the bar to tell me how he felt about the news, and if that was his true feelings, I was alone in this.

With my chin, I motioned to the open computer screen. "I'm farther along, by the way. I'm pretty sure it was the first night back in August. If it were from the road trip, the test wouldn't have worked."

A mug of coffee in his hand, he froze, his gaze darting from me to the computer screen and back again.

"Are you sure?"

I nodded, gripping the glass of water, the cold pressure centering me. "I'm either thirteen weeks pregnant or four days and, let's be honest here, that first night seems more likely, doesn't it? Remember how that condom broke in Marina Del Sol? You said it was expired?"

Color drained from his face at this revelation, and his Adam's apple bobbed.

"Three months." His coffee mug made a cracking noise as he set it down on the countertop. "That changes things for you."

For me. Not him?

Hands in his pockets, he turned to his large kitchen window overlooking the Strait of Jasper Pass. A muscle in his jaw ticked, and his shoulders rose and fell with each inhale and exhale. When he turned back to me, his expression was schooled blank. "You want to go down to the dock with me? It's almost nice out."

Yes, fresh air, salt breeze, the nip of the water before me—that would help. Nodding, I led the way. The fall day was a beautiful display of Pacific Northwest majesty. Opal skies, the writhing Salish Sea, the forest obscured mansions across the strait. The blend of red, yellow, and orange deciduous trees beside the evergreens. In the distance, a small dot of a ferry in the water. Across Puget Sound was the gleaming jewel of Seattle.

He helped me sit on the edge, taking our places exactly as we did before. Even through my thick overalls, I could feel the grit of the dock on my thighs. Crossing my legs, I leaned forward, watching over the edge into the darkness of the Sound. A clump of mussels clung to the underside and a bright patch of seaweed floated by. *Ulva Lactuca*, common sea lettuce. *Mytilus Edulis*, blue mussel.

"So, you're sure."

"I took three more tests last night." Fishing around in my bag, I produced the evidence, holding it out. "In case you want to see."

The corner of his mouth quirked up before he covered his face with his hand. "I believe you."

"Before last night, I had never taken a test before. Have you—"

Of course he had. He told me that Noemi was pregnant. They probably took the test together, cried over the results, celebrated with friends and family. Heck, maybe they had even planned the pregnancy? It was entirely possible, and this situation couldn't have been more different.

"She went to the doctor. Before Noemi and after her, I always used protection and then with her it was—" He gulped, his gaze hard on a passing sailboat making its way under the Jasper Pass Bridge. "This is new to me, too."

"This is all very sudden." I couldn't keep the hesitancy out of my voice. "I don't know what you want, if you know, even?"

We had only started whatever this was less than a week before. A week. Even if you counted the night we spent together over the summer, it was only three months. What was I thinking, wanting him to agree to this? He wouldn't want the risk, not with me.

Yeah, he said he'd take care of me, but that meant taking me on dates, introducing me to his friends, a slow build. Right now, through a half fluke, my cousin, and only one of my brothers, knew we started dating, and now? A baby before we even had the chance to settle back into life? Heck, I was still living out of my suitcase from the road trip.

He shoved his hands in his pockets, his gaze darting away from mine. "I want what you want."

From the black depths of the water, a little school of silver fish appeared in a whirl. Silver Smelt? Maybe Pacific Herring, it was too hard to tell from this angle.

"And what do you think I want, Nico?"

"To finish school, start your career, to be young." He sighed heavily, his voice dropping lower. "To be free."

My eyes snapped to his. A muscle ticked in his jaw as he inhaled through his nose, careful, slowly as if he was schooling his features.

"You think I couldn't handle it?"

With this, his head whipped toward me, his eyes wide. "Of course you could. You'd be an amazing mother."

Warmth bloomed over me. Those words. Sacred, trusting. A baby wasn't a plant. Until he said those words, I hadn't thought of the faith he had to have to say them. Had anyone ever considered me that way before?

Scrubbing a hand over his face, he shook his head at me. "But think long and hard if I'm the guy you want to waste your youth on, Autumn."

Narrowing my eyes, I studied him. I might not be the best at reading people, but with Nico, I could. Yet something else was simmering under his words. "That's not an answer."

"It's all I'm going to give you. I won't tell you what to do. It's your choice. It's only ever been your choice."

Somewhere in Puget Sound, *Enteroctopus Dofleini*, the giant Pacific octopus, lived deep in the intertidal zone, thousands of feet below the surface. They stayed stationary, or in hiding for over ninety percent of their lives.

Until a few months ago, I had felt the same way. Left behind as everyone else was moving on. Now it was as if I were barreling down a path I had no idea how to navigate correctly.

Tapping my nail on the dock beside me, I swallowed hard. That morning's affirmation repeating in my head.

My intuition guides me wisely.

"I'm keeping it. I thought about it all night and while everyone is going to question me, deep down I—" Glancing across the bay, I tried to conjure what life might be like if I made a different choice but couldn't come up with an image. When that second line appeared, I felt more resolute than ever before. "This is the right choice for me."

"Okay, let's have a baby then." He nodded as if this were all a normal conversation. As if I hadn't just made an irrevocable decision for both of us.

"You're not going to talk me out of it?" I asked.

He shook his head. "I told you; it's your choice."

"It's yours too," I reminded him.

His knuckles grew white as he clasped his hands. "Autumn, I'm thirty-eight years old. I'd be an idiot to think I have all the time in the world to have a child. I told you already, I'll take care of you. Whatever that entails."

"And what does that entail? To you? Because if last night was any indication, we are going to have some issues."

The long silence stretched before us, the lapping of the waves on the dock. "I know I told you already, but I am sorry about the way I handled the news." He leaned in closer to me, his hand raised over my cheek, not quite touching me. "I missed you last night."

"Don't"—I twisted away— "say things you don't mean; give me hope. Just. Don't."

"But I mean it. I want you to hope. To want." With a hand raised, he tucked a wayward strand of hair behind my ear, his fingers brushing against the hollow under my ear.

With one hand, I pushed against his chest, holding him still, hoping my voice wouldn't shake. "Stop it. You can't touch me like that. We need to talk, and I can barely catch my breath when you're near me."

"And I can't when you're away from me."

His voice broke through the clear fall air.

I squeezed my eyes closed, wishing away his perfect words. "Leaving you last night, not being here, it was agony without you—we are barely starting this, and now it feels so delicate. How can I miss something we never had?"

"We could. We could have it all. It was never you, Autumn, you know that, right? You are—" He clenched his eyes, clicking his tongue against his teeth before letting out a long puff of air. "You're joy and calm and steadiness, and how could I ever deserve that? After everything, to use you, for you to have my baby? To be worthy of you?"

Now here was the second crux. We'd be parents, yes. But together? In love the way I had hoped for?

I didn't know. How could I love someone who never let me truly know him? He spoke long and hard about how he was poison, how he ruined things. At what point do you let those things go? At what point does he need to save himself?

The time spent with Nico had opened me up to feeling things I never imagined I could, but it also emboldened me. For him to run when I needed him most. Without a real justification, without letting me in and giving me a reason, there was no world in which I could stay with him. Squeezing my eyes shut, I willed the words out. The urge to smooth things over, to make peace, almost overwhelmed me.

"Those are pretty words that are far too late. If I told you that one of my exes did what you did, you would tell me never to speak to him again. For the past week, you've gone on and on about what I deserve. Acting like the jokes my father made about my driving or the teasing Summer does about sea cucumbers is some affront to me. But you leave me moments after finding out I'm probably pregnant, and I'm supposed to get over that? You're the one who's been telling me I deserve better." My eyes flashed open, voice shaky. "Don't ask me to expect more from everyone else and then make yourself the exception."

"I don't. You deserve the world. But you said I could trust you, that you said you wouldn't leave me."

Snorting, I pressed my lips together. "I wasn't the one who left. I'm still here. Don't throw it back at me as if I went back on my promise. I've been here. But you—"

"Made a mistake. I know that."

"It was more than a mistake. It was everything you knew would break me." Pulling my legs up, I wrapped my arms around my knees. My eyes caught where the retaining wall met the beach, the dead blackberry leaves brown against the rocks.

Everything here was covered in them, creeping through the concrete, breaking apart driveways and the sides of houses. Cracking walls with their thick thorns.

"You told me that your saving grace is that you're nice. That it hurts you to stand up to people, to be rude to them and, yet you won't give me a second chance?"

I frowned. "It's not just about me anymore. Do you think this doesn't hurt? That everything inside me is screaming about how much easier it would be to let you back in, to forgive you for abandoning me when I needed you? It would be so easy for me to open up my arms and hold you again. I know it would be. But this isn't about me. I need to be stronger for the baby. Even if I can't be for myself. And having a father in its life who will leave us when the going gets hard? Who won't open up and let someone love them? What kind of life am I dooming them to? Don't tell me what I am, Nicolai, because no matter who I was before, now I am going to be a mother. And may have failed at most things I've set out to do, but I won't fail at this. I'm having this baby, and I will be a mother. I don't need you to—"

"But I need you." His voice broke. "You said you trusted me."

I shook my head, and my jaw tensed to the point of pain. "You can't throw my words back and guilt trip me."

"I'm not trying to—"

"But you are. What have you done to show me you mean it? Why is it always me reaching out? You told me you wanted to earn it with me? Prove it. Prove you want this."

"I want every day," he pleaded. "You and the baby every day. At the home we could share. Together."

My hand tightened into a fist. "I don't know about that. You give me all these half-truths. I tell you to trust me, but you never do. What is holding you back? Is it me? Do you not want to be with me because—"

His eyes flashed wide to mine, his mouth hanging open at my question. "Of course I want you. I want this, but when I saw you on the ground, when I was the one who put you there. It was the same. You were hurt—she was hurt." He swallowed, and wetness shimmered on his lashes. His brows screwed up, motion under his lids, each letter choked out in pain. "It's my fault that Noemi and the baby died."

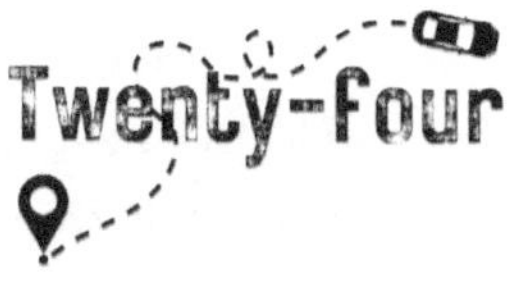

Twenty-four

POINT X-POINT OF NO RETURN

Autumn

BREATH CAUGHT IN MY throat. Beside me, his hands were bunched into fists, planted on each side of his hips. The tendons in his forearms taut as he rocked back and forth. It was as if the memory was overtaking him. Long, dark eyelashes fluttered shut as he parsed the next part out. "I think part of me didn't want you to know. To me, you're so good, so pure, and what happened that night, the part I played in it. I'm not proud of myself."

There were times to allow him his space, but in light of the night before, I couldn't do it any longer. What we could be needed absolute trust, and only he could give me a reason. "I need to know. Whatever it is, it's obviously what's holding you back."

He nodded slowly. "I told you about Noemi, how she was in a car accident. I was ashamed for you to know the truth. It was my fault she was so upset that night. That she was driving alone so late on that road. If I had only made her stay, maybe she would have—" He swallowed hard. "But I didn't. I was angry and told her to get out of my house, that I never wanted to see her again."

Between us, I set my palm over the back of his fist. "Oh, Nicolai."

Maybe it was his full name or the soft way I asked. Whatever the key was, I couldn't say. All I knew was he began to speak, slow at first and then faster, the words tumbling out of him like a river over stones.

"When I told you she was pregnant, that part was true, but that day, we had a party at the house, nothing big, a few of my friends, a few of her work colleagues. She disappeared for twenty minutes, and when I went to look for her, I found her with another man. There's always the one, right? The *don't worry about him. He's a friend, yes, isn't he so funny. Didn't I mention he's on the board of such-and-such charity? Isn't that nice?* In a way, I think I knew what I would find, but that still didn't stop my reaction. I flew into a rage. Kicked everyone out of the party. She broke down and confessed that she had been seeing this other guy behind my back for months. *Months.* They had a connection, and it *just happened.* That she still wanted to stay with me, and it was a mistake. She told me that when I proposed, she got scared and thought she had to say yes because I did it in front of all our friends." He shook his head. "Friends. They all knew about him and Noemi, by the way. Some friends."

I opened my mouth, with the question posed on my lips, but stopped myself. These were the same friends from San Jose.

Eyes far away as he spoke, Nico tapped his hand against his thigh. "And then I remembered about the baby. We found out only three weeks before, and at first, I thought maybe I could forgive her. I had always wanted to be a father, and maybe she and I could work it out. Except it wasn't my baby, was it? It was his. *Unequivocally* was the word she used. There was no way it was mine."

I froze, taking in this new information.

"When she told me this, it was like a switch flipped in my mind. I was so angry. I grabbed her bag and her coat and threw them on the lawn. I put my hands on her shoulders and pushed her out the door. I pushed her,

Autumn, that was how angry I was."

"Did she fall?" I whispered.

Nico shook his head. "No, she stumbled, but I still put my hand on her. I never thought I was capable of—"

The night before started adding up for me. The fear in his eyes at seeing me on the floor. Summer shouting that I was pregnant. The way his gaze became haunted and never ceased, how he could barely catch his breath on the side of the road.

"But you didn't actually hurt her."

"Hurt her?" he snorted. "She didn't make it fifteen miles before she crossed the double yellow and hit a truck head-on. And who is to blame for that?"

"Was it—" I swallowed, opening and then shutting my mouth. Like a movie playing out in my head, I could see it; the shouting, her getting in the car, the bright lights on the road and then nothing. "Did she—"

He shook his head. "I don't know. I'll never know if she was too emotional and couldn't see, or if it was the late conditions, or if it was on purpose. All I know is I pushed her out the door, a pregnant woman I thought I loved, and her last words to me were, *'You're such a fucking disappointment, Nic.'*"

My own words from the night before rush back. I called him a coward. And he just stood there and nodded, like he deserved it, took it, and would have accepted more. Because that was the last thing he knew.

Then I was crying. For Nico—for all the ways he could not believe in himself, for how he refused to forgive himself and take his second chance in life in stride. Tears streamed down my face for myself. For not understanding until I almost lost him, I had been doing the same thing.

"So that's what all this is about? Do you really think our situations are the same?" I asked, not bothering to wipe the tears from my face.

"No, but to see you on the ground, to hear that you were, *are*, pregnant, it was all—"

With his eyes closed, he seemed to be back in that place, eight years ago. San Jose with a beautiful but cruel fiancée. His mind so far away now. It was visceral, the way he refused to let go of the past, allowing it to burrow inside him. Once again, I glanced at the blackberry bushes. An aggressively invasive species, even as the season grew cold, it would return stronger than ever come spring. Unless you cut them back, destroy them at the root.

"I'm not Noemi. I could never do something like that. Fuck that and fuck you for thinking for a minute that I would ever hurt you." The curse was foreign on my tongue, twisting heavy and harsh. It had been years since I swore at all, let alone said fuck aloud. But if anything called for the expletive, it was the harm Noemi did to Nico. To us and the future we could have. Sucking in a big breath of air, I straightened up, my bleary eyes set on him. He watched me as if I were a caged animal. "And fuck your ex for making you feel that way."

His mouth opened and shut in surprise, his eyes clearing.

"You didn't deserve that." Rising, I wiped the grains of sand and dirt away on the legs of my overalls. How could he think I was the same as his ex? That I would ever be that kind of person? Did he not know me at all? It all made sense, yet how would we get past this? What was the next step? "But I never deserved to be left last night."

Stalking to the bottom of the stairs, I placed a hand on the railing. I couldn't look at him, with remorse coating each word, the hurt painting his gaze the deepest green. The aching to pull him close and say all is forgiven. If I didn't take a step back and breath I might drown in him. A scrambling rustled behind me and then he was there, his grip on my waist, turning me. Cupping my cheek, he leaned into my space, his eyes boring into mine.

"Please, please let me fix this. Please. Please don't . . . please don't . . . please don't leave me."

He choked out the last words, and I froze.

I was angry to a point I had never been. Not when Ryan Willnik dumped me a day before Tolo to go with Bobbie Carlin instead. Or when Tommy Holiday called Devin a slur in front of the class while we learned about WWII. Not even when Professor Caro failed me on my Chemistry of Marine Organic Carbon final because she didn't like the way I cited my sources.

Angrier than all those moments combined. But the idea I would leave him had never even entered my mind. He was going to be the father of my child. I had loved him for years.

"I'm not leaving you, Nico." The words trembled as I leaned into his palm. "Did you think I was leaving for good?"

"You stood up and walked over here and—"

"I needed a second. It was a lot to take in, and yeah, I'm mad. At you. At your ex. But I'm not some delicate flower who is going to run from this. I fight for what I believe in."

"And you believe in me?" he asked, the question full of desperation.

"Us," I corrected. "I want to. If you'll only do the same."

"How do I do that? Can I drag you down with me? How can I ask you to stay? I spent a single night away from you and already I miss you. Before you it was like I was in this stasis, go to work, see my friends, I thought I was happy enough, that my life was enough and then you—" His head twisted away, and he took in a deep inhale of the crisp fall air. "I didn't know how much I was broken until you were there to heal me. Not by the things you do or give me and not because of the baby. In a way, I think I knew that first night we spent together on my dock. Just as you are, you've saved me. No one had ever loved me the way you do. And you give it so easily. To your family, your friends. To me. Even when I never earned that love."

I tilted my head, wanting so badly to resist, to not let his words strike the parts of me that always craved them. "Love isn't something you earn. It can't be. It has nothing to do with money or status. It's being in the moment with that person every day. Choosing them repeatedly."

His arms encircled my waist, pulling my face into the crook of his neck as his fingers wove through my hair, bringing me close. His mouth was hot on the side of my cheek and an exhale ghosted over my skin as he dragged air into his lungs, then let it back out again. Each breath eased the strain, and I stroked his lower back in soothing circles as he took in uneven breaths.

"Once again, you are wiser than me."

"All I need to know is, you won't leave me again? Babies are hard. No one has ever said that having a child makes a relationship easier. So, what's going to happen in nine months when we're both sleep deprived, and I'm covered in stretch marks, and you are working two jobs to make ends meet—"

"I really don't think you understand how much money I still make from Fetch Spot, so I won't need a second job."

"—And I'm cranky, and you're cranky, and we can't go out to the bars every night."

"I'm thirty-eight. It takes me a week to recover from a single night at a bar."

"What then?"

Cupping my cheeks, he steadied my face. "Then we will alternate who naps while the other is with the baby. I'll hire a nanny, hell, even a night nanny. You want me to go to therapy, I'll go. To sleep on the couch so the baby has the whole bed to himself? I'll grab a pillow. You think there is a world where I wouldn't love every inch of your skin? That something like stretch marks would change the way I look at you?"

"You don't know what I'm going to look like in a few months. You might change your mind."

"That is our baby. Those are my marks, my proof of what we made together just as much as it's yours. I will love every scar because it is a symbol of the life we made together."

Tears were springing from my eyes as I shook my head weakly. "Why do you have to say the exact right thing? Why can't I stay mad at you?"

"Because you don't have it in you. If you truly felt nothing for me any longer, you wouldn't be this upset. I know you can raise this baby yourself. You're smart and strong and determined. I'm not asking you to take me back right away but—"

"Nico, I can't take you back because I never let you go. There is no back." I wiped my tears from my eyes. "I'm going to be angry with you for a long while about this."

"Good, that way I can spend the rest of my life finding ways to earn your forgiveness. I told you I'm impossibly selfish. I love you, and all I want to be is enough for you."

"Say it again." I urged.

"I love you."

New tears formed in my eyes. Salt brine and sweetness.

"Tactil?"

"Ti amo con tutto il cuore, I love you with all my heart."

"Ceaselessly?"

"Ceaselessly. I don't know how to do it. How to be what you deserve."

"It's a choice. Choose me once, then choose us again. Every day you repeat. Until it gets easier to trust this love. To know being you is enough for me, for this baby. You choose this family, and you don't look back on the pain you think you deserve."

When his lips slid against mine, it was with the desperation of knowing that we had started on forever. This was it for me, for him. Everything would shift beneath us, and we'd be on this path together.

"Take me to our bed," I murmured against his mouth. It wasn't ours. It never had been, but I couldn't stop the words.

Couldn't wish to take them back.

"Our bed," he hummed against my neck as his hand darted down my side to grip my ass. "I like the sound of that. It is our bed. Our house, our life."

We fumbled up the stairs from the beach, his hands on my body, his lips on my neck. I stumbled a bit on the steps, and he was there to catch me, to steady me. To whisper all the dirty things he would do once we got up to the house.

At the top of the stairs, he kissed me, his teeth scraping over my bottom lip as I rolled my hips against his. The slow sweep of his tongue soothed the sting of his bite, the filthy roll of our hips together as we walked to the door, our feet unsure, hands and mouths still connected. His hard length rubbed deliciously against my core, and I needed more. To be in his house, in his bed. For him to take all of me, and for him to know that I was never going to let him go now. For him to give me all of himself in return.

His strong hands swooped under my legs, my arms going around his neck as he carried me bridal style down the hall. With one foot, he kicked open the door to his bedroom.

The last time I was here, it was night, I couldn't appreciate the view from the window of the water, the sun heavy in the midday sky. The large white bed in the center, the plush pillow, and downy blanket on the bed he hadn't made earlier from his one or two hours of sleep. I wondered if the people across the strait in Manzanita could see us. But he could have me pressed naked against that oversized window overlooking Jasper Pass, and no one could ever know.

We fell back together, his mouth leaving mine as I bounced on the bed. His teeth scraping down the column of my throat, admissions, and endearments searing into me, more sensation than anything.

"So good, mine, all mine. Forever, forever mine. Fucking fill you up. Mine, mine, mine."

As he moved down my body, he unfastened my overalls, really the most unsexy of all garments, the corduroy and cotton being tugged down my body and thrown to the side of the room. At my exposed waist he paused under my belly button, the curve of something I had assumed was bloating for weeks, nothing noticeable under clothes but flat on my back there was a hardness to the area.

"The website earlier said it was a poppy seed, but it's bigger, isn't it?" he asked, his breath warm on my skin. "What size is it?"

"If it were fruit, it would be a plum, I think."

A vibration of affection hummed over me as he kissed the area, his nose brushing over me, his lips soft and warm. There was a low noise I couldn't quite make out until I caught half words: *love, daddy, good, take care, love, love, love.*

With one hand, he held me steady. His chanting waned as he searched me. "This is more than I've ever wanted. You—" He kissed my belly once more, ducking his head down to rest his cheek on my lower stomach. "This, us. Thank you."

An overwhelming expanse formed under my skin, swelling from my chest through my body, filling me with warmth. My breath caught in my throat as I struggled to suck in air because there was no room, no space for air when I was so full of this light, this happiness. Tears pooled at the edges of my lashes, clinging furtively before dripping over my temple and into my hair.

"Show me." Dragging my hands through his hair, I pulled his face up to look at me. "Earn it again."

"Every day, love. I'll try every day." With this, he dipped lower, pulling my underwear down. Arousal pooled between my legs as his mouth moved from my belly, lower until his breath was warm on my inner thigh. "So beautiful. You going to be my sweet girl for me?"

"Always." I gasped as his finger parted my folds, his fingers curling inside me the way I needed.

His thumb was on my clit, rubbing a small circle as he drove in and out of me.

One hand on my hip. The other laced with mine, our fingers entwined as he pressed his mouth to my core. His tongue flicked through my folds and onto my clit. Stars appeared behind my eyes as he delved deeper, licking my seam before coming back to my clit. My thighs tightened around his head, my free hand buried in his hair. His tongue rolled over me, sparking heat and pleasure through my body.

"Please, I need, I-I—" I begged for something, my vision blurring as he sucked harder, two fingers slipping inside me. His face a dripping mess.

"You're so pretty when you beg," he murmured. "Taste even better too."

I had been close to him countless times now, but this was a baring I never knew. Each flick of his thumb, each lick and dip of his tongue was an endearment.

I was coming undone—his words, his tongue, the way his hand was firm on my hip, forcing me to experience every lick and every touch. If I wasn't already his, he possessed me irrevocably.

My gasps echoed around the room, my legs a vise on his head as I spasmed under him. Bringing my hand over my mouth, I tried to stifle the cries as I came, deep and hard. Blackness spotted behind my eyelids as all strength left my body, replaced by a wave of warm tingles.

His face appeared above mine, sporting that beautiful self-satisfied smirk. Before I could say anything, he silenced me with a searing kiss. In one fluid motion, he pinned my hands above my head, his weight pressing me into the mattress as I tasted myself on his tongue; salt and musk.

I moaned into his mouth, a deep, aching guttural as his hands grasped my butt, bringing me flush with him. He swallowed down the sounds if they belonged to him. I had no words left as he thrust into me with enough force to make me cry out, and my ankles instinctively locked around his hips. He was bare, nothing between us, no condom, no fabric. I took all of him inside me and could weep at the sensation of his skin on mine.

"You come so pretty. I need it again." He rolled his hips in a figure eight, his cock hitting the spot that flared with pleasure deep inside as he murmured darkly against my lips. "You're mine. And I take care of what's mine."

"Yours," I gasped out as he sank deeper inside me, and he paused, his green eyes flashing as he stared down at me. "Take what's yours."

"Say it again."

Dragging a hand over his chest, I left little pink marks on his skin with my short nails. "Yes, take me, Nicolai. Make me yours."

He had all of me.

POINT Y-RIDGEWOOD, WA

Nico

LOST IN HOW BEAUTIFUL she is in those moments when she gives herself over to me, I savored each gasp and moan she gave. Long have I prided myself on not needing anyone close and then she gazed at me, and I was undone.

I've never understood the phrase *heart eyes* when describing a person. Not until Autumn. Because her emotions were plain on her face. The trust, the love. If I were a less selfish man, maybe I wouldn't savor them as much as I do.

With her chin on my chest, she smiled up at me. I'm sure for the first time in my life, I too had heart eyes, dopey, tenderhearted, careless love beaming out of each glance. I can't help it with her. Maybe I never could.

In the end, it doesn't matter if I don't think I'm enough for her. She did. And who was I to refuse her anything she wanted?

"Nicolai," she murmured into my chest.

I raised my head to catch her gaze. "Yeah?"

She grinned at me, that bright sunrise over the desert smile, and I couldn't help but return it.

"I just wanted to say your name. Nicolai and Autumn. Autumn and Nicolai."

"Nico, Autumn, and Nico Junior."

She swatted at my stomach playfully. "There will be no juniors."

"Not even Autumn Junior?"

"Not even that."

The sky grew dark outside my window, the pink to purple to indigo to black. The past few hours slipped over us from sex, to orgasms, talk and drift off to sleep, to repeat.

We found each other in our sleep, reaching, our legs tangling together, hands on hips and fingers on breasts. Checking, then double-checking that the other is still there, that this wasn't a dream. That we have tomorrow. When we woke, it was with the gray of clouds and the coral of dawn. How many sunrises would we have now? How many in a year, in a decade? In the rest of this lifetime?

As the clock approached ten a.m., I slipped out of bed, headed to the kitchen to make her some breakfast. Toast, barely brown, no heels—I'll eat those. Orange juice and bacon, not sausage. Eggs over hard because I can't have her get sick from an undercooked yolk.

When she joined me in the kitchen, she was wearing knee-high socks and my old college tee. I slid the platter over to her, wishing I had decaf coffee or tea to offer. But I didn't. I would need to go to the store soon and stock up on everything she needed.

Nibbling around the edge of the toast, crust first, she hummed to herself as I leaned against the counter, my legs crossed at the ankles and watched her.

"Move here," I ask.

The fork in her hand, laden with eggs and a piece of bacon, freezes in midair.

"What?"

"Move in with me. Come live here."

She sets the fork down. "We just got back together or together in the first place, depending on how you look at it—" She pulled up her bare wrist, examining it as if a watch sat there. "Sixteen hours ago."

"We're having a baby," I reminded her.

"Yes, I'm aware." Pulling her lower lip between her teeth, she cocked her head to the side. "Would you ask me to move in if I weren't pregnant?"

Fair question.

"Not today, no. But I would have soon. It makes sense, doesn't it?"

"I suppose." She picked up her fork, scooping her eggs and bacon back up again. "Everyone is going to think I've lost my mind." She paused, screwing her mouth up. "Actually, I doubt anyone would be surprised by me. Everyone will think you've lost your mind."

"My mind had never been clearer about anything, sweet."

I neglected to say what I really wanted to ask her was to marry me, a conversation for another day. One where I had a ring, and we had the chance to tell her family.

One thing at a time.

"Is that a no?"

"Yes."

"Yes, to it being a no?"

"Yes, to moving in. Let's do it, Nicolai."

An ever-expanding sensation erupts from my chest, a happiness I had scarcely believed in. Cupping her cheek, I rested my forehead against hers. "I love the way you say my name."

"Nicolai, Nicolai. My Nicolai." She kissed me, sweet but full of hunger, her tongue just this side of filthy in my mouth.

My hands found her ass, pulling her to me, her legs on each side of my hips. The times before, it was so slow, reverent in the darkness of my room, but in the morning's light reality would soon be at my door. I needed to feel her one more time before we had to face the world. Sliding my hand under the T-shirt, I found her completely bare for me.

"No underwear?" I asked, smiling against her lips.

"What's the point?" Moving her hand between us, she pulled down the front of my pants, freeing my cock. Her little palm hot on my length as she gripped it tight at the base. "I need to be ready for you."

Her legs wrapped around my hips, as I shuffled from the kitchen into the living room to spread her on the couch. In a single motion, I pulled the shirt over her head.

"My beautiful, sweet girl." I marveled as I covered her body with mine. The leather cold under my knees, I grabbed her wrists, pulling them up over her head and holding them together in one hand. Sinking slowly inside her, she fluttered around me. Her moan an aria.

"The way you grip my cock." I gasped out, thrusting deeper inside. "The things you do to me."

She buried her face in my neck, gasping as I pulled out to slide back in again.

The feeling of her moving around me, the sudden rhythm, my cock rubbing her walls from the inside, her cunt a tight glove. Nothing between us.

"I want to feel you come inside me," she murmured. "To keep you all day."

Fuck, if that wasn't the hottest thing ever. It was like a hurricane. All at once. She pulsed around me, clenching tighter, on the edge. Her moans turned to gasps then cries, her nails digging into the leather above her head. Shattering, she was covered in a pink flush. I dipped my head to nestle into her throat. Her thighs quaked around my hips, holding me steady.

I'd never get over this feeling.

Buried deep inside her, I understood why wars had been waged over a woman. The temptation between her thighs, the safety of its sweet warmth. What wouldn't I do for this? For her? Whatever it took to keep this, to keep her here with me. Anything. Everything. Tremors rippled through every muscle in my body. My breath fled my lungs as I came right after her.

Letting her hands go, she buried her fingers in my hair, our mouths coming together in a searing kiss.

"I could watch you come like that forever," I murmured into her jaw before pulling myself up to look at her body.

The flush of her chest, pink against brown freckles, constellations, and road maps. A pink scar on her elbow. Kiss-swollen lips, a jaw touched by my stubble, pink nipples, and a dark birthmark beneath her right breast. It felt like a lifetime before when we exchanged stories about our old injuries in that hot spring in California. A different life, as if I were a different man. She was pregnant that day.

With my baby.

My baby, my Autumn. My world.

The sight of her center, pink and shiny, my cum dripping from inside her. Dragging my thumb over her cleft, I stuffed my cum back deep inside her. I needed her to keep all of me as a reminder all day. To feel what she did to me.

With my hand firm on her lower belly, I studied her. "This is an intermission. I'm not done, you understand that? Give me ten minutes, and we're doing this again. Your cunt feels amazing around my cock right after you've come."

"You are absolutely filthy," Autumn huffed, although her eyes still gleamed with excitement.

I moved my body until I was face-to-face with Autumn, my forearms flexing on each side of her. "But," I said between a kiss, "you love that, don't you?"

Autumn let out an eager whimper from the back of her throat as she continued to seek my kisses, pressing her tongue against my lips until I opened for her. She tasted of the orange juice from breakfast, of the sweetness of the future. Autumn's tongue swirled around in my mouth as if she were trying to drink every drop of us from my lips.

"I love you." She gasped out as my kisses rained down her throat.

"Ceaselessly."

"Exactly."

The sound of tires crunching on my driveway was the first warning. Then the slam of a car door and the porch light coming on.

It was only a matter of time before the bubble we built around ourselves would be popped. We had it in the Eagle while we drove. In this house, when she was here with me and on the dock as I carried her one again up to the boathouse where we first came together.

It shouldn't have been a surprise when the first hammering of a fist on the door echoed through the house. Tossing her the discarded shirt off the floor, I pulled my pants back on as I approached the entryway.

I expected Victor Townsend or Summer, maybe even Ivan, at the door. But it was Oliver. Clothes rumpled as if he had gotten off the airplane only minutes before, instead of the hour and a half it took to drive from SeaTac.

"Oli—"

With fists clenched on both sides, he glowered at me. "Tell me my baby cousin was lying, Nic."

From deep in the house, Autumn called out, "Who is it?"

Oliver's blue eyes flashed at me, and he shouldered his way in, pushing me against the wall as he stalked to the living room to find Autumn sitting innocently on the couch, my computer on her lap and clad in my old UC Berkley tee-shirt and knee-high socks. The smell of sex lingered in the air, and I was sure that Oliver knew exactly what we had been up to only minutes before.

"Oliver, what—"

With his finger out, he motioned menacingly between us. "You two have five seconds to explain before I knock your teeth out, Evjen."

He hadn't used my last name since we were kids because I wouldn't let him ride with the very attractive, older, and very drunk Stacie Strickland.

As if her brother hadn't threatened to undo years of dentistry, Autumn calmly set the laptop down beside her and rose. The borrowed shirt fell to her mid-thigh. "What are you doing here? Is Janie okay?"

His eyes narrowed at his sister. "My wife's fine. She understands why I had to come up here."

Autumn snorted, "I doubt that. Let me guess, you heard the news, the *good news*, I should add, and flew up here to what, lecture me?" With arms crossed against her chest, she glared at Oliver.

"I'm here to make sure you're okay."

"And there is this handy thing called a phone. You didn't have to leave your pregnant and on bed rest wife here to ask me."

"I—" Oliver huffed, his nostrils flaring. Aware he wouldn't get far guilt-tripping Autumn, he rounded on me. "I told you to take care of her, not knock her up."

Autumn interjected. "Nico got me pregnant long before you asked him to help me drive up."

Oliver's eyes flashed, and his teeth snapped. "What?"

Taking a step back, I put my hands up. "Sweet. I don't think teasing your brother is a great idea right now."

"Sweet? Are you serious right now? Explain this to me because it makes no sense. Two weeks ago, you two were squawking about being in a car for a week, and now you're together and having a baby."

Autumn drummed a finger over her lips. "That feels like an oversimplification but essentially, yeah."

With his right eye spasming, Oliver stared at his younger sister, then back at me. "How?"

I winced. "You really want to know the details, bro?"

"Don't call me bro," Oliver warned, his finger in my face. "I'm not your bro, not after you, after—" He swallowed. "You were my best friend. How could you take advantage of her like that?"

"Whoa, whoa. Nope, you're not doing that." Autumn stepped between us, her hand on her brother's chest, and simmering in her matching blue eyes. "If anyone took advantage, it was me. I was the one who pursued him, I kissed him, I started this."

"And he could have said no. You're an adult, Nic. You could have told her to stop."

"No, I really couldn't have. I love her."

In the time since Autumn let me kiss her again, we had whispered it dozens of times. I painted her skin with the words, then sank inside her and as we drifted to sleep, wrapped in each other's arms. But this was the first time I proclaimed it for someone else.

It was better this way. At first, I was worried about Oliver's reaction, of her family and how they would view our relationship. But now, after almost losing her, losing this future family we created together, it was worth any risk. To keep Autumn close, I'd stand with her family, let her brother fake a punch. Whatever it took.

Autumn laced her fingers with mine. "And I—also an adult, in case you forgot—love him. We love each other, Oli. And yeah, the timing is faster than we anticipated, but I'm happy, Nicolai is too."

"Well, I'm not." Oliver puffed out his chest and grimaced at our entwined hands. "Ugh, my best friend and my sister." The corners of his mouth curled down, and he stuck his tongue out. "Blech."

"Sorry, man. It just happened." Bringing her left hand up to my mouth, I kissed her knuckles.

Soon I'd put a ring on that finger, but until then a kiss would have to do.

"Well, the family is pissed, Guppy, you really need to answer your phone.

There have to be at least a dozen voicemails waiting for you from the fam."

With this, Autumn dropped my hand, huffing out a small burst of laughter. "Oh crud, I bet it's dead. I forgot to charge it last night, and it was at twelve percent when I got here."

"You can't keep your phone charged, and we're supposed to trust that you can have a kid with this guy?" Oliver motioned to me.

From the walkway, Autumn paused. I opened my mouth to defend her, but she put up a hand, her blue eyes flashing. "Listen here. I am twenty-six years old. You don't get to lecture me about anything. You still don't know how to separate colors from darks for laundry and drink out of the milk carton."

"I do that, too," I reminded her, but she shot me a warning look.

"You be quiet." She glared at me before turning back to her brother. "Summer knew where I was. Mom and Dad could have figured it out. You seemed to easily, so what was the harm in spending time with my boyfriend?"

"Boyfriend," Oliver chirped sardonically, his grimace somehow growing deeper as he flung himself back to sit in the middle of the couch. I hoped there weren't any suspicious wet spots. "So, you're really doing this, with him?"

"I really am." Rising on her tiptoes, she planted a kiss on my cheek, chaste and sweet but enough to have Oliver gagging from his place on my couch.

"Okay, gross, I get it. Fuck. Don't have to rub it in." Grumbling, he leaned back, his arm stretched behind him. "Why don't you get me a beer, Nic? It's the least you can do after I didn't punch you when I found out."

A better trade-off than I expected.

"For the record, when you're the only one drinking the milk, it's fine to drink it from the carton." Oliver gave his parting shot, and behind Autumn's back I sent him a nod and a thumbs up.

The conversation with her parents went better and worse. Better in that, Lorelle cried and hugged me, saying she always considered me one of her boys, and now it was official. Worse, once Autumn told them the news, Victor's face got an unruly shade of purple and his breathing slowed.

Once Lorelle and Autumn were huddled on the couch, FaceTiming Janie together to squeals and comments of *"I knew something was going on with you two!"* Victor motioned for me to follow him to his garage. Being in proximity to a large number of power drills, chainsaws, and an air compressor, an entire wall of metal tools and what I was fairly sure was a scythe, was not the environment I should go into, but what other choice was there?

"So, you and Autumn," he said, leaning his hip against the side of his metal tool bench and glowering at me. "Can't say I approve of it, what with your being so much older and all."

"I know, sir, but I really care about her and want to be as involved as she'll have me."

"I'm assuming you'll marry her." He grunted. "Not to be all old-fashioned, but it's important to us. Me and Lorelle, we may have found ourselves in the family way with Oliver, but we were damn sure to be married by the time he came into the world."

I coughed. Autumn and I hadn't discussed marriage. Of course, I wasn't opposed. My father, whoever he might have been, certainly hadn't married my mother, and neither had my maternal grandparents, and the idea of breaking that generational cycle was a hopeful one.

"That's up to Autumn. Whatever she wants, I'll do."

I could already picture Autumn walking down the aisle toward me, a flowy white dress, flowers in her loose hair.

"I know you kids like to say you don't have to be married to be committed, long-term coupling or partnership or whatever you want to call it, but that's not for Autumn, I know my little girl, and she would want to be married."

"I only found out about the baby a day and a half ago, so it hadn't quite hit me yet. But I aspire to be a good parent and the best partner for Autumn."

He clapped me on the back. "Well, isn't that all we can ask for? I mean, hell, I was scared shitless when Lorelle told me she was knocked up. Of course, we were twenty, couldn't even drink, but still, no one knows what they're doing when they become a parent; you have to be there every day and learn together. But it can work if you have the right partner."

"Yes, sir." I nodded.

"Well, the egg has been scrambled, so there's little I can do about it, I guess." He frowned. "You know, my Autumn has always been a sweet little thing, but she's got a spine of steel. I know if she wants something, she'll get it, and that seems to be you."

"Believe me, I'm as shocked as you are."

"I don't need to tell you not to let her down."

"You, Oliver, Ivan, and Ewan, yeah, that's enough."

"Hell with us. It's Summer you've got to watch out for. Did you know she almost took a guy's eye out last year?" Victor chuckled in appreciation. "Hell of a girl, that one."

The specifics were news but not surprising in the least.

"If I hurt Autumn, I'd take out my eye."

Victor clapped me on the back, comforted by my self-immolation. "We don't need to go that far, though I appreciate the sentiment."

It wasn't acceptance, but it also left me with all my teeth, so I considered the exchange as fair as I would get from the Townsend patriarch.

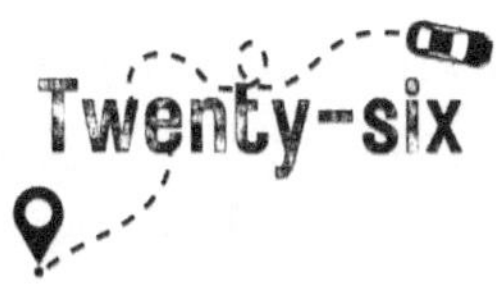

Point Z-Ridgewood Marine Science Center

Nico

I HUNG BACK IN the classroom, watching as Autumn taught her class of high schoolers. Her last class for her degree included being a student teacher in the new science class offered through Ridgewood High School and her college. In a few weeks she would graduate, and it would be only a month and a half before our baby would be born.

Autumn motioned to the screen in the front. "Now, before I move on to the next slide about everyone's favorite arthropod, I'm going to need everyone to get real cool about some stuff."

She narrowed her eyes in faux menace and waved a finger through the air at her high school students. "Do I have your word that you can all be almost adults?"

The group grumbled, while some snickered into their hands.

"Alright, I'm trusting you."

She clicked the fob, the next picture illuminating the screen. A zoomed-in video of a barnacle clinging to a rock, with a long tendril erupting from the center, undulating in the water. "In proportion to their size, barnacles have the biggest penises of all in the animal kingdom."

For a room of sixteen to eighteen-year-olds, it only took two minutes for Autumn to get the class back under control after the laughter, jokes and red-faced comments.

"Alright, I know, very funny. Like I said, I know you can be cool about this. Now, on average, the penis is eight to nine times larger than its body. Research says that the conditions in which the barnacles live can affect the length and, yes, girth of the extremity. Ones in gentle waters have been found to be longer and thinner, while ones in rougher seas are shorter and thicker. As they spend most of their time stationary on rocks, they use their penises to poke around neighboring female barnacles to spread their seed. Charles Darwin himself was quite fascinated with the reproductive methods of barnacles, spending much time researching the topic from 1846 to 1854. Though many of the naturalist's theories were later found to be incorrect, it is nonetheless a topic that has fascinated historians and biologists for years. Now, in their resting state, barnacles are simulations hermaphrodites, which means? What?"

She motioned around the room.

A girl back by the window raised her hand. "They have male and female parts."

"Good, Kamari, yes. Mating season will begin when one barnacle's egg gland swells, making it female for the time. Upon this, chemicals are released into the water that let the neighboring barnacles know it is ready to be fertilized. At this point they can become male, and thus, the oversized penis is used."

She clicked through to the next slide. "Now, onto how they eat. Can anyone tell me the name of the other appendages they used to eat? Yes, Tim."

As the class filed out to get on their bus back up Hostmark Street, and to the high school, teens glanced at me with suspicion. It had been a while since I was in school. Hell, I learned how to text using T9 on my phone, something I was sure none of these kids had any idea about. To them, I was sure I looked like an old man.

Girls giggled behind their hands, and one guy passed me whispering about Autumn. While I didn't hear what was said, I knew enough about stupid teenage boys to understand the implication. Could you smack students upside the head?

No, probably not. Hmm. Maybe I didn't want to have kids after all if this is what they turned into.

We walked to the car together. At her waddling gait, I made the mistake of teasing her about only once and got a glare so reminiscent of Summer that I shut up, and only praised her grace, which she snorted at. Her belly was big, "*like I swallowed a beach ball,*" she would say. I had to help her off the couch every night, and she had a special body pillow that she slept with. Sex was creative, to say the least. We attempted shower sex a few weeks before and Autumn's center of gravity had her slipping, so I had to finish her with my mouth and wait until later when we were in bed to have my end.

While she didn't complain about how she looked, she was getting uncomfortable. Her boobs were huge, which I enjoyed, but she said they hurt all the time, so I had to be careful.

The ring I gave her at Christmas hung from a gold chain around her neck. Her fingers had swollen up in the past few weeks, so she took it off before it became stuck.

Halfway home, she turned in her seat to grab her bag but had to flop back in with a groan. I grabbed her bag and handed it to her, and she brought out her notepad. She was constantly noting her classroom lessons and how to improve the curriculum. Upon graduation, she was offered a position at the center as a docent and teaching one class a day. She was planning on accepting for the following fall.

I was still making more monthly passive income from my deal with the app than she was offered for a full-time position, but her work was never about the money. She cared deeply about ocean conservation and wanted to teach the next group of young people to love it as well.

"I was talking to my therapist today."

Autumn's studious gaze left her notes and snapped to me.

"And it turns out having shitty parental figures, finding out your fiancée is cheating on you and then dying the same day can lead to some unresolved problems."

Autumn taking me back, despite knowing she had a myriad of reasons not to, empowered me to fix things. When I told her if she wanted me to I'd make an appointment with a therapist, she stopped me.

You can't want to get healthy for me, Nicolai, you have to want it for yourself.

She was wise.

Head leaned back against the headrest. Autumn set her hands on her belly and turned to study me, working hard not to let a smile grace her face. "Is that so?"

"Yeah, I might even have some abandonment and attachment issues."

Ronald, my therapist, was a hardass. He gave me homework to do and after worksheets and confrontation after revelations. I wondered if I should call it quits many times.

But Autumn knew better than I. It was hard work sorting myself out and according to Ronald it was lifelong work. Not so different from what

Autumn had said to me when she took me back. *You do it every day. Choose us every day.*

Forgiving myself for Noemi was still a process. Through many discussions, I was starting to see that, while I didn't handle the situation maturely, I too was flawed. I didn't put her in the car; I wasn't driving, and I didn't cross that double yellow. Five minutes before or five minutes after maybe the world would be different. But to deny myself a life based on my mistakes wouldn't change what had been done.

We had only started talking about my mom in the last session, but that would be years' worth of work and landmines.

With lips pressed together, Autumn nodded at me, her brow raised as she tried to stifle her laugh. "Fancy that, who knew?"

"Any basic Psych 101 student, probably."

"Yeah, I think you might be right."

We pulled into the driveway; the tires crunching on the gravel. As much as Autumn loved driving the Eagle, I didn't want her messing with the crank windows, and no power steering while seven and a half months pregnant. I forbade her from driving after the brakes locked a week earlier, even though pumping them helped temporarily. For now, the car was parked in our garage to be driven on special occasions, and she was going to be getting the safest new SUV on the market in a few weeks. We had gone to the dealership to pick out colors and features. At first, Autumn balked at the price tag, but I refused to allow a little thing like money come in the way of her and the baby's safety.

Until the car came in, I was taking her to and from work. It was nice being in the car with her. After our road trip, sitting side by side was our safe place. We fell in love behind the wheel, fought, she cried, I moped. She grew our baby while the tires spun beneath us. Sometimes, I would even listen to The Eagles, though not when she was in the car. The last time "Desperado" came on, she proclaimed, *cheese and rice, I do not want to listen*

Before she could open the passenger-side door, I was there, my hand on her elbow, helping her out. Our black and white Maine coon, Tactil—Taki for short—wove around our legs as we walked in the front door. Autumn insisted a house wasn't a home until we had animals and then after we got the cat informed me she couldn't scoop the litter box because of a toxic parasite.

She had done a lot to the house since moving in a few weeks after we announced our news for the family. Family pictures of her nieces and nephews adorned the once-bare refrigerator doors. A few of her friend Devin's paintings hung in the entryway. Despite Devin offering them at a discount, I knew enough about art to know whatever I paid at full price would go up in the coming years. In the living room, she hung pictures of us. At Wren and Adrian's engagement party. New Year's back in Icicle Creek, the same bar but a very different ending to the night. Christmas when I proposed and my favorite of all, one of us in Sedona, the edges of sunset on the bottom of the red rocks.

It might have been the moment I started to fall. It could have been months before on my dock. But that picture held something special. A bright promise of a future on both our faces, a lightness in my eyes I hadn't allowed in nearly a decade, captured on those dusty orange rocks.

Soon enough, our walls would be full of pictures of our new baby, of the rest of our lives. For so long my house was barren, white walls and clean cedar planks. But in a year, there would be smudges, and peanut butter and jam fingerprints. In five years, we'd have little notches on a wall for height. We'd fill my four bedrooms up with more kids. As many as Autumn wanted. She made it a home.

She threw herself back on the couch with an audible *flump* and beckoned me over to sit beside her. As I sat, she rolled to her side, laid over me, and pulled me down behind her. Our legs tangled together, she pulled my arm between her head and neck for a pillow and the other she set on her belly.

This was a nightly habit. She would make me lie beside her and then fall asleep after work for twenty minutes. I could handle the dead arm and loss of circulation if it made her comfortable. As her eyes drifted closed, I marveled at her. Pregnancy had filled her cheeks, and while she complained about it, I loved the fuller look, loved the widening of her hips and the way her hair grew thick and strong.

A fluttering in her belly started, and I froze, my eyes darting from her face down to her belly between us.

"Was that?"

She nodded. "He moved."

"She did."

We had decided we wanted to be surprised by the gender. Much to the chagrin of Summer and Wren, who wanted a reveal party alongside the baby shower, Autumn held true. Knowing Summer and her grandiose plans, it would have involved fireworks, a baseball bat, or something else equally destructive.

It wasn't the first time I felt the baby move, of course. That had been a few weeks after New Year, while we were out at the grocery store stocking up on her favorite spicy chips, despite how much heartburn she refused to admit they gave her. She had grabbed my hand and set it on her belly. The *thump, thump, thump* of a little foot or elbow against my palm and had to swallow back the lump in my throat. Crying in Ridgewood Market beside the organic veggie straws wasn't part of the plan. Until then, I had an amorphous idea of a baby. But this was bones and life and would be a person. A real person someday. Half of me made a person.

Now, three months later, I was still in wonder at each flutter and kick. The motion in her belly stilled, and she wrapped her hand around mine, bringing it up to her mouth to press her lips to my knuckles.

We had six weeks of just us and then I had a lifetime for me to earn this life she had given back to me. My nose buried in her hair, flowers, and herbs and the essence of her filled me. I wouldn't waste a moment.

Epilogue

POINT AA-HOME

Autumn

OCTOBER TWO YEARS LATER

Our story had been a series of adventures from the beginning. As much as Nico grumbled during that road trip, I knew he missed the feeling of traveling with me. When it came time to pick our spot for a honeymoon, he let me take over planning something that he rarely did after the four-by-four incident at Sedona. Australia fit everything we wanted; we just had to get married first.

The wedding planning got put off three times before it happened. First, we had planned a little courthouse thing a few days after I graduated from college but Sedona Louise Evjen made a surprise appearance two weeks early.

My parent's were thrilled at being grandparents again, though with this being their sixth, the enthusiasm was less than the first a decade before. But my not being married when I gave birth was an issue for them. Three weeks postpartum, leaking from ungodly places and still sore, my mom, and Summer brought over a bridal magazine for planning. In my most assertive tone, I let them know we would discuss the wedding when I stopped bleeding—that earned a disgusted look from Summer, who would find out in eight months exactly what I was talking about and a laugh from my mom.

The second was when I resumed work at the Marine Science Center. After two quarters of pulling double duty as a docent and teacher, I had to pull back to only teaching until Sedona was over the age of one.

Just as Sedona was walking and able to attend the local early learning center while we worked, Summer began her own planning for her and Van's wedding. A grand affair at the nicest venue Ridgewood offered. A lemon cakes and pink roses spread for the three hundred guest list extravaganza. As maid of honor, I was more than happy to delay my party in lieu of her nuptials. I was glad not to be the only Townsend woman who lived in sin and had a baby out of wedlock. Our old-fashioned fathers were aghast, but they could grumble to each other about that.

Finally, over two years after Nico, and I had shared our first kiss and promptly conceived Sedona, the day was here.

Summer, my maid of honor, stood with me at the altar. Wren and Devin stood with sunflower and yellow rose bouquets, as Puget Sound rolled below.

Sedona was there with us as we exchanged vows, and during the ceremony, she climbed up Nico's leg until he picked her up, holding my hand with the other. Bald until she was eighteen months old, a thin dusting of auburn hair was beginning to cover her head where the little floral crown sat. My mom rushed forward to take the baby, but Nico waved her off. It was right that Sedona was there with us through the ceremony; she was with us for every moment of our relationship.

The reception went into the night, with the babies going home with their respective grandparents early while the rest of us stayed up talking. Early October can still be warm during the day, but everything around the water cools quickly when the sun goes down, and our home on Jasper Pass was no exception. It was after midnight before Nico slapped the keys to the house in Oliver's hand and asked him to take care of the place while we were away.

Now standing on the edge of the white sand beach of the Capricorn Coast with the great Great Barrier Reef just offshore, was an awakening. Nico got us a car, and we planned to tour and see the sights, like the Keppel Islands and the nearby waterfalls, though I doubted we'd be able to repeat our antics from Youngs Falls years before.

Night was falling over the ocean, stars blinking into existence over us. "I can't wait to see the reef tomorrow. Did you know there are more than four thousand species of mollusks in there?"

He joined me at the window, his hand on my hip as we watched the waves crashing black over the beach and the endless dark expanse of the Coral Sea.

"You know I love it when you talk about fish." His hands moved to my shirt, pulling it over my head and discarding it on the floor behind us, my bare breasts heavier now than they had been before having our baby. Next went my leggings, travel-worn and dusty. Leaning back, I rested my head on his shoulder as his hand snaked down my stomach to part my legs.

"Mollusks aren't fish." I gasped as he ground his growing erection into my butt. "Though there are theories that fish may have evolved from—*oh*."

His fingers shoved my underwear down my legs where I kicked them off.

"Put your hands on the window and watch the ocean."

Slowly, the moon hung before me, the only light outside the window. In the reflection, I could see his face, eyes dark and glossy as his thumb rolled my nipple, pinching to the point of almost pain.

When I gripped the length of his cock, he tutted at me.

"No, no, sweet, this is your show. Stay still and hands on the window."

With his firm body against mine, I didn't move, the anticipation of him touching me and the sight ahead keeping me frozen. His fingers delved inside me, the base of his wrist hitting my clit. From this angle, my orgasm barreled down quickly.

"Oh, I'm gonna—oh . . ." I moaned as he moved faster.

He stooped, sucking the skin of my bare shoulder into his mouth, his teeth stinging me beautifully.

"That's it, sweet. Take it, take it all." His kisses rained over my throat, his tongue soothing the abraded area as he pumped his finger faster and faster inside me. My eyes fell shut, my legs shook beneath me.

He pulled the hair at my nape, bending my head to the side to look at him. "I'm going to be your last. The only one who sees you this way again. The only one who gets to marry you. To fill you up with as many babies as you want. Only me."

"Only you." I gasped out as the final crest of my climax shuddered through me.

With his thumb on my jaw, he kissed me, a chaotic, deep kiss that squeezed the last bit of joy from me, my insides throbbing around his hand.

Scanning the fingerprint smudges on the glass, I slumped against the window. Before I could catch my breath, he spun me, bruising my hips with his hands, and I was on my back on the warm bed. My legs splayed open, and he sank inside me in a single slow thrust, stretching me.

Our kiss was messy, slow and wet as he sank in deeper, his cock dragged across my g-spot deliciously and it took my breath away to be filled this way.

He sank into me, my hands wrapping around his neck as I gasped out.

"Fuck, nothing has ever felt as good," he gritted out through clenched teeth, his body stilling as I took him. I raised my hips, pulling him deeper.

"Don't stop, more, please. Feels so good." I gasped out as he slowed, slid slowly from within me to plunge back in, and I raked my nails down his back.

"Nothing. Only you."

His pelvis dragged along my clit, sparking pleasure through my body as he thrust again. As he moved harder and deeper, the headboard banged against the window overlooking the night sky.

As his hip moved faster, each thrust caused us to moan louder. His gaze opened to watch me beneath him, our matching expressions locked on each other. His teeth sank into his bottom lip as he moved. Normally, my eyes would fall shut the sensation of being filled overwhelming me,. But I watched him, the furrow of his brow, the clench of his jaw, the way his gaze darted from mine down to where we were joined. Connected forever. My legs wrapped around his waist, his fingers spread on my jaw, holding my chin up to find him. His thumb pressed into the pressure point I loved so much. "What you do to me. My wife."

Tangling my fingers through his hair, I pulled his mouth to mine, gasping as we came together. "My husband. Mine."

I cried out as I clamped down on him, wave after wave crashing over me. With a low groan, he shuddered, following behind me, his hot spend filling me. As he collapsed on me, his face rested in the crook of my neck, his kisses slowed as we both caught our breath, his hand on my hip.

"Wife."

"Husband," I echoed, grinning at him. Pushing up on his elbow, he made a move to roll to the side, but I hooked my ankles together, keeping him in place.

"Not yet. I need to feel you soft inside me until you grow hard once more."

He grinned, ducking his face down to press a kiss to my collarbone. "Since I could live in your cunt, that can be arranged."

Slowly, our breathing settled as we rolled to the side, still connected. His eyes fluttered shut, and I could see the day's travel overtake him as his breathing slowed. Minutes, then an hour passed, and we stayed like that, breathing in each other's air, his hand on my hip and my fingers in his hair.

I traced a line over his jaw. He had more gray hairs in his stubble than when we first started together—he was forty, after all, and I was six months from twenty-nine.

"I have a present for you," I murmured, and he cracked an eye open to look at me.

"Another set of cheap sunglasses for the honeymoon?"

Chuckling, I shook my head as I rolled onto my stomach to grab the bag that had fallen to the side. Fishing through it, I pulled out the little Ziploc and held it up to him.

He stared at the white stick in its bag, his vision clearing, and he straightened, leaning back on his elbows, his gaze darting from my face to the test. "Are you sure?"

"Yes, and this time I know it's early."

"Am I—" He swallowed. "Does anyone else know yet?"

I shook my head. "No, I took the test last night. I wanted to tell you first. That's how it should have been."

"You didn't need to save your pee stick."

"Yeah, kind of gross, I know. But . . ." I shrugged.

"One of these days, you're going to let me know before you take these tests."

"One of these days? How many times are you planning on getting me pregnant?"

"As many times as you want, Sweet."

I hummed as I kissed him. "We'll see how I feel after this next one. Two might be enough."

"As long as I have you, it always will be."

Halfway across the world, we drifted off, wrapped together, the ocean waves behind our eyes—the desert sunrise and sunset—colors of the blackest space and the lover's constellations in the sky.

Ceaselessly.

Also By Linnea March

Wren's Winter

A missed turn, the wrong doorstep, and the right guy?

What was meant to be a romantic retreat in the picturesque town of Icicle Creek with her boyfriend becomes an unexpected solo adventure for Wren Alexander. Newly single, she arrives on the wintry mountain armed with romance novels, canned wine, and a passion for the unexpected. Fate intercedes when a missed turn, an accidental doorstep, and an encounter with a grumpy yet irresistibly handsome neighbor challenges all her ideas of what this trip could be.

Adrian Winter, grappling with the weight of managing his grandparents' cabin after a heartbreaking loss, is taken aback by the arrival of the radiant Wren on his doorstep. Despite leaving his playboy days behind, Wren's presence sparks a resurgence of emotions, prompting him to question the depths of his heart.

As reality comes to their door, they find themselves losing the battle against their feelings. Amidst a snowstorm, a couple of canine escapades, and an unexpected plunge into a river, Wren and Adrian discover that love often appears when least expected—even on the wrong front porch. Now, they must decide if their connection is strong enough to weather all that life throws their way.

Faultless Notion

They didn't mean to get married.

Eloise Dunning ran far from her small town in the Pacific Northwest to Los Angeles with little more than the clothes on her back and a dream of being a singer-songwriter. Now she is a personal assistant to the rock band, Prevalent Notion, and leaving her songbook in the bottom of her bag.

Keller Grant is everything a rock star should be. Sinfully attractive, an enigmatic artist with a dark past, and an immensely talented drummer. He loves the revolving door of women in each city, creating music with his bandmates in Prevalent Notion, and teasing an uptight Eloise.

The night before the band kicks off their American Tour, Eloise and Keller wake up in each other's arms with wedding bands on their fingers. Forced by the record label to maintain the marriage for the public, they face a hungry press, rabid fans, and jealousy from all sides.
As they get the world to believe in their facade, they find that, maybe, this marriage doesn't feel like a performance.

ABOUT THE AUTHOR

Linnea March is a contemporary romance author who writes steamy stories about self-confident women and the rugged men who love them. She lives somewhere in the wilds of the Pacific Northwest with her husband, their two boys, and a plump dog. After fifteen years of teaching early childhood education, she put down the googly eyes and picked up a pen. When not writing, she can be found reading her way through an ever-growing pile of books while drinking copious amounts of coffee. She proudly refuses to use umbrellas.

ACKNOWLEDGEMENTS

A thank you to.

My husband, Rusty. For all car related items, being my forever road trip partner, and for building me an office in our backyard.

To my girlfriends. Laura, Greta Rose, M.J., Dillon, Kate and Shannon. Thank you for taking this journey with me every day.

To my children who will never read this book. To Cassidy for always being my first reader. And all the local books bookstores. who carry my books from the Pacific Northwest to New York. To my editor. Thank you for polishing this up to the best it could be.

This story is an homage, to the Great American road trip. I hope you enjoyed traveling on it with me.

DEAR READERS

Autumn in the Rearview is at its heart a road trip story.

My husband and I moved from our small town in Western Washington to Phoenix at eighteen. With nothing but a tank of gas, a toolbox to set our small television on, and a blow-up mattress in the back, we drove the miles through Washington, Oregon, California, and into Arizona together.

This book is an homage to that trip. The adventures of getting lost on the road beside someone you love and the discovery of who you can be when you have the right person in the passenger seat.

Using creative liberties, I have made up some of the places on Autumn and Nico's trip. Cape Rose, Sol Del Mar, and Birch Creek Hot Springs are from my own imagination. But most of the stops are real places with real sights.

Aside from the obvious ones of the Grand Canyon, Sedona, and San Jose, two real spots I wanted to incorporate into the story are Montezuma's Castle in Arizona and Youngs River Falls in Oregon.

Both hold special memories for me, and the use of them for my road trip story was intentional. (For legal reasons, I cannot recommend getting it on beside the actual waterfall. You might get arrested.)

If you enjoyed this story, I hope you'll consider leaving a quick review or rating. Your feedback helps my story reach readers.